EVIDENCE OF DESTRUCTION

"Are you saying someone set you up?" Atkins asked. "For God's sake, Carlyle, why would anyone do a thing like that? Listen! Your 'Mechs were holographed! Your DropShips were holographed! I've seen them, with the town of Durandel burning on the horizon behind them!"

Grayson shook his head. "I don't care what was photographed," he said. "Photographs, even holographs, can be faked by computer manipulations."

"Your 'Mechs were seen attacking the ruins, Carlyle."

"Witnesses can be bought, dammit! Or they can be misled! My God, someone is trying to destroy the Gray Death by turning us into outlaws ... and I can't get anyone to believe me!"

RoC

**Exploring New Realms
in Science Fiction/Fantasy Adventure**

Battletech®

BATTLETECH®

THE PRICE OF GLORY

WILLIAM H.KEITH, JR

A ROC BOOK

ROC

Published by the Penguin Group
Penguin Books Ltd, 27 Wrights Lane, London W8 5TZ, England
Penguin Books USA Inc., 375 Hudson Street, New York, New York 10014, USA
Penguin Books Australia Ltd, Ringwood, Victoria, Australia
Penguin Books Canada Ltd, 10 Alcorn Avenue, Toronto, Ontario, Canada M4V 3B2
Penguin Books (NZ) Ltd, 182–190 Wairau Road, Auckland 10, New Zealand

Penguin Books Ltd, Registered Offices: Harmondsworth, Middlesex, England

First published in the USA by ROC, an imprint of New American Library,
a division of Penguin Books USA Inc., 1993
First published in Great Britain 1993
10 9 8 7 6 5 4 3 2 1

Series editor: Donna Ippolito
Cover: Boris Vallejo
Interior illustrations: Janet Aulisio
Mechanical drawings: Duane Loose

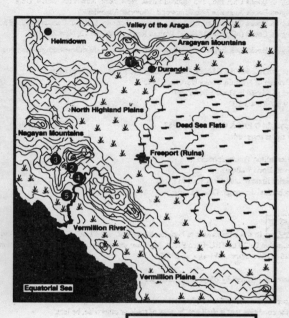

MAP OF HELM
Equatorial Sea Area

Valley of the Araga

Helmdown

Aragayan Mountains

① Durandel

North Highland Plains

Dead Sea Flats

Negayan Mountains

③
②
④
Freeport (Ruins)
⑤

Vermillion River

Vermillion Plains

Equatorial Sea

Scale

50   100   150   200   400

Kilometers

MAJOR BATTLES

① Dropships

② Drango Gap

③ Lee's Pass

④ Vermillion Valley

⑤ Vermillion Plains

BOOK I

=== 1 ===

Smoke stained an evil, yellow-green sky. There was no way that open flame could exist in the chill mix of hydrogen and methane that made up the atmosphere of Sirius V, but the wreckage and debris of the recent battle glowed white-hot in places, heat sufficient in that sub-zero chemical soup to precipitate oily, red-brown clouds of sulfur and nitrogen compounds. Those clouds hung, sluggish and sullen, in the dense and alien atmosphere.

Grayson Death Carlyle watched the approach of the city delegation through the main screen of his battle-scarred *Marauder*. The exhausts of their sealed vehicles glowed brightly against the cold on his main screen, which had been set to display infrared imagery. Beyond the delegation's convoy, the city of Tiantan brooded against a landscape of poisonous desolation. By visible light, it was a vast dome of gray metal crusted over with sulfur compounds and ammonia mud. By infrared, the city dome radiated furiously from a thousand heat sinks and ports, and looked like a fountain of heat set against the lambent skyline.

Grayson was not admiring the display, however.

"Fire lance," he murmured into the pickup at his lips. "Feed me your Sigma-Vee."

"Affirmative, Colonel." Lieutenant Khaled's voice was as dry and taut as Grayson's own throat. "Transmitting."

Four monitors along the side of Grayson's cockpit flickered and danced in static-laden bursts, then steadied into separate views of the convoy approaching from below. Lieutenant Hassan Khaled's *Warhammer*, Isoru Koga's *Archer*, Charles Bear's *Crusader*, and Sharyl's *Shadow Hawk*—each viewed the convoy from a slightly different angle. Cameras mounted in each 'Mech's head transmitted that pilot's "Sigma-Vee," his view of the unfolding situation. The transmissions continued to flash and crackle with uneven bursts of static. Sirius, this planet's sun, was a hot, young A1 star, and its raw voice easily bridged the 6 AU gulf to its fifth planet, raising periodic havoc with radio and video transmissions there.

Bear's *Crusader* was closest to the column. His screen's flickering data readout indicated a range of 2,000 meters to the nearest tracked, bubble-topped vehicle. Heavily armed and armored troop carriers straggled behind through red mud and ice-rimed puddles of liquid ammonia.

Grayson checked the console display that marked the positions of his other forces on a tactical map—three 'Mechs of the recon lance widely spaced across the rear, a fourth on guard back at the newly captured spaceport, his own command lance backing up the fire lance and deploying along the ridge facing the city.

He switched frequencies. "Command lance. Status check."

"Kalmar, *Shadow Hawk*. Check." Lieutenant Lori Kalmar sounded taut, expectant.

"Clay, *Wolverine*. Set." The laconic Delmar Clay had his *Wolverine* on a low ice ridge to the north, where he could cut off the enemy's retreat if necessary.

"McCall. Ma' wee *Bannockburn*'s ready, sair." The redbearded Davis Montgomery McCall held his *Rifleman* in reserve, as added insurance against a Liao AeroSpace Fighter strike.

The fire lance monitors all indicated ready status, and the enemy was drawing closer. Grayson's attention snapped back to the view televised from Bear's *Crusader*.

"Bear! Full mag."

The scene on the monitor obediently expanded, zeroing in on the speck of white that had caught Grayson's eye. It was a white flag rippling from the whip antenna of the lead vehicle.

Grayson shifted command frequencies. "Ramage? What's your TacSit?"

Captain Ramage's voice filtered back through the earphones in Grayson's helmet. "We're in position, Colonel. I've deployed both platoons behind Hill 103, and the men are dug in and ready."

"Good. Hold your fire, and wait for my word. I see a white flag on the lead vehicle. But watch our Six. This *could* be a surrender . . ." He let the warning trail off, uncompleted. The Sirius campaign might be on the verge of ending if those vehicles were emissaries of the city sent to parlay for surrender terms.

Grayson would have to be careful, though. The vehicles could also be part of some trap that might lead to a very different outcome for the campaign.

"Yessir. Our Six is covered." "Six" was a long-accepted battlespeech term meaning a unit's rear. Ramage's ground forces had been deployed to cover a possible enemy thrust from that direction—a good possibility if the convoy was not what it seemed.

The vehicles pulled to a halt 150 meters ahead of the fire lance, the white flag flicking this way and that in the fitful air. An amplified voice, heavily accented and carefully enunciated, echoed from a speaker in the lead machine. "This is Ambassador Gregar Chandresenkhar, Special Diplomatic Liaison of the Lyran Commonwealth to the planetary government of Sirius V. As an officially registered neutral in the hostilities between House Marik and House Liao, I have been asked to serve as Special Envoy for the City Fathers of Tiantan. I claim Privilege, sir."

Grayson flicked a switch, opening a mike to his own external speakers. "This is Colonel Grayson Carlyle," he replied. "Commander of the Gray Death Legion, in the service of House Marik and the Free Worlds League. Privilege is granted you, sir."

"Privilege is accepted, sir. May I advance?"

Grayson took a deep breath. It was unlikely that they would violate Privilege. Still . . .

"You may advance, Mr. Ambassador."

The lead vehicle stirred into motion once more, approaching the silent line of fire lance 'Mechs, meeting it, passing through. Grayson guided his massive *Marauder* forward a few steps so that the envoy would not mistake who was the Gray Death commander, then locked his machine in place.

Realizing that much would depend on the events of the next few moments, Grayson opened a private channel. "Lori?"

From her battle-stained *Shadow Hawk,* his company Exec acknowledged, "Here, boss. Are we going to trust them?"

"We have to, Lori. They've claimed Privilege."

"We never used that much, Beyond."

"Mmm. Maybe not."

Lori Kalmar had been born and raised on Sigurd, one of the half-barbarian wolf worlds in the vast Periphery beyond the Inner Sphere. For her, war had never been balanced by civilized conventions until she'd joined the Gray Death Legion.

"What's the matter?" he joked, but with a voice still taut from command. "Is warfare becoming too civilized for you?"

"No, it just makes me wonder who to trust. Heads up, Gray. Here he comes."

A lone figure stepped from the ground car, the man's face muffled by the goggles and mask humans needed to breathe in the cold, deadly Sirian atmosphere. He looked very small next to the bulk of the vehicle, and then smoke boiling from the twisted wreckage of a *Vindicator* lying crumpled on the icy gravel momentarily hid the man from view.

"Time to go," Grayson said. "Keep an eye on things, Lieutenant."

He removed his neurohelmet and hung it on the support rack above his chair, unstrapped himself, and squeezed his way aft toward the dorsal hatch, past the instrumentation that filled the *Marauder*'s cockpit. *Marauder*s have several points of entry. In the field, the one most commonly used is located on the upper back of the fuselage, just ahead of the autocannon mount. Grayson's lanky height made for a tight squeeze between the storage racks of 120 mm cassette rounds for the *Marauder*'s dorsal cannon, even though his supply of AC ammo was more than half-depleted. It would be the same throughout the regiment, Grayson thought. If the Liaos elected to continue their fight, the Gray Death Legion was going to have to pull back their DropShips to restock ammo stores.

From a small locker, Grayson removed a lightweight environmental suit and mask and began to perform the contortions necessary to don them in such cramped quarters.

So far, the Gray Death Legion's campaign for Sirius V on behalf of their current employer had been swift and unrelenting. They had been onplanet for almost two weeks now, had fought three major battles and innumerable skirmishes, and not once had their line broken in combat. This final encounter had been fought at the very gates of Tiantan—the "Heavenly Palace"—and had left the defending 'Mech force beaten and scattered.

The war should be over, and yet Grayson had to shove a deep and persistent unease from his mind. *The campaign is over,* he thought. *Now to make peace for our new lords and masters up there in orbit . . .*

The thought held no bitterness for Grayson Carlyle. The fortunes of his mercenary Gray Death Legion had improved beyond all expectations, beyond all reason or hope, since the successful conclusion of their last campaign on far Verthandi. The pathetic, forlorn revolution against the might of the Draconis Combine had ended with the impossible—independence for a people too stubborn to sit quietly while Kurita's legions raped their world. The Gray Death Legion's victory had made the unit wealthy in BattleMechs—the hardest, most secure currency that existed within the unraveling fabric of galactic civilization. Their share of the spoils taken on Verthandi had raised the Legion's 'Mech force to a full operational company, with parts and reserve 'Mechs for a company more. They also had enough captured tanks, recon vehicles, personnel carriers, and infantry weapons to create the bare-bones framework of an entire regiment. When the Gray Death returned to the mercenary hiring centers on Galatea, they found that word of their victories had preceded them. There had been no lack of volunteers for either Grayson's BattleMech or infantry companies. Every unattached mercenary warrior, it seemed, wanted to share in the Carlyle luck.

And so, it seemed, did House Marik.

Grayson squeezed into the tiny, metal-walled cubicle that served as his *Marauder*'s airlock, checked again the fit of his breathing mask, and cycled the outer hatch open. They *had* been lucky, he thought. After Verthandi, the Gray Death mercenary combined arms regiment had had its pick of prospective employers. Of the five great Houses, both Steiner and Davion had offered more-or-less standard contracts that would have continued to pit Grayson and his people against the implacable red dragon of House Kurita. Both houses had also offered tempting terms: money, of course, and the far sweeter coin of vengeance.

After Verthandi, however, Grayson found that his driving hunger for vengeance against the murderers of his father had diminished, replaced now by a vague, uneasy emptiness. Hate, it seemed, was difficult to sustain year after year. After leading his forces in a crushing victory over his old foes on Verthandi, he felt not satisfaction, but the weary realization that his personal crusade would never halt the march of evil directed from dread Luthien's Imperial Palace.

In the end, only one great House had offered what Grayson and his people could not refuse, what all of them sought with a hunger greater even than the craving for vengeance. House Marik had promised them a place, a homeworld of their own.

The victory the Gray Death had won this day would seal their right to the Legion's landhold at Helm.

A viciously cold, thin wind whipped and tugged at Grayson's protective clothing as he swung his legs out of the narrow airlock hatch and sat astride his *Marauder*. He kept one gloved hand against the support of his 'Mech's dorsal-mounted autocannon while the other hand freed a chain ladder from its storage compartment, then unrolled it in a long, clattering fall toward the ground. The air of Sirius V was primarily hydrogen and nitrogen, the "water" was liquid ammonia. With a surface temperature that rarely rose above –40 degrees C., water was always a solid here. Mountains of the stuff stretched across the stark, yellow-green skyline, glittering harsh in the actinic glare of distant Sirius.

Grayson stepped from the dangling ladder onto cold rock. Now that he stood unsupported, rather than lying back against the cushioned cockpit seat of his *Marauder*, Grayson felt the pull of the planet's 1.5 G gravity dragging at his knees and back.

Sirius V was empty of life, save what men had imported here early in the history of human expansion to the stars. At a distance of 8.7 light years from Terra, Sirius was one of old Earth's nearest neighbors in space. The first manned outpost on this frigid, barren landscape had been established some nine centuries ago, not long after faster-than-light travel had become possible. Stars as young as Sirius were not even supposed to *have* planets, according to the astrophysical understanding of those long-gone times, and so the sole purpose of the first Sirian colony was to research the improbabilities of the Sirius system. It took nearly a century before Sirius V's considerable resources of heavy metals and transuranic minerals were discovered.

The world was now a minor fief of House Liao's Capellan Confederation. Chinese warlords serving the Terran Hegemony had constructed the industrial and city complex known as the Heavenly Palace in the 26th century in order to exploit the planet's resources. Liao had taken over Sirius at the outset of the Succession Wars. The world had been a target for Marik raiders and tactical strikes during the ongoing, deathlock embrace between the two houses ever since.

Grayson stepped from beneath the shadow of his *Marauder* and onto the sunlit plain. Sirius's light held a distinctly greenish cast, filtered as it was by the planet's atmosphere, but he kept his eyes turned away from its blazing intensity. Though nearly six times farther from

Sirius V than Sol is from Terra, the tiny eye-searing disk of Sirius was a danger if gazed at directly, even through polarized goggles. Close to the horizon ahead and just above the gray domes of Tiantan, Grayson could just make out a tiny but brilliant pinpoint of light, like a planet gleaming low in an evening sky. That, Grayson knew, was not a planet, but the white dwarf companion to the far larger sun above him.

Grayson had learned during his pre-mission research that the white dwarf looped about Sirius A in an elongated orbit that brought it to within nearly 10 AU of the primary sun once every 50 years. The last such close passage had been in 2993. The next would occur in another seventeen years. The white dwarf did not add appreciably to the heat shed by Sirius A during its passage, but it was dangerous to look at the sky in those years when Sirius B was at its closest. Those twin sources of ultraviolet radiation could fry a man's retinas, despite the frigid atmosphere of this planet.

What kind of world is it, where men fear to look at the sky? Grayson wondered.

The chosen ambassador of the Tiantan Fathers stood thirty meters away, tiny against the vastness of the chill landscape and the hulking vehicles behind him, bundled like Grayson in an environmental suit and mask against the cold and poison air. The wind snatched at the man's cloak, which he had pulled around him for extra protection against the chill.

"Com check," Grayson said, speaking into the command circuit of his headgear with a voice muffled by his breathing mask.

"We hear you, Chief," Lori's voice answered in his headphones. She sounded . . . warm, just as Grayson was beginning to realize how cold were his feet, despite the heavy insulation of his boots. "We're recording. And we've got him targeted six ways."

"Right. Hold your positions. I'm going in."

He stepped forward again, willing his knees to continue to hold him up against one-and-a-half times his usual weight.

The speed of the Legion's victory over this Liao world

had been surprising. Certainly, Lord Garth, Duke of Irian, Lord Commander of the Marik support forces in orbit above Sirius V right now, had been astonished at Grayson's last combat report. *The final Liao battleline broken before the city walls,* that message had stated. *This world is yours, your Grace.*

Some members of Grayson's regimental command staff were of the opinion that Lord Garth had been deliberately throwing the Gray Death against Liao strongholds in an effort to wear the Legion down. Indeed, this last campaign had been the roughest yet, for all its brevity. The regiment had lost over fifty combat infantry, and three of its new MechWarrior recruits. During the entire struggle, Lord Garth and the full battalion of Marik Regulars under his command had remained safely in orbit, maintaining aerospace superiority, and feeding satellite recon intel to Grayson's staff, but well beyond the reach of Liao's ground defenses.

There was nothing wrong with that, either. The Gray Death mercenaries had been hired specifically to smash Liao defenses on several key worlds such as Sirius V. From the point of view of the Marik high command, military resources were precious, and it was often cheaper to hire mercenaries to expend *their* resources than to waste irreplaceable 'Mechs and equipment.

Still, it was hard to fight and die, all the while knowing that reinforcements capable of tipping the balance in your favor were only a few thousand kilometers away . . . watching it all on their long-range scanners. It was harder still to hear your own people dying beside you. Jenna Hasting's choked screams as the planet's cold and poisonous atmosphere had flooded her *Centurion*'s cracked canopy were still raw in his ears. Sirius V was starkly and brutally unforgiving during combat in a way that even enemy MechWarriors were not. There had been very few wounded on either side during the past two weeks. Breaches, however small, in combat armor or Battle-Mech pressure walls were almost invariably fatal. When oxygen spilled into this hydrogen-rich atmosphere, and heat or a spark was added . . .

Grayson stopped ten paces away from the lone man. The other, as supplicant, gave a slight, stiff bow.

"Ambassador Gregar Chandresenkhar," the man announced formally. "Special Diplomatic Liaison of the Lyran Commonwealth to the planetary government of Sirius V and the Capellan Confederation. I have placed myself at the disposal of the Tiantan City Fathers, to act as their representative. Is that acceptable to you, sir?"

Grayson returned the bow. "Perfectly acceptable, sir. I am Colonel Grayson Carlyle, Gray Death Legion, under service to the Lord Garth, Duke of Irian, and Lord Commander of the Marik Fifth Expeditionary Force. Under all accepted conventions and protocols of war, I have the authority to treat with you, and those you represent."

"I have been directed to ask for terms," the Ambassador said. "The City Fathers are willing to concede defeat."

So. The campaign *was* over. The thought held no thrill no sense of victory. It was simply that the fight was over.

"All resistance will cease everywhere on Sirius V, and throughout the Sirius system," Grayson said slowly. "All military electronics, including electronic scanning, radar, and countermeasures, are to be shut down at once. Capellan military command frequencies will be restricted to orders to cease resistance, and for emergency use alone. I am authorized to inform you that units in the service of House Marik will arrive within thirty standard hours of formal cessation of hostilities. Local civilian and government officials are to cooperate with them fully."

"Of course." That cooperation was, after all, basic to the formal protocols of war. "Is Sirius V to be permanently transferred to Free Worlds's control?"

He wants to know if this is a raid or an invasion. Grayson thought. *I guess I'd want to know the same thing myself, in their boots.*

He shook his head. "I'm afraid I don't know, sir. I'm sure His Grace, the Marik Lord Commander, will have his own list of demands. The City Fathers are to appoint a council to receive His Grace and the League officials to discuss their requirements."

"Is that all?"

"That is all I have for you under the flag of House Marik. I have requests to make in my own name."

"Yes?"

"Nothing beyond the protocol of the Conventions, Mr. Ambassador. I will need supplies, repair parts, if possible, the use of local recreational facilities for my people. I will guarantee their behavior, of course."

The ambassador nodded. "I'm sure that can all be arranged. Is there more?"

"Liao troops within fifty kilometers of Tiantan are to turn over their weapons immediately. If there are no violations, there will be no need for registration or internment."

Chandresenkhar bowed again. "That is good of you, Colonel. The gesture will be appreciated."

"You understand that I cannot speak for the Lord Commander," Grayson said. "His Grace may require internment, and that is entirely within his rights under the Conventions. But until then . . ." Grayson shrugged. "If Tiantan's people behave themselves, I see no reason to lock any of them up."

"I understand." The ambassador hesitated, as though listening. The man would be linked, no doubt, to the Tiantan Fathers themselves, through a commlink in his environmental suit. "Sir, the City Fathers have asked me to convey to you their complete acceptance of your terms . . . and to thank you on their behalf for your generosity. They count themselves fortunate to have been bested in war by the illustrious Grayson Death Carlyle."

In a sealed and heated communications vehicle nearly ten kilometers from where Grayson and the envoy were speaking, a dark man with brooding eyes leaned back from the radio console, setting aside the device he had been holding against one ear. "That's it, then," he said, the words slow and thoughtful. The four men crowding around him in the narrow compartment listened attentively. "They've agreed to Formal Peace. The Sirius campaign is over."

"We can begin, then," one of the four said. His en-

vironmental suit was open enough to show the bulky padding of a BattleMech cooling vest across his chest. The
insignia on his breast patch was a grinning gray and black
skull against a scarlet background.

The first man nodded. "I never thought anyone would
be able to move as fast as Carlyle did. In a way, it's a
shame . . ."

"What is a shame, Precentor . . . ?"

"*Never* call me that! Not even here!"

The MechWarrior's eyes widened, and he struggled
visibly to swallow. "I . . . I . . . Forgive me, Lord."

"Forgiven," the man said simply. "But don't forget
again. Your role in the events to come is most important.
You cannot afford a careless word or thought. It would
be most . . . unfortunate."

"Y-yes, my Lord. Thank you, my Lord."

"Good. You may ready yourself." He nodded toward
the other three. "All of you gather your men. The Duke
will be here in thirty hours. It is time we began."

2

"Well, our part in the contract has been fulfilled," Grayson said.

He stood with Lori on an arched bridge above the Silver Way, the high-vaulted main corridor running across the breadth of the largest of Tiantan's five domes. The other ferrocrete and steel structures housed hydroponics facilities that fed the city-colony's entire population. In this dome was the city proper, a vast, labyrinthine subsurface of warrens that housed twelve million people.

The Way below was crowded with people, citizens of the colony that had just fallen to the Legion's thrust. The Tiantan domed cities were completely encased in ferrocrete and duraplast, warmed and sealed against the frigid poison without. Outside, the domes were a sullen, cold grey. Inside, the walls had been painted in pastel shades that contrasted the crowds clash of color, costume, and noise.

The bridge, too, was crowded. It seemed that all of Tiantan's population had left their quarters today to glimpse the invaders in their midst. The Legion's tireless Captain Ramage had stationed armored security forces at strategic points throughout the main dome, but there seemed to be no need for force of arms. The crowds were not hostile, though Grayson had noted many sullen or uneasy looks among the faces. The defenders had surrendered, and so, under the protocols of war, the city of Tiantan would remain intact. The rulers of the city might be changed or reparations charged that could raise the city dwellers' taxes. All in all, though, the lives of individual Sirians would change little as a result of the recent battles in the icy fields beyond the city's domed walls.

Lori touched Grayson's hand lightly and guided him out of the jostling crowd to the railing above the Silver Way. Blonde hair fell across her eyes as she looked up at him, but she brushed it aside impatiently. "We've done our part, but you don't sound happy about it, Gray."

"What's to be happy about?"

"Home," Lori said, but her voice scarcely carried across the distance between them. "A place to call home . . ."

"At least until the next campaign, the next raid."

She took his arm in both of hers and squeezed. Her smile was infectious, but Lori's eyes held a shadow of worry as she searched his face. "Oh, come on, Gray! Aren't you excited about a place to call home? I am." The smile faded. "Sigurd is a long way away . . ."

Grayson managed a smile of his own. "I must be an honest-to-God old soldier now, love," he said. "Home is the regiment, and all that . . ."

Lori hummed something, low and sad. Grayson ducked his head closer to hear above the crowd roar. She stopped humming then and sang, putting words to the tune.

Home is the regiment, across the sea of stars,
On worlds hot, on worlds cold, where Warriors tread afar.
Though place of birth and family, though loved ones all be lost,
Home is the regiment, across the sea of stars.

She stopped, then looked up at Grayson, her eyes bright. "It's all of that, Gray. But the regiment needs a place of its own. All of us do. For us. Helm will be home . . ."

Grayson nodded, but he was thinking that the military had been his own home for as long as he could remember. As the son of Durant Carlyle, commander of Carlyle's Commandos, he had lived in a blurred succession of garrison outposts, cantonments on worlds along the marches, fortresses above alien cities. At the age of ten standard, he'd become a MechWarrior apprentice in his father's own company. From that day forward, he had been trained as a MechWarrior, raised in the expectation that one day the father would retire and the son would assume his command.

Things had not worked out that way. The betrayal at Trellwan and the death of Durant Carlyle had left Grayson Carlyle on his own. From the ashes of that loss and defeat, he had forged the Legion almost through sheer will. In the fire and blood of shared combat, he had found a kind of family to replace the one that had been destroyed.

For him, home had *always* been the regiment.

As a mercenary combined arms regiment, the Gray Death Legion was fairly typical, if still small. The Legion *had* grown since Verthandi. The backbone of the unit was still Grayson's BattleMech company, called "A" Company, or the Gray Death. Those twelve 'Mechs were arranged in three lances of four 'Mechs each, with Grayson himself as Captain, the Company Commander. In addition, they had also managed to assemble the better part of a second 'Mech company, which was now designated as a training company and replacement pool for the Gray Death. New recruits were trained in Lieutenant DeVillar's B Company, while older, more experienced recruits were rotated two at a time through A Company's recon lance.

Those who survived would eventually graduate to a permanent lance slot in a second line company that Grayson was planning.

Besides the 'Mech units, there were two companies of line infantry under the command of Captain Ramage. Organized as three 40-man platoons, each company had been unrelentingly trained and drilled by Ramage, a former Trellwanese infantry sergeant who had a knack for special commando tactics. His ability to train raw recruits into commandos able to take on BattleMechs with improvised weapons had been vital to the success of the guerrilla campaign on Verthandi, and so Grayson had promoted Ramage to the rank of Captain, despite his protestations.

A new company had only recently been created and

placed under the command of another newcomer signed on at Galatea, Lieutenant Mark Baron. Baron had charge of the Legion's armor company, which consisted of eight Galleon and twelve Vedette light tanks, most of them prizes captured from the Kuritans on Verthandi. Grayson hoped to organize the tanks into recon lance support teams, but for now was more concerned with training tank drivers to handle the balky combat machines.

Then there was the Tech Company, now under the command of Master Tech Lieutenant Alard King. At last count, the Tech Company consisted of over three hundred specialists trained to provide the technical services that kept the unit functioning. The personnel ranged from senior MechTech King, to drivers for the Legion's skimmers, combat medics who cared for the wounded, the weapons Techs, and cooks who prepared the food.

Finally, there was Renfred Tor and the twenty men and woman who crewed the starship *Invidious*. This former merchantman crew were now the Legion's Transport Division.

Counting MechWarriors, troops, specialists, and Techs, the Gray Death Legion had grown to more than 600 strong. The total approached nearly a thousand when the Legion's "family" was considered. These were the total non-combatants, wives and husbands of warriors or Techs, children, teachers, servants and retainers, barbers, private Techs in the employ of specific families, and the small army of administrators and bookkeepers who kept the business end of things running smoothly.

This minor army was not all on Sirius V, of course. For each of the Liao campaigns, Grayson had deployed to the combat zone only the troops absolutely necessary for the job at hand. A world near the border in Marik space, Graham IV, had served as a staging area. For transport, the Legion had only the one aging freighter and its two DropShips. In these merchanters converted to troop transports, conditions would have been unbearably crowded with even half that number of personnel. Besides, a mercenary unit had to feed itself when campaigning, and that task became logistically complex and devastatingly expensive on a non-Terran and hostile world such as Sirius V. This time, Grayson had with him only the Gray Death Company itself, plus several reserve 'Mechs from Company B, and one of Captain Ramage's infantry companies. The tanks, with their internal combustion engines, would not have worked in Sirius V's atmosphere, and diesel fuel was hard to come by in such places, anyway. The rest of the training company, the support personnel, even most of the unit's Techs, had all been left behind at the Legion's new home at Helm.

The Legion's contract with House Marik had promised them a landhold, a charter granting the regiment a lease on the planet known as Helm. Cold and glacier-locked, Helm was a savage world. Even the habitable equatorial region was raw and largely barren. The entire planet had a population of perhaps fifteen million, divided among numberless villages and small farming communities rather than cities. There were no factories, no mines, no massive industrial complexes, little, in fact, to make it attractive by the standards of modern galactic civilization.

The contract with Marik had been struck a year ago, and the final details of the landhold worked out six months after that. In exchange for its services against Liao, the Gray Death Legion formally received title to a large part of Helm's North Highland Plains in an investiture ceremony at Helmfast Castle, near the village of Durandel. Two months later, the regiment's 'Mech facilities had begun rising from the plains to the east.

The bulk of the Gray Death Legion—the cooks and teachers, spouses and children, the computer and logistics technicians, the army of astechs raised from among the local population, the training company and infantry reserves and Baron's tank company—all were on Helm now, building the Legion facilities at Durandel.

Despite the pessimism that gripped Grayson, he had to admit being anxious to return. *Home.*

"Uh oh. Recon lance approaching at Sector Front-Center, Colonel," Lori snapped in mock-official tones.

Francine Roget, Harriman Vandergriff, and Sylvia Trevor approached Grayson and Lori arm in arm, forging

25

relentlessly through the crowds of civilians that thronged the Silver Way.

"Ho, noble Colonel!" Lieutenant Roget raised the green glass bottle in her free hand and nodded an elaborate bow to Grayson. All three were well past the limits of sobriety. "A salute, comrades, to Colonel Carlyle, the Victor of Sirius V!"

Grayson saw black glances among the nearest of the civilian passersby, heard a change in their murmured conversations.

"Damp it, Lieutenant," he said, gently disentangling his arm from Lori's. "The celebration is over."

"Aw, Colonel . . ." Vandergriff began, but Grayson stopped him with a look.

"That will be *all*, Mister!" He glanced at his wrist-comp, noting the time. "Muster with your DropShip Captain, the lot of you."

"Vandergriff," Lori said. "I thought you had the duty tonight, walking perimeter." As the unit's Exec, she was in charge of duty schedules and watch bills.

"Aw, Lieutenant. Graff swapped with me. Said he didn't care for the nightlife here!"

"When he comes in off duty, you can tell him your whole lance is confined," Grayson said. "I'll want to see all of you logged in and ready for boost by the time I come aboard."

The lance commander came to a reasonable approximation of attention, and the others struggled up after her. Hilarity was replaced by sullenness in Vandergriff and evident confusion in Trevor, the newest member of the lance, but they obeyed.

"Is it the Colonel's orders that my lance miss out on the fun, sir?" Lieutenant Roget's words were tightly bitten off, her fists clenched at her sides. "We have been fighting hard . . . *sir.*"

"Boost is in eight hours, Lieutenant," Grayson said. He spoke quietly, but his tone and pitch carried authority with them. "You won't be missing more than a few hours' fun." He leaned forward then, voice lower rather than louder. "And I *damn* well am going to see to it that you miss out on causing a riot before we boost! Dismissed!"

The three managed a ragged salute, then turned and made their way with the flow of the crowd. Grayson turned back to Lori.

"I imagine most of our people are . . . ah . . . celebrating. It's been a rough two weeks."

"Maybe. But if they disgrace us now, with the Formal Peace . . ."

"I know. But they're good people. Gray. The whole company! They're all good people!"

What was Lori trying to tell him? Grayson wondered. He knew they were good people. The past year had seen them forged together in the furnace of a fast, bloody, hard-hitting campaign. He had watched them come together, watched them become a fighting unit. Some of them had been with him on Verthandi before they'd signed on with Marik. He *knew* they were good.

"Are you saying I'm too hard on them? Because I grounded Graff as well?" He shook his head. "A lance stands together. It suffers together. I'll not weaken it by having them resent one another. They can resent me all they want, but *not one another*!"

"I didn't mean that. You're not as hard on them as you are on yourself, Gray. But they are human. Sometimes, I wonder if *you* are."

"If I am what?"

"Human . . . or just a Colonel . . ."

Grayson suppressed an icy, internal twist at the words. With her characteristically keen inner vision, Lori had seen through to the personal devil that had been gnawing at Grayson more and more.

Full regiments were generally larger than the Legion was so far, but there was considerable latitude in the organizational tables of mercenary units, which only rarely were able to carry full combat rosters. Grayson, who had taken the rank of Captain to justify his command of a BattleMech company, was listed as "Colonel" on the organization charts to justify his command of the entire Legion. He still felt uncomfortable with *that* title. At only twenty-four years old, he was far too young to wear such rank comfortably or gracefully.

As a twenty-four-year-old mercenary who had built the

Legion from scratch in the heat and blood and fury of half a dozen hard-fought campaigns, he was beginning to realize that the job was rapidly outgrowing him, that with every order, every command decision, he was becoming less certain that what he was doing was right. In the meantime, so many people were depending on *him* to make the right decisions.

Had he been too harsh with Roget's lance? Especially Graff, who had not even been party to the lance's drunkenness, the cause for Grayson's explosion. He didn't know. Worse, he was coming to realize that he never knew, whenever he made such decisions.

He looked at his wristcomp again, needlessly. "I'd better head back to the *Phobos*."

"Why, Gray? There's time." Lori took his arm again. "The Duke won't arrive for hours yet, and I'd say that you and I are long past due for some celebrating of our own."

Her words caught him off-guard, and disturbed him more than he wanted to admit. "I . . . really don't feel like it, Lori."

"Come on, Colonel. This time it's your Exec who's giving the orders. My spies found this little pleasure place off the Silver Way. Good food. Private rooms with swimming pools for baths . . ."

"Lori . . ."

"Damn it, Grayson Carlyle. For once you and I are going to have some *fun!*"

He realized then that Lori did not know, could not know, how deeply she had touched him. He shook his head and gently pulled his arm free. For the past year, he and Lori had been close, and growing closer. In those months, they'd come to share far more than love and bed and friendship. Born of fire and pain, of death and respect for one another, that sharing had become a sharing of self.

For the first time in that year, Grayson felt that Lori not only didn't understand, but couldn't . . .

"No, Lord," he said, smiling. "The Exec doesn't always get her way. Not this time. I've got too much work to do."

THE PRICE OF GLORY

He felt her hurt as they walked back toward the command vehicle that would return them to the spaceport.

Among the rock crags and broken, ice-crusted terrain beyond the dome wall, shadows rose and moved toward a line of low-slung vehicles resting on the icy plain. An armed and armored sentry glimpsed movement from the corner of his eye and spun to issue a challenge. That challenge died with him as the white-glowing blur of a vibroblade chopped through a short arc, cleaving armor, padding, and flesh with equal ease. Blood spurted, within moments freezing where it splattered on ice and the frost-rimed surface of the guard's personal armor. Other armored figures were climbing among the vehicles even as the sentry's lifeless form slid to the ice.

Working swiftly and silently, the figures flung heavy canvas satchels one after another into the cargo compartments of three of the company's scout skimmers. First one, then another, then a third of the lithe hovercraft stirred from their resting places, then rose, balanced on cushions of air blasted into their plenum chambers by high-speed, fusion-powered fans. As their piercing whine shrieked across the frozen landscape, another sentry scrambled from the temporary pressure dome erected nearby. His voice came across the general communications frequency. "You! Who's there! What . . ."

Laser light stabbed from one of the skimmers, spearing the Gray Death sentry through the dark-tinted plastic of his mask goggles. Polarized filters did nothing to attenuate that megajoule lance of energy. Hydrogen in the atmosphere and oxygen from the mask mingled as the visor shattered, then ignited in the intense heat of the laser light. There had been no oxygen in the tight-fitting inner suit of the first sentry to react with the surrounding atmosphere and the vibroblade's heat. Here, though, the chemical reaction was immediate, and explosive. Goggles, mask, and head burst apart in a fine spray of charred debris, water, and red mist.

Heavily laden, the three hovercraft tilted forward, bows nearly scraping the ice, and raced off toward Tiantan at maximum acceleration. As they swept around a low ridge, a BattleMech, a 40-ton *Assassin*, confronted them. The trio of hovercraft did not slow but continued to race at breakneck speed across the ice and gravel toward the city looming now on the skyline.

The *Assassin* stepped aside and raised its left hand in salute as the skimmers passed. Then it turned and continued its patrol.

The *Assassin*'s pilot opened his commlink. "Graff here, on Sector Two. All clear. No activity."

Beyond the ridge nearby, two steaming bodies cooled in the frigid air.

3

Fifty kilometers west of the city dome complex, on the windswept expanse of ferrocrete and poured concrete that served as Tiantan's spaceport, Grayson and his regimental officers waited beneath the port's plex dome while members of the Irian Guard streamed from the lock leading out to the newly grounded DropShip. Captain Ramage, crisp and unaccountably sharp as always in the Legion's dress grays, muttered something at Grayson's left elbow.

"What was that, Ram?" Grayson said. The Irian Guards were forming up in twin lines, facing one another at attention on either side of the purple carpet that had been unrolled across the black ferrocrete deck of the dome. Through the port, Grayson and his men glimpsed a stir of activity in the extension tube that had just been connected to the main debarkation hatch of the towering *Union* Class DropShip.

"I was just wondering at his Mightiness arriving ahead of his fleet," Ramage replied, *sotto voce*. "There're three more *Union*s to come, and he beat 'em all!"

"Anxious to survey what he's won by force of arms," Lori muttered from Grayson's right.

"Quiet, both of you," Grayson said. "Here he comes."

Lord Garth, Duke of Irian, was a big and florid man. The Marik crest, a stylized bird of prey with wings outstretched, was tattooed on his forehead in the fashion affected by many House Marik nobles. The medals across the gold-trimmed purple of his dress tunic appeared to weigh him down in Sirius V's one-and-a-half gravities nearly as much as did his considerable girth and bulk. Flanking and following him were his senior aides, a minor host garbed in silver, yellow, and violet.

The air temperature in the dome was pleasantly cool, but Lord Garth was sweating heavily by the time he reached the waiting Legion officers. Ramage, Lori, and Grayson executed precise House Marik salutes in carefully rehearsed unison, open right hands to left breasts, palms down. The salutes were acknowledged by a slender ducal aide who seemed to be struggling to hold herself upright against the drag of several kilos' worth of gold aiguillettes.

"His Grace wishes to extend his thanks to the Gray Death Legion for a job well-executed," the aide said. "In the name of House Marik and the Governor General, he declares your mission here at an end, and your contract complete. The 15th Marik Militia relieves you, sir."

Grayson repeated his salute, adding the required formal bow, stiff and from the waist. Even as he did so, his eyes shifted from Duke Irian's moist face to the ranks of brown-and-purple-garbed soldiers behind him. The 15th Marik Militia was a standard Marik line regiment, one that Grayson knew well. The Legion had fought beside them on several occasions during the past year, in missions and raids along the Liao border. *These* troops, with their red-violet tunics and gold braid, were Irian Guards, the Duke's personal household troops.

"His Grace further directs," the aide continued, "that the mercenary regiment known as the Gray Death Legion board its transport vessels immediately and embark for Marik."

"Marik . . ." Grayson suppressed a start. "The Marik system, Your Grace?"

The Legion's operational orders had directed them to report to their leasehold at Helm upon completion of their mission on Sirius V. Marik was the regional administrative headquarters for the Marik Commonwealth, one of the vast, semi-autonomous provinces that made up House Marik's Free Worlds League. *Why Marik, instead of Helm?* Grayson wondered.

"His Grace reminds you of your duty under the terms of your contract with the Governor General," the aide continued.

"We thank His Grace for his kind words," Grayson said carefully. "And I respectfully submit that we know our *duty*. May I ask, though, why our regiment is being diverted to the provincial capital?"

"Orders, *mercenary*," Duke Irian spoke for the first time. The voice was high and gratingly unpleasant. He kept his eyes on some unseen point above and beyond Grayson's left shoulder, as though refusing to acknowledge him or his people. "I understand the Captain-General himself is planning to meet you there. Perhaps he has further—ah—matters of a financial nature to discuss with you. Or perhaps he seeks to do you . . . honor. I wouldn't know. Whatever the Captain-General's reasons, my forces will relieve you. Now."

"Do you accept relief, Colonel?" the aide prompted.

"Eh? Yes, of course. At your orders, Your Grace." Grayson saluted again. The amenities of ceremony had to be observed. "This world is yours, Your Grace."

"I don't like this one bit," Lori said. The three of them were in the observation lounge of the DropShip *Phobos*. The steel shutters normally closed against the threat of enemy attack had been rolled back, opening the small room to a view of the Sirian spaceport and the gray mass of the domes beyond. Sirius had set some hours before, and the Tiantan city domes were marked by the clusters of lights and the steady wink of air navigation beacons.

The field below them encircled the *Phobos*'s blast pit in blackness broken only by pools of work lights. Each pool revealed steady, hurried activity as the regiment made its final preparations for boarding. Most of the Gray Death's BattleMechs were already aboard, racked and cocooned in their cavernous storage bays deep within the ship. Ramage's infantry company was boarding now, a winding line of pressurized, tracked, all-terrain infantry transports. Pressure-suited traffic marshals directed traffic with circular waves of red-tipped handlights. Small, brightly lit vehicles crawled beetle-like from light pool to pool, bearing technicians intent on disassembling electronics gear still on the field, carrying support grades gathering caches of stacked and crated weapons, carrying officers making final rounds or bearing orders for harried NCOs.

"There's not much about it to like," Grayson said. He stood at Lori's side by the viewport. The lounge was in darkness, and their features were stagelit by the work lights below. "We've got damn little choice, though."

"Orders are orders, then?" Ramage asked. He was seated at a small table set back from the port. A heavy plastic headpiece embraced the back of his head from ear to ear. In the near dark, the com unit glowed and flashed with tiny lights of red, green, and amber at uneven intervals as Ramage monitored reports from his various field NCOs and Techs on the progress of the boarding. He had, in particular, been monitoring the progress of a patrol across one sector of the landing field perimeter. Two sentries had been found dead in the early morning hours—presumably the work of Liao snipers in the wilderness who had refused to surrender.

"Mmm," was Grayson's reply. "There's nothing particularly unusual about the order to report to Marik. Except, of course, that Marik is as far from here as Helm, but in a different direction. That's a long, expensive trip for us, just to pick up a new set of medals."

"If Janos Marik pays the bill . . ." Lori began, but she didn't finish the sentence. Nowhere in the contract signed with the Marik government was a provision for the Legion's transportation stated or implied. It had the taste of one of those no-win scenarios the bookkeepers and paymasters for mercenary units dreaded: resources expended to please a client, with nothing in return but the *hope* of that client's good will.

"It's not the money that's bothering me, Lori," Grayson said. "There's politics afoot, and I don't like it."

"Anytime a Marik Duke puts his foot in it, there's politics to contend with," Ramage said grimly.

"But this is unusual . . . damned unusual," Grayson said. "You know, at the procession today, all I saw was the Irian Guard, old Lord Garth's personal household troops. I didn't see The Hawk in Garth's entourage, or among the officers that came off his DropShip." Colonel Jake Hawkings, informally known as "the Hawk," was the short, red-haired and irascible commander of the 15th Marik Militia, a man Grayson and his staff had worked with before on several occasions during the Marik contract. According to the Legion's contract orders, it was Hawkings's unit that was supposed to relieve them when the operation on Sirius V was complete.

"You're right, he wasn't there," Ramage said. "I wondered about that, too. I had one of my Techs ask one of theirs about it. The 15th isn't due onworld for two weeks yet. They've only just now jumped in-system, and their DropShip is still in deep-space transit."

"Two weeks!" This was unexpected news, and Grayson wasn't sure how to interpret it. He had been informed that the 15th had arrived with the Duke's forces at the start of the campaign, two weeks before. If the 15th was not with Lord Garth, what unit *was* aboard the Dropships that had waited and watched from space during the course of the Sirius campaign?

"Maybe we shouldn't have accepted relief," Lori suggested.

"Yes? And how would you have phrased it?" Ramage said. "No, Lord Garth, I'm not going to turn over command to you. I'll just wait here for Colonel Hawkings."

"It's a moot question at this point," Grayson said. "We've been relieved, and we've received our orders. His Grace is here, and we've been gently but firmly shown the door."

Ramage brought one hand to his comset, listening intently. "The door's open," he said after a moment, as lights winked in the darkness from the set. "All infantry companies are aboard and secure. MechWarrior Graff is boarding the *Deimos* now, and that's the last of our recon lance. The last of our gear is coming aboard too. The duty cargo officer reports that we can boost in ninety minutes."

"Maybe," Grayson said carefully, "Maybe we should hurry and leave, before Lord Garth changes his mind.

William H. Keith, Jr.

There's something seriously wrong here, and I don't think I want to know what it is.''

Aboard the House Marik DropShip *Gladius*, Lord Garth, His Grace, Duke of Irian, paused in his inspection tour of the four freshly painted BattleMechs in the ship's Mech bay. Those machines looming among the shadows created by the harsh overhead work lights were newly freed from their restraints and protective locks. All four were painted in the mottled gray and black camouflage patterns used by 'Mechs in combat on airless worlds. The grinning visages of new-painted, stylized gray and black skulls on scarlet unit patches leered down at the Duke and his party from high on the left leg of each battle machine.

A tall man in an unadorned brown tunic and shortcloak approached the ducal inspection party and executed a correct but perfunctory bow. The slim dagger in his forearm sheath flashed in the light of the overhead fluoros as he straightened.

Garth licked his lips and acknowledged the bow. The man made him nervous. His manner, his bearing, the hint of power that he represented, all served to magnify the threat, real or imagined, behind those dark eyes. ''Call me Rachan,'' he had told Garth at their first meeting, on Irian, months before. ''Not 'my Lord,' not 'Precentor' Simply 'Rachan' will do.''

''You have a report, Rachan,'' Garth said. The words were a statement, not a question. Rachan had never approached Garth simply to talk, for which Garth was profoundly grateful.

''The mercenary Dropships are preparing to launch. Your Grace,'' Rachan said, without preamble. ''My agents report that all is ready at Tiantan.''

Garth nodded, his chins wobbling with the motion. ''Very well. I will come up.'' He managed a weak grin. ''This should be something to watch, eh?''

''Indeed,'' Rachan said not returning the Duke's forced smile.

By the time the Duke and his staff arrived in the large, richly ornamented lounge of the *Gladius*, the *Deimos*,

36

one of the two Legion Dropships, had already boosted. Smoke still hung heavy in the cold air above the ferrocrete launch pad in the distance. Still remaining was the DropShip *Phobos,* a solitary, silver-grey sphere flood-lit by batteries of port arc lights, and with wreaths of vapor steaming from exhaust ports and vents. The skull emblem of the Gray Death Legion was distinct under the glare of one of the port lights.

One of Garth's officers looked up as his lord entered the room. He stood, bowing, "Your Grace. The second merc ship is in the final seconds of its countdown."

Garth nodded and strode toward the broad viewing port. An intolerably brilliant blur of light appeared at the base of the Legion DropShip. Smoke, white-lit by the growing torrent of fusion sun at the DropShip's base, billowed from the launch pit's vents. Seconds later, the shockwave struck the *Gladius,* rattling faintly through from the armor of the outer hull. Balanced on flame, the *Phobos* climbed, slowly at first, then faster and faster into the night.

Garth sensed a presence at his side.

"It is time, Your Grace," Rachan said.

Garth nodded, his forefinger probing nervously at the Marik house crest tattooed on his forehead.

"Yes . . . yes. Very well. Captain Tannis!"

An aide stepped forth. He wore a comset across his ears, its lights eerie in the dazzled darkness after the *Phobos*'s miniature sunrise.

"Yes, Your Grace!"

"Now."

"As you will, Your Grace!" The aide saluted, then touched his headset, murmuring into the slender mike wire suspended before his lips. The Duke and Rachan turned to another part of the viewport, where they could see the domes of Tiantan on the horizon beyond the starport.

"The city is fifty kilometers away," Garth said, more to himself than to anyone else in the lounge. "That should be . . ."

A point of blinding, blue-white brilliance appeared against the nearest of the Tiantan domes. The flare was joined by another against a farther dome, then another, then two more. Each fireball wavered in the convection currents generated by its own heat, then expanded, with shocking speed.

The ducal party watched, silent, transfixed by the sight. The interior of the lounge was frosted in blue light, then suddenly plunged into orange and crimson as fireballs erupted from the domes exploding into the night sky.

The thunderclap roar reached the spaceport moments later, setting the DropShip's hull to rattling even harder than had the much nearer shock of the *Phobos*'s launch. The explosions went on and on, as new sequestered stores of oxygen-rich air spilled into the hydrogen of Sirius V's atmosphere and ignited. Fires raged. No fire burned for long in the Sirian atmosphere, but so long as oxygen from the ruptured city domes lasted, isolated fires raged in blast furnace infernos. Smoke piled mountain upon billowing mountain into the heavens, red-lit and angry.

Finally, the explosions had all died away. What remained of the domes were charred, broken eggshell fragments and rubble. There were also five short-lived and volcanic funeral pyres, glowing white-hot.

Rachan turned to Lord Garth. "There will be survivors, Your Grace . . . mostly in underground chambers and in work areas and outposts in the surrounding region. I suggest that your people move quickly to place the new insignias on this DropShip."

"The orders have already been given," the Duke replied softly. Who was this man whose mind could encompass such plans within plans?

"Excellent. One *Union* Class DropShip looks very much like another, but the panels your artificers created should prove most convincing."

"Yes."

"I would also unleash your 'Mechs, Your Grace. The . . . shall we say . . . the final, finishing touch to our little drama. If there are any survivors in the area, by morning, they will be convinced that this was the work of the Gray Death."

"Yes."

There was a grinding rumble from somewhere far below decks as 'Mech bay doors slid open. A moment later, a heavy *Marauder* in a gray- and black-mottled camouflage scheme similar to that used on Grayson Carlyle's own *Marauder* during the past two weeks strode out across the spaceport. It was followed by a *Shadow Hawk*, a *Wolverine*, and a *Rifleman*.

"Of course," Rachan added, smiling, "by morning, there may not be any survivors to *care!*"

4

The JumpShip *Invidious* began the maneuvers that would furl its sail. Two kilometers across and ebony-black to collect every photon for the starship's fusion-powered converters, the sail was nearly invisible save where it blotted out the stars and the searing, actinic brilliance that was Sirius.

Captain Renfred Tor had begun the process by cutting the plasma thrust station-keepers and maneuvering the kilometer-long needle of his ship stern-first into the sail's thrust eye, the circular opening through which the *Invidious* directed the magnetically boosted plasma that held her in place at the local jump point against the gravitational pull of the star. Sirius's jump points were almost 67 AU out, but the star's gravitational field, though weakened by distance, was still very much in evidence.

Grayson hung weightless on the *Invidious*'s bridge, watching Tor direct the operation. Sweat beaded on Tor's forehead, or floated free as tiny, glittering planetesimals. A mistake in calculation or execution, and the extremely valuable jump sail could be damaged, or worse, irretrievably lost. With consummate skill, Tor brought the *Invidious* gently to rest with her tail spearing through the light sail's thrust eye.

"Green," Tor said into the microphone that projected from his earpiece to a point just in front of his mouth. "Lock and furl. All departments, commence jump preparations."

Captain Tor looked up across the plot table at Grayson. "Are you sure about this, Colonel?"

Grayson studied again the network of colored lights floating in the holographic projection well of the chart tank beneath the transparent surface of the table. The stars of near space were plotted there, each in its proper position relative to the others, each with its identifying name and grid reference. Two lines, one green, one red, zigzagged through three-dimensional angles. Each began at the white gleam identified as Sirius, but the two pathways diverged. One angled sharply down toward the familiar G2 system of Graham. The other stretched upward toward the point marking Pollux.

"We're technically violating our contract if we disobey Duke Irian's orders."

"I know, Ren," Grayson said, uneasy. "But there's something just not right about this." His suspicions had first been aroused when their relief on Sirius V had turned out to be, not Jake Hawkings's 15th, as promised, but Duke Irian himself and his personal guard. Not that there was anything *wrong* there, but . . .

Then, during their passage from Sirius V to the Sirian zenith jump point, the *Phobos* had passed within close radio hailing distance of a squadron of four Marik DropShips heading the other way, in-system. The *Phobos*'s call and ID had been ignored.

Once the DropShips had docked with the old, ex-merchant freighter *Invidious,* Grayson had opened a beamcast channel to Sirius V, hoping to verify the unexpected order to proceed to Marik. Perhaps one of the Duke's staff would be willing to tell him more? That never happened because Tiantan's com beacon, the transmitter for the carrier wave that would have patched him directly to the Duke's communication network, was unaccountably silent.

Technical difficulties, perhaps, Grayson had thought. Equipment was always breaking down, and in the aftermath of the invasion, technicians and comreptechs would have their hands full, keeping city services functioning smoothly. Remembering the sullen looks on the faces of some of the civilians, he knew that sabotage, too, was a possibility.

One way or the other, the silence worried him. Something was going on back there, something involving the Duke and the unilateral changes in the Legion's contract orders. The *Invidious*'s ComTech had finally managed to open a channel to the Duke's DropShip *Gladius*, but with remarkably unhelpful results. What they were told was that the Duke and his entire staff were busy and could not be disturbed. All was secure in Tiantan, and the Legion's orders stood.

What is going on? Grayson wondered. He remembered Lord Garth keeping his eyes unfocused somewhere beyond Grayson's shoulders. *As if I didn't exist,* Grayson thought. He suppressed a shudder. That sort of thinking would get him nowhere.

"I suppose we are technically in violation of our orders," he continued after a moment. "But we're not violating our contract. Helm's only four jumps away from Marik. We can still go to the Admin capital. We'll just take a little longer to get there . . . by a little more roundabout way."

"You have a reason? The Captain-General could be waiting there to pin medals on us." Tor chuckled. "God knows, we deserve 'em! You've done a right smart job of mopping up on Liao along this border, old son!"

Grayson folded his arms, the motion setting him adrift, and moving slowly beside the chart table. "You want a reason? Let's just say I'm the suspicious sort. My father always told me that those were the kind of MechWarriors who lived the longest." He reached out and grabbed hold of a stanchion, arresting his drift. "Let's just say I'll feel better—we'll *all* feel better—after I've seen the landhold and checked in with the people there." When Tor didn't reply, Grayson continued. "Damn it, something strange is going on, Ren! Half our people are back on Helm, and I don't like being this spread out . . . exposed and vulnerable!"

"You think someone's going to attack Helm? Or us?"

"I don't think anything, right now. I just want to rejoin the rest of our people. We'll decide what the next step is after that. We'll stop at Helm for a week or two, let our people unwind, get the equipment patched up. Then we'll see about this summons to Marik."

"O.K. You're the boss," Tor said, but his voice was disapproving. "For once, though, I'd enjoy knowing that we weren't acting on one of your hunches!" He glanced up at a vidscreen that showed the activity aft along the long, slender length of the JumpShip. The sail had collapsed in a circular mass of accordion folds, guided by nearly invisible guide struts and monofilament cables. Hatch sections had closed over the sail, sealing it from the stresses of hyperspace as the manned work pods that had supervised the process returned to their storage bays in the *Invidious*'s hull. Sirius shone due aft, illuminating the blocky rear edges of the JumpShip's complex and convoluted skeletal frame.

"All stations," a voice announced over the bridge intercom. "Sail stowage maneuver complete. All stations, report readiness for jump to Navigation."

Captain Tor touched a control, and the green pathway across the stars, the one running through Pollux, zigzagging through five jumps to the Marik system, winked out. The red path, eight jumps angling down to the orange gleam of Helm, remained. "Navigation," Tor said into the microphone at his throat. "Jump route via Graham is confirmed. You have my command: jump when ready."

Moments more passed in silence. "All stations," a voice warned at last from the ship intercom, sounding throughout the kilometer-long complexity of the *Invidious* and within the paired DropShips fastened leechlike to the needle-slim backbone between crew area and reactor core. "Prepare for jump."

The voice began counting off the seconds. Grayson spent the time seeking out the pinpoint of light that marked Sirius V, but at this distance, the world was lost in the glare from its primary. *What's going on back there?* he wondered. *And why?*

Just as he was thinking that maybe a side trip to Helm would answer those questions, there came the sickening lurch and blackness of jump.

The world known as Helm was not a pleasant one for man. Fourth planet out of a mild, K4 sun, it lay on the outer fringes of its star's habitable zone. More than half its surface was locked beneath glaciers kilometers deep. Vast stretches of what had once been ocean floor were dry and bare, with much of the world's water now locked in Helm's icecaps.

Much of the land that remained was either mountainous or arid desert. Between the relentless, endless seas of ice to north and south, ice-capped mountains thousands of meters high girdled Helm at the equator.

Yet life had evolved on Helm ages before, in an epoch when Helm's star was brighter and warmer. Life had continued by adapting to the cold. The planet had been discovered and colonized by men probing out from New Hope and Tania Borealis late in the 22nd century. The principal city of Freeport had grown up around the starport on a bluff overlooking the salt flats of a dried equatorial sea. For a time, Freeport had served as a Star League naval base, then as a storehouse for Star League weapons. In 2788, however, Minoru Kurita unleashed fusion firestorms over Freeport and the other major settlements on Helm in an attempt to destroy or seize those stores. Within a single rotational period of 26 hours, the population of Helm was reduced from over one hundred million to a handful of starveling wretches huddled around campfires in the wilderness. Kurita learned that the weapons stockpiles he was seeking had already been transported elsewhere and departed.

It took three centuries for the planet to even begin to recover.

By the 31st Century, Helm was part of the Duchy of Stewart. Settlements had appeared once more in scattered clusters among the valleys and plateaus of the equatorial mountains. With its small population and non-existent industrial base, Helm was ideal as a landhold for MechWarriors in the service of the Free Worlds League. Between 2958 and 3025, Helm had served as landhold for several Marik Warriors or Warrior families, who hired or pressed local families into service to build the fortresses that marked their titled grants. In 3025, the last of those grants reverted to House Marik when the leaseholder defected to House Liao, taking his BattleMech company with him.

Then, in 3027, Janos Marik offered the largest of Helm's landholds to Colonel Grayson Carlyle in exchange for the Gray Death Legion's services against House Liao. Helmfast, the Castle in the hills above Durandel, had been a stronghold for the planet's military governor in Star League days, and had served several times since as landhold for various Warriors and their families. The practice of landholds was a common one in the neo-feudalism that had risen across the Inner Sphere in this era of continuous war and faltering technology. By taking charge of the landhold on Helm, Carlyle became Marik's "man," sworn to serve Janos Marik when summoned to do so. The arrangement worked to the benefit of both parties: Carlyle and his people had a home, and Janos Marik had a new combined arms regiment. The Legion's standard was to be raised above the long-vacant fortress above Durandel. It was understood that other men-at-arms would eventually be granted holds of their own elsewhere on the planet, but for now, Helm belonged to Grayson Carlyle.

Grayson and his entire staff consisting of Lori, Ramage, Captain Tor, and Tech Master Alard King, floated in the *Invidious*'s control center. Helm's sun shone in the main viewscreen, two hundred million kilometers distant.

"Whoever they are," King said slowly, "they don't care who hears them."

Alard King had joined the Legion on Galatea after their return from Verthandi. He was an expert Tech, who had last served with Steiner's Lyran Guard, but had left for Galatea after a "minor disagreement" with his company commander. He was Grayson's senior Tech now; as Tech Master, he was in overall command of all of the Legion's technical personnel.

King looked across the plot table at Grayson and the others. He was holding a speaker to one ear, but the babble he was listening to was coming from the general bridge speakers as well. Most of the sounds were unintelligible, broadcast in battlecode, but occasionally a voice could be heard in plain speech. "DropShip Two down, *Rapacious*!'' one excited voice cried. ''No resistance, Sector Five!''

''*Rapacious,*'' Tor said. ''I know that name. That's a Marik ship.''

''Let's get a current listing on her,'' Grayson said.

The *Invidious*'s Captain spoke to a nearby aide, watched over her shoulder as she tapped out his request at her computer console, then turned back to the others.

''Fifth Marik Guards,'' he said.

''That's a regular Marik House regiment,'' Lori said. ''What are they doing here?''

Grayson said nothing, his eyes on the orange brightness of Helm's sun on the viewer.

After jumping in-system at Helm's nadir jump point, they had realized instantly that something was seriously wrong. The combat frequencies were jammed by radio traffic, much of it in battlecode. It was immediately clear that at least one other starship was already in system, presumably at the system's zenith point and blocked from the *Invidious*'s view by the system's sun.

''It could be a sneak raid,'' he said. ''Kurita or Liao raiders could have jumped in . . . or pirate raiders. Maybe a Marik DropShip might have been passing through, and heard a call for help.''

Ramage's eyebrow crept toward his hairline. ''That's asking a bit of coincidence.''

''More's the point,'' Tor said. ''What would raiders want here? Helm is a hell of a long way from anyone's borders, and there's nothing there that any snap raider would want.''

''Since when do the Kuritans need an excuse for smashing a planet?'' Lori asked.

''Ren's got a point,'' Grayson said. ''Invasions . . . even snap raids, are *expensive*. They wouldn't pull one without a reason.'' He shook his head. ''But this doesn't feel like a raid.''

''Pirates?'' King suggested.

''Not this deep in Marik space. And not without something damned valuable to make it worth their while.''

''Which makes those Marik ships,'' Lori said quietly. ''Are *they* attacking our settlement? And why?''

"The Marik curse," Tor said.

"Eh?" Grayson said. "A rebellion?"

"What else could it be? Any time you look at them, the Free Worlds League is more than halfway to total anarchy. Maybe a rebel faction has finally gone over the line and started a civil war."

"Possible," Grayson said. "But the question remains . . . why Helm? What can they possibly want here?"

"And what's happening to our people down there?" Lori added.

The *Invidious* carried 240 people—her own crew of 20, plus one 'Mech company, one infantry company, a Tech platoon, and reserves. More than seven hundred of the Legion's men, women, and children remained on Helm.

Grayson's hands curled into fists. What was happening here had something to do with the strange events on Sirius V, of that he had no doubt. But what was happening, and what was the connection?

They had to find out, and fast. If they had indeed fallen into the midst of a revolution or power struggle within House Marik, the people they'd left behind on Helm were in grave danger.

"Ren," Grayson said. "How long to recharge for jump?"

Tor consulted his wristcomp. "Once our sail is unfurled—125 hours, if we push it. Otherwise, make it 175."

"And there's been no sign that they've spotted us?"

"Not yet. Speed-of-light propagation will take awhile to send them the news that we're here, but from the sound of things . . ."

He jerked a thumb toward a bridge speaker that had been babbling in static-ridden and unintelligible code for the past several minutes. An excited voice cut in, speaking in the clear. "Attention, unidentified DropShip bearing oh-oh-seven, vector three-one-one! We have not received your authority codes or ID transmission! Please identify! Please identify!"

"It sounds like sheer chaos down there. I think there's a good chance we dropped in unnoticed."

"O.K. Proceed with recharging the drives. Lori, pass the word. *Deimos* and *Phobos* will both be going in."

"All of us?" Ramage asked.

"Any that want to can remain with *Invidious*," Grayson said. "Anyone who wants to come with us to Helm, can."

"That will be everyone," Lori predicted. "But what can we *do*?"

Grayson's shoulders slumped as he realized the enormity of what he was suggesting. One company against . . . what? "I don't know," he said quietly. "First off, we find our people and see that they're safe. After that, we try to find out what the hell's going on. We'll improvise as we go along." He turned to Tor. "You, Ren, will get this ship out of here as fast as you can recharge."

"Now wait a minute. My people have a stake in whatever's happening on Helm, too."

"And we all have a stake in keeping the *Invidious* safe. The ship is irreplaceable. I want to know that she's out of the line of fire."

With only about twelve JumpShips produced by all the Successor Houses every year, each time a starship was lost to battle, accident, or lack of maintenance, civilization came that much closer to a time when the lanes between stars would be sundered, isolating the worlds of man from one another, possibly forever. For that reason, even warring factions were careful not to carry their fights to the starships.

Men were not always reasonable beings, however, and Grayson wanted to take no chances.

"You'll jump for Stewart," Grayson continued. "The Duke there is a good man, a fair one, and he has ears at the Captain-General's court on Atreus. He's always dealt with us fairly. Maybe he'll be able to tell you what's going on."

"Maybe . . . but you'll be here, in the thick of it."

"We'll handle this the way we did at Verthandi. We'll set a specific time and date for you to jump back in-system. We'll be waiting to broadcast a tight-beam zip-squeal. We'll let you know our condition, and what we want you to do about it."

"I won't have any DropShips," Tor said.

"No, but we will." Grayson looked at the others, each in turn. Now that they had a plan, a course of action to pursue, he felt somewhat better. From the expressions on the others' faces, he knew they did, too. "The rest of us will go in on a High-G, minimum-time run. With luck, anyone in orbit will think we're just another flight of DropShips who have forgotten to transmit their ID. We'll look for a place to set down as close to Durandel as possible." He shrugged. "After that, we'll see."

5

They arrived too late.

From the ridge west of Durandel, the BattleMech company looked down on a horror of destruction. Multiple, roiling columns of smoke boiled into a sky now heavy and black under the pall from a hundred smoldering fires. Grayson swept what had been the town of Durandel with his scanners once . . . twice . . . a third time, but could find no building still intact, no sign of life. The village had been systematically destroyed, almost building by building. The new 'Mech repair facilities on the east side of the town were gone, leaving only desolation and ruin. The Legion's fortress, Helmfast, built into the cliff face above the north side of town, was shattered, with only isolated portions still standing among gaunt, laser-charred and missile-broken towers. Black smoke curled up from behind the remnants of the castle wall.

A low moan sounded over the combat channel. Who? It didn't matter. They all felt the same way, shared the devastation of this loss. The knowledge that they had come too late to prevent this senseless yet calculated destruction burned within them.

''Clear the circuits,'' Grayson said, surprising himself with the bitterness of his own words.

In close formation, the DropShips *Phobos* and *Deimos* had decelerated on ravening tongues of fusion flame, dumping velocity under 4 Gs of thrust as they'd backed down into Helm's atmosphere. The sense that something was wrong, critically wrong, had been reinforced with every hour closer to their target.

The two DropShips had been challenged three times on their high-speed run toward Helm, but no AeroSpace Fighters or DropShips had been in positions to launch an intercept. It was soon clear that all the in-system ships were Marik forces, making it more and more likely that some sort of civil war had broken out on Helm. The knowledge had hounded Grayson's people forward, like men and women possessed.

It also made possible their wild flight in-bound. DropShips and AeroSpace Fighters patrolling the approaches were slow in their challenges, and apparently willing to ignore the pair of DropShips as they began the final leg of their deceleration in toward Helm. When they were challenged by the DropShips *Lancelot*, Captain Ilse Martinez, the intense and raven-haired commander of the *Phobos*, had announced that the Marik ship was in position for an intercept. When the *Lancelot*'s second challenge had come, Martinez responded with a blistering string of oaths, claiming to be inbound on the Duke's business.

With the Marik ship barely 12,000 kilometers distant, the *Phobos* and the *Deimos* had fallen past *Lancelot*'s orbit with no further challenges, and not so much as a query about which of several possible dukes the tiny flotilla served.

Then had come the final maneuvers for landing. Storm clouds swirled and billowed above the dead sea plain below Durandel as the Legion's DropShips streaked across heaven into Helm's ionosphere. With Marik fighters belatedly closing on atmosphere-skimming trajectories, the two Legion DropShips had applied a last, thundering bellow of deceleration and plunged into the cloud cover. Martinez in the *Phobos* and Lieutenant Thurston in the *Deimos* had timed their approaches perfectly. The ships set down less than twenty kilometers from Durandel, just on the other side of a low ridge west of the settlement. That the ships had been tracked on radar was certain. Grayson was still hoping that any Marik observers would assume that the two DropShips either bore VIPs too important to bother with formalities such as transmitting

IDs, or had pilots too stupid or too careless to identify themselves.

It might buy them time. Once on the ground, they would have to trust their ability to move fast enough to keep Marik ground forces guessing. The *Phobos* and the *Deimos* would be the weak points of the plan. Once grounded, they could not move. Martinez and Thurston would have to find rough country where something as large as two DropShips could be hidden, at least for a time.

Grayson knew, however, that time would soon be an even greater enemy to the Legion than the unknown forces they could hear over taccom wavelengths on the ground.

After an unopposed landing, Grayson deployed the command lance and the fire lance forward. The recon lance and Captain Ramage's company had remained to guard the landing zone. His command lance consisted, as always, of Lori's *Shadow Hawk,* Kelmar Clay's *Wolverine,* and Davis McCall's *Rifleman,* as well as his own *Marauder.* The fire lance was headed by Lieutenant Khaled in his *Warhammer.* Isoru Koga and his *Archer* had been in the fire lance for the past eight months, and Sharyl with her *Shadow Hawk* had come in from the recon lance when Stennman was killed. Charles Bear in his *Crusader* had replaced Jenna Hastings.

An hour after touchdown, they reached the crest of the ridge and were looking down into the smoking ruin of their home.

"Captain!" Lori said. She used the lower of Grayson's two ranks deliberately. It would serve no good purpose to alert possible listeners that a regimental commander, a Colonel, was here. "Movement at 3200, bearing 095!"

Grayson ranged in on the indicated coordinates. Over three kilometers distant and almost due east, his *Marauder*'s scanners picked up the indicated target and outlined it in green light on his HUD.

"I see, it, Lieutenant. They're still here."

Bastards, Grayson thought. The settlement's murderers moved through the rubble yet, slowly and deliberately. Perhaps no one had informed them of the DropShip landing so close at hand. Perhaps they knew and didn't care, thinking the landing meant the arrival of more Marik reinforcements—or more scavengers come to nestle down at the settlement's corpse.

Machines moved in the rubble. Grayson could make out the lithe shape of a *Phoenix Hawk* and the hulking form of a *Griffin* farther out. The *Phoenix Hawk* was mindlessly kicking at a section of ferrocrete wall that was still standing. Two kicks, and the wall toppled over in a cloud of dust, rubble, and splintered stone. The *Griffin*, moving with slow deliberation, stooped and began to use its metal hands to paw through the rubble of what had once been the community's astech barracks. Was it searching for loot? For survivors? Grayson didn't know. Indeed, a kind of numbness had paralyzed his mind and will, as well as his hands. He could only stare in horrified fascination at the raped and ravaged village.

There were more 'Mechs moving through the ruins farther off: a pair of *Stinger*s and a *Wasp*.

Grayson's eyes flicked between his HUD and a console monitor giving him updated information from his long-range passive scanners. He had seven . . . no . . . eight targets moving within scanner range. With the exception of the 55-ton *Griffin* and a pair of 45-ton *Phoenix Hawk*s, all the machines picking through the steaming rubble appeared to be lights—*Stinger*s and *Wasp*s. Grayson's lightest 'Mechs were the pair of 55-ton *Shadow Hawk*s.

The anger that had been boiling somewhere deep within him came rushing out now, a roaring in his ears and a quickening of his heart. *Murderers!* The Gray Death would sweep down on them like avenging angels, angels of death.

"We'll take them," he said over the command circuit. "Lances . . . weapons up! Arm! Deploy!"

The targets in the rubble of Durandel were unsuspecting, so absorbed were they in dismembering the last vestiges of the town. One of the *Stinger*s had uncovered a prize, a huddled group of people hiding under a blanket of sheet tin near the foundations of a demolished warehouse. The *Stinger* had just gestured those survivors out into daylight with a wave of its hand-mounted medium laser when motion or some other warning shouted across the pilot's command circuits brought the BattleMech's head up and around. Grayson's 75-ton *Marauder* strode *through* a standing wall, sending chunks of rubble cascading across the street as the almost-prisoners scattered in screaming terror. The *Stinger*'s pilot hesitated, then started to bring his 'Mech's laser up. Too late. Twin lasers caught the *Stinger* full in the right torso and arm, leaving smoking scars gouged across armor and soft, internal structure.

Grayson took another step, making certain that the unprotected humans were safely out of the way, then triggered both lasers again, this time adding the lightning fury of his twin PPCs to the barrage. Blue lightning sparked and snapped across the target. The *Stinger*'s right arm, already shattered, went spinning through the air, its laser still clutched in its metal fist. The 'Mech sagged backward, its gyros shrieking, smoke pouring from multiple, gaping holes in the light 'Mech's armor. Grayson added his autocannon to the barrage, and 120 mm shells slashed and chopped explosive mayhem through the *Stinger*'s ravaged framework. Chips of armor broke free under the explosive hail and spun crazily through the air. Grayson strode in ever closer, his autocannon hammering away, spent shell casings ringing and clanging across the outer hull of his machine.

There was a flash and then a puff of smoke. The *Stinger*'s blocky head opened as panels broke free from one another, and the 'Mech's pilot rocketed into the sky. A far brighter flash buried in the 'Mech's torso rent metal already twisted and smashed, scattering smoking fragments on the street.

Another 'Mech, a *Wasp,* strode into Grayson's field of fire. He pivoted his *Marauder* on its forward-canted leg mount, bringing both weapons-heavy forearms into line. PPC and laser fire lanced across the street, striking the *Wasp* and driving it down and back. Grayson saw that the *Wasp* had already been damaged by laser fire to its side and back.

The *Wasp* recovered, managing to swing its Diverse Optics medium laser into line with Grayson's cockpit.

Coherent light washed across the *Marauder*'s outer hull, but the heavy machine's optics blanked out light that would have seared Grayson's eyes, and the massive outer armor plate dissipated the heat harmlessly. Grayson's *Marauder* took six quick steps across the street, its ponderous forearms sweeping up and around. Like a massive club, the *Marauder*'s right arm smashed against the *Wasp*'s left arm and body. Armor plate buckled with a human-sounding shriek, and the *Wasp* tumbled backward into a crumbling pile of rubble. Three more shots from Grayson's PPCs, and the *Wasp* was still, a fire burning among the charred remnants of wiring and conduits exposed in its cratered center torso.

To make sure it would never rise again, Grayson unleashed one last barrage of PPC fire into the metal corpse. For the moment, he was beyond remembering, beyond reason. A berserker's rage had come upon him, a rage for vengeance, a rage to kill and kill and kill again until he had hunted down every last one of his people's murderers and their killer machines. His *Marauder* stalked the ruined streets of Durandel, changing the Marik 'Mechs suddenly from predators to prey.

The madness had overcome them all. Grayson came upon Lori firing bolt after blue-tinged bolt of laser light into the twisted hulk of a *Phoenix Hawk* that lay sprawled in the wreckage of a house. Delmar Clay's *Wolverine* charged the Marik *Griffin* in a fight that was even, until Bear's *Crusader* and Khaled's *Warhammer* joined Clay in an orchestrated nightmare of laser fire that all but shredded the enemy *Griffin*. As the *Griffin* went down, it was Lieutenant Khaled who guided his *Warhammer* close enough to send one massive, armored foot smashing down on the *Griffin*'s cockpit. That pilot would not survive to pillage other towns. Once the Marik 'Mechs realized their danger, they tried to escape. Ironically, it was the rubble in the streets of the town they had destroyed that blocked them, and channeled them in directions that Grayson's raiders could predict—and intercept.

The battle, if such it was, was over in fifteen minutes. Not a single Marik 'Mech survived.

It was only after the last enemy *Stinger* had exploded

in a pyrotechnic flash of light, sound, and shredded metal that Grayson realized he could barely see through the heavy HUD visor of his neurohelmet because his tears were half-blinding him.

He was still crying as the 'Mechs of his company rendezvoused in the center of what had been Durandel's market square.

The Marik DropShip *Assagai* fell into orbit around Helm. She was an old *League* Class ship, one outfitted as an orbital headquarters and communications relay vessel for Marik planetary operations. Dish antennae deployed from communication equipment bays high up near the armored bulge that marked the ship's bridge maintained two rigid lines of sight. One was directed at the gleaming brilliance of the ice-bound planet below, while the other was directed outward into deep space, toward the jump point where silently pulsing jets of hot plasma held the JumpShips *Rapacious* and *Huntress* in place against the gravitational pull of the local sun.

The *Assagai*'s captain was a veteran of many years' service for Janos Marik. During his forty-eight years in space, Fenric Javil had seen more than his share of radar tracks.

Weightless, he floated above and behind the boy who manned the *Assagai*'s number two deep radar. His arm extended past the boy's head, one bony finger probing at the green screen. "Those tracks, son. What d'you make of 'em?"

"Uh—entry tracks, Captain," replied the youngster strapped into the radar watch seat, his voice shaking a bit as he spoke. He'd hoped to escape Captain Javil's notice a while longer.

"Entry tracks is right. Whose?"

"I heard a query from *Lancelot* as they went by sir. They . . . they didn't answer."

"They didn't? And didn't you find that suspicious?"

"Sir . . . the guys on *Lancelot* said it was a pair of generals going in for a tour, see? And Shiggy said . . ." The boy's voice faltered and his eyes widened as he realized he had somehow slipped into the trap of speaking familiarly with the Captain.

Javil's eyes tracked across the bridge to meet the dark eyes of another deep-radar watchstander, eyes that suddenly ducked back behind a console as their owner abruptly became very busy.

"By 'Shiggy,' I assume you mean Junior Lieutenant Shigamura? Tell me, son, what did Lieutenant Shigamura tell you about those targets?"

"He . . . that is . . . that the . . . the targets were just bigwigs popping in from the new JumpShip, sir."

"New JumpShip?" Javil's eyes closed slowly. When they opened, it was with a snap that was nearly audible and a bellowing roar that rang through the bridge. *"What goddamn JumpShip?"*

"Sir, Shiggy . . . Lieutenant Shigamura, I mean . . . he got an echo on deep radar that might be a new JumpShip under deployed sail at the nadir jump point. But he said it must be a new arrival to the fleet from Marik . . . maybe Duke Irian himself . . ."

"Shigamura! Front and center!"

A second watch officer swam across the bridge from where he had been attempting to become invisible at his post.

"Mr. Shigamura! Would you be so kind as to explain how it is that an officer aboard a Free Worlds warship, in the middle of a complex military exercise against a possibly belligerent world, could be so . . . so careless as to note the presence of an untagged JumpShip in this solar system and not report the fact to me? Or to the Exec? Or to the senior officer of the watch? *Or to say any goddamned thing to anybody at all?"*

"No, sir! I mean, yes, sir! I mean . . ."

"Quiet! Do I further understand that the *two* of you tracked a pair of unidentified DropShips in from this untagged JumpShip and let it pass right under our noses without demanding an ID of it? Or telling somebody?"

"S-sir, things were pretty confusing, right then," Lyster said. "JumpShips had been dropping in and out at the jump points for the whole watch, and we thought it was more of the same! I don't think I've ever seen so many ships in one system before . . . merchant vessels trailing the military DropShips . . . and then there was the scuttlebutt that the Duke of Irian was coming. When those two Dropships didn't respond to *Lancelot*'s ID call, we thought . . ."

"You *thought*! When I want a goddamned junior lieutenant who can *think*, I'll goddamned well commission my wristcomp! Or a cockroach down in the galley! Good God, between the two of you, you idiots don't have the brains of a Kalidasan mosslug! You're not here to think! You're here to watch your radar screens and sing out when you see something—anything! Do I make myself clear?"

"Yessir!" The two chimed in chorus.

"Another goddamned ass-brained malf like that and I'll put the pair of you out the airlock! Now back to your posts! And *next* time you see something that just might be an enemy ship slipping in to blow us all away to hell, *sing out*!"

Javil stormed his way hand-over-hand to the podium at the center of the bridge where his private seat and control consoles were located. Senior Lieutenant Yolan Flynn, his Exec, unbelted from the seat and drifted aside to make room for the Captain.

"We miss something coming in?"

"My God, Flynn, I don't know how they expect us to manage!" He strapped himself down and began punching numbers into the console. Working carefully and with the accuracy of long experience, he coded the bridge computer to relay a playback of the deep radar tracks to his central console screen. *"Children!"* he muttered. "They're sending us half-trained, slug-brained, thumb-chewing children, and they expect us to fight wars! *Bah!*"

"Things are getting pretty thin back at reppledep. What have you got?"

Javil leaned forward, studying the paired tracks as they arrowed in low above the cloud-hooded face of the planet.

"Two DropShips. Not ours . . . not merchants. Here, Flynn. What do you make of this?"

The radar screen showed white-on-green traceries, two blips racing in across the broken surface of the planet. Clouds appeared as vague ghosts, close against the uneven ground. The blips slowed sharply, generating a cascade of computer analysis in tiny, tightly written characters that spoke of changing vectors, or mass and speed and direction.

"They're ducking into those storm clouds."

"Right. Immediately after the *Lancelot* challenged them."

"Hostiles, then? We were told there wasn't any chance that hostile warships would arrive in the middle of the operation."

"We were told a lot of things." Javil's voice was sour. He manipulated controls, speeding things forward. While he advanced the record, the *Assagai* had moved forward on her orbit around Helm, and the twin blips were barely visible, settling to the surface a few kilometers west of the village of Durandel. He began comparing the radar image on the record with stored radar views taken of the surface on previous sweeps.

"That settles it, Flynn. They're grounding right outside the town all the fuss is about."

"Interesting."

"It's a damned sight more than interesting." Javil bent over the readings for a moment. "Hah! Got it! I've got them spotted relative to that mountain range to the south, and to Durandel itself. That'll pinpoint them—right to the mark, or close enough!"

"But they'll have been down for hours!"

"True . . . true . . . But a DropShip! Ah! That *is* a prize, Flynn. One worth fighting for! And here we've got two of them cold, with a small army on the surface already, plus AeroSpace Fighters and some DropShips of our own." He looked up at his Exec. "Open a line to the Colonel for me."

The Exec glanced at the bridge chronometer. "Aye aye. Captain. He's over the horizon now, but we can hit him with a relay off Comsat Twelve." Lieutenant Flynn used his throat mike to contact the *Assagai*'s communications department.

It would take long minutes for Javil's request to reach his superiors aboard the *Rapacious* at the system's zenith jump point, and more time again for a reply to make its way back to Helm. While he waited, he decided to get things moving. As the ranks of naval Captain and MechForce Colonel were approximately equivalent and their areas of authority did not overlap, he could not pass orders on to the Colonel in charge of surface operations on Helm, but he *could* pass the news on in a friendly and unofficial fashion. Javil rubbed his hands together with satisfaction. This was *big*! After relaying the orders to ComDep, Flynn looked back up at Javil. "Captain? What about that JumpShip?"

"I doubt that there's much we can do. If it's hostile, it'll be jumping soon. It would surely be gone by the time we could get ships out there. So, we'll ignore the JumpShip for now, though I want the *Rapacious* notified and I want a twenty-four-hour watch put on it from here. I want to know the instant that JumpShip does *anything* out there. Got me?"

"Yessir." The Exec touched his earpiece, listening. "ComDep has the Colonel on the line for you, Captain."

"Good." Javil adjusted his own earpiece, then touched a control on his console. "Colonel Langsdorf? Captain Javil here. Fine . . . fine . . . no problem. But we *do* have some news. We've picked up a pair of targets for you, over closer to Durandel. Move fast, and you just might catch yourself a real prize!"

6

Until now, Captain Ramage had been happy with his life. Fourteen standard years, he had been a senior NCO in the militia of a Lyran Commonwealth world called Trellwan, where he had honed his combat skills leading ground infantry against raiders and pirates from the Periphery, the distant, vast reaches of space beyond the so-called "civilized" worlds of the Inner Sphere. He was good at what he did, and the young mercenary warrior hired by the Trellwanese to create a BattleMech force to combat an invasion by the Draconis Combine had recognized it. The mercenary had drawn heavily on Ramage's talents, particularly in special forces techniques for using common infantrymen to bring down BattleMechs. When a world had no 'Mechs of its own, it was up to these ordinary troopers, armed with flamer, skimmer-mounted laser, or satchel charge explosives to defend his people from the predations of the 20- to 100-ton armor-clad monsters that dominated the modern battlefield.

The young mercenary's name was Grayson Death Carlyle, and when he left Trellwan after successfully completing his mission, Ramage chose to go with him.

Ramage's talents had once again been invaluable during Grayson's campaign with the rebels on Verthandi. Armed with only a few battered, captured BattleMechs and AgroMechs jury-rigged with machine guns, the rebel forces had fought the Kurita occupying forces to a standstill, while House Steiner stepped in to guarantee Verthandi's semi-autonomy. It had been Ramage who had trained those ragged ground troops, Ramage who had led them in raid after raid that killed at least ten of the Kurita 'Mechs, and damaged many more.

Ramage had tried his best to retain the rank of sergeant, even when, for all practical purposes, he carried a captain's authority in command of a full infantry company. "The men wouldn't know what to do if they couldn't come grouse to Old Sergeant Ram," he had told Grayson on more than one occasion. When a Captain's commission had come his way despite his protests, Lori Kalmar had pointed out, "The time'll come when you have to rub some fresh-face lieutenant's nose in it . . . *Captain*. You'd better have the rank to back it up!"

Ramage's leadership technique could best be described as tough, but he was no less hard on himself. Known only by his single Trellwanese name, or affectionately as "Ram," he had earned both the respect and love of the troops under his command.

"Red Two, what do you have for me?" Ramage was crouched in a hastily dug slit trench in the boulder-strewn woods near the valley where the Legion's two DropShips had come down. Behind him were the foothills of the Aragayan Mountains farther to the north. The communicator earpiece spat static at him, then cleared.

"Red One, we have incoming 'Mechs!"

The Lieutenant listening in on a separate headpiece next to Ramage raised his eyebrows. "Ours?"

"Not a chance, Dulaney," Ramage replied. "Not from that direction. Red Two! Red Two! Give me an ID!"

"Red One, this is Two! Company strength! We count twelve. Repeat twelve! We see a *Warhammer* . . . two *Archers* . . . a *Thunderbolt* . . . and listen, Red One! We see infantry and armored vehicles as well!"

This was bad, Ramage knew. All the 'Mechs that the Legion patrol had named were heavies, a match or more for any of the 'Mechs in the Gray Death 'Mech Company, and far superior to the four light 'Mechs in the recon lance pulled up alongside the DropShips.

"Red Two! This is Red One! Mount up and pull back. Keep us posted on their Twenty!"

More static crackled in their headsets, this time pulsing in a regular, almost hypnotic surge of hiss and pop.

"They're jamming," Ramage said, removing the headset. "I don't know if our patrol heard or not. But those 'Mechs they spotted are moving our way, and fast!"

"What does it mean, Ram?"

"It means they have the DropShips nailed and they're moving in to get 'em!"

"How long do we have?"

Ramage was already studying a map of the area unfolded across his knee. His forefinger marked a point on the map with a smear of mud. "Twenty minutes . . . if that. We've got to get word to the Colonel!"

A quick check proved that all radio bands were clogged with the same melodic surge and hiss of enemy jamming. "Damn, and we don't have fiber optics strung yet, either." That meant no field telephones. He looked up out of the trench. "Runner!"

A young trooper in a gray-green camouflage smock dropped into the trench next to the two officers. Ramage switched on a recording device built into his wristcomp and hurriedly dictated his report on what Red Two had observed.

"Situation critical," he concluded. "I strongly urge that main body Gray Death 'Mech company be alerted using jam breaker techniques from DropShips. Estimate infantry and recon lances not sufficient to more than delay approaching forces if hostile."

He switched off the recorder, then pressed a button and caught the thumbnail-sized mini-clip that popped up from its recess, placed it in a small waterproof canister, and handed the package to the soldier. "This is for Captain Martinez, Lieutenant Thurston, and Lieutenant Roget," he said. "For their ears only . . . and urgent! Report back to me with their reply."

"Yessir!" The runner scrambled out of the trench and was gone.

Ramage moved over to where long-range infrared binoculars were mounted on a tripod at the edge of the trench, facing southwest. The land sloped gently in that direction, leading down out of the hills and woods and onto the broad sweep of the North Highland Plains.

Helmdown was in that direction . . . and the main Marik forces.

"I wish the Colonel were here now," Ramage said, more to himself than to Lieutenant Dulaney.

"Can they get a message to him?" Dulaney asked.

"Eh? Well, the transmitters aboard the DropShips will punch through the jamming, if anything can. And if the Colonel picks up the fringe of the jamming, he might figure out what's happening on his own and high-tail it back here. He's a smart one, that boy."

But Ramage did not feel as confident as he sounded. Even if Grayson Carlyle immediately force-marched his two lances at top speed back from Durandel, they *might* arrive in the area of the DropShips at about the same time as the 'Mech force that Red Two had spotted. And after a march like that, Grayson's men would be in poor condition for a fight, especially against an enemy force composed of heavy 'Mechs.

He adjusted the telephoto zoom on the binoculars, scanning the empty horizon to the southwest. No, things did not look good at all.

Grayson tried again. "*Phobos, Phobos,* this is Amber, do you copy? Over." He strained against the speakers built into the earphones of his neurohelmet, but could hear only a faint, distant hiss like the heavy surge of an ocean against its shore.

"Lori, what do you make of it?"

Across the ruined plaza, Lori's *Shadow Hawk* paused in its slow and deliberate movements among the rubble, as though the battle machine itself were listening. "It's not natural," was her reply. "Deliberate jamming, Gray. I'm certain of it."

"That's what I thought, too."

The horror of finding Durandel deliberately obliterated had left the Legion's MechWarriors in a state of dulled shock. They were finding bodies now, forms crushed beneath fallen rubble or sprawled in laser-seared or trampled gore on the town's ferrocrete walkways. The survivors were emerging, slowly, as word spread that it was the Gray Death Legion's 'Mechs descending like avenging angels on the Marik BattleMechs that had occupied the town. Each survivor had a similar tale. Word had come five days earlier that a force under the command of Lord Garth, Duke of Irian, was landing at the Helmdown starport, that a great victory had been won at Sirius V, that the Gray Death was due some special, spectacular honor.

Durandel's leaders and Captain Baron, who had been left in command at Helmfast, had gone to Helmdown to talk with the Marik representatives.

They had never returned.

On the following day, the BattleMechs of the Hammerstrike Company of the 5th Marik Guards had secured Helmdown and swept into the countryside, seizing strategic crossroads and what few industrial facilities existed around the planetary capital. A clear but incomprehensible radio message had been received at Helmfast: ''Your leaders have been declared in rebellion against the legal government of the Free Worlds League. Surrender to your lawful lords, or be destroyed.''

After Captain Baron's disappearance, a young Lieutenant named Fraser had assumed command of the garrison. The recent chain of events had been so odd, so confusing, that it was a real possibility that the Helm invaders were not Lord Garth's people at all, but renegades, enemy raiders, or even the vanguard of some rebellious Marik faction. Helmfast had been given into Fraser's keeping. He would not surrender it without certain knowledge of who his attackers were, or what was the legal status of the Gray Death Legion.

Helmfast's first line of defenders consisted of the armored vehicles that had been under Baron's command until his disappearance. There was infantry, too, local Helman militia for the most part, called up to serve with the masters of the Durandel landhold. There were also MechWarriors at Durandel, including Lieutenant Gomez DeVillar, a *Phoenix Hawk* pilot named Kent, and several recruit trainees, but their 'Mechs had been packed aboard the *Phobos* months before to serve as reserve 'Mechs in Liao space.

Lieutenant Fraser met the Marik BattleMechs on the

plains west of Durandel, where the enemy 'Mechs crashed through the defender's line. The militia had remained in Helmfast Castle preparing for a siege, while B Company, the twenty vehicles of the armored company, and the infantry deployed.

So far, none of the survivors that Grayson interviewed had been able to give a coherent picture of what happened after that. Some reported seeing the Marik Hammerstrike Company deploying beyond Fraser's line. Most of the enemy 'Mechs were lights, but well-handled and well-disciplined. Though low, heavy clouds of drifting smoke tended to obscure what was happening, within thirty minutes, there were Hammerstrike 'Mechs firing into the walls of the castle and prowling through the streets of Durandel. There were reports of panic among the trainees of Company B fighting on foot, of the Marik BattleMechs sweeping like a whirlwind of flame and destruction through the lightly armed vehicles facing them. A doctor found working among row upon row of injured soldiers and civilians at the edge of the village said that he had treated a soldier who reported that a Marik *Griffin* had crushed Lieutenant Fraser's Vedette light tank under its feet.

Grayson remembered the young and eager officer. He had not been more than 20 years old, and sported a wiry mustache whose obvious purpose was to make its owner look older. Fraser had joined the Legion, as had so many others, on Galatea. He claimed to have heard so much about the exploits of the Gray Death Legion that it made him want to join. "I want to win some of that glory myself," Fraser had told him.

Grayson had sat the young Fraser down in that Galatean bar and bought him a drink. Glory was the wrong reason to join the infantry, he'd explained. There was glory, certainly, in the military traditions and the camaraderie, the bravery and the sacrifice of combat. But such glory came only at a price. A steep price.

Though Fraser's training at a military academy on New Exford had marked him for a commission, he continued to insist that the Legion was for him. He was so determined to wait for an opening among the 'Mech apprentices that he would even give up his Lieutenant's commission. Fraser told Grayson that one day he would be a MechWarrior, a bearer of the *true* banner of glory . . .

Grayson had nearly turned him down, but something in the young man's eagerness reminded him of his own green apprenticeship. Fraser had signed the articles that brought him in as a junior lieutenant, and been posted to Baron's armored company, a first step in the long training that might one day lead to piloting a 'Mech. Within a year, he had become a Senior Lieutenant and been entrusted with the authority of Baron's Company Exec.

And now Fraser was dead. Grayson wondered how much glory the boy had found, in being smashed by the foot of fifty-five tons of armored steel. He may have died a hero, but he had also paid the highest possible price. And the battle had continued on after Fraser's death, as though the young man never existed at all.

Sergeant Burns, of Ramage's Special Ops force, had witnessed the final action in the town. With the defending force clearly beaten and scattered, the remaining town leaders of Durandel had decided to surrender. After seeing a white flag flying from the town council's office dome, the militia in Helmfast, themselves mostly citizens of Durandel, had followed suit. The gates to Helmfast had been opened, and the Marik conquerors welcomed according to the usages and conventions of war.

Grayson let his gaze linger on the outcome of those conventions. Not a single building had been left intact. The gates, walls, and turrets of Helmfast Castle had been burned and blasted and torn by laser fire . . . *from within*. The destruction had been complete and deliberate. While looking at the ruins around him, he pondered these deceptions leading to more deceptions, a twisting of the Conventions that seemed aimed directly at the heart of the Gray Death, and Grayson himself.

The burden weighed heavily on him now. Had it been his stupidity that had put the Legion in their current position? Or had he been too cockily assured that whatever he faced, he could certainly handle it? Of seven hundred people left at Durandel, his men had found less than four hundred so far, and many of those were injured. The fighting efficiency of his unit would be seriously compromised by the knowledge that many of their wives, husbands, children, or other loved ones were dead, or else hiding in the woods and the mountains, possibly wounded and dying.

And if the enemy took his DropShips, Grayson and his men would be trapped here on Helm.

There had been tricks . . . and tricks within tricks.

As he gazed up at the ruins of Helmfast, his fists clenched around the *Marauder*'s control grips. There would be no more such tricks.

Hours later, Lori found Grayson, in what had once been the briefing room in Helmfast Castle. The south wall had been blasted in, the ceiling timbers charred, the two-story windows smashed. The tile floors were ankle-deep in broken glass, plaster dust, and chunks of stone.

Grayson had brought a small, two-seat skimmer right through the hole in the wall. Cables stretched from the hovercraft's auxiliary generator and into the computer built into the conference table in the center of the room. Above him, a pair of large display screens were mounted on the east wall. Somehow, some way, much of the Castle's electronics had remained intact, though the power generator had been destroyed and fire had consumed many of the circuit controls.

"Grayson?"

He didn't respond at first. His back was toward Lori as he hunched over the computer keyboard.

"Gray?" she said, a bit louder. "Sergeant Burns has uncovered a supply of plastic explosives buried in a warehouse in Durandel."

Grayson turned to looked at her, but his eyes were unseeing, almost as though he didn't recognize her. Then what she was saying seemed to penetrate. "Good," he said, with a nod. "Good."

"You've got the briefing room computer working!"

"There's not much else left up here that works. It was built into the table, and this room survived pretty much intact."

"So I see," Lori said. She looked up at the maps. The

one on the left was blank, but the one on the right displayed expanses of green, ocher, and blue arrayed as a photographic map. "Plans?"

"Options."

She crossed the rubble to a point behind his shoulder, staring up at the screen. "What map is this? It's not . . . is that a map of Helm?"

"A very, very old one, yes. It's the computer display map that came with Helmfast, the one the Janos Marik gave me as part of the Title Ceremony. It's a computer-enhanced map, based on photographs taken from an orbital satellite . . . but it was made something like three centuries ago, so it's a bit out of date."

"I should say so!"

Now Lori understood why she'd been confused by the sea on the map. The Dead Sea Flats of today's Helm were bone-dry and barren, mineral-encrusted deserts. But on this map, a small sea still lay south of Durandel. Glowing letters identified it as the Yehudin Sea.

"Want to see how it works?"

She nodded.

"The operation is simple enough. An extremely detailed set of high-imagery photographs are digitized and stored in the computer's memory. The computer creates a referent grid." He turned to the keyboard and typed an entry. Lori now recognized the terrain on the right-hand screen, the southward sweep of the land from the Aragayan Mountains to beyond the Nagayan Mountains. Forests showed as dark, mottled, scratchy-looking grays, greens, and blues. The West Equatorial Sea was a deep and crystal blue, except near the shore along islands, where shallow sandbars created smooth strips of green and green-blue.

He used a display pointer on the screen to indicate a gray patch north of the dead sea bottom. "That," he said, "is Durandel. It's at coordinates 456 dash 076, mag level three. The smallest object we can see here is perhaps a kilometer across."

"Gray . . . I *know* how to read a map."

"I'm sorry, Lori. It's been a long, long night." He keyed an entry, and the perspective of the map changed, the ground leaping forward on the screen. The broad sweep of land was now dominated by the tiny gray patch of Durandel. Individual buildings could be made out, and everywhere else, rubble. Helmfast clung to the rim of the bluff above the town.

"There is level five, a one hundred-fold magnification. The smallest object we can see at this enlargement is about a meter across, one thousand times smaller than at level three." He leaned back, looking up at the map.

"It doesn't help us tactically, of course," he said. "It's a bit too far out of date for that. But I have found us a valley across the Aragayan Mountains to the north. The terrain is not difficult. There's a valley . . . the Valley of the Araga, about eighty kilometers from here. We can set up a camp there, and keep it out of sight of the Marik ships in orbit."

"Then what?"

"Then we get our refugees up there. I want you to find DeVillar." As one of the two MechWarriors with any experience at Durandel when the attackers had struck, Lieutenant DeVillar was the closest they had discovered to authority among the survivors found so far. "Put him in charge of rounding up all the survivors, plus any vehicles they can get to run. He is to take command of the group and organize an encampment, but he must also continue the search for other survivors."

There had to be survivors, Grayson thought. They had uncovered perhaps fifty bodies so far. They couldn't *all* be dead! In the meantime, that river valley would provide shelter, plus food and water, for as long as the group remained undiscovered.

"I'll alert the 'Mechs," he added. "The Company will head back to the LZ at full gallop."

"You're afraid for the DropShips."

"Damn right I am. We lose our DropShips, and we're stuck here . . . and we don't even know who's mad at us yet—or why!"

He didn't add what Lori must already know—that if their communications with the *Phobos* were being blocked, it had to be because hostile forces were moving against the DropShips. Grayson knew that if he wanted to act, it had better be fast. Time was running out. Maybe it had already run out, and the Legion would be too late once again.

Grayson simply wouldn't think about that. With luck, they had a chance.

═══ 7 ═══

For the past two years, Colonel Julian Langsdorf had been the regimental commander of the 12th White Sabers, an understrength regimental assault group assigned to garrison duty on Thermopolis, along the Free Worlds League frontier with the Lyran Commonwealth. That had changed less than two weeks before when none other than General Kleider of Janos Marik's House Command Staff had approached him.

Kleider was a heavy-set man, one of those court functionaries given to wearing torso armor in the form of rank upon glittering rank of military medals and awards. His eyes were deep-set under bushy, gray brows that seemed permanently drawn together in the strain to concentrate. His fat lips, too, seemed always to be puckered, though it could as easily have been in deepest thought as at the remembered taste of something particularly sour.

"I am here at the behest of Lord Garth, Duke of Irian," Kleider had said without preamble, moments after entering Langsdorf's staff briefing room at his garrison headquarters. "His Grace has formulated a plan, and your participation is deemed essential to its execution." The general spoke with the smooth assurance of one who knows that his words cannot fail to impress the listener.

And Langsdorf had been duly impressed. Irian was a minor dukedom, located on the border of the Marik Commonwealth Principality. Its once extensive industrial facilities had been ravaged and raided time again by both Steiner and Liao forces. Garth, the current Duke of Irian, was nevertheless reputed to be highly placed in the webwork of relations, favors, and favorites that permeated the Marik court on Atreus all the way to the Center Seat of the League Staff Command of the Captain-General himself. Any plan involving Garth was certain to be the result of high-level planning, indeed.

"I will serve His Grace in any capacity, sir," Langsdorf had replied, and he meant it. His loyalty was—had always been—to the person of Janos Marik. In the neo-feudalism of the current era, with its interconnected personal allegiances and oaths of military support, any service rendered to Lord Garth was service rendered to Captain-General Janos Marik himself.

Kleider had pursed his heavy lips and gone on to explain that a plot had been discovered with the Free Worlds League, one threatening the very foundations of the League's delicate balance of principalities. Should this plot succeed, Kleider said, the bonds holding together the principalities would dissolve in the blood of civil war. The Free Worlds League would be reduced to anarchy, and the greedy dogs and jackals that pressed so close from every border would surely see it as their chance to seize anything they could.

The plot, it seemed, had originated with a House Steiner mercenary who had managed to secure a contract with Janos Marik for a protracted campaign along the Liao border. Fortunately for the Free Worlds League, Lord Garth had discovered evidence that this mercenary had betrayed Janos Marik and was organizing a rebellion on the very planet granted to him as landhold. The name of that world was Helm.

Thus had Julian Langsdorf now come to Helm. On Kleider's orders, he had landed and seized the planet's starport and its capital of Helmdown. Through a simple ruse, he had also captured the highest-ranking members of the rebellion and dealt with them appropriately. Then, when the rebels had deployed their 'Mech garrison to meet his approach to their castle stronghold, Langsdorf had personally led the 5th Marik Guards in a wild fight to utterly crush the rebels' resistance, smash their capital, and overrun their castle.

THE PRICE OF GLORY

The Colonel's orders were to hold his prize until either Kleider or Duke Irian relieved him.

Though he'd done well, Langsdorf was unhappy with his command. It was fine to be hailed as Defender of the League, to know that he was preserving the rule and power of Janos Marik himself, but his operational orders from Kleider offered scant room for his own judgement. Worse yet was that his judgement told him that he was doing a thing that was wrong.

According to the unwritten but quite powerful Conventions of War, themselves descendants of the far older Ares Conventions, civilian populations were not the proper targets of war. Only if a civilian population should rise in revolt, should take arms against its lawful ruler, was that ruler allowed, even *obligated,* to treat the civilians as an enemy army.

When a civilian population was unarmed, and its army had announced formal surrender by an acceptable agency such as a white flag or neutral messenger, then those people became wards of the conquering army's commander, who was now charged with their protection.

Kleider's orders left little room for the rebels' formal surrender, however. Langsdorf was to answer any resistance, however token, with an overwhelming blow, using every bit of force at his command. The rebel army was to be destroyed even if it meant leveling the village of Durandel and the castle of Helmfast. Furthermore, Langsdorf was ordered to ignore any white flags or other formal declarations of surrender, which were sure to be tricks by the perfidious rebels.

Langsdorf had been horrified. "General! You are making it impossible for these people to surrender to us! Surely a living population is more valuable than one that has been trampled and destroyed! A town whole and productive is more valuable to us than . . . than burned-over rubble!"

Kleider had laid his hand on Langsdorf's shoulder in a fatherly way, his bushy eyebrows rising toward his forehead. "Son, there is more to this than you know. These . . . orders . . . they're distasteful, I know. But His Grace, Lord Garth, has accumulated evidence suggesting that this . . . this foul mercenary is guilty of abominable atrocities in Liao space."

"Atrocities? What atrocities?"

"I don't know the details, Colonel. But from what I've heard, from what His Grace was able to confide in me, this mercenary band planned to commit an atrocity while in the service of Janos Marik, with the sole intention of laying blame for the incident at the Captain-General's own hand!"

"God is heaven . . ."

"God had little to do with this scheme, I fear. Imagine! By making the Captain-General responsible for this atrocity, whatever it is, the mercenaries sow the seeds of civil war. The various factions leap to support or denounce Janos Marik. In the chaos, the mercenaries hope to seize power for themselves. And they could, too, with the League falling to pieces, the army in shreds, our worlds open wide to invasion by Liao and Steiner."

"The mercenary and part of his force are in Liao space now. It may be too late to stop whatever terrible deed the man has planned. But we do hope to lure him and his band to a place where we can deal with him. His Grace is already preparing an overwhelming force to trap and deal with this monster.

"You, meanwhile, must seize the mercenary's landhold. And you must be ruthless about it, single-mindedly and bloodily ruthless!" Kleider had smacked one of his fists wetly against the palm of his other hand for emphasis. "It may well be that the perpetrators of this scheme are among those at Durandel. Certainly, there are no innocents among them, for the mercenary leader would need the full support of his people before even contemplating such a scheme. No . . . you must *not* consider these people to be *innocents*, Colonel."

Being a good, loyal soldier, Langsdorf had played his part. Langsdorf's father, Rolf Langsdorf, had been a personal friend and confidant of Janos Marik, had supported Janos in the recent, bloody fratricidal struggle between Janos and his brother Anton. As reward, Janos had named Rolf as Count Valik, with a patent of nobility that made Langsdorf's brother a viscount, and Julian himself a minor noble. Julian Langsdorf had been raised by his sternly correct father to believe that nothing was more important than absolute loyal and faithful service to one's liege lord.

Langsdorf opened his hands and looked at them, turning them under the light. He still believed that, but the shrieks and death screams of the slaughtered civilian of Durandel still rang in his ears. The enemies of the Captain-General *had* to be rooted out . . . the perpetrators of such a monstrous scheme *had* to be exterminated with utter ruthlessness . . . And yet . . .

Was there reason and purpose to such slaughter? He remembered the woman, half-naked and golden-haired, who had fled from beneath the shadow of his *Warhammer* when he'd smashed aside the walls of her house. He had had the woman in the sights of his *Warhammer*'s left machine gun when he realized she was carrying a baby in her arms.

He had let her go, still torn between duty and morality.

It was one thing to destroy monsters bent on the destruction of his culture and his people, on tearing down the government and the lord he was sworn to serve. The indiscriminate machine-gunning of a defenseless woman and her child was another matter entirely. At that point, Langsdorf had turned over command of the operation to the Hammerstrike Company's Captain Prosser. He had returned alone to Helmdown, where he was greeted with the unconfirmed reports of landings by unidentified DropShips.

Langsdorf sat now in the cockpit of his *Warhammer,* leading his 12th White Sabers toward what Captain Javil claimed was an enemy DropShip LZ. He wanted desperately to speak with someone, but the same interference that was blanketing enemy communications was blocking his own. Things had started to go very seriously wrong almost from the beginning of the operation. First, there had been this struggle between loyalty and right, a struggle that threatened to paralyze Langsdorf by making him question each order, each movement, if only to himself.

Then had come word that eight 'Mechs—*eight 'Mechs*—of the 5th Marik Guard were out of contact and presumed destroyed in Durandel. The only clue to their fate was a confused radio message received by a regimental command listening post in Helmdown, a fragmentary and panic-ridden warning of unknown agencies hunting down the Hammerstrike Company. The transmission had broken off before the radio operator could get a confirmation on it. Then, only silence came from Durandel. Langsdorf had to assume that the 'Mechs he had left there under Prosser were destroyed. What he did not know was how and by whom.

The answer had come moments later, in the call from Captain Javil in orbit. He informed Langsdorf that a pair of DropShips had set down outside of Durandel, probably at about the time the Colonel's *Warhammer* was returning to Helmdown. The news answered several questions, but was disturbing, too. It suggested that things were going very wrong, indeed. Had not Kleider promised that the first-line combat forces of the renegade mercenaries would be diverted to another system and apprehended there, that all Langsdorf would need to worry about was a handful of rebellious civilians, trainees, and third-rate troops?

Third-rate troops did not dispatch eight 'Mechs so quickly that they scarcely had time to call for help. The grounding of a pair of *Union* Class DropShips meant that as many as twenty-four 'Mechs could be on the ground at this moment—far too many for his small combined unit to face. At the moment, assuming that all eight of the Hammerstrike 'Mechs were destroyed, he had fifteen 'Mechs at his command, and the majority of those were lights.

Langsdorf had assembled what 'Mechs he could—his own *Warhammer,* plus three lights left by the Hammerstrike Company at Helmdown when they'd left for Durandel, together with two full lances from his own 12th White Sabers. That would leave only three more 12th White Sabers 'Mechs to watch Helmdown, but he'd be needing as much firepower as possible to have a chance against the enemy DropShips.

The road between Helmdown and Durandel was broad and flat, and so progress was rapid. A pair of ECM ground vehicles detached from his infantry reserves raced alongside the 'Mech column, broadcasting the static that would scramble the enemy's radio transmissions. It would also tell the enemy of their approach, but that didn't matter. Langsdorf's Warriors already had detailed instructions, with little need for further communications once they were in the field. The jamming should hamper the enemy more.

With luck, his force would arrive at the DropShip landing zone before the mercenary raiders could even return from Durandel.

With luck, they had a chance.

Captain Ramage adjusted the focus on his ranging binoculars. Numbers flickered across the image plate within the eyepieces as the device probed targets with rangefinder laser beams. The far end of the gently sloped valley was already obscured by dust, making it difficult to get a precise fix on the most distant targets, but the nearest were only eight kilometers away.

Casting long shadows through the low-lying dust cloud, the two lead machines were moving at nearly eighty kilometers per hour. One was the odd, stilt-legged shape of a *Locust*. The other was a more human-shaped *Wasp*.

He opened the tac frequency and heard the harsh, rattling hiss of static.

"Runner!"

"Sir!"

"To Captain Martinez. At least two 'Mechs are closing on this position. Range eight, speed eighty."

"Two 'Mechs! Eight-Eighty! Yessir!"

"Good! Go!"

Ramage looked up and down the line of the trench. Other soldiers crouched along its sinuous length every ten to fifteen meters, their weapons poking out beyond hurriedly erected front-cover masses of logs and rocks. Further up the hill behind him, and farther down in front, other slit trenches took advantage of the boulders, the low, scraggly trees, and whatever other scant cover the hill had to offer. In a few cases, the occupants had had time to create rough-and-ready bunkers, with logs and light armor plate covered with dirt providing overhead cover.

Eight kilometers, eighty klicks per hour. There was no arguing with the arithmetic. The two metal monsters would be on top of their position in one tenth of an hour—six minutes. The chances that Grayson and his pair of lances would make it back from Durandel in time were microscopic. Shadows loomed and moved with surreal menace deeper within the dust clouds across the valley.

Ramage tried to penetrate the murk. Three . . . four . . . six . . .

They were out in force. Ramage could make out a big, battlescarred *Warhammer* now, and a *Thunderbolt* close behind.

The enemy 'Mechs lumbered out onto the flat central field of the valley, stepping easily across the narrow, dry stream bed that marked its center. The half-glimpsed shadows seemed to be spreading out to left and right in a classic combat deployment. *They must know we're here,* Ramage thought. *They must know the DropShips are just on the other side of this hill, and it's right here that we're going to have to hold them. They're sending their light stuff against us, while their heavies sweep around us and over the hill.*

Straight into the LZ.

One soldier, a teenaged boy with a garish mixture of camouflage paint and dust smeared over his face, scrambled down into the trench, nearly knocking aside the makeshift flag that marked Ramage's battlefield position. He wore the green armband of a runner. *Flags and armbands.* Ramage thought ruefully. With the unexpected use of ECM jamming, they'd had to improvise quickly in order to keep their field communications open.

"Sir! Captain Martinez reports they have three *Boomerangs* on radar. And . . . and there's no sign of the Colonel yet, either."

Ramage glanced at the sky, trying to penetrate the high, hot haze. *Boomerang* spotter planes would explain how the enemy had known their positions. The trenches were well-camouflaged from the front, but it was next to impossible to shield them from aerial infrared cameras.

Stifling a sudden, half-crazed urge to smile and wave at the sky, he turned back to the runner. "Right. Take a message to Captain Martinez. At least eight 'Mechs, including heavies. Targets' range now . . ." He checked the rangefinder again. "Two kilometers, and closing. Main body seems to be deploying north and south, and may be getting ready for a double-flank run. Got it?"

The boy's forehead furrowed in concentration. "At least eight targets, with heavies! Two kilometers . . . main body deploying north and south. Maybe getting ready for a double-flank run. Yessir!"

"Go!"

As the boy scrambled up the back of the trench, Ramage chambered a round into his TK assault rifle. "Hold your fire, people," he commanded. "Flamers and SRMs, keep hunkered down until you have a target in range! I want you to shoot hot, tight, and close! On my word!"

There was a stir along the trenches as weapons swung slightly this way or that, as men keyed to the highest possible pitch began to chamber rounds or open the fuel valves on their hand flamers. These troops were his best, trained in his every trick of counter-'Mech warfare. He knew they would give a good account of themselves. He also knew that their chances of inflicting any serious damage on even one BattleMech lance under these conditions were virtually nil.

The BattleMechs loomed closer, their pace increasing, their strides longer. Now he could see the glint of sun on visors and upraised weapons.

Ramage raised his TK, searching for accompanying infantry. *Here it comes,* he thought.

8

ComStar had come into being during the 28th Century, almost three hundred years before. At that time, it was merely—merely!—an interstellar communications network stretched across most of human-explored space. Its founder and chief organizer was then-Star League minister of Communications, Jerome Blake.

It had been Blake's machinations that had preserved ComStar as a separate, and neutral, entity during the civil wars that tore the Star League asunder and laid waste to hundreds of worlds. Any one of the Successor State pretenders to the old Star League throne would have won a powerful advantage over its rivals if he, and he alone, could have controlled the hyperpulse generators that were the key to interstellar communications faster than the JumpShips themselves.

Blake established ComStar as a power in its own right by using a mercenary army to seize Terra in 2788 and to declare it a neutral world under the protection of ComStar itself. In a rapid round of negotiations and politics, he won guarantees from each of the Great Houses: ComStar would continue to operate as a commercial enterprise, one that was an absolute neutral in the on-going wars. Each of the Successor Lords could see the advantage to such an arrangement. If any one of the Successor States controlled ComStar, that state would soon dominate all of known space. If no one controlled ComStar, then all would have access to ComStar's unique—and invaluable—services. In almost three centuries, there had been various incidents of one or another of the Successor

Houses attacking ComStar facilities, however. ComStar's inevitable retribution was to cut off all interstellar communications services to the world or worlds involved until the offender inevitably decided that it was better to respect ComStar's neutrality.

ComStar served well in its role of providing interstellar communications, but it had another, stranger side as well. After Blake's death, the organization had undergone a reorganization that many saw as the rise of a new religion. Its leaders now believed that ComStar held the key to the rapidly vanishing technology of the old Star League, that ComStar alone would be able to guide civilization into a path that could lead ultimately to peace and plenty for all. It was not long before the organization, its members, and its beliefs became shrouded in mystery, mysticism, ritual, and superstition. Most Techs outside of ComStar held the Order in some derision. Recite the words of Blake over a hyperpulse generator before enabling the transmit program? Ridiculous!

Yet only ComStar Techs, the Adepts of the Order, knew how to repair or run the hyperpulse generators. If they wanted to chant over the damned equipment, let them! Those same Technicians who laughed at ComStar Adepts might be just as likely to rely on one particular transit wrench because that wrench was "lucky," or "knew the job," or because its absence would "jinx the malfing job." In three centuries, so much had been lost to the devastation of war. Though men struggled to regain what they had lost, it was inevitable that ignorance and superstition should rise to fill the void.

Under the direction of the Primus and the First Circuit on Terra and, led by the administrative Precentors, ComStar held together what was left of the Empire of Man. Believing that they were a bastion against the abyss that threatened to engulf mankind, the followers of the Way of Blake grew and flourished and spread the Word of the Eternal, the Blessed Blake.

The Precentor searched the thronged ballroom until he found the stout and beribboned form of Lord Garth. He had been giving some thought to the crisis of the moment and had considered summoning Lord Garth to his private office aboard the JumpShip *Mizar*. In the end, he had thought better of it. In front of his own people, a high-ranking noble like the Duke of Irian deserved respect and deferral even from a ComStar Precentor, who, after all, held no noble title or other rank.

Yet, the power behind the Precentor is what gave him sway over such men as Garth—a power far greater than any mere titles or rows of campaign medals and ribbons. It was a power best used in subtle ways, and the Precentor understood that fully. The steel fist within the velvet glove would never be anything less than steel, and he appreciated that the disguise of softness could make it even more potent.

The Precentor smiled and raised his glass of carved crystal to his lips. Overhead, the transparency of the ballroom dome looked out on wheeling jeweled splendor, as the stars seemed to sweep past the motionless *Mizar*. In fact, of course, it was the ballroom's unfelt motion that made the stars appear to move. The passenger DropShip in which Duke Irian's party travelled could be extended from the *Mizar*'s central axis on a webwork of monofilament strands, counter-balanced by a second DropShip on the far side of the ship, with the entire structure set rotating in order to generate artificial gravity aboard the DropShips through centrifugal force. Short of using the main ship's station-keeping thrusters to accelerate at 1 G—impractical while the jump sail was deployed—it was the only way of generating gravity so that the assembled multitude could strut about in their jeweled and beribboned costumes rather than float helplessly. The thought of some of these fat toads (or their helpless and bedecked mistresses) thrashing about in midair broadened the Precentor's smile.

They are so useless, all of them . . .

Well, not entirely useless, perhaps. Even Garth had his uses, which would continue to be true for some time. The Duke had already failed badly in one minor way, however, and had to be brought to account for that. Too, Garth needed a reminder of who really was in charge of this project that he seemed to think was his. Indeed, it was for just such a discussion that the Precentor had considered summoning Garth to his room.

But no, this was the time for the veiled fist and the soft approach. Later, should Garth prove stubborn, there would be time enough to lay bare the naked steel behind the Precentor's words.

He approached the Duke, the smile still playing at the corners of his hard mouth. Garth's face went pale. *Good,* the Precentor thought. *He does fear me still. I will give him more reason than he dreams . . .*

The Precentor's bow was curt, obviously a formality and nothing more. "Your Grace."

"Rachan." Garth's voice was weak, with the hint of a stutter. His eyes looked bleak, as though he already regretted his liaison with the Precentor and those he represented.

So much the better. Such men could be more easily twisted to one's will. "I have news, your Grace," Rachan said.

Gathered around Garth were an obscenely fat merchant from the minor trading house of Mailai, half a dozen minor functionaries, and a gaggle of young women wearing makeup, plumes, jewelry, and little else. Garth's eyes flitted uneasily around the group. "Can it wait?" he said.

"No, Your Grace."

The Duke took another swallow of the blue liquid in his glass, then handed the empty crystal to a servant. "I'll come." Mustering his dignity, he stepped past the Precentor and led the way across the glittering floor toward a curtained alcove where the two of them could speak in private.

"What is your news, Rachan?"

"Communications have reached me from our station here." In private, the Precentor quickly dropped the perfunctory "Your Grace." There was no advantage to undermining the man's own authority in front of his people, but it was an excellent way of reminding the Duke of whose was the greater power. Rachan gestured toward the transparency overhead, beyond the silvery gleam of the *Mizar.* Somewhere beyond lay the world of this star system. Garth's own duchy, Irian. The *Mizar* had stopped here en route to Marik, which lay one jump deeper into the Free Worlds League, and it was here that Rachan had been informed of events that could twist the current crisis in directions unforeseen.

"Yes?"

"The hyperpulse station on Irian has relayed a message from my agents on Helm." Not *our agents*. *My* agents. "They sent it under a Priority Alpha code, so great was the importance attached to it." He sipped again at his drink, enjoying the obvious turmoil behind Garth's fat, blank features. "As I warned you, Grayson Carlyle has not gone to Marik. He is at Helm . . . now."

"Helm! But . . . but . . ."

"I warned you that not all men jump when you command them. He disregarded your order to proceed to Marik. You should have foreseen that."

"It shouldn't matter. There are still two full companies of 'Mechs on Helm, as well as the air and space forces. Carlyle will not get past them."

"Fool!" The time had come to remove the velvet glove. "My agents report that two of Carlyle's lances—*two lances*—interrupted eight of your 'Mechs in the destruction of Durandel. All *eight* of your 'Mechs were destroyed. Apparently. Carlyle's force suffered no damage worth noting."

Garth's mouth made gulping motions, as though he were struggling for air. "He can't evade the rest of my forces there . . ."

"He can and he has. My sources report that your field commander there is moving against Carlyle's DropShips now. Your forces, however, are outclassed in this. There are not enough BattleMechs on the planet to run a fox like Grayson Carlyle to ground, even if the move against his transportation succeeds. A hard, stand-up fight could wreck your garrison forces completely. Grayson Carlyle is a . . . capable fighter."

"We couldn't cover every eventuality, Rachan! We couldn't! All I could spare for the Helm operation were two depleted regiments! An understrength battalion! *You* said it would be enough for the job at hand."

"Pardon me. I said it was adequate for the job of destroying a civilian community and rounding up the Techs and MechWarrior recruits who lived there. I said nothing about facing Carlyle's seasoned warriors!"

"All the rest of the forces at my disposal are here, or on Marik, waiting for him."

"Obviously."

Garth showed new determination, one fat fist smacking into his open palm. "The units stationed on Marik can be shifted. They will be shifted. We can still trap Grayson Carlyle . . . and exterminate him!"

Rachan drained his glass, then studied the emptied crystal, rotating it against the light provided by the drifting stars. "Exterminate him or not as you will, Garth, but the man and his mercenaries *must* be neutralized, one way or another. The operation on Sirius V was not enough. You must finish the job."

"It will be finished, Precentor, I promise you!"

"I don't want promises, Your Grace." Rachan judged it was time again to observe the amenities. "What I need now are results. Results that you have promised . . ." He held out one hand, palm up, and closed his fingers into a fist. "To me! If you wish to share in what we have discovered, you must do your part!"

Garth closed his eyes and nodded. "Believe me, Pre . . . Rachan, I want it as badly as you. This is a delay, nothing more. Within days, I can have the better part of three regiments on Helm. Grayson Death Carlyle and his whole band of mercenaries will not be able to face such an army as that!"

Rachan nodded, satisfied. Garth was his creature, of that he was certain. "Very well, Your Grace. But do not fail us." It was good to remind the man of those who stood behind Rachan. "Those with me do not tolerate lack of faith . . . or failure. Especially failure."

"I understand."

Surging up out of the dust-filled valley, the House Marik BattleMechs struck, laser beams and machine gun fire probing the Gray Death infantry defenses. As Ramage had expected, their lightest 'Mechs took the center, smashing forward against the infantry hiding in trenches and rough-made bunkers, while the larger, heavier 'Mechs flanked the infantry positions to north and south.

Ramage's men held their fire until the last moment, then unleashed a barrage of short-range anti-Mech missiles and laser bolts and billowing plumes of orange flame, seeking weak points in the armor of their gigantic targets.

Ramage did no shooting. There was no enemy infantry on the field as yet, and his assault rifle would be exactly as effective against BattleMech armor as so many wads of paper hurled by hand. What he could and did do was to direct those troops within earshot, pointing out possible weak points in armor, leg joints, and motivator arms, encouraging his men with a steady stream of invective, steadying those who wavered with either encouragement or curses, depending on the individual's personality.

The 'Mechs in the enemy's van strode across Ramage's trench lines without slowing. Short-range missiles arced up from a dozen emplacements, striking armor in flares of light that scattered great chunks of metal across the hillside. The *Locust* paused once, the medium laser slung from its chin turret pivoting down and around to seek out the launch site of a stinging swarm of SRMs. White light flashed, dazzling even through the dark-tinted visors that Ramage's troops wore, and then dirt, smoke, and fire boiled from the shattered log roof of a hidden emplacement. Now the *Locust* was striding forward again as Ramage's men began to turn small arms fire against the machines. The air was filled with the sigh and ping of hurtling rounds and ricochets. Once, something heavy smacked Ramage squarely in the center of his padded armor jerkin, then rattled off the top of his boot. He spared the object with a glance. It was a 10 mm rifle bullet, its nose mashed almost flat where it had struck the side of the *Locust* fifty meters away.

Sounds of battle erupted sharply up the ridge both to the north and to the south. *The flanking* forces going over the top, Ramage thought. They'll have us surrounded pretty damn quick if we don't do something about it.

THE PRICE OF GLORY

The Gray Death's line was crumbling. There was no way for unsupported infantry to do any more than slow these monsters. If looked as though the enemy commander had already evolved a plan to nullify Ramage's defensive line by pinning his infantry with a few light 'Mechs, and sending the heavy stuff around to the rear.

It was time to go.

Ramage reached into the bulky holster at his hip and withdrew a flare gun. Breaking open the breech, he inserted a 35 mm red round, snapped the gun closed, aimed it at the sky, and fired. There was a dull thump, and the red star rose in a hissing arc that fell out over the valley and slowly drifted toward the ground. Here and there, isolated clumps of men began falling back from their positions. The signal, prearranged as they'd taken their positions, was the order to fall back to a second line of defense along the crest of the hill.

A flash of light caught his attention. White smoke trails stabbed out from a bunker thirty meters downslope and toward the north, reaching toward the *Locust* as it lumbered up the slope below. One of the shoulder-fired missiles struck the machine squarely on the plate armor across its cockpit, but left no visible sign of damage beyond a blackening of the 20-ton 'Mech's tan and brown camouflage paint pattern.

"Number three, fall back!" Ramage yelled. The *Locust* was almost upon the hidden bunker now. There was an agonizing pause, and then two men broke from under their sheltering tarpaulin and bolted up the hill, just as the *Locust*'s massive foot smashed down on their roofing, splintering the roof logs into spinning white slivers.

The *Locust* paused, its turret tracking side to side. The pair of machine guns mounted high up above its back on either side of the massive, round leg actuator casings swung around and down, falling into line with the running men. There was a high-pitched rattle and a twinkling fall of spent shell casings. Geysers of dirt stitched up the hill toward, through, and then past the two men, slamming into boulders and leaving white scars on trees. Ramage heard one of the men scream as heavy-caliber rounds shredded flesh and bone, spun them around and

down, and left them as torn, bloodied, rag-limp forms
still on the ground.

Enough is enough. Ramage thought. *War is hell, but
gunning down fleeing, unarmed troops isn't part of it!* He
stooped in his trench, grasping a heavy canvas satchel.
He would take on this particular bastard by himself.

The *Locust* had taken three more uncertain steps forward, then paused again, towering on its spindly legs.
Ramage bent low as he raced along the trench, twice
stepping across the twisted, broken shapes of Gray Death
troopers cut down by the advancing 'Mechs. At the end
of the trench, he rolled out onto the ground, rose in a
low crouch, and raced the remaining thirty meters toward the enemy BattleMech.

Farther up the hill, near the crest now hidden by smoke
and low, scrubby trees, the insistent, deep-throated voice
of a heavy machine gun began yammering above the general roar of battle. That would be the 15 mm Spanner
machine gun he'd ordered set up at the crest of the hill
above the center of the line. The gunner must have spotted the *Locust* and be trying to bring it down.

At the moment, the machine gun was far more dangerous to Ramage than it was to the 20-ton BattleMech.
Even armor-piercing explosive rounds would have to
score many hits before they could do more than scratch
that armor plate. As he ran, Ramage heard the snap and
whine of heavy-caliber bullets high above his head.

The goddamned idiots, he told himself. *They're firing
too high again. Drop your aim, you bastards!*

Fortunately for Ramage, they didn't heed his unspoken
advice, and the rounds continued to bark and snap among
the tree branches overhead, an occasional round flashing
in miniature pyrotechnics against the hull of the *Locust.*
The *Locust* was holding its ground, its hull canted back
to give its medium laser a clear shot at the machine gun
nest on the hill above. The laser fired, a beam of white-
lit fury boring through smoke, haze, and branches, toward the brush at the top of the hill. After a moment,
the machine gun fired again, to be answered again by the
laser. The battle was like a game of double blind man's

bluff, with two clumsy and half-blinded opponents feeling for one another through the fog.

The exchange also meant that the *Locust* pilot was too busy to see the man running through the swirling smoke toward its feet.

*Locust*s do not have vulnerable knee joints as do *Stingers*, *Wasps*, and similarly constructed humanoid 'Mechs. A *Locust*'s weak point was in the joint between foot and leg, where the ankle joint allowed the four broad foot flanges to fold and flex as the machine took each step.

The *Locust* took a step forward, Ramage put on a last burst of speed, leapt, and came down on top of the 'Mech's right foot just as it began to sweep forward in its next step. He reached up and grasped the slender leg above the lower leg sheathing, hanging on as he swung dizzily forward. Somehow, he hung on without being knocked clear as the foot came down on the grassy hillside. Ramage took the canvas satchel and waited, watching for his moment. The *Locust* fired its laser again. The white-hot bolt discharging six meters above Ramage's head sent a wash of heat across his body. Then the machine took another step, and a narrow opening between foot and ankle sheathing opened as the machine's right foot flexed closed. Ramage jammed the satchel into the narrow opening, letting the closing of the joint itself wedge the package into the weak point in the *Locust*'s foot. Then he grabbed the pull-ring igniter, let go with his left arm, and tumbled toward the ground. The igniter ring yanked free of the igniter, leaving a curling trail of smoke as the 'Mech lurched forward. Ramage hit the ground with a thump, and rolled. Then he was up and running as fast as possible down the slope.

Five seconds passed, then the air at his back was rent by a shrieking blast, and bits of metal whipped past his ear. Ramage flopped face down to the ground as metal rattled through the grass. He rolled to the side and looked back. The *Locust* had settled back on its haunches, its spindly legs folded high above the cockpit. It was evident that the 'Mech had sustained serious damage to the foot, but, so far as Ramage could see, the foot was still attached to the leg.

He cursed. A five-kilo block of C-4 should have sheared the foot off cleanly, crippling the vulnerable light 'Mech. As it was, the damage could probably be repaired in a few hours.

The top of the *Locust* broke open as the twin escape hatch panels swung apart. A helmeted head appeared in the opening. Ramage cursed again. His TK was back in the headquarters trench, and his holster carried an empty flare pistol. Except for his combat knife sheathed high on his armored tactical vest, he was unarmed.

Idiot, he told himself. *what do you expect, chasing after 'Mechs and leaving your sidearm behind? Ramage, old son, it's time you retired . . . before these unfriendly people do it for you.*

The *Locust*'s pilot swung his legs clear of the hatch and dropped to the ground. He was bare-legged and bare-chested, wearing only red shorts and his incongruous, massive visored helmet, but the subgun clenched in his hands was short, mean, and deadly.

Time to go, Ramage thought. Keeping his eyes on the Marik pilot, he began to work his way backward down the hill, toward the shelter of some heavier brush twenty meters further downslope.

Another trench lay concealed there within the brush, but it was empty now, its occupants long since fled. Looking about him, Ramage realized that he was now quite alone, cut off from any friendly troops. He scavenged through the bottom of the trench, searching for a weapon. Apart from some spent shell casings, there was nothing. He glanced back up the hill. The *Locust* was still there, its pilot on the ground in the shadow of the crouching body, apparently working on the damaged ankle joint.

As he turned away, movement caught his eye farther down the hill. The *Wasp* strode forward out of the dust and battle fog, its Diverse Optics medium laser cradled high in its metal arms. Ramage watched it come, helpless to do a thing about it. From seventy meters away, he could see the missile pod cover above the joint of its left leg pop up, exposing a pair of stubby black tubes.

My God, the bastard's after me, Ramage thought. *He's*

got me nailed! The machine's pilot had seen him—or his trench—and was preparing to open fire with deadly, short-range missiles.

Ramage scrambled back up out of the trench. The tubes spat fire, and a pair of SRMs shrieked across the short distance between the *Wasp* and Ramage's temporary shelter. The twin explosions caught Ramage in the back, lifting him clear of the ground and hurling him with un-imaginable violence up the hill.

The universe was engulfed by an all-consuming darkness before he hit the ground.

9

Static continued to crowd the tactical frequencies, growing louder and harsher as Grayson's 'Mech column closed on the DropShips. There was no way a message could be punched through that interference even to alert Ilse Martinez that his 'Mechs were on their way. The interference was so bad that communications between the 'Mechs of the two lances was becoming difficult.

"Motion, Gray," Lori warned from her *Shadow Hawk*. He could barely hear her through the jamming noise. "Sector front-center. Reads like a skimmer, at range . . . eight hundred meters."

Grayson's *Marauder* paused, its weapons-heavy forearms swinging into combat attitude. An armed skimmer posed little risk to a BattleMech, but it was never wise to take chances. Skimmers loaded with plastic explosives had been known to make suicide runs that had shattered 'Mechs or caused massive damage to control and actuator systems.

Brush thrashed aside 500 meters ahead, and a small, two-place skimmer whipped into view. Grayson removed his hands from the *Marauder*'s firing controls. The skimmer was a Legion scout craft. The lone pilot wore the camouflage greys of a Legion trooper.

"All units, hold fire," Grayson ordered. "It's a messenger!"

The messenger echoed the sentiments with a message of his own. "Don't shoot, Colonel!" he yelled, his light voice transmitted by the *Marauder*'s external audio pickups. "I've got a message from Captain Martinez!"

THE PRICE OF GLORY

It was easier for Lori to unbutton her *Shadow Hawk*'s canopy and hope to get it sealed again than it was for Grayson, whose *Marauder*'s egg-shaped body was massively armored and sealed. The hatch on top of her cockpit swung aside, and Lori's helmeted head appeared in the opening. "We recognize you! What's the message?"

"The Captain says the DropShips are under attack! She says the infantry line isn't holding, and the 'Mechs at the ship aren't going to last long! The enemy's attacking with at least ten 'Mechs, maybe more! She sent me to try to find you . . . to warn you . . ."

"You did well," Lori said. "Fall in behind our column, and stay clear when the shooting starts." A moment later, her voice came across on the tac band, heavily filtered by the static. "We don't have much time, Gray."

"I know. Let's pick up the pace." He could hear the firing, like the distant rumble of summer thunder coming from straight ahead, over his 'Mech's pick-ups.

As his *Marauder* surged into motion again, Grayson fretted about the lance of BattleMechs he had left on guard with the DropShips. Lieutenant Roget had some combat experience, as did Graff, but Vandergriff and Trevor were unknown quantities. Though they were no longer apprentices, their lack of actual combat experience meant Grayson could not rely on them in a BattleMech firefight. That was why he had left the lance behind to mount guard. He had expected a fight at Durandel.

He had not expected the Marik forces to respond as quickly as they had, however, with this headlong race to seize his DropShips.

The 'Mech column crested a low ridge, and suddenly the battle noise was louder, a thundering roar that rumbled on and on, the crackle of small arms fire interspersed with missile explosions and the rapid-fire thud of BattleMech autocannons. The DropShip LZ was less than a kilometer away now.

The jamming was louder, too. Grayson heard Lori saying something over the radio, but he couldn't make out her words. He recognized other voices as well—Davis McCall's and Hassan Khaled's among them—but the words were drowned in the hissing sea of static.

Grayson thought furiously. It was obvious that the enemy had elected to fight according to a set plan. Indeed, that was the only possible approach when using jammers, for there was no way either side could communicate changes of plan or issue new orders. Though the jamming put the Gray Death at a disadvantage, the attackers were operating at a handicap as well. With no way to issue new orders, they would be slow and cumbersome in reacting to the unexpected.

And Grayson Death Carlyle was a master of doing the unexpected in battle.

His motion sensor was chirping a steady, monotonous pinging at him, showing something large moving across his front. He twisted the *Marauder* five degrees right and stepped up the speed. The land here was gently sloping, but heavily screened by light woods and boulders, some of them as big as a house. It was impossible to see more than a few tens of meters in any direction.

Trees parted for Grayson's *Marauder.* A *Thunderbolt* rose above the low-twisting trees eighty meters ahead, its out-sized arms hanging apelike on either side of its massive, black-painted body.

Grayson's *Marauder* outweighed the other 'Mech by ten tons, but the *Thunderbolt* had the edge in armament. Its right arm-mounted Sunglow Type 2 heavy laser was one of the largest lasers ever carried by a BattleMech. It was backed up by a massive, tube-shaped LRM rack slung across its left shoulder, a battery of medium lasers and short-ranged missiles in its torso, and a pair of heavy machine guns in its left arm. The *Thunderbolt* was armored to match its weaponry, with heavier armor than the *Marauder*'s in some key places.

Grayson knew that the *Thunderbolt*'s weakness was that so much weaponry generated a hell of a lot of heat. *Thunderbolts* suffered more from heat build-up than many other 'Mechs, and that fact would work to Grayson's advantage.

Or rather, it *could* work to his advantage, if he had the time to exploit it. Grayson's immediate concern was the situation back at the DropShips. This Marik *Thunderbolt* had obviously been thrown past the LZ positions to block just such a movement as his. Grayson did not have time to play tag with the *Thunderbolt,* and it would take time to wear his opponent down to the point where heat became a serious concern.

The one certain way to knock out a heavy 'Mech fast was to concentrate overwhelming firepower against it. Grayson knew that such a maneuver took quick timing and good communications. The Gray Death Company had no communications at all at the moment, but they did have a considerable body of shared experience and training to draw on. It might work, but it would have to be done quickly.

There was a rippling flash, and long-range missiles lanced from the *Thunderbolt* toward Grayson's *Marauder.* Grayson twisted at his 'Mech's controls and trotted to the left. Savage explosions shredded trees and ripped across the floor of the woods. A giant boulder ahead offered shelter, and Grayson made for it.

More explosions shattered through the woods behind him. Lori's *Shadow Hawk* was in the *Thunderbolt*'s line of fire now. Her autocannon dropped across the shoulder of her 'Mech as she engaged the heavier 'Mech in a stand-up slugging match. McCall's *Rifleman* stepped into line at her side, his paired autocannon and lasers hurling fire into the larger 'Mech. The *Thunderbolt* responded. Missiles exploded on the *Rifleman*'s flank and on the *Shadow Hawk*'s right shoulder and leg. Autocannon shells slammed into the *Thunderbolt*'s upper chest, scoring the armor and gouging it with deep, ragged craters.

Grayson paused behind the boulder, checking his weapons systems and estimating the *Thunderbolt*'s position from the sounds of gunfire and explosions. Then, when the *T-Bolt* was concentrating completely on Lori and Davis, he lunged around the boulder.

The *Thunderbolt* filled his sighting scanners, barely ninety meters away. Grayson's 120 mm autocannon began slamming high-explosive armor-piercers at the enemy machine, scoring hit after hit on its arm and upper chest. Grayson's PPCs cut loose with a twin torrent of blue-white fire that barked and crackled as discharged electrical current leapt like blue lightning from the stricken *Thunderbolt* to the ground.

The *Thunderbolt* turned to face this new challenge, but Grayson was already pulling back behind the boulder. Lori and McCall continued to pour fire into the enemy 'Mech, with both Khaled's *Warhammer* and Delmar Clay's *Wolverine* also joining the action.

Grayson saw missile fire strike Clay's *Wolverine* on its left arm, leaving scarred and broken plates of armor. The *T-Bolt's* heavy laser fired, lighting up the woods with a supernatural radiance that edged every leaf and limb in blue-white light. Grayson winced as he saw that fire touch McCall's *Rifleman,* melting armor across the Scotsman's torso. Swinging his *Marauder* around the rock again, he targeted on the *Thunderbolt,* and opened fire with everything he had.

Smoke billowed from a savage gash in the *Thunderbolt's* side. Autocannon shells smashed into the heavy 'Mech's right arm.

The *Thunderbolt* pilot was quick to respond. His heavy machine spun, the right arm heavy laser swinging up to point directly at Grayson's cockpit. Looking down the black maw of that lethal weapon, Grayson knew what it was to stare into the throat of Death.

But nothing happened. Sparks arced and snapped at a power connection high up on the T-Bolt's laser mount. Either Grayson's autocannon shells or perhaps an earlier hit scored by one of the others had damaged the laser and made it inoperable.

Grayson shrieked a victory yell and fired his PPCs again. Great chunks of armor spun from the stricken *Thunderbolt,* which was now backing slowly toward the cover of heavier woods to its rear. Grayson urged his *Marauder* forward.

The two antagonists stopped, facing each other across fifty meters. For a moment, Grayson thought the other 'Mech was going to rush him, putting Grayson at a severe disadvantage in hand-to-hand combat with a handed 'Mech.

Then the *Thunderbolt* lurched to the left, turned, and vanished into the woods in full retreat. Grayson couldn't be sure, but the 'Mech had probably taken enough hits that even this brief combat had begun to threaten the pilot with heat overload and an automatic shutdown.

The way was clear. Grayson and his seven Warriors swept through the woods and up the hill.

The DropShips were down in the valley beyond.

Accepted military doctrine had DropShips ground in a broad, open field with an unobstructed field for fire. The reason is obvious. Typical military *Union* Class Drop-Ships mount as many as twenty lasers of various sizes, as well as missile launchers, PPC turrets, and autocannon. Though the range of those weapons is sharply reduced from what it would be in the free reaches of space, in strategic terms, a grounded DropShip still represents a small fortress that BattleMechs treat with great respect.

Grayson had ordered that the *Deimos* and the *Phobos* set down in the rocky notch of a saddle valley for a reason, however. With no sure knowledge of how strong were the unknown but probably hostile forces on the planet, he had to assume that an open landing could result in the LZ being surrounded by enough BattleMechs to eventually overwhelm even the DropShips' firepower and armor.

The presence of a storm system over the area around Durandel had given the DropShips pilots their chance. By plunging into the clouds during the final moments of their approach, they had been able to mask the exact point of their landing among the confusing ground clutter echos of the ridges and hills in the region. Ilse Martinez had spotted the rocky saddle, and Grayson had agreed to it. The DropShips' fields of fire would be sharply restricted among those boulders and ridgelines, but there was a good chance that the location of the LZ would remain secret until the Legion could figure out what was going on. If the enemy ships tracking his approach to Helm in the first place could be kept in the dark about the Legion crafts' identity and exact LZ, the DropShips might never be found. DropShips stand out like flashing red beacons in the emptiness of space, but it was a different story on the ground. Surrounded by hills, woods, and boulders, the ships became insignificant and almost impossible to

find unless the searcher were using extremely sophisticated instruments with square-kilometer-by-square kilometer finesse, determination, and patience.

Altogether, it had seemed a worthwhile gamble.

As Grayson crested the ridge east of the LZ, he knew
the gamble had failed. There had always been the chance
that one of the Marik ships in orbit would tag the two
ships by radar or other means. Perhaps they had been
spotted by an orbiting picket suspicious enough of the
"ducal party" to survey the area where the DropShips
had gone down after the storm cleared. Or perhaps a
long-range infantry patrol had seen the flare of their jets
and reported it to headquarters. Any of a hundred minor
giveaways could have revealed their precise LZ to the
Marik forces on the planet.

And now those forces here *here*.

Both the *Deimos* and the *Phobos* were fully engaged
in the battle in the valley. The two ships were grounded
500 meters apart from one another, which gave them
excellent control over the ground between them. Inevitably it also created "fire shadows" on either side, which
meant that one ship could fire some of its weapons while
the other was blocked by the first ship. The attackers
were making use of this, with two groups of BattleMechs
engaging the DropShips, one in each fire shadow on opposite sides of the pair. More BattleMechs still struggled
along the crest of the valley's western ridge. The 'Mechs
of the Gray Death's recon lance were there, firing wildly
at several light enemy 'Mechs, but it was obvious that
the main enemy force had swept around both flanks to
attack the DropShips.

A Marik *Archer* and a *Wolverine* moved among the
boulders 300 meters in front of Grayson's *Marauder*.
Missiles arced up and across and into *Phobos*'s hull,
smashing at laser turrets, and flashing among the damage
that had already marred the armor along the Dropship's
flank. A *Centurion* and a *Panther* crouched nearby, providing supporting fire. Grayson's *Marauder* kicked up
boiling clouds of dust as it raced down the valley's slope,
his autocannon hammering into the battle's din.

His first rounds struck the *Centurion* in its right side,

smashing armor plate and tearing a gaping hole high in the 50-ton 'Mech's shoulder. The Marik 'Mech spun to face him, its right arm Luxor D autocannon barking fire in return. The *Centurion*'s 80 mm rapid-fire rounds struck home on the *Marauder*'s upper hull. The sound inside Grayson's cockpit was hellacious, a crashing that would have deafened him except for the high noise cutouts in his neurohelmet earpieces. He took the fire rather than trying to dodge, bringing his 'Mech's forearms to the point. Twin medium laser bolts lanced out and caught the *Centurion* side by side, high on its chest. Grayson's PPCs fired an instant later, knocking the *Centurion* backward off it feet as gobbets of half-molten armor sprayed from blossoming impact craters in its torso.

Lori's *Shadow Hawk* dueled with the enemy *Wolverine*. With the two 55-ton 'Mechs so closely matched in both armor and weaponry, a stand-up battle between the two could have gone on interminably, until both machines were reduced to scrap. McCall's *Rifleman* stepped down off the hillside seconds later, however, and added his massive firepower to Lori's. Side by side, the two Legion 'Mechs began to advance on the *Wolverine*, drifting apart slightly to force the enemy pilot to choose between one or the other for his targeting. After multiple hits on the *Wolverine*'s legs and lower torso, the Marik pilot decided that discretion was the better part of valor, and fired his jump jets. The 'Mech vaulted backward across the boulder field, landing eighty meters farther on and partway up the west slope of the valley.

Farther up the valley, Charles Bear's *Crusader* and Hassan Khaled's *Warhammer* engaged a Marik *Shadow Hawk*, a *Warhammer*, and the *Thunderbolt* damaged moments before by Grayson. The two *Warhammer*s seemed bound for a toe-to-toe struggle, each massive machine delivering bolt after searing bolt of star-hot energy from their heavy PPCs, scoring hit after armor-boiling hit.

Then the Marik *Warhammer* began to withdraw, backing up the slope step by step, and the 'Mechs with it followed.

Charles Bear followed, too, his *Crusader*'s arm-mounted medium lasers burning away at the *Warham-mer*'s massive body. Inside his neurohelmet, his features remained as stonily impassive as ever, but the muscles of his jaw clenched in anticipated frustration.

Charles Bear's ancestors had been colonists on Tau Ceti IV, a loose coalition from among eight of the surviving Amerindian tribes of North America. On Tau Ceti's South Continent, the People's Nations had established a federation dedicated to preserving and continuing the ways of life of their ancestors. That cultural heritage rode with Charles Bear. He was a warrior and the son of a warrior, though his sense of the word was subtly distinct from its use in 31st-century technic society. For Bear, "Warrior" was a spiritual concept that could be fully realized only through hand-to-hand combat with one's personal enemy.

In the vast majority of battles, however, a Mech-Warrior fought unknown foes, and he remained unknown in return. Indeed, there was a comforting anonymity within the steel hull of a BattleMech. So few Mech-Warriors survived long enough to become well-known that most of a warrior's opponents were reduced to the level of targets. Dangerous targets they might be, but targets on tracker screens and HUD displays, nonetheless. It became easier to press the fire button when your target was a 50-ton steel monster, and not a man of flesh and blood, with his own hopes, fears, ambitions, and berserker's battle lust.

MechWarrior Bear's training and cultural conditioning had given him the need to face a known enemy, to prove himself in hands-on combat between worthy foes. Bear's ancestors on Terra had kept the custom of "counting coup," a way of winning glory, status, and warrior's rank by actually touching an opponent. In the past seven years, since his apprenticeship under his father in the Ceti Rangers, Bear had served as a mercenary MechWarrior with both the Ceti Rangers and the 21st Centauri Lancers. He had racked up a score of seven kills and five assists, but never, *never*, had he destroyed an enemy 'Mech in hand-to-hand combat. Until he had counted coup, however, Charles Bear would never consider himself a true warrior, the son of a warrior.

Now once again, the enemy was withdrawing as he advanced, pulling back beyond the reach of his *Crusader*'s outstretched mechanical hands. He triggered laser fire again, scoring hits on the *Warhammer*'s left arm and side. The *Warhammer* dodged left and returned fire, a PPC bolt striking Bear's *Crusader* squarely in the chest, knocking him back a step.

This was a worthy opponent, one skilled with his weapons, and courageous in battle. The scars in its armor, the evidence of patches and old repairs, a line of white-stenciled kill marks on the 'Mech's armor to the left of the cockpit all spoke of this warrior's prowess in combat. Bear ignored the other Marik BattleMechs, concentrating on this one machine.

They exchanged fire again. The *Warhammer* retreated, placing itself close beside a house-sized boulder. Bear triggered his Magna Longbow long-range missiles, sending a salvo lancing across the valley and into his foe. For a moment, smoke and swirling dust blocked out that portion of the hillside. Bear urged his *Crusader* forward at its fastest speed, thundering across the valley floor toward the enemy's last position.

When the dust settled across ground torn and cratered by Bear's salvo, the *Warhammer* was gone. Before Bear had a chance to wonder where, missiles smashed into his *Crusader* from behind. Bear dropped his *Crusader* in a roll toward the giant boulder. As rocks and dirt flew around him, he brought his machine around to face the rear, prone on the ground. In that position, supported by his left arm, he could only bring his right-arm weapons to bear, but he was targeting and triggering both the LRMs and the medium laser mounted in his right forearm before his 'Mech had stopped moving. The enemy *Warhammer* had moved with superhuman speed and agility, ducking behind a nearby boulder and circling around to hit Bear from behind. Now he circled again, moving and firing with lightning speed. Bear's 'Mech took another hit across the right shoulder, while his own fire missed. Dust from the explosion began closing in again. Bear pulled his *Crusader* to its feet, but rather than charge the hidden enemy, he circled to his right, seeking the shelter of the rock the *Warhammer* had used moments before.

Hoping to catch his enemy while he was moving, Bear readied his weapons, composed himself, then moved with lightning speed back into the open.

The dust was clearing, the *Warhammer* gone. Sharyl's *Shadow Hawk* moved across his line of sight several hundred meters farther on, dueling with an enemy *Commando.*

Bear remained expressionless, but his hands closed slowly into rock-hard, tendon-strained fists above his controls.

10

The Marik *Wolverine* had fired his jump jets, and vaulted backward eighty meters up the slope of the valley. In response, Grayson raced after the enemy 'Mech. The Marik pilot triggered short-range missiles that hissed at his *Marauder*, exploding in gouts of flame-shot fury on all sides. Two struck Grayson's 'Mech in the left leg, staggering the heavy 'Mech and almost making it stumble.

With the enemy forced back from the DropShips, it might be possible for the Gray Death 'Mechs to keep them divided, holding part of the Marik force at bay while they crushed the other. Grayson doubted that the enemy commander would care to keep the fight going if such a large part of his available forces was in danger of destruction. Grayson's one hope was to threaten the enemy commander with enough damage and destruction that he would chose to withdraw. Wasn't that, after all, the central tenet of any military tactical doctrine?

As a commander, Grayson, too, had to be concerned with preserving his own company. The Gray Death's recon lance was now at the top of the valley's western ridge, engaged in a long-range duel with unseen Marik BattleMechs on the far side of the ridge. The retreat of the heavy Marik forces in the valley could overwhelm the recon lance, or at least cut it off long enough for serious damage to be inflicted on those lighter 'Mechs. Grayson wanted to get at least some of his heavier 'Mechs up the western ridge and among the company's light 'Mechs there, partly to support them in their duel with the Marik forces, partly to allow them to rejoin the company's main body.

Reuniting with the recon lance was more important at the moment than dealing with the Marik *Wolverine*. Grayson dropped his *Marauder* into a low-bodied crouch and discharged a savage left-right-left-right volley of PPC and laser fire that staggered the enemy 'Mech and forced it to retreat again, but he did not follow up his advantage. Instead he sprinted up the ridge toward the isolated recon lance. He could make out three of the lance's 'Mechs at the crest of the ridge, heavily engaged with Marik forces on two sides. There was Roget's 35-ton *Panther* in the thick of the action, with Vandergriff's *Commando* and Trevor's *Wasp* close beside her. Their 'Mechs looked impossibly small, struggling in silhouette against the skyline of the ridge perhaps two kilometers away.

But where was Graff's *Assassin*?

If one of the lance's 'Mechs was down already, the others must have absorbed plenty of damage as well, and could now be on the verge of being overwhelmed. He increased his *Marauder*'s pace, racing up the ridge.

Behind him, battle swirled through the valley close about the DropShips.

The Marik pilot's name was Gordon Wilcox, and he had been a *Locust* pilot in Captain Prosser's Hammerstrike Company of the 5th Marik Guards regiment. When word had come down for the Hammerstrikes to move on Durandel, he had been ordered to remain behind at Helmdown, guarding the DropShips.

Wilcox had accepted the assignment with relative equanimity. He was young still, as were most Mech-Warriors, and eager to come to grips with the enemy. He had seen enough action in his short career, however, to know that even a relatively simple operation like mopping up on rebel civilians and a handful of light armored vehicles could be a risk to life and limb. How much more true when life and limb were sheltered within the relatively frail armor of a 20-ton *Locust*.

He had walked his *Locust* on sentry-go around the spaceport perimeter and been on patrol when the news

had come. Of the nine 'Mechs that had gone to Durandel, only one had returned. That the one survivor was
Colonel Langsdorf's *Warhammer* was significant. Every
other one of those eight 'Mechs had been lights. Despite
its martial name, the Hammerstrike Company had originally been conceived as a fast recon company, and so
the heaviest 'Mech in the unit had been Captain Prosser's
Rifleman. Then Langsdorf—the man wasn't a Hammer-
striker, but the regimental big-wheel of the 12th White
Sabers—had come in and shaken everything up. The
Captain had been bucked down to lance leader of the fire
lance, and Nakamura's *Griffin* had been shuffled to the
recon lance. None of it made any sense, except perhaps
for the decision to leave Gordon's *Locust* back at Helmdown.

Now Langsdorf was back, and the word was that the
eight 'Mechs he had left behind at Durandel would never
return. There were vague hints and dark rumors, the usual
mix of fantasy and maybe-fact inherent in all military
scuttlebutt. It was said that enemy DropShips had
grounded near Durandel, and a regiment of renegade
mercenaries had wiped out all eight of Gordon's
comrades-at-arms.

Almost before Gordon could absorb the magnitude of
this personal disaster, new orders had come again. He
had been ordered to attach his *Locust,* along with Fred
Kilpatrick's *Wasp* and Hernando De Cruz's *Stinger,* to
part of the 12th White Sabers and to move out against
the rebels at Durandel.

He followed orders, but with a growing hatred. Because of the jamming, there was no way to talk things
over with De Cruz or Kilpatrick, though he was sure the
other two felt as he did. Not that he would have wanted
to discuss all this over a comm frequency! The thoughts
Wilcox bore in his heart bordered on outright mutiny.

As they approached the target area, Langsdorf had used
arm gestures of his *Warhammer* to deploy the troops, and
Gordon had found himself and his two friends in the center of the line, with the heavies of the 12th Sabers on
either flank. What was the man trying to pull? It was
obvious that the renegade mercs had deployed in en-

trenchments along the slope of the ridge facing them, that the enemy was dug in and waiting for them. Could it be that the Colonel was actually trying to eliminate every last 'Mech of the Hammerstrike Company? They'd started off one short of a full company, and then eight had been junked at Durandel. That left the three of them, light 'Mechs all, and Langsdorf was sending them right up the enemy's center, where his firepower and armor were bound to be thickest. *The man must be crazy!*

Then Gordon was too busy to think. The hillside had been a warren of cleverly dug and concealed trenches and bunkers. Though no single strongpoint masked enough firepower to seriously threaten even his *Locust,* the danger was acute, the battle an endless, nerve-twisting fight against fear and an unseen opponent, against rugged ground and hidden pitfalls and the sweat streaming into his eyes. A missile launcher had lightly damaged one leg of his *Locust.* The troops who had fired on him bolted from cover, then raced up the hill. Gordon's anger had surged out in a need for release. His hands had closed on his machine gun controls. He'd tracked his heavy Sperry-Brownings up the hill after the fugitive mercenaries, and triggered a long, satisfying blast that cut them down kicking. An enemy machine gun had answered from the crest of the ridge, and he had engaged it, trading round after rapid-fire round.

He didn't see the enemy sapper on his combat view-screens until it was too late. He'd spotted the man racing away from under his *Locust* seconds before an explosion all but severed the 'Mech's foot. He had pulled off his neurohelmet and replaced it with a combat helmet. Dressed only in shorts and combat boots. Gordon's only body protection was the dark visor that would shield his eyes on a battlefield where stray laser beams were still flashing low across the ground. Anxious to find that sapper, eager to kill, he climbed out of his crippled machine while cradling the Rugan subgun.

It was strange, some detached portion of his mind told him, how his hatred of Langsdorf had been channeled into an all-consuming hatred of the enemy. Had *that,* after all, been Langsdorf's idea, to take men already so angered at the deaths of their comrades that they would pilot their 'Mechs into the very heart of the enemy's defense, and in the fury of their attack, buy time for Langsdorf to flank and surround them? The DropShips, by all accounts, lay just on the other side of this ridge, a place marked as Cleft Valley on the Company's orbital recon maps. Langsdorf's 'Mechs must be over there now, fighting among the renegade's DropShips in an all-out attempt to take them before the enemy's main force returned from Durandel.

He had seen the enemy sapper an instant before Kilpatrick's *Wasp* had fired two SRMs into the enemy's trench. He recognized the man's tactical vest, the camouflage pattern of his combat helmet. It was the same man he'd glimpsed on his screens just before his *Locust* had been crippled.

Gordon hoped the enemy soldier was not dead. Killing him with the submachine gun—or better, with his bare hands—would be far more satisfying than the deaths of the two running soldiers on the hill. His anger was out of control now, a torrent raging against the injustice that had cut down eight of his friends and left him stranded on a fire-swept hillside light years from his home.

The thought of home moved him forward. He had a sister and a mother and his fiancee Mirinda all on Marik, loved ones whom he had not seen in three years. Sometimes, the desire to see them was so intense that he could almost taste it. Yet here he was, twenty light years from home, hurled blindly into combat against murderous renegades by an insensibly stupid Colonel who didn't even know Gordon's name.

There were tears coursing down his cheeks as he hefted the subgun in his sweaty, trembling grip and started down the hill toward the still form of his enemy.

"You bastard," he said. "You filthy bastard . . ." The mercenary lay unmoving, face down in the grass. Gordon was about to raise the subgun to his shoulder, ready to empty his 40-round magazine into the man, but something made him pause, then walk cautiously forward.

The man's tactical vest had torn across his back, and his tunic was bloodstained and torn. A ragged gash across the man's left shoulder was thick with fresh blood. Gordon reached one arm out, took the man's right arm, and rolled him over. The mercenary's chest rose and fell with his breathing. His face was a mass of caked blood. Bubbles swelled and popped under his nostrils as he breathed.

Gordon did not even note the passing of his anger. It wasn't that the hatred was gone, and it certainly was not that he no longer wanted to kill. Somehow, though, the soldier's blood mask had transformed him from target to human being. Gordon groped at the wounded man's throat for a pulse.

The dark eyes snapped open through the drying blood, and with a speed that Gordon could not quite comprehend, the man's right fist came up, one knuckle extended in what should have been a killing blow to Gordon's throat. The man was weak enough, and just slow enough, that the blow caught the edge of Gordon's combat helmet, knocking him backward.

He kept his feet and his grip on his Rugan. He fumbled, though, as he tried to bring the SMG around to point at the enemy. Moving with a speed Gordon did not think possible for a man so badly wounded, the blood-masked mercenary surged up from the ground, the wicked, black blade of a combat knife materializing almost magically in his hand. The man stepped inside the firing arc of Gordon's weapon and slashed with the knife. Gordon didn't even realize he was wounded until he felt something hot splash across his bare chest. He looked down, startled, and wondered why the whole world was turning red.

Then he was on the ground, on his back looking up at red sky through red trees. "Damn you, Langsdorf," he tried to say, but the words wouldn't come. Then red faded to black and he died.

Captain Ramage leaned against a tree, holding himself upright as he stropped the blade of his knife on his trousers. He felt sick and weak. The wound in his back throbbed in agony. From the feel of it, his tactical vest had absorbed most of the blow from a piece of shrapnel the size of his fist. The material had torn, but it had reduced the projectile's speed to the point where it had gashed the flesh behind his left shoulder—and not carried away his entire arm. But that didn't mean it didn't hurt.

His face felt stiff and cracked. The concussion of the SRM explosions had burst a blood vessel in his nose, and he knew that what he felt was dried blood. *I must look a fair sight,* he thought. *It's a wonder that Locust pilot didn't run screaming at the sight of at me.*

Consciousness had been returning with a slow, burning pain in head and back when the enemy trooper had rolled him over. Ramage had opened his eyes to see the insect-visaged helmet of the *Locust* warrior bent close to his own face, a vicious Rugan submachine gun gripped tightly in his left hand. Ramage had neither hesitated nor favored his own wounds. He had launched himself into combat, ignoring the tearing pain in his shoulder, ignoring all but the need to kill this enemy as quickly and as silently as possible. His first blow had failed to kill; it had been a difficult thrust requiring precision and accuracy. Being flat on his back and scarcely able to see should have made it a nearly impossible thrust. Through blind, dumb luck, the blow had staggered the enemy enough to give Ramage an instant's grace. He had forced himself to his feet. The wound in his back shrieked white agony with every movement, as he pulled out his knife while rushing inside the soldier's fire arc, and then slashed the man's throat.

Waves of sick dizziness lashed furiously at his mind, and Ramage thought he would faint from the pain alone. His movement had torn something open in his back. He could feel the fresh trickle of blood down his spine, could feel fresh damage grating under the blood with each move he made. The stabbing pains in his left side that accompanied each breath suggested that he had cracked at least one rib as well.

To take his mind from the pain and nausea, he looked around in an attempt to assess the tactical situation and his chances for survival. Meanwhile, the battle raged on. His ears told him that much as he'd first begun climbing back to awareness. The whole crest of the ridge above him to the east was a mass of flame and thundering explosions. From the sound of it, Marik 'Mechs had gained the top of the hill and were fighting there with the Gray Death recon lance.

When he caught the deep-throated thunder of a DropShip's autocannon, Ramage knew that the *Deimos* and the *Phobos* were also in the fight. They would be hard-pressed to target in that narrow trap of a valley, but deep trouble awaited any Marik 'Mechs unlucky enough to wander into their field of fire.

His ear caught another sound, the familiar thud of a 120 mm autocannon. The timber of those rounds was the same as the 120s aboard the DropShips, but the rate of fire was slower, more measured. Ramage had heard the sound often enough to identify the gun immediately as the autocannon slung across the dorsal hull of Grayson's *Marauder.* The volume of explosive thunder from the far side of the hill convinced him that the entire company must be committed to the battle.

Ramage would have cheered had he not been so close to fainting. *Everything would be O.K. now. The Colonel had made it in time!*

He heard another sound through the cacophony of battle, the grinding of engines from another direction. Clinging to the tree for support, he turned to see a pair of low-slung wheeled vehicles moving slowly along the base of the hillside. He recognized the model. They were modified Packrats, 20-ton, eight-wheeled combat cars mounting complex, omnidirectional broadcast antennae. Those cars carried no weapons, but proper use of the electronic countermeasures gear they packed into those low, squarish bodies could be enough to turn the tide of battle.

Ramage's experienced eye could see that they were not being properly used, however. Those two Packrats should have been set up far from one another at opposite ends of the battlefield. They would have been just as effective sitting on the crest of the next ridge to the west, instead of venturing so close to the battlefield. Where they were now, any stray BattleMech, even some isolated trooper left behind by the flow of battle, could damage the ve-

hicles enough to stop their broadcasts and to clear the
tactical frequencies again.

More movement and the rustle of thrashing underbrush
brought Ramage's head around again. There were the
Marik soldiers, hundreds of them! He saw a wheeled
APC making its way steadily up the slope, and heard the
keening whine of a hovercraft off through the trees and
smoke to the south. With the west face of the ridge secured, the Marik infantry was moving up and bringing
the ECM vehicles with them. Why? The soldiers he could
see were advancing with grim determination up the slope.
It couldn't be that they were going to try to tangle with
the Colonel's 'Mechs. What then . . . the remnants of
Ramage's infantry?

Something turned to ice in the pit of Ramage's stomach.

The DropShips?

So far, the Marik infantry had not noticed him. He
had to do something. But what?

He bent over to retrieve the Rugan SMG from the dead
pilot's fingers and nearly passed out. He couldn't stop an
army with a submachine gun, but it steadied him a bit to
feel the cool plastic surface in his hands. The Rugan fired
80 caseless rounds, and from the heft of the weapon, the
magazine must be full, or nearly so. One glance at the
dead pilot's scantily clad body told Ramage that *he* was
carrying no spare magazines. Perhaps there were some
at his disabled 'Mech.

An idea stirred within Ramage's pain-dulled mind, and
he struggled to capture it. The Marik pilot's *Locust* was
parked where he had left it, hunkered down among the
scrub brush and trees partway up the west face of the
hillside. With the damage to its foot that Ramage himself
had inflicted, that 'Mech would not be going anywhere
soon. Ramage had a nodding acquaintance with
BattleMech operation through his work with the Gray
Death.

That *Locust* was still a potent weapon, intact except
for the damage to its right foot.

Step after painful step, he made his way back up the
slope, using the SMG as a walking stick, making his way

from tree to tree. He was afraid that if he fell, he would be too weak to get up again.

Ramage knew more about the operation of *Locust*s than he did about most other BattleMechs because of his friendship with Lori Kalmar. They had first met back on Trellwan, when the two of them had joined the fledgling 'Mech force that that was to become the Gray Death Legion. Except for Ramage and Grayson, Lori had felt isolated among the other unit members, who continued to treat her with suspicion long after she had defected from the forces of their enemy. He had used what technician's training he could muster to get her *Locust* battle-ready, back before the final, climactic battle at Thunder Rift.

The *Locust*, like all other 'Mechs, would have a computer-oriented cutout to prevent unauthorized personnel from using the machine. However, the cutouts in all but the largest, heaviest 'Mechs would disengage the 'Mech's fire control or drive systems only after the machine had been completely shut down. It was unlikely that the Marik pilot had done so, considering how much time it took to power up a dead 'Mech, and so Ramage thought its control and fire systems might still be operational. As he drew closer to the still form of the machine, he could hear the gentle hum from its power routers and cooling fans. The 20-ton 'Mech was still idling, and its boarding ladder dangled where the pilot had left it. Though Ramage's shoulder throbbed with pain, he grasped the chain link ladder in one hand, set his boot onto a rung, but then nearly sagged to the ground as he tried to pull himself up.

Mustering all his will, he tried again. With the *Locust* hunkered down this way, its dorsal hull was only three meters off the ground. As Ramage made his way up one dizzying, swaying, pain-ridden rung after another, those three meters might have been three hundred.

Or three thousand.

When he paused, panting and clinging to the chains, he could feel the warm blood flowing down his back again. At the rate his clothes were becoming soaked with blood, Ramage wondered how long before he would pass out from loss of blood alone.

Vaguely, he heard shouts, someone yelling something about the *Locust*. When he swung the chain ladder around enough to look back down the hill, he saw Marik soldiers charging through the clearing. They would know he was not a Marik MechWarrior by his uniform and tactical vest, not to mention the blood and his evident weakness.

A bullet sang off the metal hull beside him, which somehow galvanized Ramage into action again. He continued his climb, until at last he could roll over onto the dorsal hull of the *Locust,* clinging to the machine by dropping one arm and one leg into the open cockpit. He was lucky that the pilot had elected to open the broad, swing-panel dorsal escape hatch instead of the smaller hatch at the rear of the vehicle. Ramage would not have been able to maneuver to squeeze through the smaller regular hatch.

He dared not stop now for fear of passing out before his task was complete. More bullets spanged against the *Locust*'s hull. He unslung the machine gun from his right shoulder, pointed it toward the noise and flashes, and let loose a long, rippling burst of heavy-caliber autofire. Though he couldn't see if he'd hit anything, the running man-shapes down the hill were gone now, and so the Marik troops must have been driven to cover by his fire. Ramage dropped down into the *Locust*'s seat and checked the controls.

With the damage to the 'Mechs foot, he didn't dare try to set the BattleMech in motion. He didn't even bother bringing down the pilot's neurohelmet from its rack above and to one side of the seat. The neurohelmet would have to be tuned to his own brainwave patterns for him to use it, and its primary purpose was to provide sensory feedback on the 'Mech's attitude and balance anyway. None of that would be needed for what he had in mind.

The controls were identical to those in Lori's old, Sigurdian *Locust*. He touched a control and felt the vibration as the chin turret directly under the cockpit swung 90 degrees, sharply to the right. A screen on the instrument console showed him the target feed from the *Locust*'s medium laser. He could see the troops cautiously moving forward again. Beyond them, brightly lit in the clearing at the bottom of the slope, he could see the two Packrat ECM vehicles, with soldiers swarming around them.

Ramage keyed two buttons, bringing up the screen's targeting display and charging the Martell medium laser. A green light flashed full charge; a second winked readiness. The firing computer closed the target brackets down around the near vehicle. Ramage adjusted the aim up off the heavy armor along the combat car's flanks, and brought the Omni-D antenna into the tracking lock.

Got it! His palm slapped the big red button on the right-hand steering rip. The laser fired, the glare brilliant through the tinted combat screen of the *Locust*.

White fire washed across the ECM car. Without waiting to see if he had scored critical damage on the machine, he traversed the *Locust*'s turret, further right and higher. The second combat car was moving, making a tight turn to get out of the line of fire of this unexpected menace. Green lights flashed, and Ramage's hand came down on the firing switch again. A hit!

The first car was moving now. There was damage to its upper hull, but the antennae appeared intact. Ramage retargeted, locked, and fired. Chunks of metal hurtled from the antennae, leaving twisted wreckage dragging on the ground behind it.

Just then, something big and heavy hit the *Locust*'s outer hull, and smoke boiled in through the still-open escape hatch, but Ramage didn't care. The exertions of the last few minutes were catching up with him in a violently tossing storm of blackness and nausea. The pain was fading now, mercifully, but the dizziness was whirling him up and around and down into oblivion. He wondered whether he had damaged the second Packrat's antenna enough to break the enemy's ECM jamming. He started to reach for the controls again in order to find out.

Somehow, that small movement was just too much for him. He could see his hands dimly through sweat and blurring vision and blood and smoke . . . but he just couldn't make them do what he wanted. Then it no longer mattered, for he couldn't see anything at all.

11

The shrill hissing in Grayson's ears stopped with a suddenness that was astounding. For a moment, he wondered if it were some enemy trick, or was the enemy commander about to broadcast a demand for Grayson's surrender? Or make his own request for terms?

But no, neither side had suffered that much in the fight so far. The Marik commander was pulling his 'Mechs back up the ridge west of the DropShips, but he was moving in good order and his 'Mechs were still fast and dangerous. Chances were that the withdrawal was a tactical movement only, an effort to win better ground on which to continue the fight, clear of the DropShips' fire.

"All units!" Grayson shouted over the taccom frequency. "All units! Coordinate on me! Fire lance, rally between the DropShips. Command lance, form on me!"

He shifted frequencies. "*Phobos! Phobos!* Ilse, are you there?"

Ilse Martinez's voice came through his headphones. "We're still here and buttoned up tight, Colonel!"

"How bad's your damage?"

"Thurston is still checking his. The *Phobos* lost a couple of laser turrets and took some hits in the main armor belt, but she's holding together just fine. Need any help?"

"Yeah! Monitor for enemy transmissions. I don't know why they've stopped their jamming, but it may be to pass on new orders. You hear something uncoded, let me know!"

"Right. Anything else?"

"Cover our tail. You got infantry?"

"Two squads of Specials. They were mounting guard close in and pulled inside when things got rough. You want 'em?"

"Just deploy them. Have them watch our tails. We're going to kick these people back over the ridge!"

"Kick 'em hard for me, Colonel! You know where!"

Combat excitement tingled in Grayson's body. A Marik *Archer* moved among the trees ahead and above him. He angled his forearm weapons up five degrees and triggered his PPCs together. The *Archer* whirled, released a salvo of missiles that went wide, then scuttled for cover, smoke and tattered wiring trailing from damage low on its left arm.

What had become of the enemy's jamming? Sweeping through the frequencies, he could pick up bits and pieces of communications between enemy units, but so far, it was all uncoded. His foe seemed as surprised about developments as Grayson was. What then . . . mechanical failure?

His motion sensor peeped alarm. Grayson slewed his *Marauder* around, facing a new threat bursting through the scrub brush fifty meters uphill and to his left. He swung the *Marauder,* weapons ready. His hand nearly closed on the firing trigger before he realized that his sights had locked in on Graff's *Assassin.*

"Don't shoot, Colonel! Thank God you made it!"

"Graff!" Suspicion edged Grayson's voice. If Graff were skulking away from the recon lance's battle line . . . "What the hell are you doing down here?"

"My coolant seal blew, Colonel! I don't know if I took a hit, or just had a major malfunction, but my board's lit red like you wouldn't believe! The Lieutenant said I could retire to *Phobos* and have the Techs there put in a quick fix."

"Right." Grayson gestured with one of his 'Mech's arms. "Move it, Graff, and get back to the line. We need you."

"Yessir!" The *Assassin* scrambled down the slope in a cascade of dust and broken tree branches, moving past the *Marauder* and on toward the silvery dome of the *Pho-*

bos partly visible through the trees a thousand meters up the valley.

Grayson's *Marauder* continued his climb. His own heat indicators were flashing red as his heat sinks struggled to dump the heat accumulated from his brief clash with the enemy *Wolverine* and *Centurion.* He had been pushing his 'Mech hard ever since they'd begun the forced march from Durandel almost two hours earlier. His heat levels were back within safe levels, but they would continue to be one more small but nagging worry.

Of more concern was the status of his recon lance. The three light 'Mechs had gone to ground on top of the ridge, lying down among the boulders and broken ground to better conceal their machines and to enable them to draw steady sightings on the approaching enemy forces.

"Lieutenant Roget!" he said into his throat mike. "What's your Twenty?"

"Colonel! Are we glad to see you!" Francine Roget's voice sounded tired, and nearly broken with strain as she gave him a rapid rundown on the recon lance's condition. Her *Panther* had taken serious hits to its front torso, left leg, and right arm, but was still functioning well. Missile fire had smashed the SRM rack in the chest of Vandergriff's *Commando,* which had caused considerable internal damage, but the arm-mounted laser and SRM launcher were still in the fight. A Marik *Archer* had blasted away the left leg of Sylvia Trevor's *Wasp*—and with it her SRM-2. Roget had helped drag the *Wasp* to a good position, however, from where Trevor continued to fire with the light 'Mech's medium laser.

"And the enemy?" Grayson moved his *Marauder* to get a view down the slope. Before him, he could see smoke rising from burning vehicles at the bottom of the hill, and what looked like the still, broken form of a knocked-out *Locust.*

"There have been at least four separate attacks, Colonel. All light stuff from down there. I think we knocked out a *Stinger,* earlier on." The arm of Roget's *Panther* pointed off to the northwest, and Grayson could see a still, silvery shape there, inert among the weeds. "The *Archer* surprised us from the rear, but I think you frightened him off. We've been taking a lot of fire from all directions.''

"The rest of the command lance is moving up behind you now," Grayson said, "so don't shoot them as they come in. I also ran into Graff and he told me you cleared his withdrawal to handle his malfunction. He'll be back up here as soon as that's taken care of.''

"*What* malfunction!" Her voice was rimed with ice, the tension showing through again.

"Eh? he told me you cleared it.''

"That coward! He vanished just before the first wave hit, like he made his 'Mech invisible. I'll *give* him a malfunction, next time I see him!''

Grayson felt cold. So Graff had run during the battle, had left his comrades on the ridge to face overwhelming odds, while he skulked among the trees on the slope below. Under the rules of war, a man could be shot for that, if he were caught and convicted under a general court. There was no time to think anymore about that now.

"You've done well, Francine. You may have held their center long enough to save the DropShips.''

"There's more, Captain.'' She still sounded taut, as though she were holding herself together by sheer force of will. "I think they're bringing up infantry.''

"Where?''

"There were vehicles moving that way, a little bit ago. Our infantry took out that *Locust* . . . I think maybe they captured it, because it looked from here like that *Locust* was firing on those vehicles down in the valley. That was a few minutes ago, when the jamming went off.''

"You think those are jammer vehicles?''

"Can't tell from here, but I think so. Anyway, there was a lot of infantry—APCs, skimmers, mostly light stuff—moving through the trees down there. I think they were deploying up to the top of the ridge, but they went to ground when that *Locust* opened up.''

"Anything more from the *Locust?*''

"It took some hits a few minutes ago. It's been dead since.''

Damn. Whoever had turned the *Locust* against the

Marik ECM cars may possibly have saved the Legion.
And while Graff was running, at that.

"O.K. Hold your position here. I'll get a handed
'Mech up to help with Trevor's *Wasp* as soon as we're
sure the enemy is really pulling out."

"Yes sir! And . . . sir?"

"What?"

"It's good to have you back!"

Harris Graff pulled his *Assassin* up outside the main
'Mech port under the towering overhang of the DropShip
Phobos. He broadcast his ID, which brought a response
from one of the bridge officers aboard. "Graff? What is
it you want?"

"Major malfunction here, Lieutenant. My coolant
seal's blown, and it's leaking like a stuck grivit. My
Lieutenant said I could come back and have it patched
up by your Techs."

"Stand clear, then. We're opening up."

With a loud sound of metal scraping metal, the massive 'Mech port ground open, its steel-treaded ramp extending out to the ground like an extruded tongue. Techs
gathered on the main 'Mech bay deck, looking curiously
at the lone *Assassin*.

Graff started the 'Mech up the ramp.

Janice Taylor crouched in the weeds 200 meters from
the *Phobos* and watched the *Assassin* move up the ramp
into the 'Mech bay, then turned away to watch the woods
around her. She had been born and raised on a Kurita
frontier world called Verthandi. While a professor of history at Verthandi's prestigious Regis University, she had
been witness to the bloody revolution against the planet's
Kurita overlords. In one attempt by the planetary governor to restore order, she had been chained up with fifty
other female captives, and marched under the ready guns
of Kurita BattleMechs out of the city. Their destination
was to unknown points offworld, where they would
doubtless have become chattel joy girls through out the
Combine.

It had been Grayson Carlyle and his men who had liberated the captive women. From that day on, Janice Taylor had become a member of Sergeant Ramage's Special Ops Force, and had participated in the last, wild battle to free Verthandi's capital from the Kuritans. When victory and independence had been won, she chose to follow the Gray Death Legion elsewhere among the stars.

Janice still wondered about her decision. Her first determination to fight had been born of a love for her world and a willingness to give her life to free her homeland from monsters like the Governor General Nagumo who had ruled it. She did love her world, and her people, and because of that love she often wondered why she had left.

She thought she might know now, though it had taken her a year to see. Verthandi's freedom had been purchased at a terrible cost of lives of friends and loved ones, and thousands of other Verthandians whom she didn't know but who had also been caught up in the struggle to free their world and had paid the final, highest price possible for freedom. In the end, of course, one lone rebel world like Verthandi could never hope to stand against the armed might of the Draconis Combine. Victory had come when House Steiner had recognized in the rebels' victory at Regis a means for the Lyran Commonwealth to win a political victory without firing a shot. Verthandi's independence was one that existed on paper only, the end result of treaties and concords between House Steiner and House Kurita.

Janice, a student of history, knew how fragile that independence was. She had been saddened during those last days on her homeworld to watch the newly won freedom become one more bargaining chip in the three-way negotiations between Steiner, Kurita, and Verthandi's new government.

With liberty only a few days old, there had been people willing to trade away the blood-purchased freedom in the name of expediency—or profit.

And that, she decided, had been why she left. Janice loved her world and her people, but she could not have borne the sight of her countrymen, trading away their victory through cupidity.

She had found a new home of sorts with the Gray Death

Legion. For a time, she had even believed herself in love with the regiment's young commander, Grayson. It had been with some bitter inner pain that she eventually realized that Grayson had a strong and absolute relationship with the company's Exec, Lori Kalmar. In the end, though, she and Lori had become close friends and confidantes, instead of rivals for the attentions of the same man.

Janet knew that she still loved Grayson Carlyle, but perhaps in a different way. Maybe that was why she couldn't leave.

A sound brought her around, the TK assault rifle high in her arms. There were men moving throughout the woods, but her section had been ordered to secure a close perimeter around the two DropShips to prevent anyone from approaching too close unchallenged. Someone was approaching the perimeter through the dense underbrush a few tens of meters in front of her.

"Halt!" she challenged. "Identify . . ."

But she got no further. A burst of submachine gun fire tore through the brush, chopping the air just above her head. Reacting with reflexes and training instilled in her by Captain Ramage's endless training sessions, she dove for the ground, rolling hard to her right. She immediately bounced to her knees to fire a short, spattering burst toward her attackers, then hit the ground and rolled again. Something hurtled through the air and thumped among the bushes to her left, where she had been a moment before. She rolled again, then hugged the ground. The grenade exploded with a sharp concussion that set her ears to ringing and shredded the tops of the grass reaching just above her head, but the explosion left her untouched. Men in combat armor were rushing through the brush now, firing as they came.

She was close enough to see the troops' eagle insignias on the right breasts of their armor. From her position flat on the ground, she triggered her TK in quick, three- and four-round bursts. Two of the soldiers kicked forward and fell to the ground. A third skewed around and opened up with a long, rolling blast from his submachine gun, blazing away across a ninety-degree arc that clipped branches and leaves far above Janice's head. She fired again and brought the man down. Now other Marik soldiers were charging out of the trees. Dozens were already between her and the *Phobos*.

Janice opened her personal transceiver to the *Phobos*'s tactical channel. "*Phobos! Phobos!* This is perimeter five! You are under attack by ground troops charging your 'Mech bay hatch!"

There was no answer, but machine gun fire was blazing now from the open hatch. The troops replied, and a running figure up in the brightly lit 'Mech bay tumbled down the ramp in an untidy sprawl. She heard the grinding machinery that marked the closing of the big hatch panels.

There was an explosion inside the DropShip bay, then the thunder of more explosions in a tightly confined space. Smoke belched from the open hatchway. Janice watched in dawning horror as ten Marik troopers raced across the open ground, mounted the ramp, and raced up and into the 'Mech bay itself.

More Marik soldiers followed. Janice opened fire, but the soldiers ignored her, so fixed were they on their target—the mercenary DropShip. Others of her squad fired from hiding places nearby, cutting down eight . . . ten . . . fifteen Marik soldiers, but more jut kept on coming.

For a long time, there were no targets.

Then the Marik BattleMechs returned—the big, damaged *Thunderbolt*, the *Archer* still trailing debris from one forearm, a *Panther* that limped and looked as though its torso had been peeled open with an explosive can opener. They came in firing, not at the DropShip, but at the Gray Death troops in the brush and weeds outside. Janice saw Vince Hall cut down by a laser burst twenty meters away. As smoke from burning bushes roiled across the valley between her and the advancing 'Mechs, she decided it was time to withdraw.

There seemed to be no reaction from the *Deimos*, half a kilometer off to the north, but she did note with a curdling chill that as many as the *Phobos*'s weapons as could be brought to bear were twisted around to point north.

The *Phobos* had the *Deimos* under its guns, and so if

there had been no firing as yet, it must mean that negotiations were going on. Janice knew what negotiations meant when the freedom of a world was at stake. She didn't want to learn the results of these negotiations, at least not at close hand. She joined other members of the Gray Death Special Ops forces and retreated into the woods to the east.

Behind her, a hatch high upon on the flank of the *Phobos* opened, and a radio antenna became a convenient mast for a flag that broke open in the gentle breeze. Armored troops moving among the BattleMechs in the DropShip's shadow stopped and cheered.

It was the Marik eagle. The *Phobos* had been captured.

12

Lieutenant Thurston's voice bore witness to the strain the man was under. "Colonel, I've got to do what they say. I've *got* to!"

Grayson closed his eyes and leaned back in the seat of his *Marauder*. It was not like him to simply accept such a decision without fighting, and yet there seemed to be absolutely nothing he could do about it. Nevertheless, he could not bring himself to say the words. *Go ahead, Lieutenant. Do what you have to* . . .

"No, Thurston! You're condemning all of us if you do! I *order* you to refuse terms. We'll be down there to support you within five minutes."

"No, sir. I can't do it. Don't you see?"

"The cowardly bastard," Grayson heard over his tac-com. He thought the voice belonged to Delmar Clay, but he couldn't be sure.

"He's not being cowardly," a new voice spoke over the line. "He is being quite sensible."

"What . . . ? Who is this?"

"Captain Harris Graff, of the 5th Marik Guards."

"Graff . . ."

"Not my *real* name, of course."

"Okay, Graff . . . or whatever your name is. What is it you want?"

"I have what I want, Colonel. I have your DropShips . . . as planned. If you would care to surrender now, I'll put in a good word for you with my superiors."

Rage surged within Grayson. "You have *Phobos*, Graff.

You don't have *Deimos*. And when we come down there and dig you out . . .''

"You'll do nothing of the sort, Colonel. As I have already explained to Lieutenant Thurston, his DropShip has been . . . tampered with. Nothing severe . . . or noticeable, but a certain coded radio signal will start a meltdown of the *Deimos*'s fusion plant. No explosion or anything spectacular, but it will generate enough heat to reduce that DropShip to molton scrap.''

Grayson listened in sick horror. The Conventions of modern warfare forbade destroying technology, and most warriors abided by the injunction. From time to time, there were still raids against an enemy's factories or industrial complexes, but such installations were spare whenever possible. A factory or a manufacturing center or even a DropShip might be captured in battle, but there was always the possibility that it might be recaptured later. Warriors who wantonly destroyed something as precious as a DropShip were viewed as barbarians by most other 31st-Century warriors. As the steady, grinding attrition of war continued, there were fewer and fewer Technicians who understood enough to rebuild or even repair something as complex as a fusion reactor or an automated BattleMech plant. Grayson was not one of those superstitious, mystical-minded followers of the Way of Blake, but the idea of a centuries-old DropShip being reduced to scrap at the touch of a button filled him with horror.

"Release the crew, then.''

"Colonel, Let me assure you that you are in absolutely no position to bargain! These people are legitimate prisoners of war. They are safe, and will remain safe until they are tried.''

"Tried? Tried for what, for God's sake! You . . . you say you're Marik 5th Guard! We're working for Janos Marik, for God's sake! We're under contract to Janos Marik!''

"Why don't you come down here and we'll talk about it? I have information you may find . . . interesting. We can discuss it at leisure, and perhaps we can find a way out of this impasse. Maybe there has been a misunderstanding somewhere along the line.''

Grayson closed his eyes, suddenly very tired. He had no intention of walking tamely into Graff's parlor. The Marik forces had been using deceit and trickery at every turn of this campaign, and Grayson's own liberty would last just as long as he remained outside the *Phobos*'s hull.

If he survived at all.

''No deal, Graff. Tell me over the comline.''

''I don't think we have anything further to discuss, Colonel. But Lieutenant Thurston *is* surrendering the *Deimos* to me, or I will melt that ship down around his ears. Will you give him the order, Colonel? Or shall I deal directly with him?''

''Yes, dammit.'' Grayson's voice was scarcely audible. ''I'll give the order.''

A truce settled across the battlefield after that, arranged by radio between Grayson and Colonel Langsdorf, the Marik commander. Such truces were common in the formalized usages of modern warfare. It was not unknown for two commanders engaged in a protracted battle to call a halt while both sides salvaged damaged 'Mechs, recovered injured or lost pilots, and allowed for individual warriors and Techs to trade with each other on the field. A MechWarrior might trade a kilo of rare coffee or tobacco for an enemy Tech's spare actuator adjustment wrench and calibrator set, or a length of number nine reflex tubing for a working percolator. Such entrepreneurial activity was frowned upon by unit commanders everywhere, but was impossible to stop.

Grayson's men and women used the time to comb the woods for their wounded and to locate what scattered elements of Ramage's infantry company they could. When the line on the ridge to the west had broken, most of the Legion soldiers had attempted to form up at the top of the ridge, then scattered east when the enemy 'Mechs closed in. They were hiding now in the woods throughout the valley. Those who still had radio communications through to the Legion's 'Mechs were already coming in, but it would take time to round up the stragglers.

Grayson dispatched a team down the west face of the western ridge to recover the unknown trooper who had turned a disabled *Locust*'s weapon against the Marik ECM cars. When he learned that the "unknown trooper" was none other than Captain Ramage, it didn't surprise him. Ramage was badly wounded, unconscious, and in serious danger from loss of blood. Dr. Morrison on the *Phobos* was the closest medical man around, but Graff would not permit even the ship's doctor to leave. Soldiers with first-aid experience cleaned Ramage's wounds and bandaged them, but no one wanted to predict the Trellwanese's chances of recovery.

Silently, Marik soldiers moved through the valley and along the hillsides as well, searching for their own wounded, gathering up their discarded equipment. A team of Techs was seen busily at work on the two disabled ECM Packrats. Another team of Techs had descended on the damaged *Locust* as soon as Ramage had been removed from it. With some Marik troops posted nearby on guard, they could now be seen working on the severed connectors of the *Locust*'s right foot.

Grayson stood in the open, leaning against his *Marauder*'s foot and lower leg. Helm's sun had dropped low enough that the valley was now in shadow, though the sky was still light and hours remained before sunset. Delmar Clay came up alongside.

"Colonel?" He spoke softly, as though afraid of being overheard. "I've got a real bad feeling about all of this."

"Yes, Del?" Grayson had felt it, too. There was something wrong here . . . but what?

"Look . . . you know that usually, during a truce, the troops sometimes'll swap stuff. Tobacco. Gum. Spares. You know."

Grayson nodded.

"If there's nothing to trade, at least they trade news. God, Colonel, soldiers are the most news-hungry creatures in the universe. They *always* want to know whatever the other guys knows . . . Who's your C.O.? What's happening on Atreus? What kind of punishment details do you guys have? Stuff like that."

Grayson exhaled. *That was it.*

"It's all wrong here. I went up to two of their MechWarriors and five PBIs. Not one of them would talk to me. They ignored me, like I wasn't there. The ones farther off . . . and the officers, they watched me, and I could see their fingers twitching on their guns . . . but the guys I talked to acted like I wasn't there."

"He's right, Gray," said Lori as she and Janice Taylor approached from behind. Janice's face was still smeared with gray-green camouflage paint, and she looked tired.

"Janice just came in through the lines," Lori continued. "She was telling me that they let her past, but there wasn't any of the usual bantering or joking that you hear during a formal truce."

"It was scary, Colonel," Janice said. "You know, I've been asked for *dates* by Liao soldiers during a truce . . . asked to cook breakfast . . . asked to give up soldiering and become a kept woman . . . but those people out there act like we're . . . we're *zombies* or something!"

"I think you've put your finger on it," Grayson said. "They're behaving . . ." Grayson's eyes widened as he saw the implications of what he was saying. "My God, they're acting like we're *outlaws!*"

Though civilized warfare followed certain codes strictly observed by each side, there were always those who chose not to obey the Conventions of War. The half-barbarian raiders from beyond the Periphery, the pirates and bandit kings who looted worlds for water or transuranics or machine tools, the occasional renegade mercenary who exacted revenge on an unfaithful employer or won a campaign by destroying a foe's JumpShip . . . All those could be lumped together into the amorphous group known vaguely as outlaws. Civilized folks had no dealings with such animals. More, they were fair game for the adherents of civilized warfare anywhere. The rules of "civilized" warfare, including formal truces and honorable dealings in negotiations, simply did not apply.

"Outlaws," Janice said. "God, no wonder they won't have anything to do with us."

"Worse," Delmar said. "What if they decide to terminate the truce . . . unilaterally?"

"I was just wondering about that," Grayson answered.

"O.K. Janice, you go back to where the unit is gathering and pass this on to whoever is in command there now."

"Lieutenant Dulaney."

"O.K., good. Tell him the Marik people may think we're outlaws, and to be ready for a surprise attack. Hell, be ready for anything! Keep someone tuned in on the taccom frequency. Have someone organize stretcher-bearers for the wounded. Have them ready to move. Most of our vehicles should be rounded up by now. Tell Dulaney that priority goes to the wounded on the vehicles."

"Yessir!"

"Lori, Del . . . same drill. Round up the Mech-Warriors. Have them unobtrusively move to their machines, and be ready to move. Uh . . . better have half of them go ahead and mount up. Make it fire lance. Command lance stay outside your 'Mechs like nothing's happening, but be ready to jump, fast. The recon lance is still up the hill?"

"They're working on Trevor's *Wasp*," Clay said. "Trying to patch on the leg."

"She may have to abandon it. Have someone walk, *walk*, mind you, up there and fill them in. Nothing by radio, They'll be listening. Right? Move!"

The trio vanished into the gathering shadows, leaving Grayson by himself. Though he was a member of the Legion's command lance, he elected to climb into his *Marauder* just the same, in order to monitor a wider selection of radio frequencies than were available in the small, left-ear headset he was wearing.

There was nothing on the radio frequencies, and that worried him, too. It was as though the Marik forces already had their plans worked out and were simply awaiting the signal to put them into operation.

The signal came less than ten minutes later when a white star flare arced high above the *Phobos*'s hull. Instantly, machine gun fire erupted from the woods, slashing into a small group of Legion troopers who were moving across the valley with three wounded men slung between them in blankets. At almost the same instant, the Mark BattleMechs opened fire. Multiple laser bolts hissed and burned in rapid succession past or into Gray-

133

son's *Marauder.* He was returning fire an instant later, PPC bolts searing back down the valley into the enemy *Archer* that had opened fire on him. The range was nearly three hundred meters, long-range combat targeting of medium lasers. Grayson's heavier PPCs scored twice as blazing beams of charged particles tore into the *Archer's* heavy armor.

Graff's *Assassin,* Grayson noted, was nowhere about. *Probably still aboard* the *Phobos,* he thought. *He wouldn't dare show himself outside now!*

"Colonel!" Francine Roget's voice cut in on the tac frequency. "Colonel, they've jumped us! Five heavy 'Mechs are on the west side of the slope, driving toward our position!"

Damn! There'd been no time to organize a proper watch to keep track of all of the Marik BattleMechs. The valley was too large, the trees too thick. Five of them had slipped away in order to jump the already badly damaged recon lance 'Mechs.

"I'm on my way, Francine!" he said.

"Colonel! What's happening! They're breaking the truce!"

"Lieutenant . . . didn't you get word by runner? He should have been up there by now!"

"No, sir. No word! Everything was so quiet . . ."

Too quiet. *Too goddamn quiet!* Had Marik troopers watched, then killed the messenger as he climbed the slope? Had that been the signal to start the attack, once they knew the Legion was becoming suspicious?

Grayson guessed that he would never know. For now, though, the failure of the message to get through was threatening the recon lance. It was already a 'Mech short and had one 'Mech crippled. With all three badly damaged from the fight earlier in the day, the recon lance was the weakest part of his whole command. Now it was they who had not received word that the Marik forces might be planning a sneak attack!

He opened the power governors wide on his *Marauder* and urged his 75-ton mount into a lurching, two-legged gallop toward the west ridge. Missile fire arced in from the north, splintering trees behind him and sending chunks of rock and metal rattling from his upper hull. He did not reply, but concentrated instead on the placement of each of his *Marauder*'s massive feet as it began leaning into the slope of the hill.

Flashes of light, dazzlingly brilliant in the fading daylight, flared and sputtered along the skyline of the ridge. He saw Roget's *Panther* standing against the sky, loosing bolt after bolt from her particle beam weapon at unseen assailants on the far side of the hill.

Rockets struck the ridgetop, sending black gouts of smoke and earth skyward. For a moment, a laser beam from downslope played against Roget's 'Mech, which was outlined by luminous particles of dust in the air, refracted and scattered by the *Panther*'s armor. The light show sent dazzling beams and streaks of blue-white light chasing across the sky, broken by the moving shadows of the *Panther*. The vision, inexpressibly beautiful and horrifying at the same time, lasted only an instant. Then an explosion slammed against Roget's 'Mech, and the 35-ton *Panther* stumbled back off the crest of the ridge.

"Roget!" Grayson yelled into his mike. "Get your people off that crest!"

"I can't!" Her reply was faint over the searing hiss of static. Her antennae or her transmitter, or both, had been damaged. He could barely hear her over the roar. "I can't leave Sylvie!"

Sylvia Trevor must have still been up there trying to get her 'Mech functional. Missiles were raining onto the ridge now from at least a dozen launchers. The Marik infantry must have trained shoulder-launched missiles on the recon lance's position as well as five BattleMechs. Explosions tortured the landscape as mortar fire began dropping from the sky.

Grayson was halfway up the hill when a Marik *Centurion* rose to face him, battle scars carved gruesomely across its torso. He recognized the machine that he had exchanged fire with earlier in this longest of days, and triggered a burst of PPC fire at it.

It skipped aside as he fired, unleashing its own laser and autocannon salvoes at the same time. Tracking quickly, Grayson snap-fired a laser at the lighter machine, then pushed ahead. He didn't have the time now to exchange shots with a suicidal *Centurion* pilot.

More shots were slamming home into Grayson's *Marauder*. Blue electric discharges danced and snapped from his *Marauder*'s hull into the ground as his instruments went wild under the momentary surge of an electrical overload. Another PPC bolt struck him from behind. He heard a grating crash from behind his head as a chunk of his rear armor was torn away. Lights flashed on his console, warning of damage to his electrical system and the loss of two of his heat sinks.

This was damage he couldn't ignore. He pivoted his *Marauder* on the hillside. The enemy's *Warhammer* stood fifty meters downslope, stepping from behind a boulder. In a flash, he realized that the *Centurion* must have been bait, that the Marik had expected him to engage the *Centurion* in order to destroy the machine he had damaged earlier. In doing so, he would have exposed himself to a crippling, close-range attack from the rear. His decision to move on had upset the Marik pilots' timing, but they had gone ahead and sprung their attack anyway.

Though the *Warhammer* was still at long range, Grayson fired on it, more to discourage it from coming closer than in hopes of damaging it. Then, closing his eyes to better sense the input from the neurohelmet through his middle ears, he leaned the 'Mech into a spinning turn, ducking as he moved. PPC charges flared brightly overhead. Three quick steps and he had closed the range on the *Centurion* to thirty meters and brought the enemy machine between his *Marauder* and the distant *Warhammer*. He discharged his own PPCs then, one after another. Great, flaming holes opened up in the *Centurion*'s torso armor. A strike in the left torso must have landed squarely in the *Centurion*'s ammunition stores of 5 cm SRMs, because the first flash of light from Grayson's PPC shot was followed by a much brighter flash of exploding ordnance . . . and then another . . . and another . . . and another. Rockets arced skyward on aimlessly twisting trails of white smoke. A final explosion gutted the *Centurion*'s torso, blasting away huge chunks of armor and leaving the machine's hull a flaming skeleton, an empty framework of struts and half-glimpsed masses of machinery behind the remaining fragments of armor plate. For an instant, Grayson held an image, burned into his brain, of the *Centurion*'s pilot smashing wildly against the inside of the plastic transparency of his cockpit. Then another explosion sent a gout of flame hurtling into the air, fragmenting the cockpit into tiny, glittering slivers as it burned a gaping hole between the 'Mech's shoulders. Burning wildly, the 'Mech fell forward to the ground, its fall marked by a dense contrail of black smoke.

The pillar of smoke boiling from the wrecked *Centurion* formed a screen almost at once. Turning his back on the enemy *Warhammer,* Grayson resume his race up the slope.

There he found disaster.

Trevor's *Wasp* lay sprawled on the ground, its left leg still missing, its head crumpled as though by a multi-ton swing of an armored BattleMech foot. Vandergriff's *Commando* had exploded. Nothing remained but scattered limbs and a hull as torn and gutted as the *Centurion* just dispatched by Grayson. Francine Roget had her *Panther* fifty meters further along the slope, firing gamely at the 'Mechs that were closing in on her. Through the smoke, Grayson could make out the monstrous forms of the damaged *Thunderbolt* and *Wolverine,* as well as three smaller 'Mechs. Roget scored hit after hit on the advancing army until the *Thunderbolt* reached her position and raised one massive, black fist.

Grayson heard Francine's scream over the taccom line as the fist descended.

BOOK II

13

For Grayson, the retreat from Cleft Valley was a nightmare of pain, loss, and the knowledge of total defeat. Not since the night of his father's death in a Kurita surprise attack had he known such desolation.

The BattleMechs of the Legion's command and fire lances, the 'Mechs that had had warning, were able to regroup below the western ridge. The Marik 'Mechs had come thundering toward them from three sides to meet the unerring fire of the now thoroughly aroused mercenaries. Twice they had charged, and twice their charge faltered under that hail of laser, PPC, and missile fire. With several of their 'Mechs limping or showing blast-cratered scars and metal wounds leaking smoke, the Marik forces drew back to the valley where the DropShips maintained silent vigil.

In that respite, Grayson got his troops away.

The infantry went first, with the seriously wounded crowded aboard a trio of cargo skimmers, and the rest walking or piled onto the turtle backs of a small menagerie of scout cars, hovercraft weapons carriers, and APCs. The fire lance moved with the column, providing cover from enemy infantry or AeroSpace Fighter raids. The command lance remained in place, a rear-guard against further Marik treachery.

No more came, however. It seemed that the Marik forces—Graff and Colonel Langsdorf included—were content to allow the Gray Death to escape. At least for now.

The problem was that the Gray Death Legion was in

serious trouble. All of their reserve 'Mechs, and much of their infantry equipment and heavy weapons, had been aboard the two DropShips. At least three-quarters of the Techs who had returned with the Legion from Sirius V, all of the ship's personnel, both ships' doctors, and most of the regiment's logistical personnel had been captured. Even the regimental cooks had been taken.

Nor did the Legion have any food beyond a few days' worth of emergency rations aboard various 'Mechs or vehicles. It was certainly not enough to feed the survivors for more than a short time. There were both wild and domestic animals on Helm, but it would take time to find them, to hunt or gather and slaughter them. The meat would have to be processed, a way found to preserve it. Salt? Was there salt? Salt for preserving meat could be found along the shores of the dry sea bottom some fifty kilometers to the south, but ways would have to be found to separate sodium chloride from the various other salt compounds that encrusted the rocks along the long-dead beaches there.

And water. What would the survivors use for water? There were springs up in the hills, and the Araga River wound its way through the wooded valley where most of the Legion's survivors were already encamped. Grayson knew that an encampment of hundreds of people uses huge volumes of water, and can easily ruin what it does not use through poor waste management or hygiene. Water was not a serious problem, at this point, but it was another worry in a growing list of them. The water in the tanks aboard the *Deimos* and the *Phobos* would have lasted for months, and the recyclers continuously produced more from wastes and the moisture in the air.

And ammunition. The infantry was down to a few tens of rounds per man for some weapons. Just after a major battle, special rounds such as inferno warheads were vanishingly scarce. The shortage ran right up to the projectile weapons of the various 'Mechs. Grayson himself had fired fourteen ''rounds'' of a hundred 120mm shells each. That left him with eleven ammo cassettes—enough, if he conserved his shots, for one battle. He had already checked with Davis McCall and found that the *Bannock-*

burn, the Scotsman's *Rifleman,* was down to six cassette rounds—600 shells—for each of its autocannons. And the way a *Rifleman* went through AC ammo . . .

And the wounded. Fifteen men and women, including Captain Ramage, were too seriously wounded to walk. Without a doctor, without medical supplies, antibiotics, plasma, or blood, without even clean bandages, their chances for survival were not good. Another twenty-one had less serious wounds, but their fighting efficiency would be impaired unless they could be treated, and soon.

Grayson almost yielded to the impulse to call Langsdorf and ask for terms. The only thing that stopped him was the chilling knowledge that, for whatever reason, he and his men were being treated as outlaws. To surrender would not mean the usual repatriation by an employer, or a ransom posted by a patron. To surrender to Langsdorf would most certainly lead to a trial for some crime or crimes for which the Legion had apparently been found guilty already.

What crimes, though? And who was accusing them? The Legion had fulfilled their contract to Janos Marik on Sirius V! Why were the Marik forces now persecuting them?

Outwardly, Grayson had remained calm. He'd given the orders that set the column moving rapidly toward the north until the sophisticated D2j tracking system aboard McCall's *Rifleman* informed them that the last of the *Boomerang* spotter planes had returned to the Marik encampment at Helmdown. Presumably, they were now leaving the task of shadowing the column to ships or satellites in orbit. Grayson had then led his people into the forest that blanketed much of the land fringing the North Highland Plains, and begun moving toward the northeast. In the foothills of the Aragayan Mountains north of Durandel was the Valley of the Araga, the river valley to which he had directed Lieutenant DeVillar and the rest of the survivors from Durandel. The place was well-hidden and secure. There they could rest and make their plans.

No matter what the outward show, Grayson carried with him a growing certainty of his own failure. What he had dreaded for so long had now finally come to pass. It was inevitable that a 24-year-old regimental commander would eventually come face to face with his own limitations through errors of judgement so serious they brought the entire regiment to ruin.

The column raced northeast, as Grayson thought of the soft and inviting comfort, the sweet oblivion, of suicide.

The House Marik JumpShip *Mizar* materialized at the Helm jump point. Nearby, the other ships of the squadron hung motionless, poised on the gentle, invisible streams of particles from their plasma station-keeping thrusters. Orienting under gentle shoves from her thrusters, the *Mizar* maneuvered until her stern pointed toward the orange glare of Helm's star. It was then that the vast jump sail, absolutely black in order to absorb every stray quanta of energy possible for the starship's conventers, began to unfold from the *Mizar*'s external sail lockers. Light from the sun streamed through the sail's central hole, an adaptation that allowed the *Mizar*'s station-keepers to maintain thrust without damage to the delicate fabric of the sail.

On board the ducal DropShip *Gladius,* in the almost palatial suite of rooms assigned as his personal quarters, Precentor Rachan strapped himself into the chair behind his desk, and touched the key that ran his personal decoder program through the computer mounted on his desk. The *Mizar*'s parabolic antenna had trained on Helm IV almost from the instant the JumpShip had emerged from hyperspace into the system; within the handful of minutes necessary for speed-of-light communications to bear news that the *Mizar* had arrived at Helm, a coded message from Rachan's brothers in Helmdown was on its way skyward.

The *Mizar*'s communications operator noted the receiver's code and routed the stream of meaningless garble to Rachan's screen. There, the decoder turned garble into meaning, and a printed message flowed across the monitor. As he leaned forward to read, the screen lit his features with its phosphor glow. Rachan began to smile as he read, for the news from Helm was good, very good, indeed.

Under the shelter of darkness and trees, the endless rows of bubble tents were nearly invisible. Inside one of them, two people shared closeness . . . and pain.

"Well, Lori, I've made a real a mess of it this time."

Hearing past the lightness in his tone, Lori knew that Grayson was worried sick—and that he blamed himself for their current predicament. Her feelings for this man had flip-flopped so many times in the four short years of their comradeship, but love him or hate him, Lori had come to know Grayson Carlyle better than anyone in the Legion did. No one else saw the sorrow in his eyes now. Neither Ramage, who'd been working for Grayson the longest, nor Renfred Tor, who had known him longer, could read him so well. Only with Lori did the young mercenary commander let down his guard, and even that was rare.

"Gray." Lori's soft voice was pleading. "Gray, it's not you. We were betrayed. That damned Graff! There's nothing you—"

"Nothing!" He turned to face her, grey eyes flashing. Even in the dim light from the tent's glow panel, she could see his torment. "Nothing I could have done? I've made mistakes, grave mistakes, every step of the way! And now we've lost . . . everything . . ."

Lori reached out, touched his arm gently. He grabbed her, clung to her desperately. "Lori, Lori, what're we going to do? What in God's name can we possibly do?"

Lori held him, grateful for his outburst. It wasn't often that he showed his need for her, and she knew it wouldn't last long. Soon they would be making love and he would be passionate and strong. By tomorrow, he would have figured out what they should do next, once again the courageous leader of the Gray Death Legion. But now, for just these few moments, he was vulnerable, and he needed her, not just as his Exec, not just as a fellow Warrior, but as a woman. And oh, how she needed that needing!

As happened so often when she was in his arms, Lori

remembered the first time she'd seen Grayson Death Carlyle. If anybody had told her back then that one day she would be in love with the man who was aiming an inferno launcher at her . . .

As a 'Mech apprentice in the Sigurd Defense Forces, she'd been working for the Bandit King Hendrik of Oberon. A difference of opinion with her training sergeant got her assigned to a Special Expeditionary Force that was actually under the command of a Kurita noble. After they'd set down on the first planet of a star called Trell, she'd gotten her first taste of real combat. Piloting a fast but lightly armed *Locust,* Lori had been assigned to attack the palace of Sarghad, but she and her comrades couldn't even get through the city. Wes had bought it, his *Wasp*'s head smashed, then Garik had fled, asking her to cover him. Well, she had, and he escaped. Then Grayson Carlyle stepped out from the cover of an alley and threatened to set her already-overheated 'Mech on fire.

Lori shuddered. Ever since her parent's death in the fire that destroyed their home, she had been deathly afraid of fire. As a MechWarrior, the thought of death in combat was all part of the job, but the prospect of death by fire had broken her, shattered her nerve. There had been no choice. She *had* to surrender when faced with Grayson's inferno launcher.

And then Grayson had made her first a Tech, and ultimately a MechWarrior under his command. They'd managed to win on Trellwan, through a combination of superb tactics and sheer luck, and had then gone on to form an independent mercenary unit. Already the unit was something of a legend. Against unbelievable odds, the Gray Death had helped the rebels on Verthandi win their independence, and at the same time, Lori had won a personal victory. In the torture chambers of Regis, she had finally overcome her fear of fire. More, she had come to realize that she did, indeed, deeply love this young, sometimes exuberant, sometimes exasperating man beside her.

Gently, she rubbed Grayson's back and felt his trembling subside. She reached up and stroked his blond hair, moving stubborn wisps away from his rugged face. At her touch, he roused, lifted her face to his, and kissed her with a sudden, desperate eagerness. She responded ardently, fiercely glad that of all the women in the Legion, she was the one to whom Grayson turned for love and comfort.

Strange. She still wasn't entirely sure that he loved her, nor if he was capable of loving any one woman. For now, it was enough that he needed her.

The early morning sun filtered through the trees, creating mottled shadows on the ground that the bubble tent's camouflage pattern mimicked closely.

It's a lot like Sigurd here, she thought, cupping her hands around a hot mug, and taking occasional careful sips. Cold . . . rocky . . . mountainous—but beautiful. There were mountains to the south, she knew, three thousand meters tall, the tallest spires capped with eternal snows, with endless glaciers. So much like home.

She stood up abruptly and strode to the edge of the clearing behind Grayson's tent. Home! She hadn't thought of Sigurd that way for a long time. Yet Helm reminded her so much of the land of her childhood, reminded her of a time before Hendrik of Oberon's troops had arrived in fire and fury and death to force that isolated planet to join his confederation. After her parents were killed and she had been orphaned in a conquered world, Lori had joined the Defense Forces partly as a way of combating her intense loneliness. She had found friends—comrades— that helped replace her lost family, only to see them torn from her, too.

It had been harder to make new friends in the Legion. At first, on Trellwan, the men hadn't trusted her, didn't respect her; she'd had to maintain distance in order to retain authority. Then, by the time they had begun to accept her as a fellow warrior, everyone assumed that she was the Chief's woman and so avoided getting close to her all the more. It wasn't until Janice Taylor joined up on Verthandi that Lori really found someone she could talk to.

Lori looked back at the encampment. There were signs of stirring now in the other tents, though Grayson apparently still slept. As one of the early risers this morning, she had enjoyed the solitude. In a close-knit community like the Legion, it was sometimes difficult to find a private moment. She walked back to the fire, refilled her mug, and sat down on a log, hoping that a good night's rest had refreshed Grayson's mind as well as his body. She, too, was wondering how they would get out of this fix, yet felt confident that Grayson would find a way.

A soft rustle and a low moan from the tent told her that he was waking up. A moment later, he poked out his head, sleepily trying to focus his gray eyes. Seeing her, he pushed some recalcitrant strands of straw-colored hair out of his eyes, and grinned.

"Morning, woman," he drawled. "Is that coffee I smell?"

"It sure is, Gray." Lori smiled back. "If you're good, I might even have a mug for you by the time you get out of that sack."

"Oh, I'm good, Lori, I'm real good." He pulled his head back into the tent and a moment later, emerged fully dressed. He sat down on the log next to Lori to pull on his boots.

"Did you sleep well?" she asked.

Grayson stretched luxuriously and then took the proffered mug from Lori's hand. "As always, after one of your delicious . . . ah . . . treatments, my love." He rested one hand on her thigh. "You're good for me, Lori. You know that?"

She smiled, but felt an inward twinge. She was not as free with endearments as Grayson was, and somehow could never fully believe his tender words. Few relationships in the Legion, or in any similar combat unit for that matter, lasted as long as theirs had already. She kept expecting Grayson to grow tired of her one day, but the thought always brought a tiny, distant chill.

"Do you have a plan, Gray? Do you know what we're going to do next?" She took a last sip of coffee and tried to steer her own thoughts away from matters personal.

The tall, blond leader took a deep breath, held it, then let it out slowly. "Yes," he said finally. "I know what I've got to do next."

Lori looked at him sharply. He had said "I," not

"we." Whatever Grayson planned, it was something he planned to do himself. She knew that he still tended to view every action too personally, blaming himself if anything went wrong. Lori's own position as the Company's Executive Officer was endlessly complicated because Grayson had never learned to *delegate* his responsibility.

At times, the burden of command seemed far too heavy for those broad twenty-four year-old shoulders. At others, he acted as though he might take on the universe and win. Lori didn't know which attitude exasperated her the most.

"So?" She reached for the battered coffee pot on its self-powered hotplate, and poured herself another cup, more for something to do than anything else. Coffee was already in short supply, but *that* was certainly the least of their worries. "So . . . what's your plan?"

Grayson's studied cheerfulness was another of his masks, one she had come to know well in four years. He knew she wasn't going to approve of whatever it was he had in mind, and so he assumed this outrageously cheerful façade. Of course, he couldn't assume the façade if he wasn't truly sure of which course of action to pursue, but following his shifts of mood could be frustrating.

"First and foremost, Lori, we need information. For one thing, do this Colonel Langsdorf and our friend Graff really represent the Marik government?"

"You still think we could be caught in a civil war?"

He shook his head. "I doubt it, but it's a possibility. We've got to know where we stand with these people, and with Janos Marik, before we take another step. Then, we must contact our friends."

"Friends? What friends do we have here on Helm?"

"Oh, you'd be surprised, Lori. Back in the old days, governments kept embassies in one another's countries. The idea was to have people there to keep an eye on what was going on in the other fellow's backyard, and to have someone convenient as a mouthpiece to that government when the need arose." Grayson sipped his own coffee, and scowled at its bitterness. "No sugar? Well, never mind. There's not much sense in embassies today, of course," he went on, "not with everybody fighting everybody else half the time, and with the Great Houses controlling so many worlds.''

"There are embassies . . . and ambassadors. That negotiator on Sirius V, the Steiner Special Envoy . . .''

"Right, but they tend to come and go only as they're needed, say, when a trade treaty or a defense pact has to be negotiated and signed. A world like Sirius V would probably have a regular envoy from House Steiner, and House Davion, and Kurita and Marik, just because it's a fairly important world on the Liao trade lanes. But an out-of-the-way rock like Helm wouldn't have anything like that.

"Still, every one of the Great Houses has to keep tabs on what's going on in everybody else's backyards, even including backwaters like Helm. You never know when something big is going to pop in an unlikely spot.''

"Spies.''

"Well, sure, but there are spies . . . and there are spies.''

"What do you mean?''

"Everybody uses spies, of course.'' His mouth tightened, and his eyes regained some of the wintry bleakness she had seen in them the night before. "Like Graff. He must have been planted on us at Galatea. God only knows why he turned on us . . . or was turned on us.

"But nearly every world has a resident agent or two from one or another of the Great Houses. They're nothing like an official ambassador, but then, they're not required to perform a regular ambassador's duties. They're just there to make a report once in a while, and maybe to provide help, advice, or maybe communications to someone who might ask for it.''

Lori's eyes widened. "House Steiner!''

"Exactly. The Lyran Commonwealth government has got to remember what we did for them on Verthandi. Hey! We beat Kurita and won free a world that had been stolen by the Dracs a few years before . . . then set up things so that House Steiner could regain some lucrative trade rights there. Yes, I think Katrina Steiner's government remembers that and I think they'd be glad to help us.''

"Do you know the Steiner . . . ah . . . ambassador?"

"The Steiner spy. I was told, lives at an address on Hogarth Street. It's a local merchant firm that deals in offworld trade."

"So, how the hell did you find out about him?"

"One of Janos Marik's aides told me back when I signed the contract that gave us Helm. He gave me the address of a House Davion agent, too." He grinned. "Hell, he even offered me addresses for agents for Kurita and Liao as well, but I turned him down. I didn't figure we'd be wanting to talk to *those* people, much!"

"I should think not." Lori's voice betrayed her surprise, and her amusement. The so-called civilized peoples often acted in ways that continued to amaze and confound her. There were many things in life for which distant, cold Sigurd had not prepared her. "And Marik's people actually know about this guy?"

Grayson shrugged. "Hey, like I said, he's just a merchant with ties to the Lyran Commonwealth. Nothing flashy . . . and nothing illegal. It's just that his merchant connections give him a means of sending messages offworld unobtrusively from time to time, and so House Steiner pays him a little on the side to keep an eye on things that might interest Katrina here."

"Like a Marik invasion of the Lyran Commonwealth? That could be a dangerous job."

"It has its rough points. Of course, I doubt that Janos Marik's generals would tell this guy about their invasion plans. It's the spies you *don't* know about that can cause you trouble."

She saw his jaw tighten again. "Like Graff," she said.

He nodded. "Like Graff."

"So why you?"

"Eh?"

"Why do you have to go? Any of us could make contact with this guy. Give us the address, and we'll do it."

"No."

"Ah. Grayson Carlyle against the universe . . . once again?"

"It's not like that, Lori. But it *is* something I have to do."

"Is it, Gray?" She stood suddenly, her eyes flashing in the early morning light. "Is it? Or are you tripping over your damned pride again?"

He started to answer, but she had already turned and crawled back inside their tent.

She didn't know whether to feel happy or furious that he did not crawl in after her. When Lori heard his boot-steps moving away from the tent after a time, she felt the loneliness from long ago welling up inside her once again.

14

The skimmer resting in the sun-broken shadows of the woods was an ancient one, scratched, marred, and with only the faintest trace of brown-on-gray patterns to show where coats of paint had once been. The engine access panels that had borne the grey-on-scarlet death's head of the Legion had been removed, leaving the grease-black convolutions of the engine visible through gaping openings on either side of the turbine nacelle. More scratches had been added up forward, where a vibroblade had been used to scrape off the battered little craft's serial numbers. The Magna CC light laser and its pintle mount in the cargo well aft of the driver's seat had been removed, and the mounting rack unbolted from its brace struts and folded onto the deck. The craft had been carefully inspected by four of the Legion's Techs, including Alard King himself, to make certain that there was nothing about the vehicle that would call attention to its real identity.

While the demilitarized skimmer had been undergoing transformation, both Grayson and King had been undergoing a similar transformation.

"There's something, I suppose, for going native," King said. He spread his hands and looked down at himself. "But I feel a little out of place, don't you, Colonel?"

Both men wore workboots, trousers, and simple tunics—little more than coarse-woven bags with holes for arms and heads—belted at their waists.

"Oh, I don't know, Alard." Grayson plucked lightly

at the front of his tunic. "If our mission doesn't go well, we may have to retire and dress like this all the time."

The men and women of the Gray Death Legion, like the personnel of all but the largest and most prosperous mercenary units, had no one uniform in common. Many wore items of clothing acquired during previous service. Charles Bear, for example, had once been with the 21st Centauri Lancers, and usually wore the gray and green helmet and jerkin that was standard-issue for that regiment, though the unit insignia had been removed or painted over. Delmar Clay still wore the green and brown summer campaign jacket used by Hanson's Roughriders.

Grayson's own uniform varied from day to day. In the nearly four years since Trell I, he had outgrown or worn out the few pieces of uniform left over from his days as a MechWarrior Apprentice. Though he had made an effort to acquire a standard Legion uniform on Galatea after the successful conclusion of the Verthandi campaign, there had not been enough money—or time enough—to carry the idea very far. His usual campaign uniform, then, was gray tunic and trousers with the unit patch on his left breast and upper left arm. When Grayson needed to impress someone—such as a prospective employer— he added a gray shoulder-half-cape lined in scarlet and a black beret from a shop on Galatea to transform his plain grays into service full-dress. For daily wear, Grayson favored fatigues of no single traceable ancestry. Still, their brown and green camouflage pattern defined them as military-service issue. For what Grayson had in mind now, he had to look the part of a civilian. Hence, the rough, almost shapeless local garb.

"I don't suppose we can talk you out of this," Lori said. McCall and the rest of the command lance warriors stood with her. A variety of chirrings and chirpings sounded from the woods around them.

"Aye, sair," Davis McCall said, scratching his reddish beard and smiling. "There'd be aye plenty a' th' lads that'll be wantin' tae go doon t' town, Colonel."

"You're volunteering, I suppose?" Grayson said.

McCall's smile widened to an open grin, and he drew himself up taller. "Aye, sair, for one . . ."

"Forget it." Grayson said, shifting to a rough impersonation of Davis's broad Scots burr. "Tha' idea is tae go in wi'oot bein' noticed, laddie! An' how you'd manage tae ask questions wi'oot speakin', I dinna' ken!"

All of them laughed, including McCall, but Grayson could hear the tension behind their levity.

"But why *you*, Gray?" Lori said as the laughter died. Her anger had receded since the morning, but she still felt irritated at his stubbornness. "Any of us could go. We all know Helm at least as well as you do!"

That again. "For one thing, I know some people here . . . as so does King. We've been over this before."

His voice carried warning, but Lori's answering expression said, *Don't give me that.* He turned away and climbed into the skimmer beside Alard King.

During staff discussions of the plan, King had mentioned that he knew several people who might be able to help them, besides the Steiner and Davion contacts that Grayson had in mind. He had been insistent—as insistent in his own way as Lori, and Grayson had finally agreed to his argument that two of them together had a better chance of finding someone who could help them.

Grayson smiled at Lori. "Hey, look! There shouldn't be any danger. We're just a couple of farmers, in from the boonies for some sightseeing. Right, Alard?"

"You got it, Colonel."

"You'd better lay off that 'Colonel' stuff," Lori said, looking straight past Grayson at the senior Tech. "You get this guy killed and you'll answer to *me!*"

King looked as though he were going to make a joke of it, then changed his mind. "We'll be back, Lieutenant. Both of us. I promise."

She turned to Grayson. "Gray, what do you hope to find out?"

"I'd like to know what's going on, mostly. What we've found so far just doesn't make any sense." . . . *House Marik line BattleMechs operating under the assumption that the Gray Death Legion was a renegade unit—outlaws, pirates, or worse.*

"Well, it doesn't make sense for you to get yourself killed."

"Lori's right," Delmar Clay said. "If you two get captured . . ."

"If we get captured, we might learn what this insanity is all about!" Grayson said. "But we *won't* be captured. Even if this is a full-fledged invasion, they're not going to be rounding up farmers. Even invaders have to eat, right?"

"The Conventions again, Gray?" Lori's eyes were bleak. It looked as though she'd been crying.

Grayson was certain that the Marik troops would not bother a pair of farmers if their commanders had taken it into their heads to invade one of their own planets. By the conventions of warfare that had held throughout the past century—with isolated and instantly condemned exceptions—civilians were safe from attack by soldiers, so long as they stayed out of the fighting.

That had not always been the case, Grayson knew. Once, whole civilian populations, whole countries, even whole worlds had been held hostage, subject to annihilation in war as the enemy sought to smash the target government's supply lines, destroy its communication centers, and batter down the will to resist through stark terror. The 25th-century Ares Conventions had risen above that barbarism, declaring that only military targets were legal game on the battlefield, that civilian populations were to be spared. Those accords had also made warfare a way of life, but they did offer some hope of mitigating the savagery of war.

The horrors of the First and Second Succession Wars had reintroduced the nightmare of blood-soaked, unrestricted warfare, with whole worlds laid waste and genocide occurring on a planetary scale. The Kentares Massacre was perhaps the most infamous of these atrocities, but there had been others.

So far, though, in this third round of struggles for supremacy among the five Successor Houses, something akin to the old Ares Conventions was once more in force. It was as though a war-exhausted humanity had now tacitly agreed, for perhaps the first time in its bloody history, that the proper occupation of warriors was to fight other warriors, and that civilians should be spared whenever possible. The practical reason behind this was the brutal fact that if all the cities and trained mechanics and 'tronicists were dead, if all the BattleMechs and vehicles and DropShips and JumpShips were destroyed or broken down from lack of trained hands to repair them, there would, quite simply, be nothing left to fight over.

The neo-feudalism that was rising throughout the worlds occupied by humanity was, like the feudalism of 2,000 years earlier, based on ownership of the land—in this case, whole worlds. Even a green and verdant world, one with clean, breathable air, and plenty of fresh water—even such a paradise was worthless to the Duke who controlled it unless there was a population to make it productive. Throughout the Successor States, it was the MechWarriors who bore the mantle of honor and glory, like modern knights who fought for their Lord's cause. It was the Techs who worked the magic by which technic civilization survived, piecing together the bits and pieces of an earlier, more advanced science in a struggle to keep the machines—and the culture—alive. But it was the peasant farmer, the laborer, the astech, and the craftsman who made civilization possible at all.

As Grayson had reminded Lori, even soldiers had to eat. Few MechWarriors knew much about planting crops or harvesting them. Fewer still were in a position to transport those goods, or to see that they were distributed on a planetary—on an *inter*planetary scale. No duke, no army, however greedy for land or worlds or power, would destroy the population on which that power rested.

"Believe me, Lori," Grayson said gently. "We'll be safe. We'll be careful not to attract attention to ourselves."

King grasped the skimmer's tiller. When he switched on the turbines, the little hovercraft's engine keened into life, spilling clouds of dust from the scarred plenum shrouds. The vehicle shifted, skittered to the right until King could bring it under control, then dipped its nose and accelerated out from under the dappled sunlight and shade of the woods.

Considerable thought had gone into their disguises. Helm had no export industry to speak of, and little in the way of textile manufacturing. Though there were a number of mechanics and machine workers who kept those pieces of machinery native to the planet functioning, the majority of Helmans were farmers. An AgroMech plant outside the capital of Helmdown turned out small, four-legged Harvester and Planter 'Mechs that were used locally, and hovercraft similar to the disguised skimmer were still manufactured in small numbers in Glovis, south of the Nagayan Mountains. Production of this equipment was fairly limited, however, and provided machines only for local use. The Kurita raid that had smashed Helm over two centuries before had so thoroughly leveled local Helman industry that only now was it struggling back to a shadow of its former life. To look the part of native Helmans, Grayson and King had decided on the disguise of peasant farmers come to town in their centuries-old hovercraft to buy supplies.

The trip took almost two hours.

Helmdown, an untidy sprawl 400 kilometers northwest of Durandel, was more village than city, but it functioned as both principal starport and capital for the planet. What little industry did exist on the world was centered here, and it was where trader DropShips came infrequently to barter offworld manufactured goods for wheat, ice plums, and ferris grass from the Highland Plateau. The population numbered 50,000, if the census included the farmers who lived in the rural communities within fifty kilometers of the town's dusty streets and whitewashed ferrocrete block buildings. The AgroMech factory on the outskirts of town provided work for perhaps a quarter of the citizens of Helmdown proper. The lives of the rest revolved around the spaceport and the freighter DropShips that made their infrequent calls there.

For once, business was good in town. It looked as though the fleet was in.

Helmdown's starport was a dried lakebed that had served as landing field for space-borne commerce in the days of the Star League. In those times, Helm's principal port was Freeport, some five hundred kilometers to the southeast. Helmdown had had a port of its own, too, one that needed that expanse of lake bed to handle the merchanter ships from space. With the grounding of the Marik DropShips, it seemed as though the prosperous times had returned. Grayson and King stood beside their skimmer, staring through a chainlink fence at six massive *Union* Class DropShips.

"They've got their guard posted," Grayson said. Even at a distance of over a kilometer, he could identify the massive, insect-like silhouette of a 70-ton *Archer*.

"O.K.," he continued. "We accounted for eight at Durandel . . . and we ran into twelve at Cleft Valley . . . twenty. One more here. Six DropShips means they could have a total of seventy-two 'Mechs on Helm . . . or fifty-one more we haven't seen."

"You use a pessimistic version of arithmetic," King replied. "Some of those DropShips must have brought in the infantry we ran into."

"Agreed, but we don't have a good estimate on how much infantry they have here, either. They could still have another twenty . . . thirty 'Mechs down. Not good odds."

"Not the sort of odds I'd care to face." King looked thoughtful. "I suppose it could still be a rebel faction claiming to be the Free Worlds League government."

"Possibly . . . if Janos Marik was dead, and his two top generals were at each others' throats, squabbling for the title of Captain-General. But you'd think they'd identify themselves as one faction or another, just to avoid confusion."

"We should probably move on into town. They'll have perimeter security people out." King nodded toward the distant heavy 'Mech. "And *those* things, too."

Helmdown was crowded. The streets and mallways between the low, white buildings were crowded with native Helmans, most in the baggy, coarse-woven tunics that King and Grayson also wore. Some native vehicles were evident, but most Helmans were on foot. Interspersed through the crowd were crewmen and soldiers off the Marik ships. The soldiers' pale green trousers, light torso armor, and soft purple caps made them stand out in the crowds. Most of them armed, but their weapons were holstered, and the way they walked in small groups through the crowds, pointing and talking among themselves, suggested that they had come to town more to see the sights than as an invading army. Occasionally, Marik skimmers or wheeled vehicles made their way slowly through the throng on some errand or another, but the sense of an official *presence* such as a conquering army would bring, was absent.

Grayson and King left their skimmer in a dirt lot filled with similar vehicles several streets away from the main thoroughfare.

"Not much of an invasion," King said.

"I was just thinking the same thing."

"We've got to find out what's happening. Now, you have your contact on Hogarth Street . . ."

"Hey, when you want to know something," Grayson said. "You go to the source and ask."

He left King on the walkway and made his way toward a lone Marik soldier he had already spotted a few meters away.

"Hey, soldier!" Grayson said. He had considered affecting the slight drawl of Helman speech, then thought better of it. Caricatures of speech were easily recognized as such, and the local speech patterns were not that obtrusive.

The soldier turned at Grayson's call and watched him warily, but without evident hostility. He kept his hands on his hips, however, his right finger close by the butt of the holstered sonic stunner. "You talkin' to me?"

"Yessir. Ah, you see, I just got into town, and I was wondering what all the fuss was about."

Grayson was watching carefully for signs that he had said the wrong thing—the flaring of nostril or pupil, the tensing of muscles in hand or shoulder—but the soldier just grinned, his teeth very white through his beard. "You must be from the other side of the damned planet," the man said.

"You boys come in for maneuvers? I don't think we've seen this many spaceships landed all at the same time out there on the lakebed for years." Grayson's choice of words was deliberate, though casually spoken—he hoped.

Spaceship instead of *Dropship*. *Landed* instead of *grounded*. The differences should mark him as a grounder, a farmer who had done more than look at the stars in the night sky.

The soldier snorted. "Maneuvers? Yeah, I guess you could say so. You got your papers?"

The words were spoken so casually that it took a fractional moment before Grayson registered. "Papers?"

The soldier's hand was out, gesturing. "Yes, grounder, your papers. The notices have been posted all over the district for a week. Let's see 'em."

Grayson had a choice. He could pretend to reach for nonexistent papers while watching for an opening to break and run, or he could claim blank innocence. Thinking quickly, he elected the second course. He might be able to learn something more that way.

He set his jaw at what he hoped was a stubborn angle. "I ain't seen nothing about papers. What kind of hustle are you trying to pull on me?"

Grayson had half-expected the man to pull his gun, but the soldier simply looked tired. "No papers?"

Grayson decided to try the offensive. He leaned back on his heels and bellowed. *"What* damned papers?"

Throughout the crowd, heads turned toward them. The soldier reached forward, dropping one hand on Grayson's shoulder. Grayson tensed, ready to counter or deliver a blow, but something in the Marik trooper's manner made him hesitate. The man was relaxed . . . and wide-open for a killing hand-to-hand attack. And he was smiling . . . !

"Look, see that flag up the street?" The soldier pointed toward the center of town. "What used to be the Planetary Council's offices? That's the Planetary Administrator's headquarters now. Right in front, there's a booth set up. You go talk to the officer there, and he'll give you your papers. O.K.?"

"I see it. Now would you mind telling me what it's all about?"

"The planet of Helm is under the direct rule of House Marik, now. The Captain-General has appointed an Administrator to run things for the duration of the crisis."

"The Captain-General . . . Janos Marik?"

"You know another Captain-General?"

"Uh . . . no, I just don't have the damnedest idea what's going on. Crisis? What crisis?"

"You just go talk to Captain Biggs at that booth in front of the Helm Council building. He'll tell you all about it."

The soldier's tone suggested that he thought Grayson might be simple-minded, and Grayson decided not to press the man further, or to disabuse him of his notion. "Yessir," he said.

King was waiting where Grayson had left him.

"Well, I suppose that's one way to remain inconspicuous," the Tech said. "Scream and shout and get everybody looking."

"It seemed like a good idea at the time." Grayson sketched in what little he'd learned. "Looks like Janos Marik is still in power, and these troops are loyal to him. They've moved in to run things during the . . . crisis, whatever that is. Damn! I wish to hell I knew what was going on!"

"Think it has something to do with us?"

"It must. Those were Marik regulars at Durandel. We've got to find out why . . ."

"Watch it!" King's eyes flashed warning, staring past Grayson's shoulder. "Company!"

Grayson turned and saw the bearded Marik soldier he'd been talking with moments before coming toward them.

"I was just telling my friend . . ." Grayson began.

"Right, I saw that," the soldier said. "I just thought you'd like me to walk you up to the documentation center myself, so you wouldn't get lost."

"That's kind of you," Grayson said, smiling. "We know where it is, and we *are* going . . . right now."

The soldier's right hand rested lightly on the butt of his holstered stunner. Grayson noticed that the safety strap was off, permitting a fast draw, if needed.

"I assure you it's not necessary."

"I insist." The soldier's friendliness was gone now.

If Grayson and King were taken as far as the documentation center, their chances of escape would be considerably reduced—possibly to nil. There would certainly be more soldiers there, soldiers better-armed and more watchful than the isolated bands of soldier-tourists that dotted the crowds around them. The time to make a break for it was now, before this trooper became thoroughly alarmed, and before they ended up someplace where their chances of escape were as nonexistent as their papers.

"Well, fine, then," Grayson said. He exchanged glances with King and was certain from the Tech's guarded expression that he had assessed the situation and arrived at the same conclusion as Grayson. "Shall we go?"

Grayson turned to go up the street in the direction of the Council House, but the first two steps he took also brought him closer to the soldier, and to the man's left. King also started in the same direction, but he stepped to the right on a course that would take him behind the soldier as he walked past.

Realizing that the two other men were splitting up, the soldier took a quick step backward, and turned to his right to face King. The stunner slid from the holster, as the soldier started to say, "Now, hold it right there . . ." He never finished the sentence. Grayson lunged forward, shoving the Marik soldier hard toward King.

The Tech had already moved by that time, and his booted left foot was sweeping the air in a stiff-legged roundhouse kick that landed squarely behind the Marik soldier's ear. Grayson had been trained in hand-to-hand combat as an apprentice, but there had never been reason or time to sharpen his skills with much practice. It looked as though Alard King had had plenty of practice, for he moved with lighting speed and precision. The fight was over before it had even properly started. The soldier lay sprawled on the pavement, face down. Grayson picked up the man's sonic stunner, which lay close by, but dropped it when he realized it was still attached to its owner's belt by a wire-bound dummy cord.

"Let's move it!" King's said, his voice low but penetrating.

Grayson nodded. The disturbance had impinged on the crowd around them like ripples from a pebble thrown in a pond. Most of the civilians were crowding back and away from the two warriors and the Marik soldier's still form, while other Marik soldiers were forcing their way in against the flow. Grayson saw several guns already in hand and plainly in sight. The soldiers weren't close enough to see the unconscious soldier yet, but a few moments more, and they would be.

"We'll split up." It would be safer traveling separately, Grayson decided quickly. One of them, at least, might be able to make the inquiries they needed. "Try to meet me at the skimmer lot in . . . five hours. We each wait an hour, and if there's no rendezvous, we make our own way back to the camp."

"Right! Five hours! Wait an hour and then we're on our own!" Then the Tech was gone, fading into the crowd with a suddenness that startled Grayson. Not only was Alard King an ace Technician, but he seemed to be skilled in other arts as well. Grayson hoped King would make it as he himself twisted away into the crowd in another direction.

"You! Stop where you are!"

The new voice had the snap of authority behind it. Grayson didn't bother to look, knowing full well that the soldiers had spotted him walking away from the first soldier's body. He threw himself past the corner of a building, dodging through a deserted alleyway lined with refuse cylinders, a cool, dank semi-darkness leading down a slight hill toward the next main parallel street.

"Stop! Stop!" came the shouts, but fainter now. The mouth of the alley opened ahead, bright with sunlight and the moving figures of civilians. A quick turn into that next street, and . . .

Shadows moved against the light, blocking the way. One dropped into a crouch as the figure whipped a gun to bear on Grayson's chest.

"Halt where you are, grounder!"

15

Veering suddenly, Grayson vaulted a garbage can, then dove directly toward the Marik soldier. A sound buzzed under his chest as something struck his left leg a numbing blow. "Watch out!" the standing man yelled, and then Grayson was rolling across the ferrocrete pavement in a tangle of legs and arms.

He came up with all of his strength and mass behind the outthrust heel of his hand, smashing up into the jaw of the standing man and sending him sprawling back into the refuse cylinders in the alley. A plastic radio handset splintered on the walkway at his feet. Grayson spun and started to run, but his left leg nearly gave out.

Marik soldiers were shouting from down the alley. Grayson noted quickly that at least two were down, caught by the sonic bolt that had nearly felled him in mid-flight. His own left leg tingled where it had caught the fringes of that beam. Forcing himself to stay on his feet, he hurried his way down the street and into the crowd with a lurching gait.

There was no safety in the crowd, he knew. There were people all around him, farmers and laborers for the most part, all dressed as he was, but his limp made him stand out from the rest. If that weren't enough to give him away, then the wild-eyed look of desperation on his face would probably do it better. He was going to have to find a place to hide until the effects of the sonic bolt wore off.

Following a side branch of the street he was on, Grayson came to a broad, ferrocrete plaza, with an open park beyond. Though the park was close to the center of Helmdown and its unexpected crowds, it would provide him with temporary sanctuary. There were people here as well, but not so many of them. Many were couples, strolling slowly or lying on the gray-green grass under spreading hostlepines, while they talked, read, or kissed. A low stone wall along the edge of a sculpture garden was occupied in various places by couples or solitary figures enjoying the shade from the surrounding buildings.

Seated on the wall, Grayson felt he would not look out of place. Neither would the dragging limp of his leg, now tingling furiously with the pins and needles of returning sensation, mark him out. He leaned back and pretended to study the art displayed in the sculpture garden. Grayson knew little about classical statuary, though these looked like something he'd once heard referred to as Rim Worlds Neo-Realist. The forms seemed to represent either nude women or dying warriors, and they must once have been colored in realistic tones. That would have been in the days when the garden had first been opened, long before the nuclear death of Freeport and so much more of this world. The colors were faded now, except for bits and pieces, and the forms were waterstained, pollution-marred, and overgrown with moss and weeds. The shade trees that once had surrounded the garden had long since been cut down, and except for the half-hidden statues, the place had the look of an overgrown abandoned lot.

A pair of soldiers hurried purposefully across the ferrocrete plaza from the direction Grayson had just come. He ignored them as he pretended to admire the statuary, but kept his head angled in such a way that he could watch the soldiers out the corner of his eye. The chances were that none of them would recognize him, for no Marik trooper had seen him except as a blur or a running form in the distance. Still, the man holding a radio, the one he had hit—and probably the man who had been crouching at his side as well—had gotten a good look at his features. If they were sharp enough, either of those two might recognize him.

These were two different soldiers, however. They wore

heavy black-purple clamshell armor and dark-visored combat helmets instead of felt caps. Each carried an assault rifle cradled uncertainly in nervous hands. They entered the park hesitantly, their helmeted heads turning this way and that. Twice the sun glinted from their visors as their gaze swept past him, but Grayson remained calm and unmoving. After a second, one of the troopers took his comrade by the arm, and pointed across the garden toward the buildings beyond. Then the two broke into a trot, parting waist-deep weeds as they zigzagged past still forms of nymphs and dying warriors in what they imagined was the direction of their prey.

Grayson didn't move, but continued to survey the park. He wasn't sure how intelligent was the search being mounted for him, but he was taking no chances. A moment later, two more armored and helmeted soldiers followed with slow deliberation along the trail of the first two. Grayson couldn't tell for certain whether all four were working together, but it was a possibility he could not afford to discount.

He decided to stay put for a while.

A man walked up to a spot on the wall some five meters from Grayson and sat down. He was an old man wearing the tunic and boots of a laborer, and holding a knobbed walking stick in his veined, gnarled hand. His beard was white, his scalp bald, but his eyes were clear and remarkably blue. As Grayson looked across to him, those blue eyes caught his. There was no recognition on either side. Grayson had never seen the man before, but he did detect a flash—the merest suggestion—of comradeship. Or was it simple curiosity?

The man's eyes tracked back across the park in the direction the soldiers had gone, then back to Grayson. He shrugged then, as if to say, *It's a strange world.*

With that brief eye contact to lead him on, Grayson decided to venture further. He stood up, gingerly putting his weight on the hit leg, happy to find that the numbness and tingling were almost gone. He walked a few steps over to the old man, then sat down again. "Good morning."

" 'Morning to you, young feller.'' The man's voice was clear and strong.

"I'm new in town,'' Grayson said. "What's with all the soldiers?''

"Them? Some sort of flap with the new landholder, they say. They came in a week ago and took over. I hear the landhold at Durandel's been leveled.''

"I've . . . heard that too. But why?''

"Beats me. I don't care for politics, myself. 'Long as the new landlord keeps the peace and keeps the tax collectors off my back, I'm happy.'' The man's eyes narrowed. "Wouldn't be that those soldier boys were after you, son, would it?''

"Not that I know of. Why do you ask?''

"Oh, I don't know. You come in here, limping . . . like maybe someone had nabbed you with a tingler. Then you sit there showing a truly remarkable interest in these perfectly awful sculptures while the Captain-General's best line troops go racing past. I don't know. Call it a hunch. Or a wild guess.''

Grayson decided to change the subject. "What's all this about papers and a document center?''

"You *are* new in town. That's the first thing these johnnies did when they came in. Everyone has to have papers, like this.'' He reached into his tunic, fumbled with an inside pocket, then withdrew a flat wallet. Opening it, he withdrew a single, folded sheet, printed on one side. "Actually, this is all there is. Paper . . . not papers. Name . . . date . . . birth . . . mother . . . father . . . occupation . . . the usual bureaucratic dreck. You don't have yours yet, eh?''

"First I've heard about it.''

"Might explain why those soldiers yonder were interested in you . . . but then, they weren't after you at all, were they?''

Grayson rubbed his leg. The numbness and tingling were nearly gone. "Well, I'd better get a move on.''

The old man watched him with a keen, lively intelligence. "You'd better, eh? And where to?''

Grayson smiled. He could picture himself telling the

gentleman that he was setting out in search of the resident Lyran Commonwealth spy!

"Oh, just a guy I have to see. Business."

"Ah. Business. Well, you find any business in this town, you come back and tell me." His eyes twinkled with the beginnings of a smile. "The again, if you don't find any business, you might want to tell me, too. Mebee I can help."

Grayson had the strange feeling that the man was laughing at him. His words made no sense, probably the maunderings of an old man on the verge of senility. Nodding toward the gentleman, he stood up. "Yes, well, I'll see you later."

"Yes, I daresay you will."

His confrontation with the old fellow left Grayson shaken. The trip into Helmdown had been so carefully planned, but the man's careful banter, his apparent or pretended knowledge of Grayson, was unsettling. Grayson abandoned any attempt to look the part of a Helman farmer and hurried back toward the center of town. Hogarth Street was not far from the Council House, and he found it easily after consulting one of the electronic maps positioned at strategic corners throughout the town. The crowds were thinner there, though plenty of people were still about. Grayson wondered if so many strangers were in town because they had come to get papers, or because they were curious about all the Marik soldiers from the DropShips. Perhaps it was both.

The name of his contact was Jenton Moragen, whose Moragen Emporium was reputedly one of the most respected mercantile firms in Helmdown. Though not large—the company's personnel register recorded 52 people on its payroll, including those working offworld—it had been an important part of Helm's economy under Moragen's great-great-grandfather, almost two hundred years before.

According to Grayson's informant, it had been Moragen's grandfather who had begun to act as a conduit of information from Helm to the Lyran Commonwealth. Jenton was merely carrying on the family tradition, both as businessman and as spy. Little enough happened on

Helm to warrant the attention of Katrina Steiner or her officers on Tharkad, of course, but there had been occasions for Moragen to show his usefulness. Once, when agents of the Draconis Combine had been showing an unusual interest in Helm several years before, he had written up a report for transmission to Commonwealth space, then thoughtfully sent a copy to the District Office of the Captain-General.

The Marik aide who had told all of this to Grayson had laughed. "Jenton is an old friend of our governor there on Helm. Listen, you want to get to know the governor, go ask Jenton to introduce you. They'll sucker you into a game of three-handed trovans and clean you out!"

Grayson found the Moragen Emporium without any trouble.

Posted over the door, with its tack-welded electronic lock, was a notice that could be read from clear across the street: CLOSED BY ORDER OF THE MILITARY GOVERNOR.

Closed! There was fine print on the notice, but Grayson did not want to appear too curious about that door or its sign. A sudden chill gripped him. All around him were tall, blank-windowed buildings, behind where there might be hidden watchers, men with vision-enhancers, recorders, and radios for alerting other men on the streets. As casually as possible, Grayson continued his walk along the opposite side of the street from the Emporium. The building had been freshly whitewashed, and the electric sign above was intact, though the power was off. It looked as though it might have been closed only the day before.

He made his way on down Hogarth Street until he found its junction with Victory Way. Then he walked north for several blocks, back to where the crowds were thickest, not far from the Council House and the booth of Captain Biggs. The plaza known as the Condordiat joined Victory Way, and on the corner was the sign advertising the Skyway Travel Bureau.

Skyway Travel had been located on this corner for nearly seventy years. The manager was a respected Helmdown businessman named Wilkis Atkins. Atkins had been born and raised on Helm, though his parents had come to that world fifty standard years before from Robinson, in the Federated Suns. The same aide who had told Grayson of the owner of the Moragen Emporium had described Wilkis Atkins as Helm's resident agent for House Davion's Federated Suns.

It was less likely that House Davion would be willing to help an out-of-luck mercenary company on a world as far removed from Davion territory as Helm. Yet, without being immodest, Grayson knew that the Gray Death Legion had made a name for itself in the past three years, and the rich and powerful House Davion was bound to have noticed the Legion's rise. If Grayson could make contact with someone well-placed on a Federated Suns world, perhaps the Gray Death Legion could win a mercenary ticket serving Hanse Davion. It was reputed among mercenaries that House Davion did not pay as well as the other Great Houses, but were fair in dealing with those in their employ. Certainly, it would be worthwhile to talk with Atkins.

That was not to be, however. Skyway Travel had the same "CLOSED BY ORDER OF THE MILITARY GOVERNOR" sign that had been posted over the Moragen Emporium. This was too much to be coincidence.

The words of the old man in the park came back to him, and Grayson knew a moment of stark terror. The man had known, had known that Grayson was looking for Moragen or Atkins, had known that their businesses were closed down!

"Mebee I can help," the old man had said. *Mebee, indeed!* Grayson turned so sharply that he collided with a laborer in the crowd close behind him, mumbled apology, and made his way south again along Victory Way. The old man had said to go see him, and Grayson intended to do just that!

Alard King paused in front of the weathered, native stone building and looked both ways. The crowds had nearly vanished in this, a residential portion of Helmdown on the northern outskirts of town. The land here rose sharply, and King was breathing heavily after his stiff, fifteen-minute climb up the narrow streets. Behind him, the open street gave him a view of the town spread out below the hill, and of the spaceport beyond. He could make out the forms of all six DropShips there, glittering gray-silver in the sunlight.

King had removed his bulky tunic and traded it for an elegantly cut merchanter's blouse and cape from a canvas bag he had worn under the baggy tunic. With the tunic now in the bag, and the bag slung over his shoulder, he felt considerably less conspicuous than in the farmer's garb. Alard knew he looked the part of a good-looking young merchanter come to town on business.

The buildings in this hilltop district tended toward pastel colors and open architecture rather than the unrelieved whites and browns and blocky façades of the city proper. By Helman standards, most of these residents were wealthy. The area, known as Gresshaven, was largely reserved for the owners of businesses, members of the professional elite, and the wealthy merchants of Helmdown.

King touched the door announcer and an electronic voice said, "Yes?" Slowly and precisely, King replied, *"Shogyo de kite imasu."*

"Dare desu ka?" the voice behind the speaker said.

"King desu ga."

"Wait."

There was a long stillness, and then an electronic lock clicked and the door slid open. A young man with hair so blond it was almost white looked out, glanced past King into the street, then looked back at the Tech.

"You are here on . . . business, you said?"

"Please. I need to see the mistress of the house."

The blond man's eyes narrowed. "Things are . . . difficult, just now."

King smiled. "You don't believe I have business here?"

"Oh, your use of Japanese, your mention of the word 'business'—they were perfectly correct. But there has been some trouble. The military occupation forces have been rounding up all foreign agents in Helmdown, real and suspected. Madame's house in town has already been closed down.''

King's face showed alarm. "Is Deirdre all right?''

''The Mistress is well. As yet, they do not seem to have made the connection between Madame's business interests in town with those here in Gresshaven, but we must be . . . cautious.''

''Understood,'' King paused, considering. Then he removed a ring from his pouch, one he had had kept hidden from his Gray Death comrades. It was a heavy, ornate gold ring with a raised relief of a dagger set against a fleur-de-lis. "Then give her this. Tell her that Alard King, special personal representative of Duke Ricol, of the Draconis Combine, *must* see her.''

The servant's eyes widened when he saw the ring.

''Immediately, sir.''

''Tell her it is a matter of life and death,'' King added.

16

Grayson followed his guide down the winding stairway. The old man walked slowly, but the light here was so dim that even with a far younger and more nimble guide, Grayson would have had to move with caution. The ceiling was low enough that he had to stoop to keep from hitting his head. The stone walls were dank with moisture.

It had not, after all, been luck that had brought Grayson together with Victor Wallenby on the stone wall along the statue garden. Wallenby had seen Grayson making his way from the alley where he had escaped the Marik soldiers, and had been sufficiently intrigued by the younger man's appearance to decide to investigate more closely.

"Of course, I knew you were needin' help," Wallenby had explained when Grayson found him again in the park. "I could tell you weren't from around *here*."

"But how did you *know*?" Grayson had asked in exasperation. He'd looked around the plaza area at the other civilians, most wearing shapeless, homemade clothes identical to his own. "I'm dressed just like a farmer . . ."

"Ah!" Wallenby's eyes had twinkled. "But that's just it, young feller. You obviously *weren't* a farmer. Look at those hands! Not a callous on 'em."

'Oh, come on! You couldn't have checked my callouses from across the street, when you said you first saw me!"

"Nope. But I could see a young guy *dressed* like a farmer. And I asks m'self . . . why's a young buck come to town wearin' his everyday work clothes from the farm?

174

An old guy like me . . . sure! I wear this because it's comfortable . . . and I'm too old to play dress-up! Your father, forty standard years old and hands calloused like these''—he held up his own gnarled hands—''Who does he have to impress with his clothes? But you? I could see as the farmer's son, maybe . . . but not in *that* outfit. No, the farmer's son would wear his good clothes to come to town. Impress the girls! Show off to the other farmers' sons how much money he has in his pockets! You? You don't even *have* pockets in those baggy things!''

''So, how did you know I was looking for the Steiner . . . ah . . . representative?''

''The Steiner spy? I *didn't* know, for sure. But I figured it had to be either the Davion or Steiner folks. They both have their businesses here, in the central part o' town. I didn't figure you were lookin' for the Liao spy. He's clear over by the spaceport. And the Kurita spy, well, she does her business out in the well-to-do part of town . . . and if you was to wander in over there wearing hick clothes like those, I'd figure you were a lot crazier than you looked! Course, she's got a place in town—or had one, until yesterday afternoon—but she still mostly caters to the rich folks. I doubt that you could get past her front door looking like *that*.''

''Well, I'm not interested in any spy of Kurita's. Or Liao's. I was told that a man named Jenton Moragen might be able to help me, but when I found his place closed up, I thought I'd try Wilkis Atkins.''

''Steiner or Davion . . . right. I knew it! I had you spotted from the moment I laid eyes on you! You *are* new at this kind of thing.''

The twinkle in the old man's eye robbed his words of any offense, and so Grayson smiled. ''I'm afraid so. You claimed you could help me. Can you tell me if Moragen was arrested? His emporium was closed.''

''Yep. Marik soldiers went in and shut him down two days ago. But he'd heard they was comin' and lit out before they got there. Same for Major Atkins.''

''Why did the soldiers close them down?''

''I dunno . . . except that something hellacious big has been happening here, ever since the Marik troops came in. I wouldn't wonder if the Marik generals have something big cooking here, and they don't want the other House governments to get wind of it. Of course, the best way to stir up a feller's interest is to try to arrest all his friends in the very town where you're tryin' to keep a low profile, but . . . Well, governments ain't generally known for their brains, I guess.''

Grayson had stared at the man, hands on hips. ''But who the hell are *you,* anyway? Another spy?''

Wallenby had broken into laughter at that. ''Hell, no! But I got eyes, ain't I? They ain't shut down yet! And this is a small town . . . for all that, it's the biggest city on Helm! I've lived here all my life, which is sayin' something, and when you've been in a small town that long, you get to know everyone. Lots of people from out of town are here the past few days, o' course, but you were different . . . dressed like something you weren't.''

''But you know the Steiner representative.''

''Yep. Know him well.''

''I don't suppose you know what's been going on, here? Why all the Marik troops . . . the fighting out at Durandel?''

''Nope.''

''Can you get me in to see Jenton Moragen?''

''I dunno. I'll have to talk to him, see if *he* want's t' see *you.* As you can imagine, they're both a bit hesitant about talkin' to strangers, just now. Who should I say is callin'?''

Grayson hesitated. If he told Wallenby his true identity, the old man might be tempted to turn him over to the authorities in hopes of a reward. He didn't want to believe that of the friendly old man, but he'd been badly shaken by how easily Wallenby had seen through his disguise, and he didn't want to take any chances.

''I'd really rather not say. I know Moragen is taking a chance if he sees me. As far as he knows, I'm with Marik counterintelligence. The hell of it is, I learned his name from a Lieutenant Gainsborough, on Janos Marik's staff!''

Wallenby's bushy white eyebrows crowded toward the top of his forehead. ''Tell you the truth, old Jules Gainsborough's word'll get you farther with Moragen than lots of others. He wouldn't have told you about either Jenton or Wilkis if he didn't think you had a reason to know. Tell you what. You stay here and let me make a call. Don't talk to anybody." He'd leaned forward on his walking stick, his eyes laughing. "There's too damn many *spies* loose out on these streets, and you never know when you'll find y'self talkin' to one!"

Fifteen minutes later, Wallenby had returned, and the two men had walked east, toward the part of town dominated by the old AgroMech industrial facility. The place where they were meeting Moragen wasn't within the plant itself, but located in an AgroMech storehouse close by, where the heavy farming machines were arrayed for inspection and sale by the company that manufactured them. A palm electronic key won them admittance to the main warehouse, a dimly-lit room dominated by row upon row of huge, spindle-legged agricultural 'Mechs. Another locked door had led to a narrow hallway, then to a spiral stairway running down a dank stairwell with wet stone walls.

The room at the bottom looked as though it had been carved from native rock, and it was chilly so many meters below the level of the street.

Two men waited under the pale light of a ceiling fluorostrip, seated at a plastic table in an otherwise empty room. One of them caught Grayson's attention immediately—tall, silver-haired, hawk-nosed, and lean, he had the look of a MechWarrior. The man opposite him was small and plain to the point of dumpiness. He was bald and rubbed the palms of his hands slowly back and forth in an incessant revelation of the strain he was under.

Wallenby gestured toward the nervous one. "This, sir, is Jenton Moragen, of Moragen's Emporium. This other gentleman is the director of Skyway Travel, citizen Wilkis Atkins. Or should I say 'Major'?"

The one identified as Atkins turned his mouth in a sour expression. "I'm not sure you should say anything, Wallenby, in front of this person." Atkins looked sharply at Grayson. "Who are you, sir?"

Grayson took a deep breath. If he had been betrayed—

again—there would be no help for him here. He would
have to assume that these men were who they claimed to
be. If they were deceiving him, he could not see their
purpose. Marik soldiers could have taken him easily
while he sat in the park, a waiting for Wallenby's return.
The thought that Wallenby had gone to call the soldiers
had turned that fifteen minutes wait into an eternity.

"My name, gentlemen, is Colonel Grayson Carlyle.
Until yesterday, I was lord of the landhold at Durandel,
Helmbold. My regiment, the Gray Death Legion, is en-
camped some distance from here, near what is left of
Durandel. I am here to try to learn what . . ."

He broke off as both Atkins and Moragen rose to their
feet.

"Carlyle!" Moragen said "I *told* you, Atkins! I told
you it had to be him . . ."

But Atkins was descending on Carlyle, his forefinger
raised. "You . . you scum! You have the audacity to
seek us out here . . . *now*?"

Even Wallenby looked shocked. "Him!" was all he
said.

"Whoa, there, people," Grayson said, moving back a
step. "Every since I arrived on this planet, people have
been treating us like renegades, like outlaws, but I can't
figure out why. Why not let me in on the secret! Just
what the hell is going on around here, anyway?"

Atkins stopped short. "What? You don't know?"

"Damn right, I don't know! That's why I sneaked in
here, why I wanted to see you! Somehow, we seem to
have pulled the whole Marik army down on our heads . . .
but we don't know how, and we don't know why! I came
here to talk to you, Moragen, to try to get passage offworld
for my people." He didn't mention the loss of the
DropShips—there was no reason to admit that particular
weakness—but it was common for mercenaries to dicker
with prospective employers over transportation.

"You bastard," Atkins said. "You're going to stand
there and deny what you did on Sirius V?"

Grayson felt himself growing cold all over, as though
suddenly transported to the chill surface of that ice-locked
world. "*What* did I do on Sirius V?"

"You murdering bastard, you accepted the surrender of the city of Tiantan! You negotiated the surrender, trooped aboard your DropShips, and then blew the living hell out of all five city domes! Damn you, your 'Mechs were holographed smashing through the rubble after the explosion! You blew open five domes! There were twelve million people in that city! Women! Children! Old men! Babies! The ones who didn't fry when you blew the domes choked to death in the frigid, poison air. Have you tried breathing ammonia at fifty below, mercenary? It's not healthy!"

Grayson listened to Atkins' diatribe with growing horror. "I give you my word, Atkins, this is the first I've heard of this," he said when the Davion agent had run out of breath.

"And what is the word of a renegade merc worth these days? I hear they're still digging frozen bodies out from under the rubble. They're finding survivors, too. That you can believe. You might have wiped Tiantan off the map, Carlyle, but you missed enough people that they'll be able to nail you flat out on the ground! And God, I hope they do it . . . if I don't do it first!"

"Hey! Listen to me, man! We took the surrender of the city! We turned command over to the Duke of Irian! We talked to the man's headquarters from the jump point days later, and everything was fine!" Grayson's horror took an even keener edge at the memory of his communications people aboard the *Phobos* unable to find the Tiantan transmitter carrier wave, and that no one in the Duke's command had wanted to talk with him. He remembered the peculiar behavior of Lord Garth, and struggled to fit that behavior into the pieces of the puzzle that he was hearing now.

"You're saying someone set you up?" Atkins said. "For God's sake, Carlyle, why would anyone do a thing like that? Listen! Your 'mechs were holographed! Your DropShips were holographed! I've seen them, with the Tiantan domes burning on the horizon behind them! The story's been running for two days over the Helmdown news services! Don't you bother to monitor the news?"

Grayson shook his head. In point of fact, BattleMechs

179

were not generally equipped to picked up televised signals. The *Deimos* or the *Phobos* could have done it, but there had been no reason at the time. They had been too busy dealing with the Marik forces at Durandel . . . and later, at Cleft Valley.

"I don't care what was photographed," Grayson said. "Photographs, even holographs, can be faked by computer manipulations."

"Your 'Mechs were seen attacking the ruins, Carlyle."

"Witnesses can be bought, dammit! Or they can be misled! My God, someone is trying to destroy the Gray Death by turning us into outlaws . . . and I can't get anyone to believe me!"

"I don't think anyone is going to believe you," Moragen said quietly. The disdain was heavy in his voice. "You were assigned here as our protector, but that kind of protection we can do without! And I can assure you that House Steiner will want nothing to do with a man or a unit capable of such a monstrous act!"

"The same goes for House Davion, Carlyle. I won't even put in the request, because I know what they would say. Hanse Davion doesn't associate with renegade city killers!"

Grayson thought that Atkins was about to attack him then and there, but the big man seemed to relax slightly. "You can take your filthy so-called regiment and hike it," Atkins said. "Civilized warriors will have nothing to do with you now. Get out of my sight!"

Grayson turned to Moragen, but the small man folded his arms. "I suggest you leave, Carlyle. I am not a violent man, but your actions at Sirius V ignore every tenet of modern warfare . . . of common decency! There was no reason to destroy that city . . . no reason to massacre those people! Your actions have placed you outside the pale of civilized men . . . and of law."

The silence that followed was as cold as the glacial ice on the mountaintops of Helm. The behavior of the Marik BattleMech forces on that planet was explained at last. The Conventions of War dictated certain formal ways for troops to behave toward one another in war, but renegades—city killers—they were beyond the pale of even unspoken and unwritten laws.

Wallenby had been silent, too, as he led Grayson back to the stairs to the surface.

"Wallenby . . . you believe me, don't you?" he said, stepping out into the light. There was no response, for the old man had already vanished back inside the warehouse, leaving Grayson alone in the lengthening shadows of the Helman afternoon.

17

Grayson waited as long as he dared at the rendezvous, but when Alard King did not show up, he returned alone to the Valley of the Araga.

Upon his arrival, word spread quickly through the encampment along the banks of the Araga River. The Gray Death Legion had been proclaimed as renegades—an outlaw regiment—and the Marik forces were trying to hunt them down. It was small consolation, but now that they knew the "truth," other pieces of the puzzle no longer seemed so strange. They understood Colonel Langsdorf's unorthodox tactics of seizing Durandel's military and civilian leaders, the sort of treatment usually reserved for renegades or rebels, and not for respected military adversaries.

When Alard King returned to camp nearly three hours later, he was piloting a stolen civilian skimmer, and bearing the same news as had Grayson. And more.

"I think I know why Marik is interested in this planet," he'd said, and so Grayson had called a meeting of the regiment's senior people.

"We all know that the Star League was the last time mankind even came close to having a single interstellar government," King began. "Many of the Houses we know today . . . Kurita, Marik . . . they were part of the structure of the League."

"Some of them thought they *were* the League," Clay put in.

"Yeah, well, in 2786, Minoru Kurita started the First Succession War by declaring himself First Lord."

McCall folded his arms. "We all ken our history, laddie."

"Helm was an important target when Kurita led his fleets against the Marik Commonwealth. There was a League naval base here, at Freeport, and a storehouse of military weapons intended for the League forces.

"Now, when the Star League dissolved, there was quite a vicious political fight within the Free Worlds League over who would get those weapons. Kurita moved to grab them while the squabbling was still going on."

"Yes?"

"They weren't there."

"That's right," Grayson said. "They were probably moved someplace else, after being split up into a dozen smaller caches that fell, one by one, to various contestants in the war."

"Maybe." King smiled. "That's what everybody thought."

"Go on."

"Minoru Kurita's troops scoured the planet, but they could find no sign of the League weapons cache. Certainly, it had been moved out of Freeport. In frustration, Minoru nuked Freeport and left it in radioactive ruins, then nuked most of the other major population centers, leaving Helm a dying world.

"Kurita wrote a report on his action for his council back on Luthien. He proposed what you did . . . that the cache had been removed."

"So?"

"So, the cache couldn't have been moved!"

"Why not?"

"Think about it! We're not talking about ten or twenty BattleMechs. We're talking about hundreds! Enough for a regiment . . . for ten regiments! No one knows how big that cache was! Tanks! Heavy artillery! Ammunition! Do you know how heavy a 'Mech repair gantry is?"

"I have some idea," Grayson said drily.

"The garrison commander on Helm was a House Marik officer, a major in command of an engineer battalion. Apparently, he was a Star League idealist, too, one who wanted to see the League reborn to its old glory.

He had already put off the various Marik commanders by suggesting that they settle among themselves who had the proper authority to remove the weapons before he relinquished control to them. By invoking chapter and verse of certain military articles, he was able to stop them from walking in and carrying everything off.''

"So why couldn't *he* carry everything off?'' Clay asked.

"What would an engineering battalion commander use for ships?''

There was a stunned silence. King paused, then plunged ahead. "The officer—his name was Edwin Keeler, by the way—Major Keeler had been ordered to provide a garrison force for Helm, but he had no ships. Even if he had, he wouldn't have had access to a fleet big enough to transport even a fair percentage of the weapons elsewhere. And at the time, Kurita's invasion fleet was closing in. All available ships were elsewhere—fighting at the front.''

"So the cache had still to have been on Helm,'' Grayson said.

"Exactly. If it was an incontrovertible fact that the cache was here before the war began, and if it was also an incontrovertible fact that there were no ships available to move the cache once the war began, it follows that Keeler didn't transport the cache offplanet. He *must* have simply . . . hidden it.''

Grayson looked thoughtful. "*Hidden* it? Then it's still here.''

"And somebody is going to a hell of a lot of trouble to get us out of the way so that they can find it.''

"How are we in the way?''

"Perhaps . . . because you are the military governor of the district,'' King said, with a shrug. "My source wasn't sure.''

"And . . . just who is this source?''

King rubbed his jaw, then shook his head. "Colonel . . . I can't tell you.''

"Laddie,'' McCall said. "Ah think ye damn weel better . . .''

"Save it, Davis,'' Grayson said. He studied King narrowly. "You're satisfied with this information?''

"I am, Colonel. But my source . . . doesn't want to have his part known in this."

"You'll have to tell us sooner or later, Alard. If it's the integrity of the regiment . . ."

"Give me some time on that, Colonel. Maybe . . . maybe one day I'll take you in to meet . . . him."

Tracy Maxwell Kent stood on the rocky bank above the Araga River, clenching her fists so hard that her whole body trembled. her angry gaze took in the rushing water, the huge, tumbled blocks of sandstone along the shallow river, the wooded hills that enclosed her on every side. This shouldn't be happening to her! It was the final blow in a long series of setbacks that had brought her . . . here. Here!

This slim, dark-haired, pretty young woman was the eldest daughter of one of the wealthiest noble families in the Federated Suns. Though she had been raised to become a cultured, elegant lady, her sheltered and proper life had been shattered by the combat death of her adored older brother, Captain Sir Roderick Fitzroy Kent, when she was twenty. Tracy promptly decided that the only way to redeem his death was to join the Davion Military Academy, and become a MechWarrior like Fitz. It was all well and good for the eldest son of the family to become a MechWarrior, but Tracy's father protested that properly raised young ladies of good families and noble background simply did not do such things.

Tracy stubbornly entered the Academy anyway. Stubborn in his own way, her father had used his influence to have her expelled on a technicality.

Infuriated by these high-handed tactics, Tracy decided to join the line infantry as a private instead of returning home to her family. Within two years, she had worked her way up to Tech sergeant, attempting to become a MechWarrior the hard way—from the ground up. After two more years of training and serving as an astech for Blackely's Blackguards, she had the chance to replace a 'Mech pilot killed during a particularly hot action on Proserpina. Her skill and daring so impressed Colonel Blackely that she won a battlefield commendation and was allowed to stay on as a *Phoenix Hawk* pilot in the Blackguard's recon lance.

The Blackguards had been forced to disband after losing over fifty percent of their strength in the debacle at Cassias, leaving Tracy as a free agent with her own *Phoenix Hawk*. After making her way to Galatea in the Lyran Commonwealth, she had made the acquaintance of Sharyl.

Like Captain Ramage, Sharyl had no other name. Her culture on Dahar IV, like that of Trell I, used given names only. Another fiercely independent soul escaping an oppressive family, she had somehow drifted into the world of BattleMech mercenaries. Recognizing in Tracy a kindred spirit, she had taken her to Lori Kalmar, Executive Officer of the Gray Death Legion. Thus had the Legion become Tracy's new home.

That was only four standard months before. The Gray Death had been engaged in Liao space at the time, and Lori Kalmar had been present on Galatea solely for the purpose of recruiting new mercenaries to the fast-growing Legion. Instead of being thrown directly into combat, Tracy had been assigned to the Legion's Company B and sent to the new landhold on Helm.

"Our people are being transferred right now from our temporary cantonment on Graham IV to our new home on Helm," Lori had explained. "We're putting you in with the trainees there, under Lieutenant DeVillar. Not because we think you don't know your business, but because we want to give you a chance to settle in, to get to know us . . . and for us to know you. You'll help build our new home at Durandel, on Helm. You'll help train the new recruits . . . including the MechWarrior apprentices in B Company. When the Liao campaign is over, we'll either bring you into A Company to fill a hole, or we'll turn B Company into a second first-line 'Mech company, and create a new one—C Company—for trainees and new recruits. Colonel Carlyle is looking to expand the 'Mech Company into a full battalion as soon as we have the warriors and machines to do it. It won't be long before you're in a line regiment again."

"And how long will that be?" Tracy had wanted to know.

"When the Liao campaign is over, probably. Not long, another five months maybe."

Five months! That was an eternity! Tracy had tasted enough combat to know that she was good, damned good. With experience, she would be fantastic, a terror of the battlefield whose reputation would make her father's jaw drop open when he heard of it. But five months of raising walls and training raw recruits! She'd almost turned Lori down right then, but knew she was better off accepting a ground floor chance in the Legion than spending many more months hanging around Galatea's seedy starport bars looking for work with another merc force.

The Gray Death already had a bright reputation as a fast, hard-hitting, brilliantly deployed merc unit, one that had taken on outrageous odds and won. Its young commander had his own reputation as a brilliant, unorthodox, and perhaps visionary tactician. If Tracy Maxwell Kent was to make a name for herself as a warrior, Grayson Carlyle's unit could give her the chance.

Since making her decision four months ago, she had worked tirelessly at Durandel, overseeing the rise of the new community there, readying Castle Helmhold for the regiment's return. She had even permitted her beloved *Phoenix Hawk* to be shipped out aboard the *Deimos*, when the *Invidious* had called back at Helm for spare parts and supplies. After the debacle at Cassias, the *Dutiful Daughter* was all she'd had to keep alive the hope of becoming a renowned warrior one day. When the Legion needed the *Hawk* as a reserve 'Mech for A Company in the fighting on Sirius V, Tracy had let them take the *Daughter* because she believed in the unit and what it was doing. She had come to accept the other members of the regiment as a kind of extended family. After all, they accepted Tracy for herself and not because she was the daughter of Lord Rodney Howard Kent of New Avalon.

The Liao campaign had ended sooner than expected. The last word they'd had on Helm was that the campaign for Sirius V was nearly over, and that Carlyle and the regiment would be returning in another few weeks. When

DropShips next descended out of Helm's sparkling blue sky, however, they were not the *Deimos* and the *Phobos*, but six House Marik ships, armed and arrayed for war. The attack on Durandel had taken them all by surprise. During that night of fire and horror, Tracy had cowered inside a shelter created by the collapse of a machine shop wall across the sunken well in the shop's floor used for lubricating and repairing the armored company's wheeled vehicles.

That night of terror had brought Tracy face to face with herself. Disgusted by her own fear, she wondered how she would ever live up to the standard of her valiant brother. Even worse was that she had cried out for her father at one point when burning debris from an exploding Galleon had come crashing down on top of her shelter. The memory still made her burn with shame. How would she ever find the steel inside her own soul to become a real MechWarrior like Fitz?

Grayson Carlyle had arrived the day after the surprise Marik attack, and she had witnessed the extermination of the Hammerstrike 'Mechs from a hiding place on a rocky, wooded bluff north of the ruins of Durandel. The Colonel was back! With him were the DropShips and her *Dutiful Daughter* still aboard the *Deimos*—and intact! Tracy had seized on that fact with an eagerness approaching passion. Now, perhaps, she would have her chance! She would go into combat against the Marik troops who had killed so many of her new friends. She would redeem herself in her own eyes! She would prove to them all that Tracy Kent was a MechWarrior, and that nothing could stand in her way . . .

Things certainly hadn't turned out as she planned. Rounded up with the other dazed, bruised, and battered survivors of Durandel, she had been told to help Lieutenant DeVillar take the ragged band north to the Valley of the Araga, there to await the return of the Legion. There was no time, she was told, to get her 'Mech from storage, power it up, tune its controls, and ready it for combat. The Legion had to march now because the DropShips were in danger.

The word had come the next day. The DropShips had been taken, and with them, her *Phoenix Hawk.*

Damn them! Damn them all! Damn Grayson Carlyle for taking her BattleMech from her, for giving it . . . *giving it* to the Marik bastards who had slaughtered the people of Durandel! And now she was left with nothing.

Tracy moaned softly at that thought, sinking to her knees at the river's edge until she was nearly hidden by the slender, grasslike vegetation. Her shoulders shook with sobs. Nothing! She had *nothing!* First she'd lost Fitz, then she'd been cut off from her family, and now the Legion, her new family, was disintegrating around her. With the *Daughter* gone, too, so was Tracy's hope of becoming a warrior that her brother would have admired.

Her parents and younger sister were still alive, of course, but they were nearly 130 parsecs away, on the other side of the Inner Sphere. Besides, she had long since severed any hope of help from that quarter far more completely than light year upon light year of distance ever could. She was *alone.*

"Oh, Fitz!" The cry burst from her, and she wept bitterly.

Outlaw!

The word had a special meaning for the man who went by the name of Hassan Ali Khaled. He'd known it with a searing inner pain that had remained with him all the way from Shaul Khala. His Saurimat brothers—his former brothers—knew the word as well. And now he was an outlaw again.

Though his comrades considered him a kind of emotionless machine, the truth was that Khaled concealed emotions that burned with the heat of a planetary core. It was the discipline of controlling his feelings that enabled him to behave as a coolly efficient warrior who never made an error in judgement. Inside that cool shell were locked both a fierce pride and a deep, burning shame. He had told no one in the Legion why he had left the Saurimat, and he never would.

Do I start running again? If I could . . . should I?

No! he told himself. *Honor compels me to stay, to show*

loyalty to this young man, my sworn commander. This time . . . this time I will follow the way of honor.

Delmar Clay leaned against a tree at the edge of a clearing, and gave a long sigh as he slowly slid down the trunk. Seated on the ground at the base of the tree, he wearily laid his head on his knees. *Was there any hope left?*

An unmistakable Scots burr interrupted his thoughts. "Eh, laddie, what do you make a' it all?"

Clay looked up to see the brawny Scotsman sit down on the log opposite, holding a steaming mug in each hand.

"Davis, my man, you're a lifesaver!" Displaying considerably more cheer than he felt, Clay reached for the proffered mug and cupped both hands around it, relishing its warmth.

"Dinnae be expecting it to be Terran standard brew, Delmar. No doubt it'll rot your pipes on the way down." McCall's grin was infectious.

"Right now, Davis, I don't think I give a damn about that." He gave a wry laugh. "I don't think I give a damn about much."

McCall looked at his fellow warrior and shook his head. "I dinnae like to tell a friend that he's lyin', Del, but ah somehow doubt you're ae' tellin' me all, just noo."

Clay took a sip of coffee to avoid answering and swore as he burned his tongue. *Dammit,* he thought. *Why does the man have to know me so well?* He glanced over at the red-bearded giant and shrank away from the pity in those eyes. He felt a hand on his shoulder and shuddered.

"It's Terri you're thinking about," the Caledonian said gently.

Struggling to control the emotions he had been holding in check, Clay nodded. "I'm . . . I'm worried sick about her, Dave." It was as though a damn had burst. Having admitted his fear, now he couldn't stop talking about. "Ever since we got here last night, I've been searching the whole encampment. I asked Gomez DeVillar, I asked Bill Burns, I asked Tracy Kent, I asked every one of the

Durandel survivors I could talk to. No one has seen her since . . .''

He took a few sips of the coffee, grimacing at the bitter taste.

''I never wanted to get so close to anyone before, Dave. Our kind of life is too . . . too uncertain. I sure fought hard against it when I first started to . . . to care for her.'' He swallowed hard, then continued. ''But . . . but just knowing we were going to have a place to call home—that made things different, you know?''

McCall nodded. ''I understand, laddie. You could feel sure that she was safe while you were off fightin'.''

A harsh, bitter laugh erupted from Clay's throat. ''Yeah. Safe. That was a joke. We were safer on Sirius V!''

''But Del, you dinnae ken for sairtain that . . .''

''But don't you see, Davis,'' Clay interrupted. ''Don't you see that that's the worst of it? That I *don't* know? She *could* still be alive. She could be hiding somewhere in these hills and be perfectly safe. But I . . . don't . . . *know*! And *that*'s what killing me.''

Clay stared at the ground in silence for some time.

''There's another thing, Dave.'' He spoke so low that McCall had to strain forward to hear him. ''She was . . . our . . . it's our son.'' Despite his anguish, he couldn't keep the pride out of his voice. ''Gomez said he looks just like me, poor kid.''

He thought back to the night on Graham IV when Terri had told him that she was pregnant. He'd been angry at first, not wanting to bring a child into the world. It was bad enough—after so many years as a loner—feeling responsible for Terri. But she'd been so obviously happy, so full of love for the new life inside her, that he couldn't help joining her in joyful anticipation.

''The wee bairn, he'd be . . .'' McCall rubbed his red beard in concentration. ''What, two months now?''

''Nine weeks yesterday.'' Clay looked sideways at his friend with a shadow of a twinkle in his eye. ''Guess what Gomez said she decided to name him?''

McCall shrugged and shook his head, then saw the twinkle. ''No, Delmar, she didn't. She wouldn't do that to me.''

"Yup." Clay grinned at the man's discomfiture. "Davis Carlyle Clay, after you and the Chief."

"Well, she got it half right, then. The Carlyle name's a grand one, for ae' it'll take some living up to." McCall looked deep into his comrade's eyes. "We may yet find her, laddie, and my young namesake as well. She's a spunky lass, that Terri. If she escaped the initial raid, she'll find a way to survive."

"I want to believe that, Davis. God, how I want to believe that."

18

Janice Taylor eased her weary body down onto the ground, closed her eyes, and sighed. It'd been a long, long day. Somehow the waiting times were the worst.

"Hey, Corp." A fresh-faced boy with carrot-colored hair sat down next to her. "You heard anything about the Old Man?"

To Corporal Taylor and the others of the Grey Death's infantry, whether Special Ops or ordinary PBIs, "the Old Man" referred to only one person—the steel-eyed, dagger-voiced Captain Ramage. Far less isolated from the ordinary soldier than was Colonel Carlyle, Ramage was one of them.

Janice opened her eyes. "Hi, Niklas."

"I . . . I saw you were coming from the direction of the med tent, and, well, I just . . ." He broke off and looked down at his feet.

"You're right, Nik, I just came from there. I'm afraid he's not looking good. Burke says his condition is stable right now, but he doesn't know how long can he last without proper treatment."

"And he's sure not going to get that here!" Niklas interrupted angrily. Like all those trained by the former Trellwanese, Private Niklas Chen felt a deep admiration for and a passionate loyalty to "the Old Man," who was, in fact, all of 32.

"What do *you* think we should do, Corporal Taylor? I mean. . . ." Chen jerked a thumb in the direction of a row of bubble tents at the edge of the clearing behind him. "Some of the guys are saying as how we ought to pack it in. You know, we could, well, become farmers or something?''

Janice looked at him sharply. "You mean, disband the Legion?''

The redhead gulped and nodded. "You see, I figure we could take the Cap'n in to . . . to . . . what's the name of that town? And maybe get him to a hospital, see? And . . . and they could patch him up?'' His words stumbled all over themselves in their eagerness. "Anyway, I bet I could be a good farmer. My dad was one. Did I ever tell you about him? He could never figure out why I wanted to be a soldier. Hell, right now I don't have the damnedest idea either! 'Scuse me, ma'am." He flushed.

Corporal Taylor smiled. After being in the infantry for over a year and a half, she was amused at this young private treating her the way he would probably treat his mother.

"Tell me about your father, Nik'' she said gently.

A soft, faraway look came into Private Chen's eyes. "I bet he was just the best da . . . er . . . best darned farmer there was in Norberia. That's where I grew up. It's on Winter, out by Trentham. You know where that is?''

Janice shook her head.

"Well, it's pretty far out, so I guess not too many folks'd know about it. But it's sort of like this place, you know? Kinda cold most of the time. But pretty.'' Chen absentmindedly picked up a stick and started scraping the ground with it. "I guess I didn't think too much of it back then. I kept angling to get offplanet, see new worlds, do new things. I sure do miss it now.''

He looked up at Janice with a shy smile. "But you were asking me about my dad,'' he said suddenly. "You know, the Cap'n kind of reminds me of him. I don't mean he looks like him or anything. It's just that, well, when the Old Man chews us out about something, I can sort of picture my dad, like when he chewed me and Gunter—Gunter's my brother—chewed me and Gunter out for sliding down the meergrass stacks or chasing the naf-fers until they got sick.'' He laughed, a high boyish chuckle. ''They sure did look funny!''

Then his face clouded over, and his eyes grew dark. ''Corporal, how're we going to get out of here?'' Janice could hear a thin edge of panic in his voice. ''First they blow up our . . . our home, and now they say we're *outlaws*! Why are they doing this, Corporal? What'd we do? We didn't do nothing!''

''Private Chen! Control yourself,'' Janice struggled to keep from showing the sympathy she felt. Chen was on the verge of hysteria, and he needed to hear authority in her voice. ''What do you think the Old Man would say if he could hear you right now? Do you think he'd be proud? We're soldiers, Private. Did anyone ever tell you that a soldier's life is easy? Well, if anyone did, then anyone is a malfing idiot!''

Chen swallowed hard as he worked to regain his composure. Janice softened her voice.

''We've just got to hold on, Nik, and make the Old Man proud of us.'' She smiled. ''Make your dad proud, too.''

Chen nodded, the corners of his mouth twitching in a weak attempt at a smile. ''Thanks, Corp.'' He got up slowly and brushed himself off. ''I reckon I'll go over to the med tent, see if Burke needs any errands run or anything.''

Janice watched as Niklas Chen walked away between the trees, and shook her head. *If this is what the burden of command is like, I don't ever want to be a sergeant!* She hadn't answered any of his questions, questions that burned just as fiercely inside her brain. How the hell *were* they going to get out of this one?

Would they have to disband? She didn't even want to think about that possibility, but she forced herself to it. She'd watched the Grey Death go from a handful of 'Mechs on her homeworld of Verthandi to a full-scale mercenary unit, almost a full battalion, though they all thought of it as ''the regiment.'' She hated to think of the Legion that Grayson . . . that all of them had been working for so hard to build being dismantled.

But did they really have any other option? With the

DropShips captured, they were marooned on the planet that should have been their home. They had lost so many people, and those remaining felt shattered by their losses. From what Grayson had said earlier, they didn't even have the option of surrender. As outlaws, they would not be treated according to the Conventions. In fact, they could be summarily executed. How long could they hold on out here, with food supplies dwindling, with so many wounded needing expert medical attention, even if the Marik forces didn't make any moves to root them out of their hiding place? And even if they *could* get offplanet by some miracle—recapture the DropShips or something—what good would that do them? The evil reputation that had been foisted on the Legion would precede them wherever they went. No one would hire them.

Corporal Janice Taylor clenched her fists in pain and anger as the thought struck her full force. *The Legion was as good as dead.*

Grayson Carlyle walked through the encampment, noticing the many small groups huddled together in earnest conversation. The usual light-hearted banter typical of a soldier's campgrounds was missing. It was always bad after a battle, when so many were wounded, but there was more than that here. This time, it was the whole Legion in danger, not just individuals.

Most people fell suddenly silent when Grayson walked past, but he had overheard enough to know that many were afraid the Legion would disband, and that many more thought it *should* disband.

Maybe they're right, he thought.

Grayson had been raised to be a soldier, a Mech-Warrior, and so he was used to fighting. He was also used to being able to see his enemy, too. How did one fight a rumor, a lie? The story had been running on the local news service, Atkins had said, and had probably been vised on a thousand other planets as well. Even if the Legion managed to get off Helm—and right now he had no idea how to accomplish that—what chance would they have of ever getting employment again? The lie would precede them; they'd be branded forever.

Yet, if they disbanded, then what? A few of his people might be able to obtain passage offworld, but most would be stuck here forever. Not that Helm was such a bad place. In its cold, severe way, it was actually a beautiful planet. But it wasn't home. Not anymore. And even assuming that Marik left them alone, what could ex-mercenaries do for a living?

Even if the Legion did disband, how many of them would be able to make it offworld . . . or strike bargains with new employers? More to the point, how many would escape the Marik nets? If Marik had gone to this much trouble to crush the regiment, they were not going to be content with the mere dissolution of the unit. From the look of things, they were bent on annhilation. Was it possible that the whole thing had been created just so they could seize an ancient Star League weapons cache?

Grayson stopped just then, letting his gaze travel around the encampment, watching as men and women cleaned their weapons, prepared food over low fires, worked or talked or simply rested in their tents.

There had to be something they could do!

The biggest question was whether there was enough of the regiment left to do it.

"We are *not* disbanding."

The men and women of the Gray Death Legion were drawn up in ranks under the trees along the Araga River. The Aragayan Mountains, tipped in gold and ice, crested to the north against a chill sky of blue crystal.

The Legion stood silent as Grayson addressed them from the open dorsal hatch of his *Marauder,* using the *Marauder*'s external speakers as amplifiers to carry his words throughout the crowd. All eyes, from those of Clay, Sharyl, Bear, and the other MechWarriors to those of the older children of the astech families whose homes had been torched in Durandel, were fixed on him; every member of the Legion stood waiting, expectant, and very still.

"I've heard all the arguments," Grayson went on. "We could disband, and go to ground. We could live here as farmers, as machinery techs and factory laborers, until the Marik troops go away. Maybe someday a few of us could hope to buy passage to Galatea, or some other mercenary hiring center, and join new regiments. But we're not going to go that way, people. And I'm going to tell you why.

"Disbanding the Legion is not the answer . . . not the answer that will help every man and woman in the unit. If we go to ground, maybe . . . *maybe* a few people will put together enough C-Bills in a few years to buy passage offworld . . . *but where will that leave everybody else*? Can *any* of you plan to work toward getting offworld, when you know that nine out of every ten . . . that ninety-nine out of every *hundred* of your comrades are going to be stranded here on Helm for the rest of their lives?

"And the Marik troops aren't going to be satisfied if they pick up just a handful of us. I would . . . I would . . ." He paused, momentarily unable to continue. He was no longer trying only to rally his people. These words came from the core of his own heart and will.

When Grayson found his voice again, it was quiet with certainty. "I would turn myself in to Colonel Langsdorf this afternoon if I thought that act would set the rest of you free. But they aren't going to leave it at that. They've convinced the Inner Sphere that we are murderers, renegades, bloody-handed monsters . . . and they won't be content until we are hunted down and exterminated.

"And even if we could get offworld, past the Marik troops, out of Marik space . . . could we live out there among the stars with the reputation they've branded on us. *We are the Legion.* Our name, our reputation . . . those are as much a part of who we are as our eyes and hands. If we lose that, as a unit or as individuals, we are *crippled*!"

He paused again, searching among the faces below him. From the altitude of a *Marauder's* cockpit, it was hard to read individual expressions. What he could see was Lori almost directly below and in front of him, and she was smiling. McCall was next to her, grinning, too. Sharyl looked grimly determined. Tracy Kent looked drained, pale and expressionless. Khaled appeared as motionless as a statute, and as cold. Clay's face was unreadable as ever, but his hands clenched and unclenched rhythmically at his sides.

"I am not ordering you to stay," Grayson continued. "Any of you, *any* of you who want to can go, with no restraint and no bad feelings. As long as Langsdorf has some kind of unified force to chase after, he'll probably leave you alone. Perhaps you can eventually pick up your lives offworld. Perhaps you can find a home for yourself, here. Helm is a good world . . . a place for a good life. If that is your choice, I sincerely wish you well.

"*But the regiment will not disband!* The *regiment* will prepare to break camp and move out. Tonight!" Grayson's gaze swept the ranks again. No one moved or spoke. The only sound was the rustle of wind among the leaves of the trees.

"I need volunteers for a special mission tonight, one that will give the rest of the unit a chance to get away. If you're interested, speak with your team leaders. The rest of you . . . you who are staying, pack your things and prepare to move at dark." He paused and swept the group with his eyes once more.

"That is all."

Normally, it would have been up to Ramage to take his cue from Grayson by smartly swinging about-face to give the order to dismiss. With Ramage still unconscious, Grayson did it himself.

"*Reg*'ment . . . dis . . . *MISS*!"

There was no movement among the ranks. Not a man or a woman moved in all those ranks upon ranks.

Somewhere, off to Grayson's left, a thin, reedy voice rose in song, trembling, though whether in fear or emotion, Grayson couldn't tell.

Home is the Regiment, across the sea of stars . . . Another voice, a deep bass picked up the tune.

On worlds hot, on worlds cold.
where Warriors tread afar.
Though place of birth and family,
though loved ones all be lost,
Home is the Regiment, across the sea of stars.

Then they were all singing it, the entire regiment together, the song buoyed by a surge of emotion that
swelled and rose, sweeping the Legion forward, together.

Home is the Regiment, though warriors travel far.
They cannot take our home from us,
our home is where we are!
With brothers under arms we share
a bond that draws us where
Home is the Regiment, across the sea of stars.
Home is the Regiment, the price of glory high.
We stand with brothers at our sides
to pay that price, and die!
The blood of comrades cries to us
long after glory's past:
"Home is the Regiment, across the sea of stars."
Home is the Regiment, in honor's proud refrain—
blood brothers forged together as
drawn steel quenched in flame!
They stand by us in blood and fire
and share with us the cry:
"Home is the regiment, our family and our own!"

Then the song was gone, and there was only the rustle
of wind among the leaves. The regiment remained for
another full minute, then gradually dissolved, its members breaking away toward the tents, alone or in small
groups.

But Grayson knew that the regiment remained.

═══ **19** ═══

The mobile headquarters rested just off the ferrocrete roadway ten kilometers south of Helmdown, its parabolic antenna trained on an invisible point in the sky above the southern horizon. During the days of the old Star League, mobile headquarters trucks had been built with small but highly efficient fusion power plants beneath their forward cabs. There were probably still a few fusion trucks scattered here and there across the worlds of Man. The majority were like this one, however, its fusion core removed centuries before to replace some light 'Mech's damaged power plant. In its place was a rattling, clanking monster of an aging, twin gas turbine-charged internal combustion diesel. Vent stacks crudely welded along the armor belched volumes of sooty black smoke as the driver gunned the engine. Above the cab, the low turret mounting a single Hesperus B3M medium laser slowly traversed the horizon.

At the rear of the long, heavy, eight-wheeled trailer, a door swung open between a pair of armed sentries standing watch, dropping a shaft of white light into the night and across the gravel on the ground. A lone man in a tattered jacket stepped down the ramp, returned the sentries' salute, stood for a moment staring out into the darkness, then began to walk forward past the trailer. The door closed behind him, chopping off the rectangular pool of light.

A *Thunderbolt,* brutal scars still marring its right arm and shoulder and the heavy laser mounted along the outer forearm armor plate, turned at the man's motion, then resumed its patrol of the area. An *Archer* stood guard on the far side of the trailer, silent and unmoving. The air stank with the foul miasma of the diesels, and the night trembled under their heavy rumble.

Grayson lay on his stomach in the dark, his black-painted face and hands and black Special Ops uniform invisible within the shadowy foliage from only a few meters away. A whisper of movement stirred next to him. Lori placed her mouth close to his ear, but her words were scarcely more than a subvocal murmured. "Only two 'Mechs. Six sentries. No patrols."

He nodded, letting her sense the motion in the dark. Their assault force had taken nearly three hours to creep into position at this spot, ringing the huge mobile headquarters van. They had taken special care to make sure that enemy PBIs—ground infantry—had not been deployed as roving patrols and to identify the locations of any sentries with absolute precision. Lori's report meant that the last scout had reported in. Six sentries, two 'Mechs, and no patrols, at least none out at the moment.

It was time to move.

Mobile headquarters vans were frequent fixtures with regiment-sized units, though some regimental commanders, such as Grayson himself, preferred to lead their regiments from the pilot's seat of a BattleMech. Certainly, a mobile headquarters gave a skilled tactical commander a valuable tool in conducting a battle or a campaign. Colonel Langsdorf, it seemed, commanded both ways: from his *Warhammer* when engaged in relatively small, localized actions, or from his headquarters truck when conducting a far-flung, widely dispersed operation. Langsdorf's search for the Gray Death Legion was becoming frantic in its intensity.

Using Davis McCall's D2j tracker patched into an amplifier salvaged in Helmfast's ruins, Gray Death communications Techs had picked up radar signals from a high-speed multiple source rapidly inbound toward Helm. A new, higher volume of radio traffic suggested that Langsdorf's superiors were even now decelerating for a landing on Helm. Perhaps they included Lord Garth himself. If that were true, Langsdorf's activity on the ground could mean a last-ditch attempt to capture or destroy the rest of the Gray Death before the Duke's arrival.

Grayson began to crawl forward, his passage leaving little trace as he crept toward the rear of the van. As per plan, he crawled to a point some twenty meters from the ramp, then froze in position. Around him, behind him, he sensed more than heard the sounds of other raiders moving into position.

Seconds dragged.

Any sudden motion would be detected by the motion sensors of the twin BattleMech guards. Any closer, and the infrared sensors on board the 'Mechs would pick up the raiders, despite the special clothing and paint that helped cut down their body-heat signatures on an IR screen. Scarcely daring to breathe, they waited in the darkness.

Grayson had explained that the raid was necessary, vital, in fact, if the Gray Death Legion was to have a chance of getting away. If they could somehow destroy this mobile headquarters that their scouts had spotted moving south from Helmdown that afternoon, the enemy's pursuit of the Legion could be hopelessly complicated. With luck, they might even catch Langsdorf here, though the Marik Colonel seemed to spend less time in the headquarters truck than he did in the field in his *Warhammer*. If they could catch him, though, they might be able to bargain with his second-in-command, to win time enough for a fair hearing, or a confrontation with their accusers.

There had been no shortage of volunteers after Grayson's speech from his *Marauder* at the Araga River. The problems did not begin until he had begun choosing who would go. He had ruled out any of the MechWarriors, insisting that they were not expendable and that this mission would very likely result in heavy casualties.

But Grayson nevertheless found himself facing a minor mutiny, one led, he suspected, by Lori Kalmar, but enthusiastically supported by David McCall and the other men and women of A Company. They told Grayson bluntly that if he were going to be considered expendable, then they *all* were expendable and they *all* were going on the raid. It had taken an hour of argument before Grayson would relent. He would lead the dangerous raid, but the warriors of A Company would join him, along with thirty troops chosen from among the ranks of Ramage's Special Ops force.

Now they waited near their target, motionless, soundless, listening to the raucous mixture of shouts and song that carried across the compound even above the rumble of the van's twin diesels.

The *Thunderbolt* seemed to stiffen, its upper torso rotating slightly as it zeroed in on the sound. The heavy 'Mech's left arm came up, zeroing in on the noise, the stubby twin barrels of its paired Voelkers 200 machine guns protruding slightly above the steel-armored wrist. Light spilled from a searchlight mounted above the *Thunderbolt*'s cockpit, glaring into the darkness. Grayson and his comrades were careful not to look at the light or what lay in its beam. They could not afford to ruin their night vision.

Grayson didn't need to look because he knew what the searchlight had caught. Three men wove their way arm-in-arm toward the van. They sang drunkenly at the tops of their voices, and clutched half-empty bottles in hands draped across each other's shoulders.

"Halt!" The amplified voice from the *Thunderbolt*'s pilot boomed into the darkness. "Halt where you are!"

"Hey . . . ya wanna drink?" came the reply. The voice was that of Sergeant Burns.

"Aye, ye grand, fell Laddie!" There was no mistaking *that* voice "Ye'll be wantin' jes' a wee li'le drop ae scotch tae warm ye, an' we'd be aye *honored* i' . . ."

"What the devil? Captain, you'd better come and . . ." The pilot's voice boomed puzzlement before he realized his external speakers were still on. He cut them off. Grayson moved his head slightly. With one eye tightly closed, he risked a look toward the spotlit men.

Sergeant Burns, Sergeant Clay, and MechWarrior Mccall stood side by side, blinking into the light. They were unarmed, were not even wearing knives, but they had on the slightly baggy fatigues common to technical personnel in the military forces of all the Successor States. They were the very image of a trio of astechs who had gone out to share a bottle and then wandered back to camp, roaring drunk and barely able to stand.

The door at the back of the van opened, spilling light onto the gravel once more. Two men stepped down onto the ramp, the light silhouetting them against the brilliance.

Grayson came to his feet, his TK assault rifle held high, his booted feet pounding against the gravel. Lori, Lieutenant Khaled, MechWarrior Bear, Alard King, and the others in the assault group followed close behind, flying toward the open door.

The two men in the light turned at the sound of running feet. One groped for a holstered weapon. The other gasped and jumped back into the van. The sentries on either side of the door brought their weapons down, but the man drawing his pistol on the ramp partly blocked their fire.

Grayson's TK thuttered as silenced, 3 mm caseless slivers spat from the heavy barrel. One sentry's face vanished in a trio of tiny, searing explosions as soft metal and high explosives impacted in flesh and bone. The man with the pistol shrieked and kicked back as explosive rounds chopped across his chest and arm. The second sentry plunged off the ramp, his submachine gun firing wildly into the night.

Lori's SMG stammered in her hands, picking up the second sentry and spinning him back against the trailer hull. In the same moment, the *Thunderbolt* swung ponderously around to face this new disturbance. A fractional instant later, a small, furiously burning projectile arced from the woods, exploding the air ten meters short of the *Thunderbolt*. The explosion grew, unfolding in liquid flame that washed across the *Thunderbolt*'s upper hull, Inferno rounds are designed to explode halfway to their target, spraying it with a concentrated fuel mixture that burns at a temperature sufficient to melt alloyed steel. The "drunken technicians—" Clay, McCall, and Burns— had unlocked arms and ran for cover the instant the inferno round shrieked over their heads.

The night on the north side of the trailer also lit up as a second inferno round bathed the *Archer* in living flame.

Between twin fountains of radiance, Grayson and the others raced up the ramp.

The door at the end of the van was closing; once closed, there would be no way to open it without heavy cutting tools or a 'Mech's laser, neither of which they had at the moment. More even than the Marik officers inside the headquarters van, time was their enemy now. Grayson ran faster. The door, swinging shut, fouled on one of the bodies at the top of the ramp, giving Grayson the instant he needed to plunge through into the lighted interior.

A sergeant rose from a communications console, a pistol already in his hand. Two communications technicians sat behind him, their faces frozen in fear. At the far end of the narrow, instrument-crowded room, a Marik officer was heading for the massive steel door that led to the forward chamber of the van.

Grayson's TK bucked and hissed again, spraying the room with death and destruction. The sergeant pitched back into a console, smoke and blood boiling from the pulsing hole in his chest. Grayson was past him before he fell, was past the technicians before they could even react. The Marik officer at the far end of the van was opening the steel-armored hatch there. If he got through and sealed it, the raiders would be isolated in this rear portion of the trailer. Yet, if there was a chance to capture the van's inner sanctum, this was it.

The Marik officer stepped through, the door closing behind him. Still running, Grayson swung his TK over his head and hurled it spinning end for end down the length of the room. It clattered across the low sill between the two chambers, and the heavy door smashed down on it. Plastic splintered and the massive sound suppressor barrel bent, but the door jammed open. An instant later, he was at the door, hauling back on it with his bare hands. King was beside him, adding his strength to the effort. The door cleared the smashed rifle, then swung open.

Gunfire barked from the inner chamber. Lori's submachine gun fired past King and Grayson, shell casings from her weapon ringing against consoles and across the waffle-molded steel deck. Then Bear pushed past her, his own submachine gun looking like a toy in one of his massive hands.

"Gray!" Grayson had not heard such shock and surprise in Lori's voice before. He squeezed past the half-open door and joined Lori and Bear inside the inner room.

It was a smaller room than the rear part of the headquarters, with fewer instruments. A planning and conference table dominated one end. On three bulkheads, there were wall-sized, fully-color, satellite-projection computer displays showing the entire area from north of the Aragayan Mountains to the Vermillion Plains beyond the Nagayan Mountains in the south, and from the Grodon Sea to the west to the Dead Sea Flats to the east. Computer terminals glowed, their screens crowded with words. A Marik Lieutenant lay sprawled on the floor, cut down by Lori's gunfire.

Lori stood there above the body now, her gun leveled on a second officer cowering against the far wall of the room. Grayson knew from the uniform that this was the man he had first seen outside, and whom he had chased back through the trailer. His eyes widened in shocked recognition.

"Graff!"

"Don't . . . kill me! Carlyle! Don't kill me! I'm valuable to you!"

Bear reached one massive first forward and easily plucked Graff from the deck as though he were a bundle of rags.

"Don't hurt him," Grayson said. "Bring him!"

King and Khaled were in the outer room with a half-dozen of Ramage's Special Ops people. Grayson recognized Janice Taylor under layers of camouflage paint. Lieutenant DeVillar and a Legion infantry-man came through the door, each lugging three canvas satchels. Each satchel held ten kilos of plastic explosives and a set of fulminate of mercury detonators.

Grayson gestured at the two technicians who still sat in their chairs, their fingers carefully interlaced on the tops of their heads. "You Techs," Grayson said. "Out!

If you stop running any time in the next five minutes,
you're dead!'' The two squeezed past the Legion troops,
their hands still above their heads. Grayson heard their
booted feet break into a run as soon as they touched the
metal ramp outside.

''O.K. Everybody out except the explosives people!
Bear! You take Graff! Mind the 'Mechs outside!''

DeVillar was already placing each satchel of explosives where it would do the most good, and running long
wires clipped to the fuses from bag to bag. The man had
been a mining engineer long before becoming the commander of the Gray Death's B Company, and professed
to know something about explosives. This, Grayson had
told him, was his chance to prove it.

A long burst of machine gun fire sounded distantly
from outside, followed by the keening hiss of 'Mech laser fire. The inferno rounds fired at the two 'Mechs would
not be enough to disable them. The hope was that the
clinging, liquid fire would distract the pilots for the few
moments that Grayson's raiders needed to complete their
mission. Precious seconds had been lost already, chasing
and catching Graff. But if they could get *him* back to
camp, it would be worth it!

The hollow thunk of bullets striking armor rang
through the van. Within seconds, the two 'Mechs would
have their fires under control, and the Legion people firing infernos at them would be out of ammo. Marik infantry must be in the area already. They had to go *now*!

Grayson hurried to the van's forward room. Time to
go or not, something was nagging him about the map
display he had seen there. He studied the maps for several long seconds. The Legion had no up-to-date satellite
scans of the area, had nothing, in fact, but old hardcopy
maps of the land south of Durandel to the Nagayan
Mountains. His hope was to force-march the Legion by
night, starting the following night, travelling across the
Dead Sea Flats and reaching the Nagayan Mountains before sun-up. In the Nagayans, they might be able to elude
their pursuers a while longer, for the land there was broken with wild, forested stretches, isolated glacial valleys,
and rugged passes. If they could confound their pursuers

by destroying this mobile headquarters, then make the trip in a single night, they just might be able to buy some time.

A current satellite scan, complete with computer enhancement, would help.

Reaching a decision, Grayson sat down at one of the terminals. He was skilled with computers ever since his days as a teenaged apprentice with his father's mercenary company. The computer was an Omnistar 4000, a standard-military issue type that took both keyboard and voice input. He had worked with them often before, and so he sat down and rapidly began to type.

"Colonel!" DeVillar's voice came from the next room. "Colonel! She's ready to blow!"

"Don't light her off yet," Grayson said, still typing furiously.

The Lieutenant stuck his head through the inner door. "Colonel, we've got to go *now*!"

Grayson punched a final key, then waited. The map projections on the wall screens winked off, plunging the room into complete darkness except for the glow from the terminal displays. A slotted box nearby bleeped, and a narrow memory clip rose from the slot with a slight whir.

"Right!" Grayson grabbed the clip and turned to face DeVillar. "Let's go!"

Grayson left the van first. DeVillar pulled the igniter ring on one of the satchels, and followed.

Outside the *Thunderbolt* burned furiously against the night. Gunfire lanced among the trees, and here and there, the still, bloodied forms of dead men sprawled in the wierdly flickering light of the flames. The *Archer* had doused the fires that had fallen on it, and was now sweeping the woods with laser fire, the beams blue-white and sun-brilliant in the darkness. Perhaps its pilot did not realize that Legion troopers had broken into the headquarters van, for the 'Mech's back was to the van and its pilot was directing his fire toward the woods to the north, in the direction from which the inferno rounds had come.

The *Thunderbolt* still burned, the fire roaring across its already damaged right arm and shoulder, flaring hotter and brighter as each move force-fed the flaming fuel with more oxygen. In the woods to the south, Legion troops fired with machine guns and small arms, plinking useless rounds against that thick-armored hide in an effort to distract its attention away from the trailer close beside it.

It almost worked. The gunfire from the woods ceased when Grayson and DeVillar burst from the rear of the van. The *Thunderbolt* thrashed around to its left, then paused as its pilot caught sight of two men racing through the half-light away from the headquarters. From the corner of his eye, Grayson caught a glimpse of the left arm coming up, caught sight of those twin barrels embedded in the armor above the battle machine's wrist.

Then the *Thunderbolt*'s paired machine guns were firing, licking the air around them with tracers that danced and wavered into the woods ahead. Grayson and DeVillar threw themselves face down as the *Thunderbolt* descended on them from behind. Grayson rolled over, looking up at death. The *Thunderbolt*'s fire was almost out now, and there were no more inferno rounds coming in. Bullets whanged and keened off the armor from the south as soldiers tried futilely to turn the machine. It took another step, towering into the night, machine guns levelling for a second, final burst.

20

Then the night exploded with a brilliance far exceeding that of a burning BattleMech. Flame mounted into the sky, consuming the mobile headquarters. DeVillar and Grayson rolled face-down, covering their heads. A hurtling wall of flame belched from the open door like the blast from a flame thrower, searing the night just above their heads. A chain of explosions ate its way through the van as DeVillar's munitions erupted in a succession almost too quick to follow. Then the reserve of diesel fuel sealed in a tank underneath the cab blew off with the force of a high-explosive bomb.

The *Thunderbolt,* standing with its back only meters from the explosion, was thrown to the ground like a toy. The fact that that toy weighed sixty-five tons made the ground tremble, and the crash competed with the roar of the exploding van. One outflung metal arm whooshed through the air as the BattleMech toppled forward, its fist gouging into the soft ground three meters from Grayson's feet. Grayson and DeVillar were on their feet again in an instant, racing for the woods.

By the time the *Thunderbolt* pilot regained his senses enough to bring his machine to its feet, the two men had rejoined their unit in the woods, and the Gray Death assault force was already slipping away to a rendezvous many kilometers to the east.

Once the immediate danger was past, Graff changed his piteous air for defiance. Perhaps the fact that his captors had bound and gagged him instead of killing him outright had made him bolder. While the assault team

213

was racing back to their new encampment in the hills above the Dead Sea Flats, southwest of Durandel, they had kept Graff under close guard. They had him now inside the large bubble tent Grayson had been using as a headquarters, tied to a chair in the middle of the floor.

Grayson could see calculation glitter in the man's eyes, and knew precisely what he was thinking: *If the commander of the Gray Death Legion is keeping me alive, it's for a good reason . . . probably his own survival! He won't dare hurt me if he thinks he can use me to save his own skin!*

Graff's words confirmed Grayson's thought. "So, what makes you think I'll tell you one damned thing? You're history . . . all of you. You must know by now that the Duke of Irian is almost here. He'll arrive in another day, and then your pathetic force will be hunted down and crushed!" Suddenly, his tone turned conspiratorial. "Of course, if you want to make a deal, maybe I can help you! There's still time, you know, before the Duke gets here with his army! I can talk to Langsdorf, you know."

Grayson felt sick as he listened to the man's attempts at manipulation. McCall stood behind Graff, his arms folded, his normally smiling features twisted into a frown. Clay paced by the door, darkness etching his features. Khaled sat on a stool in a far corner, cool and unexpressive as ever. Lori sat behind the table they had set up nearby, and rubbed at her eyes.

"Are we going to step on this worm, Gray . . . or what?"

"I vote for 'Or what,' " Clay said. "A slow, lingering 'or what.' "

"Aye." McCall added. "Colonel. Just gi' me thirty wee minutes wi' tha' laddie, an' . . ."

"Quiet, all of you," Grayson said. He leaned forward until his gray eyes were level with Graff's brown ones. "Graff, to tell you the truth, I don't think you could buy me a ride into town, much less any kind of deal." He reached forward and flicked one of Graff's collar rank tabs. "What kind of pull does a Captain have over a Colonel?"

"More than you'd think, Colonel," Graff twisted against

the ropes that held him, then managed a shrug. "There are things in this that even the Duke doesn't know . . . As for Langsdorf, he doesn't know a damned thing!"

"And you do, I suppose?"

The man smiled nervously. "Like I said, Colonel. I'm valuable to you. Play things right, and you might even get off this dirtball alive!"

Grayson allowed scorn to color his voice. "Well! Gentlemen . . . and Lori! It seems we have captured ourselves someone important! The mastermind of the whole operation!"

"Laugh all you want! Tomorrow afternoon you'll be laughing at Duke Irian's assault BattleMechs!"

Grayson considered the bound man. He was a mass of contradictions. Boastful, yet secretive. Unwilling to help Grayson, yet desperate to prove that he could be valuable. Above all, there seemed to be the driving need to appear important, a powerful figure, someone his enemies would have to contend with.

It was this last motivation that Grayson sought to use against the man now, in combination with Graff's own fear.

"Gray . . ." Lori began, but Grayson silenced her with a wave of his hand.

"I'd hoped we would be able to capture Colonel Langsdorf," he said, despite the fact that the object of the attack had been to destroy the mobile headquarters, with Langsdorf's death or capture a minor goal. "You know, Lori, I think we missed the one we really wanted. That man who came out just before we attacked . . ." He turned on Graff. "That was Langsdorf, wasn't it, Graff? The man in the old leather jacket, with no rank insignia?"

Graff nodded slowly. "He was there. He left a few minutes before you came in. He doesn't care much for the protocol of rank."

"You know, I think we could have talked with him. It's a shame that all we came up with was . . . this."

Graff snorted. "You don't know what you're saying."

"No? You're honestly claiming a Captain knows more about the mission than the Colonel in command of the whole planetary expeditionary force? Come off it, Graff! You're nothing . . . nothing! And you're worth less than that to me.''

McCall came to stand next to Grayson, where Graff could see his face. He was smiling warmly through his beard. ''Shall ah takit tha' wee beastie oot for a lit'le walk, Colonel sair? A one-way walk?''

Grayson sighed. ''No, Davis. He's not worth it.''

''We're not taking him with us!'' Lori said.

Grayson shook his head. ''No.'' He gave a calculated pause as he looked at the trembling quisling. ''No, I think we'll let him go.''

''What?'' Lori was first to voice the outrage all of them shared.

''You can't do that, Colonel!'' Clay said.

Grayson started to speak, but he was interrupted by Hassan Khaled, who had not moved or spoken during the entire interrogation. When he spoke now, it was with the measured, emotionless tones of Death itself. ''I think the Colonel has made an excellent decision,'' he said. ''Somehow, sir, I did not expect you to be so . . . inventive.''

''Thank you, Khaled—I think. Davis, cut the man loose.''

Davis hesitated, then caught the look in Grayson's eye. He drew his combat knife from its boot scabbard and went to the back of Graff's chair.

''What . . . are you doing?'' Graff said as he stood, rubbing his wrists. His glance shifted from face to face around the tent, and the uncertainty in his eyes was rapidly becoming sheer terror.

''You are free to go.'' Grayson said. ''You know nothing we need to know. We can't afford to take you along, not when our food is short, and we need every man free to fight. And despite the stories that are being circulated about me, I am not a bloodthirsty killer. You will not be executed.'' Grayson allowed himself to smile, though the effort turned his stomach. ''At least . . . *I* will not be your executioner.''

Graff's eyes widened until the whites stood completely revealed around the brown of his irises. ''You . . . you want me to go out there; in the middle of this camp? But if I'm seen . . .''

Grayson shrugged. "You might not be seen. At least, not right away."

"I wonder how far he'll get," said Khaled, measuring Graff through narrowed eyes.

"Wait . . . Carlyle! You can't do this! If your people catch me, they'll . . . No! Wait! You can't do this! It's not human! You know what a mob can do . . ."

"Do I? Well, maybe I do. I've been accused of murdering twelve million defenseless civilians. For a man like that, a little mob violence is nothing. Get out of my sight! We'll let your former comrades-at-arms, the ones you betrayed, decide your fate."

"No!"

"There are a lot of people who liked Francine Roget a lot," he said thoughtfully. "And Sylvia Trevor. They were good people, and they died because of you. And there were the DropShips . . ."

"Wait! You don't understand!" Graff was pleading openly now. "You can't send me out there! They'll tear me apart."

"Slowly," Khaled added. The single, cold, drawn-out word made Graff begin to shudder uncontrollably.

"You don't understand," he said again. "It's true that I'm only a Captain in the Marik House Guard, but I'm also . . . much more!"

"You haven't told me anything I care to hear, Graff. Out."

"No! ComStar! I'm ComStar!"

The word caught Grayson totally and completely by surprise. He had not been sure what revelation he sought to break from Graff, but of all possible revelations or confessions, he had not expected *that* one.

Grayson stared hard into Graff's eyes. The man was purely, starkly, and openly terrified. There was no sham to his trembling.

Somehow, Grayson made himself dissemble. He smiled. He let the smile grow into a chuckle, and then into a laugh. "You? A ComStar agent?"

Clay smiled. "Maybe he wants to send a message just now, eh, Colonel?"

"Look, Colonel, you've got to listen to me!" The words came tumbling forth now. "I was approached months ago by someone . . . someone very high up in ComStar! His name is Rachan, and he's a Precentor. A high-level one! Do you know what that means? He's a high-ranking administrator within the ComStar organization! They say he's a confidant of the Primus himself, on Terra! It was Rachan's idea to disgrace you . . . to disgrace the Gray Death Legion!"

"Why?" Grayson's lips formed a hard, tight line. "Why would ComStar want to do that?" He was genuinely baffled.

"Yeah, what the hell does ComStar have to do with it?" Clay asked. "That bunch of superstitious cowl heads and their . . ."

"Gently, Del, gently. Let's not insult the gentleman. Tell us, Graff, what interest does ComStar have in us? ComStar's neutrality in inter-House disputes is proverbial."

Graff looked from face to face, bracing himself. All of the MechWarriors had drawn closer, ringing Graff in.

"It's . . . it's because there's a storehouse . . . an old, old Star League storehouse, here on Helm someplace."

"A storehouse," Lori said. "Of weapons?"

"Weapons," Graff nodded. "And BattleMechs. And spare parts. Ammunition. Heavy equipment. Repair gantries. A whole Star League naval base storehouse, and it's someplace near Freeport."

"Someplace," Grayson said. "In other words, you don't know where it is.

Graff shook his head. "It's like this. There are records, old, old records from Star League days that talk about the naval depot here. It was actually located in Freeport."

Grayson nodded. "I've heard. And chances are, it's still someplace close by. There was no way for the local garrison commander to ship so large a cache offworld."

"You've heard?" It was Graff's turn to look surprised. He seemed to fold back into himself, his sudden animation failing. "Well Colonel, your military intelligence is better than I gave it credit for."

"Is that all you can tell us? That Marik wants to find the League storehouse?"

"It's not just House Marik. *That's* what I'm trying to tell you! It's ComStar!"

"So what's ComStar's interest?" Lori asked.

Graff shrugged. "ComStar has access to old records . . . including Minoru Kurita's reports on the Helm raid."

"The reports to the Council back on Luthien."

Graff nodded. "The Council on Luthien could accept his report at face value, for they weren't actually *here* to put things together, you see. But when ComStar researchers read those reports, they had plenty of time to wonder. That cache must have been *huge!* Where could so many BattleMechs, so much war materiel, be hidden? ComStar maintains armies too, you know, to defend its own interests. Such a large, secret installation . . . that is of enormous interest to ComStar.'

"Hmm." Grayson studied Graff intently. "All very interesting. But none of it explains why this Precentor you mentioned wants to disgrace my regiment."

Graff hesitated until McCall said, "Come, laddie, speak up, or will ye be takin' tha' walk we mentioned a wee bit ago?"

"It was Rachan's idea . . ."

"So you said."

"You, Colonel . . . you and your people, were in the way."

"Of what?"

"Of ComStar. This planet, Helm, is divided into administrative districts. Your contract with Janos Marik specified that the landhold of Durandel would be yours in exchange for your service to Marik."

Grayson nodded. "Yes."

"As Lord of Helmfast, you are, in effect, the governor of the whole stretch of territory from the Araga Mountains southwest to the sea. Governor, in fact, of everything on this part of the continent, except Helmdown itself, which is a special reserve of the Duchy of Stewart, under the planetary title.''

"I am familiar with the legal aspects, Graff.''

Graff shrugged. "Precentor Rachan was bringing his plan along. Durandel was to have been given to Garth for . . . oh . . . services to the Commonwealth. Helmfast had been vacant for some years, its last landholder gone . . . disgraced. Perhaps that was ComStar's doing, too. I don't know. Rachan had been maneuvering for a long time to get the legal title to Helmfast.''

"Which would give him legal title to the lost cache.''

"Mostly it was a matter of timing. Rachan figured that it might take years, perhaps decades, to find the lost cache. It has to be within a few tens of kilometers of the ruins of Freeport—*has* to be—but he didn't expect the search to be easy. It could be anywhere in an expanse of thousands of square kilometers. One guess is that it's in the Dead Sea Flats. That vast, empty depression was filled with water until quite recently. It's possible that the mining efforts to create a hidden chamber for storing the weapons resulted in the sea's draining into cracks in the bedrock. Another possibility is that the cache is still buried under Freeport, but deep under meters of ferrocrete and steel, where it can't be found. It would take years of drilling and probing just to check all the possibilities in just that one location. And there were other cities in the area. You see what a task it is? Rachan expected the search to take years.''

"And when he found it,'' Clay said, "He'd need a small fleet to move it. That meant the cooperation—and the silence—of the Lord of Helmfast.''

"He figured I wouldn't be cooperative.''

Graff smiled wanly. "You were studied quite closely, Colonel, for some time before the decision was made to disgrace you. It was determined that your personality was not . . . suitable to their purposes. Lord Garth met their criteria perfectly.''

Lori tossed her head. "Well, Garth is a lot fatter than Grayson . . .''

"He is also more malleable . . . and he has a certain handle that allows others to manipulate him.''

"Which is?"

"He is greedy."

"Ah."

"In any case, Helm was to have been given to Garth, not you. But in order to get you and your Legion out of Durandel . . ."

Grayson closed his eyes. "The . . . the people on Sirius V . . . Was that for real? Or is it just a story that's been circulated?"

"Oh, it's quite real. Lord Garth was in charge of *that* aspect of the operation." As Graff saw the expression hardening on Grayson's face, he grew more agitated. "That wasn't me! I . . . I told you! I was a Captain in the Guard! Rachan approached me almost a year ago. He told me about the cache and asked me if I would help him. I was . . . flattered. ComStar Precentors rarely have dealings with mere Guard Captains!"

"And what, exactly, did he want you to do?"

"I was to join your regiment as a MechWarrior. The contract assigning the Helm landhold to you and your regiment had not been signed at that point, but Janos Marik and his staff had been discussing it. Rachan didn't want that to happen. But if it did, he wanted someone already in your regiment, someone who could keep him informed of your movements, your plans."

"A bloody spy," Clay began. "As well as a traitor."

"I'm no traitor! I was in the service of ComStar . . . for the good of humanity."

"Ah, it's the good of humanity now!" Grayson said. He was suddenly angry. "Millions of people slaughtered . . . and it's for the good of humanity!"

"That wasn't me . . ."

"Wasn't it? I wonder . . . I happen to remember that last day on Sirius V. You had the duty, on patrol in your *Assassin.*"

"Well . . . yes . . ."

"And you swapped around with Vandergriff," Lori said, her eyes widening. "There was some comment about it, I recall . . . that you would prefer standing sentry-go to enjoying the fleshpots of Tiantan."

"Why did you *want* to stand duty that night?"

Graff compressed his lips and shook his head. "I didn't blow up that dome."

"No, but two sentries were found dead, killed at close range by laser fire and vibroblade. Do you remember?" Lori shook her head slowly, as if she couldn't quite believe what she was saying. "We questioned you about it because it happened on your watch, but we assumed it was the work of Liao soldiers who didn't want to turn in their arms. But there was someone else there that night, wasn't there? Someone who had to steal a pair of hovercraft in order to move in and . . . and what, Graff? Plant explosive charges on the domes? Charges that could be detonated once we were away, but before most locals would realize that we had gone . . . to make it look like *we* had done the deed?"

Grayson said. "They had to get past you, didn't they?"

Graff nodded, his expression one of lost misery.

"And you stand there and claim you didn't kill those people? The responsibility was yours!" Grayson turned from him in disgust. "Del! Get him out of my sight!"

"No!" Graff cried. "You promised . . ."

Lock him up in the stores tent, Del."

"Yessir. C'mon, you."

As Clay took Graff by the collar and hustled him from the tent, Lori stood up and walked around the table to Grayson.

"It still doesn't help us, does it, Gray? I mean . . . knowing who and what we're up against. I don't see any answers."

"I wonder . . ." Grayson said absently.

"It's late," she said. "Or early, rather. Daylight in another couple of hours. Why don't we get some sleep."

Grayson shook his head. He had pulled a small, black computer clip from his jacket pocket and was looking at it thoughtfully. "You all go ahead. Get some sleep."

"What's that?"

"Something I picked up tonight. You go on," he told her. "I've got some studying to do."

21

Lori found Grayson four hours later, after two infantry-men on perimeter guard told her that he had checked out a hovercraft and was last been seen heading down the road toward Durandel. She had taken a skimmer herself and followed.

When she found him, Grayson was sitting inside the ruin of the briefing room in Helmfast. The ceiling was open to the sky, and shafts of early morning sunlight sliced through the gaps in roof and wall, brilliant in the mist of plaster dust that Grayson's activity had stirred up during the night.

He had maneuvered the hovercraft inside the room through the hole in the south wall. A pair of power cables snaked their way from the idling generators in the rear of the powerful little vehicle across the rubble-covered tiles. Then he had connected a pair of large computer display screens to a terminal and to the impromptu power supply aboard the skimmer. As Lori watched, it seemed that Grayson was intent on bringing up the magnification on the orbital maps he had displayed on the computer screens. He would study one or another of the maps closely, then tap out new commands on the keyboard in front of him. While he typed, the display on one of the screens would shift, change, or suddenly expand as he increased the magnification factor.

A charred piece of wood fell with a clatter when Lori brushed against it, and Grayson spun suddenly, obviously startled. His eyes were sunken and shadowed by exhaus-tion and had a wild look about them.

"Lori! What are you doing here?"

"I might ask the same question. Grayson, what do you think you're doing?"

He gave her a thin, tight-lipped smile. "Learning some things, for one thing. Graff told us more than he knew."

"He was holding something back from us?"

"Oh, no. I think he was scared enough that he was telling us everything he knew. No, I meant that literally. He told us more than he, personally, knew about."

"How did he do that?"

Grayson pointed to one of the maps displays.

"Remember how the map works?" She nodded, but he continued talking anyway. His words were slurred to the point where, at first, she thought he had been drinking. Then she realized that he must be at the point of utter and complete exhaustion. "We can key in the desired magnification at the terminal and study any part of the terrain we want. We can increase the magnification a tenfold step at a time and zoom in to where we can resolve objects about a meter across."

"Grayson . . . why don't you come and get some sleep?"

He continued as though he hadn't heard her. "This"— he indicated the left-hand screen—" is the map that was here in Helmfast . . . remember?

She nodded.

"It's out of date, based on data recorded . . . oh . . . three centuries ago. Things have changed a bit since then. For one thing, the Dead Sea wasn't dead." He used a screen pointer to indicate the pale green body of water south of Durandel, running hundreds of kilometers almost to where the Nagayan Mountains hooked to the east.

"It's shallow," Lori said. The difference between the two bodies of water on the photographs was startling. The West Equatorial Sea was mostly a deep, royal blue, except for the light-green or green-blue streaks where sandbars rose near the surface along the coastland or surrounding islands.

"Calculating the Equatorial Sea at sea level, what we call the Dead Sea Flats, and what they called the Yehudan Sea 300 years ago, lies at almost 200 meters above sea level.'' Grayson slipped the pointer to a gray patch on the Yehudan Sea's western shore. ''That is Freeport, before Minoru Kurita came calling. And yes, I've looked for the original Star League weapons complex. I think it must be inside a number of monstrous warehouses north of the city, but I can't tell for certain. Obviously, the cache would have been hidden from orbital observation.''

''Obviously.''

''Right here''—the pointer moved again—''is a river. The Vermillion River.''

''It's red.''

''Pretty much. There's some kind of pollutant, or maybe algae or some other plantlife that grew very thickly along here.'' He indicated the coastline near Freeport. ''It concentrated in the river enough that they named it the Vermillion.

''Now, Vermillion empties out of the Yehudan Sea at the site of Freeport. It flows this way, toward the west, and vanishes . . . here.''

''Vanishes?''

''Goes underground. Watch.'' He typed in new commands. In response, the river flashed into extreme magnification, so that the view looked like a photograph taken from an aircraft only a few hundred meters up. The river wound across a level plain crisscrossed by the dark ribbons of ferrocrete highways. As it approached the mountains, it gradually sank into a deepening valley, until it took a sudden twist and vanished under a massive boulder.

''Rivers don't generally flow toward the mountains, Lori,'' he said. ''But this is a special case. The Yehudan Sea is quite a bit higher than the West Equatorial sea over there. The mountains between them are raw and new, the result of mountain-building along the border between two tectonic plates, I imagine. As the plates collide, they're in the process of punching up these mountains. That means the area is not entirely stable. There must be earthquakes here from time to time, really big ones.''

''Interesting. But so what?''

Grayson returned the left-hand view to the first magnification. ''Now. Look over here.'' He indicated the right-hand map display. It showed the same view as the first, but changed. The area of the Yehudan Sea was cast in ochers, grays, and the stark white swirls and splotches of mineral incrustations.

''This is the copy of the map I took from the mobile headquarters van last night. The program notes show that it was made by a DropShip—the *Assagai*—in orbit over Helm five days ago.''

''Before we got here.''

''Right.'' Grayson used the screen pointer again. ''Here's Freeport . . . in ruins, of course, courtesy of Minoru Kurita. Up here is Durandel . . . not in ruins yet.'' His voice sounded brittle. Lori knew what he was thinking: that aerial view of Durandel was of the village before the Marik forces had come.

He leaned back in the chair, rubbing his long, bony fingers down across his eyes and face. He sat there for so long, head thrown back, eyes closed, that Lori thought he might have fallen asleep while talking her. ''I came here last night,'' he said at last. ''This morning, rather . . . because what Graff said was nagging at me. We'd heard about the Star League cache from King, of course. I confess I was curious about its never having been found . . . but I had other things on my mind at the time, and I just didn't think about it long enough. Then Graff said that ComStar had that same information, and was . . . interested.''

''Interested enough to try to turn us out in disgrace.''

''Damn it, Lori . . . interested enough to coldly arrange the murder of millions of people, just to establish a legal pretext! God, Lori . . . do your realize what that means? ComStar has billed itself all this time as the perfect neutral, above any of the petty politics and squabblings between the major houses! Mercenaries out of every Successor State use ComStar's services as broker and banker in arranging contracts! They control the communications services on every world in their net from Apollo to the Pleiades! Now they callously condone—arrange!—the murder of ten or twelve million civilians . . . *to establish a legal pretext?*''

Lori had trouble finding her voice. She had not followed the reasoning behind Graff's words as far as Grayson had, and the meaning was only now dawning in her. "They . . . ComStar . . . must want Helm very badly . . ."

Grayson looked at her. The dark circles under his eyes were alarming. "It makes me wonder how many other political pies they've had their fingers in during the last few centuries. I have this . . . this picture . . . of ComStar as the sixth Great House, unseen, invisible, but working behind the scenes, manipulating the other Houses toward its own ends."

"What ends?"

"God, but I wish I knew. Or maybe I don't! If they can order the deaths of twelve million innocent people . . ."

Lori stepped across to a point behind Grayson's chair and circled his neck with her arms. He leaned his head back against her breasts, his eyes closed.

"It's possible," he said at last, "that this Rachan that Graff kept talking about is operating outside of ComStar authority."

"A renegade? An outlaw?"

"Something like that. But it's also possible we've stumbled across something much larger than the scheming of one man."

Lori heard the certainty in Grayson's voice, and knew he had already arrived at a decision. "What are you going to do?" she asked.

"The first thing we have to do is guarantee the security of the regiment. But after that . . . I'm beginning to think we might be able to upset Rachan's . . . or ComStar's . . . plans."

She caught the excitement in his voice. He swiveled the chair around so that he could face her. There was a fire behind those cool, gray eyes that she had never seen in all the time she had known him.

"Lori! I think I know where the Star League cache *is!*"

She looked into his eyes for a long moment. Their feverishness worried her. *Is he grasping at any hope?* she thought. *He's desperate to save the Legion . . . and so*

227

tired! He can't so quickly have found what others have been seeking for so long!

It was impossible that he, working for a few hours, and without sleep, should solve a puzzle that had apparently been occupying ComStar scholars for years.

"Gray . . ."

His exhaustion made him vulnerable. She could clearly read the disappointment in his face.

"You don't believe me, do you?"

"Gray, you're wiped out . . . exhausted."

And then she realized he was laughing at her.

"Think I've punched out, do you? Well, so did I, when I first saw it. Look."

He swung his chair back to face the terminal and began pecking at the keyboard. Both map displays shifted slightly, expanding to show the broad sweep of plain from the Nagayan Mountains to the shores of the Yehudan Sea. On the left, the Yehudan Sea was green and blue-green, the gray sprawl of the city on its shore an obviously live and growing entity. The faintly red-tinged Vermillion curled across the landscape toward the mountains. The thin, black streaks of ferrocrete roads and skimmer pathways crisscrossed the land.

On the right, the Yehudan was dry and mineral-encrusted. The city was still an untidy grey sprawl, but it had been rearranged, with a distinctly circular pattern where Kurita's weapons had vaporized the central area and reduced everything beyond the crater to rubble. Sections of roads were still visible, but broken by stretches where dirt had covered the pavement and grass had covered the dirt. The river was visible as a faint ocher track winding west from the ruined city, as dry and empty as the dead sea bottom itself.

"Now . . . see the difference?"

She studied the maps, her eyes shifting from one to the other and back again. "The Yehudan Sea is gone."

"Of course. What else?"

"Freeport is in ruins."

"What else?"

Lori started to say she was too tired to play guessing games, but the words froze in her mouth. "The river," she managed at last. "The river east of the mountains is dried up."

"Exactly."

She stepped over next to Grayson, leaning forward to study the map more closely. "When Freeport was nuked, perhaps the river was blocked off."

"Possibly. There is evidence here of some sort of massive construction across the mouth of the river right on Freeport's waterfront, but the blast destroyed whatever it was. But look. The Vermillion River used to flow out of the Yehudan Sea, here." He traced the course with a display pointer on the screen. "The Yehudan is quite a distance above sea level, up here on the North Highland Plains. It flowed toward the Nagayan Mountains and vanished underground, probably into a subterranean cave system. It re-emerges here, on the western face of the mountains and drops—here—nearly 2500 meters to the West Equatorial Sea.

"What first caught my eye was that if the sea had dried up, then the river would dry up, too." He shifted his pointer to the right-hand map, which showed the area as it was in the present.

"But right here, we see the Vermillion emerging from underground on the west wide of the mountains. It's not nearly as big as it used to be. You can see that it's only a trickle compared to what it was 300 years ago."

"Well, the river could have dried up between Freeport and the mountains," Lori said uncertainly, "but the western half is still being fed by melting glaciers or underground springs."

"Agreed." Grayson nodded vigorously. "Still, it was unusual enough to make me curious. I started examining the old Helmfast map carefully, using full magnification to explore the valley, here where the Vermillion flows off the North Highland Plains and underground." He typed rapidly, and the left-hand map expanded sharply. The red-tinged waters of the river could be seen flowing through a shallow valley. After winding through a kilometer or so of wild and rocky terrain, the river turned sharply right and vanished under a slab of granite the size of a large building.

Grayson kept typing, and the right-hand map expanded to the same scale, centered on the same area. "And I started examining the map we took from the mobile headquarters, the one made five days ago. The hardest part was using the computer to reconcile two different coordinate systems, so that I can punch one set of coordinates into the terminal and have the same spot displayed at the same magnification on both maps, new and old."

Lori looked from one display to the other, feeling more and more confused. It was hard to believe that the two were centered on the same coordinate system, as Grayson claimed. The outline of the Vermillion River Valley was clearly the same on both displays. The one on the left had water in it, the one on the right did not, but the general lay of the surrounding land, the shape of the banks, were all clearly the same. The vegetation was different, of course, sparser in the modern view. There was also a building in the modern view that was not on the older one, a low, structure of metal and ferrocrete, set into the side of a hill overlooking the bank.

Such changes were to be expected in three centuries, and so were easily discounted. What was confusing was the shape of the land where the river vanished under the rock. In the one view, the river flowed into what might be a cave mouth under a vast slab of stone. In the other, the empty river valley ran up to that same slab of stone—only now, the slab of stone was standing on end, a sheer, polished granite cliff face thirty meters tall. It was as though the river had flowed straight up to the foot of a cliff—and vanished, passing into solid rock. The land around was largely unchanged, except for places where the formerly gentle slopes of the valley walls had become steeper, almost vertical, in the area immediately around the slab. *It looks like it's been dug out deliberately,* Lori thought.

"That makes no sense at all," she said. "It looks . . . deliberate! An earthquake? You said there could be earthquakes here . . ."

"I estimate that that stone slab weighs something like ten billion kilograms . . . ten million metric tons. Yes, an earthquake *could* have moved that large a weight . . . but could it have moved *only* that slab of stone, and not brought down these cliffs here . . . or here? Or made the river banks collapse? What about this building, in the modern view? Maybe it was built after the . . . earthquake . . . but when you put it together with the lack of changes elsewhere in the area, well, I'm having trouble believing in an earthquake *that* selective.''

''That *is* the same rock, only turned on end?''

''I'm convinced of it. It's not very thick, actually, from what I can see. It looks like it was deliberately pulled up and stood on end. I've been wondering if it wasn't trimmed a bit to fit here, across the river valley. And it looks to me as though the river valley itself was dug out some, to make the stone fit.''

''Then what you're saying—.'' She stopped. *He's right! He really has found it!*

Grayson set the pointer on the enigmatic, vertical rock clif. ''Lori, my love, I think that what we are looking at here is a door. A very large, very strong, and very deliberately placed door.''

'The Star League weapons cache.''

''Makes sense,'' he said. ''It's only about a hundred kilometers from Freeport. The fact that the river flowed down into the mountains suggests that there was some sort of a cave entrance there. I think that Star League engineer . . . what was his name?''

''Keeler.''

''I think Major Keeler and his people diverted the river somehow, maybe by damming it off in Freeport. The river bed went dry, and left a large, clean, dry cave or tunnel, right through the mountain. When things were getting bad, and the Star League was falling apart, he *moved* the weapons cache up here. Put it into that tunnel, then sealed off the entrance by putting a cliff across the front of it! Minoru Kurita comes along a little later, looking for an old Star League cache, and finds it's gone. He searches all over, but can't find a clue. He would have made satellite recon maps at the time that would have shown the dry river bed, even the cliff, but he wouldn't have had older views showing that the river had actually been flowing here or that the cliff here was different, only a few months or years before!''

"So he destroyed the world . . .''

"And in doing so, probably killed everyone who actually knew the secret of where the weapons were.''

"So how come ComStar couldn't figure this out?''

"I doubt that anybody thought to compare the two maps, side by side. Maybe they worked with old maps that showed things as they were before the cache was hidden. They probably worked mostly with maps made after the destruction of Freeport. But you have to see them both, side by side, to realize that *that*''—he used the pointer to indicate the out-of-place cliff—''simply doesn't belong there!''

"Next question. How do we get at it? That *is* your idea, isn't it?''

He smiled, but exhaustion distorted the smile into something closer to a grimace. "How does brute force sound?''

"I can just see you walking your *Marauder* up to that cliff and kicking it in.''

"I doubt that would do the trick. But we do have a healthy supply of explosives from the storehouse down in Durandel. And we have a former mining engineer who knows how to use it.''

"You think we could bring down the cliff?''

Grayson used the pointer again. "I don't know geology that well, but I'm engineer enough to know that this cliff has to be supported . . . braced somehow . . . and it looks to me like that might be here, and here, on top of the cliff and at opposite sides of the valley. Or maybe our real engineer can come up with something better. And if DeVillar can't take three tons of high explosives and bring that cliff down, I'll be willing to tunnel in using a spoon!''

"But why? Oh, sure . . . we could use some new 'Mechs . . . and there're spares and repair facilities in there, certainly. But we can't use all that stuff, and I doubt that Langsdorf will give us time to enjoy it. All the equipment on Helm won't help us if all we have is our under-strength regiment . . . and no time to work out a decent defense.''

"For whatever reason, ComStar wants those weapons, Lori. I daresay they've promised a share of them to the Marik people working for them. Garth, for example, must be convinced he's going to get something out of all this, and that something would have to be pretty valuable.''

"Like a regiment or so of mint-perfect BattleMechs.''

"Right. Whether it was ComStar or Rachan working on his own, millions of people were slaughtered simply to get *us* out of the way, so that they could get their hands on that stuff.'' Grayson's mouth set again in an unyielding, bitter line. "They will *not* get away with that. If the cache is that valuable, let's see to it that they don't get it!''

"You're going to destroy it?''

"We'll see what Lieutenant DeVillar says. I suspect, though, that we'll either be able to break in, or we'll be able to so smash up the face of that mountain so that no one will *ever* get in. If we can enter, perhaps we'll be in a position to bargain with Langsdorf, and still cut out ComStar so that *they* don't profit from . . . from Sirius V. If we can't get in, we'll ruin it so that neither Marik or ComStar will ever find a way to get at the cache.

"One way or another, Lori, Rachan is going to pay for Sirius V!''

═══ 22 ═══

Grayson still had not slept, and only the fire burning within his mind and heart kept him moving. He and Lori had returned to the encampment, where he had explained his discovery to the senior people, including all of A Company. The Legion was about to attempt something very difficult, he explained, and it would be good if the men knew just what would be expected of them.

It had taken him five minutes to sketch an outline of the proposed plan: move south, find the cache, and seize it either as a bargaining tool or to prevent the Legion's betrayors from getting it. When DeVillar saw a printout of the cliff face area from the Marik map, he was confident that it would take only a small amount of explosives to bring it down. What he could not promise was whether or not the collapse would also cave in the cache tunnel. From the exterior, there was no indication of just how well-braced the hidden chamber might be.

Grayson did not go into details about the possible location of the weapons cache, of course. There was too much chance that someone who knew the cache's secret would be captured, and fall into Rachan's or Garth's hands. Right now, the Legion had a slight head start, and Grayson would need every instant of it. If they could race south to the Nagayan Mountains as they'd originally planned, if they could reach the cliff face where the empty river valley ended, they might claim the mountain's secret before Garth or Rachan even knew what Grayson was up to.

Whoever controlled Helm's secret would be in a powerful bargaining position and Grayson knew it. He was also tactician enough to realize that it would not be difficult to defend the approaches to that artificial cliff, perhaps making it possible to strike a deal with Langsdorf.

If Langsdorf can keep Garth and ComStar off our backs, we could agree to split the cache with him, Grayson thought. *Or maybe we could make a separate deal with Garth.* That thought revolted him, because Garth had apparently been a willing participant in the destruction of Tiantan. It was Garth's report, and holographs taken by men in Garth's employ, that had shown the 'Mechs masquerading as Legion 'Mechs among Tiantan's ruins.

First and foremost, though, he had to do what he could to save the regiment.

But what is the right *thing to do?* he wondered. *If I can save the Legion by striking a deal with Garth—or even Rachan—should I? Or should I try to use the weapons to strike a deal with someone else? Who, though? No one on Helm believes we didn't destroy Tiantan. So far as Steiner or Davion are concerned, we're outlaws. They won't even talk to us!*

"Colonel?"

Grayson turned at the sound of Alard King's voice. The senior Tech had moved up so quietly that Grayson had not heard him.

Or maybe Lori was right, and he was asleep on his feet.

"Yes, Alard?"

The Tech looked uncertain. "Sir, I've got to talk to you. It's about what you told us just now."

"Yes?"

"It's . . . well, I may have some additional information for you, something else to figure into your plans."

"O.K. What is it?" It was not like King to be so indirect. It almost seemed that he was afraid.

"I'm not entirely sure how to tell you this, Colonel . . . but I'm an agent."

Grayson looked at him blankly. "Agent? What kind of agent?"

"A spy, sir. I'm a spy."

Grayson found himself laughing, somewhat to his own surprise, and certainly to King's. "What's so funny, sir?"

"It's just that I don't think I've ever seen things get so complicated! Graff was a spy for Marik, *then* it turned out he was really a spy for ComStar. We've got spies running around in Helmdown that everybody knows about, and spies in the regiment that no one knows about. You and I go off into Helmdown to look for spies, and then it turns out that *you're* a spy yourself! O.K. . . . who are *you* spying for?"

"Duke Hassid Ricol."

Grayson's smile vanished instantly, his amusement suddenly gone, and even his exhaustion, too. He stared at King with a hard, cold expression. The Tech moved uncomfortably under his gaze.

Duke Ricol! The man was a Kurita noble, whose power extended across several worlds on the Steiner-Kurita frontier. This gave him the actual power of an archduke, for dukes generally had responsibility for only a single world. Ricol had a reputation as a warrior, though he had not been in combat for many years. Along the Steiner border, he was well known, though, as "the Red Duke" or "the Red Hunter."

It had been Duke Ricol who had conceived the plan four years before, one that had burned Ricol's name and face into the memory of one young Grayson Death Carlyle. That plan had begun while a combined-arms mercenary force consisting of a BattleMech company and several platoons of infantry prepared to withdraw from a small and relatively unimportant world called Trell I, or Trellwan, near the Kurita border. A pirate raid struck the world in a surprise attack that destroyed the mercenary force and conquered the world's principal city and starport. With the civilian populace ground under the heel of the conquering marauders, it was planned that a House Kurita 'Mech force would eventually land, secure the city, and destroy the pirates. The citizens of the liberated city, it was thought, would be grateful to the Kurita forces who had rescued them, and disdainful of the Steiner-hired mercenaries who had let them down—who had, in fact, been preparing to depart the planet just as the pirate raiders had struck.

The mercenary force had been Carlyle's Commandos, and its commander, Captain Durant Carlyle, had died during the initial landing of the pirate force. Grayson had been injured, and left for dead while the remnants of Carlyle's Commandos fled the planet. Stranded on Trell I, Grayson ultimately discovered that the pirates were in league with Duke Ricol in a clever ploy to conquer a world *and* the hearts of its people in a single operation.

It was on Trellwan that the Gray Death Legion had been born, child of Grayson's determination to win vengeance against the bloody Kurita Red Duke.

Grayson had won a small measure of vengeance on Trellwan. He had won a second measure of revenge on Verthandi, a world nominally under Ricol's suzerainty, though the planet's actual ruler had been a Kurita Governor-General named Nagumo.

Since then, Grayson's driving need to avenge his father's death and the destruction of Carlyle's Commandos had dimmed. Perhaps it had been tempered by the growing realization that what he had here and now—the Gray Death Legion, and friends like Ramage and Lori—were more precious to him than vengeance on a minor Kurita duke.

Now, though, mention of the Red Duke's name roused memories, thoughts, and emotions that Grayson had thought long-buried. His eyes bored into King's as though trying to open the Senior Tech's soul. "What . . ." He had to stop and bring his voice under control. "What is Ricol's interest in me now?"

"You needn't be modest, Colonel." King regained a small measure of his accustomed confidence, perhaps realizing that Grayson was not going to kill him outright. "His Grace has been interested in you since Trellwan. You created a BattleMech force out of nothing . . . and went on to beat a much larger 'Mech force with it, singlehandedly. On Verthandi, you were even better. What did you have there? Something like a company of 'Mechs?"

"Seven. Plus the local militia."

"And then you trained the rebels and the militia, with almost no equipment at the start. The Verthandians could never have won free without your help."

Grayson crossed his arms, watching King warily. "So what's your point?"

"I told you the other day about what I had learned in town. I was not able to tell you who I learned it from."

"Yes?"

"The local agent for the Combine is a woman named Dierdre Ravenna. She operates several business establishments in Helmdown, including a place up in the fancy Gresshaven District. Like Moragen and Atkins, she keeps an eye on things locally for House Kurita.

"But she also knows Duke Ricol. You see, Ricol has been interested in Helm for a long time."

"Helm? Why?"

"According to Deirdre, a number of Kurita nobles and officers have been intrigued by the place. You see, they've all read the report Minoru Kurita made at the conclusion of the Helm Campaign in 2788. And they reached the same conclusion you did, in the same way you did. The Star League cache had to be here. It couldn't be moved . . . and yet it was gone when Kurita arrived with his battle fleet. It has not surfaced in almost three centuries. Therefore, it has got to be around here . . . somewhere."

"And Ricol was one of those nobles."

"He was. He also had an advantage over the others. He is wealthy and powerful, even for a Duke, and he maintains a JumpShip—the *Huntress*—as his personal vessel. And don't think he hasn't been keeping an eye on you ever since you bested him—again—at Verthandi last year."

"You."

"Me. He sent me to Galatea a year ago, with instructions to seek you out, impress you with my technical skills, and to join the Gray Death Legion." King smiled. "I didn't realize you would make me Senior Tech . . . and your own personal Tech as well. That was an unexpected bonus. When His Grace realized that you were being granted the Helmfast landhold, that you would become, in fact, the key to the lost Helman cache, he grew very interested, indeed.''

''All of which brings us to the key question,'' Grayson said. The exhaustion was returning, now that the shock of revelation had ebbed. He rubbed his eyes, then looked up at King. ''Why are you telling me all this? If you want me to tell you where the cache is so you can tell Ricol, forget it.''

''You know where it is?''

''If I do, don't think I plan to tell you.''

''Somehow, I didn't expect you to. But I do think I can help you.''

''How?''

''Come with me.''

''Where?''

''To Helmdown.''

''How?''

''I have the necessary papers. We can dress as businessmen, run into Helmdown, see who we have to see, and then leave.''

''To see this Deirdre person?''

King looked Grayson up and down, as though measuring him. ''I want you to talk with Duke Ricol.''

''You don't trust me.''

Lori stared across the headquarters tent at Grayson, shook her head, and said again. ''You don't trust me.''

''It's not that, Lori.'' The pain in his soul was like a knife's twisting. ''It's better if you don't know, that's all.''

''But you calmly walk in here and tell me that if anything happens to you, I'm in charge . . . and to go through with the plan as we've discussed? God, Grayson . . . I *love* you! Doesn't that count for *anything?*''

''Yes, Lori. It does. And it's why I . . . why I can't go into it, right now.''

He had wrestled with his conscience all the way to the tent after he left King to ready the ''demilitarized'' skimmer. His moral dilemma had suddenly become more complex. It was unacceptable, from Grayson's point of view, to negotiate with either Garth or Rachan. It had occurred to him that finding the cache and offering it to either of those men, with certain safeguards, might be a means of guaranteeing the safety of the Legion: the Star League weapons in exchange for the safety and freedom of the regiment.

How could he even bring himself to do such a thing, though? Rachan—with or without ComStar's knowledge, but certainly with Garth's connivance—had slaughtered millions of civilians merely to seize those weapons. For Grayson, giving someone like Rachan the weapons in exchange for the lives of even his own people was like dealing in the blood of those murdered civilians. To do so would go squarely against everything that Grayson Carlyle was. The only alternative, it seemed, was to destroy the Star League cache and await the onslaught of Garth's legions. Once the cache was destroyed, there would be nothing left but a final, hopeless battle in which the Gray Death must certainly meet destruction.

He had tried to convince himself that the Marik forces might leave the Legion alone if the cache were destroyed and there was nothing left to fight for, but Grayson realized finally what a delusion that was. If he destroyed the cache, Rachan would guess that Grayson knew of the whole plot. Grayson's death, and the death of every man and woman with him, would be absolutely necessary to keep quiet the fact that Rachan—and possibly ComStar itself—was involved in the massacre on Sirius V.

It was a dead end, then. He might preserve the unit's honor, but he could not preserve their lives.

Now the equation had become even more complex. King thought that Duke Ricol might have a way out for the Legion, and Grayson knew what price Ricol would demand for his help.

Should he bargain with Ricol? Grayson was still wrestling with the moral aspects of that question. For nearly four years, he had thought of the Red Duke as his father's murderer. Yet Ricol's stratagem on Trellwan had been a legitimate ruse of war. If Grayson looked at it that way, Ricol had simply been trying to minimize casualties among his own forces and the civilian populace of Trellwan by arranging it so that Trellwan's inhabitants would not *want* to rise against their conquerors.

Where was the right all this? What was right? What would Grayson's father have wanted him to do?

There was no clear answer yet, but if Grayson told Lori where he was going and who he was going to see, her protests would make the decision that much more difficult. At that moment, Grayson realized how much he *did* love Lori, no matter how poorly he expressed it to her. Because he did love Lori, he could not tell her where he was going and what he was planning. Lori's hurt at his own hurt would keep him from doing what he had to.

"I love you, too, Lori. More than I can say. And I would tell you . . . if I could." He shrugged. "But I can't. All I can say is . . . please . . . trust me." Grayson knew there was a chance he would not come back, but it was remote. From what King had said, he was sure that Ricol did actually want to talk to him, that it was not a trap. But to see Ricol, he would have to enter Helmdown once again, and Garth's fleet was nearly upon them.

"Don't forget that I need you as the Legion's Exec to get things rolling here." He shook his head sharply, cutting off her protest. "No! You've got to see to rounding up any last survivors that might be hiding out there in the woods. You'll have to saddle up the regiment, have it ready to move. Strike the camp, and be ready to go an hour after sundown. I should be able to do what I have to do and return by then. But if I'm not back, you must get the regiment on its way. If I know I'm going to be late, I'll adjust my course accordingly, and catch up with the column along the way. You can have one of the trainees pilot my *Marauder,* so it'll be with you when I get in."

Lori smiled softly. "Are you sure you shouldn't take your *Marauder* with you . . . wherever you're going?"

Grayson took Lori in his arms. She resisted at first, then molded herself to his body, clinging to him with all her strength. He raised her chin, then sought her mouth with his. They kissed, long and lingeringly. "I must go. But I will see you . . . tonight, I promise."

23

"**Y**our Grace." Grayson gave the bow proper for a MechWarrior in the presence of a man of Ricol's station.

Duke Hassid Ricol was an impressive figure, as tall as Grayson was, but broader across the shoulders, with larger, heavier hands whose grip took Grayson's in a powerful clasp. He still wore the same, thick full black beard, and his teeth were very white against the beard when he smiled.

When Grayson had met Ricol before, the man had worn the full-dress reds for which he was famous, but such garb would be too conspicuous here on Helm. He was dressed instead in the ruffled blouse and richly patterned trousers of a merchant. His high-topped boots were also ornate and expensive, the mark of a wealthy man showing his worth through tasteful ostentation.

Grayson was fully aware that Ricol used clothing, as he used all else, for his own purposes. He had heard once that the dress reds were the Duke's way of instilling awe in those he ruled, a kind of psychological advantage because men's minds so easily associated the color red with blood, danger, and death.

So, too, the ornate civilian dress had let this Duke of the Draconis Combine ground his DropShip, stroll through an occupied city, and visit this house on Gresshaven's hill without attracting the least bit of unfavorable notice—and without giving anyone a clue as to his real identity.

"I am glad to see you again," Ricol said. "though you probably don't believe that."

"I have endured a number of surprises of late, Your Grace," Grayson replied. "One of the biggest was learning that you were here."

"Events . . . required it," the Red Duke said. "Things were happening too quickly for me to oversee their progress from elsewhere."

Ricol's ship the *Huntress* was in the Helm system, had been insystem for nearly five days, but no one had questioned it. The Marik forces gathering now at Helm numbered dozens of ships, ranging from the *Rapacious* and her consorts at the jump point, to DropShips like the *Assagai* and transports such as those on Helmdown's landing field. Like most modern military organizations, the Marik government relied on private merchants and traders to carry the vast amounts of food necessary to provision a fleet as large as the one that had descended on Helm during the past week. The *Huntress,* and the DropShips with her, were carefully disguised as lightly armed merchanter vessels. Ricol's DropShip *Alpha,* grounded now at Helmdown's landing field, would excite no more comment than any other civilian merchanter now in port. And Ricol himself looked the part of the *Alpha*'s merchant-owner.

Deirdre Ravenna stood across the room. A tall, handsome woman, she was one of Helmdown's best-known courtesans. She did not look like a spy, Grayson thought, but then, neither had Atkins or Moragen . . . or King, for that matter. He glanced across at King, seated comfortably in a soft chair and wearing the semi-formal civilian trousers and tunic he had chosen for this visit to the city. *What* is *a spy supposed to look like?* Grayson wondered.

"It was a surprise to learn that His Grace has been so close, all along," she said. "I thought my reports were being taken by occasional merchants . . . gods! How many hundreds of light years? And then Alard comes to me with His Grace's ring and tells me that the Red Duke has spent the last two months parked right next door!"

Grayson shook his head. This was not the way Dukes, not even Kurita dukes, behaved. He reached up and touched the thin packet resting in an inside pocket of his tunic, the papers Ricol had provided so that King could bring Grayson for a meeting. This was not the way *Kurita* dukes behaved at all.

"Why, Your Grace? Why the interest in me?"

Ricol smiled, stroking his beard with one massive hand. "A fair question, but not one I can answer easily. Suffice it to say that when Alard reported to me that Helm was to be the price of your service to House Marik against Liao, I became extremely interested in you. I had reason—strong reason—to believe that the Star League arms cache was still here . . . within your landhold. If you were to become lord of this . . . this treasure, then perhaps I could win a chance at it."

Grayson remained skeptical. Ricol's answer had not answered what he *really* wanted to know, which was why the Duke had decided to assign King to keep an eye on him in the first place. Certainly, Ricol would have had no way of knowing that Marik was going to give the Helm landhold to Grayson before the fact!

"What made you think I would help you?"

Ricol pursed his lips, as though considering. "I didn't think you would, actually. Not willingly. But my studies had convinced me that something very, very big was going on in this sector. From what my agents could gather from the ComStar hyperpulse generator traffic, the Order was showing a keen interest in Helm. Let's just say that I decided the *Huntress* ought to be nearby, just in case an opportunity presented itself."

"That would have to be one hell of an opportunity," Grayson said. "If I'm reading you right, you were planning a snap raid in the middle of a joint ComStar-Marik recovery of the Star League cache!"

"That is precisely what I was planning. At the same time, I knew that you would not simply stand aside and let them take it, and I felt that perhaps you and I would be able to come to some . . . arrangement. I was more certain that the situation was . . . ah . . . fluid when I received word that you had been declared an outlaw." Ricol looked narrowly at Grayson. "I have known you, have fought against you for four years, Colonel. I did not . . . I *do* not believe the stories I heard about your massacre of a surrendered city.''

The transformation in Ricol's face at the mention of the Tiantan massacre was startling. The man's bushy black eyebrows came together like miniature thunderclouds, and there was a wintry look in his dark eyes.

''I could not believe the report at *all* at first.'' The Duke's voice matched the look in his eyes. He reached across to a low table where a bowl of fruit was displayed, and pulled a large, ripe xenogrape from the golden cluster. ''A city, already surrendered . . . destroyed as callously as a man crushes a grape.'' His thumb and forefinger closed on the grape, spattering yellow juice across his fingers. ''Pah!''

The thundercloud passed, and Ricol looked momentarily embarrassed. He wiped his hand on his blouse, then continued. ''When Alard here made contact with me through Deirdre the other day, and told me you couldn't possibly have done the things of which you were accused *because he had been with you the whole time*, I decided it was time to come to Helmdown personally. They were using tactics on you that I had every reason to believe would . . . fail. And I don't want to see these city killers win.''

''All very flattering . . .''

''It's not meant to be flattering, Colonel! Even if I had time for such foolishness. I know it wouldn't work on you any more than attacking your reputation would!''

''I stand corrected. What is it you want?''

''Isn't it obvious, by now?'' the Duke said drily. ''I would like a share of whatever you find in the Star League cache.'' King had already explained to Ricol that Grayson seemed to know the cache's location. Ricol had not questioned that certainty.

''And in exchange?''

''I will intercede with the force at my disposal in an attempt to rescue the Gray Death Legion. I will provide transport for your regiment to . . . to wherever you would care to go. I will also provide transport for whatever treasures we can recover from the cache.''

Grayson only nodded, still not sure what he wanted to reply.

Ricol glanced at the corrected local time function on his expensive-looking wrist computer. "I warn you, we haven't much time. Garth's ships will be grounding at any moment. I don't know where your people are now, Colonel, but if they are heading toward the cache, it's going to be a race, even now. Garth's orbital surveillance will be certain to pick up your force's position sooner or later. You will not long be able to disguise the cache's location once you reach it."

Grayson paced the luxuriously furnished room, thinking. What Ricol proposed made perfect sense. The Legion's crisis gave the Duke the opening he had been waiting for. Ricol would get a share of the Star League weapons, and Grayson and the Gray Death Legion would have a ticket offplanet. It was the perfect solution for all involved. There was only one problem that Grayson could see. Could he, in fact, *trust* Duke Ricol?

To do so meant turning upside down all his previous beliefs. It had been Ricol's treachery—or so Grayson had always read it—that had killed his father and destroyed his unit. And Grayson had always associated Ricol with the Draconis Combine and House Kurita, a regime known across the Inner Sphere for its callousness, its brutality, and the Machiavellian nature of it politics. If such a government could not be trusted, how could such a man be trusted?

Yet Grayson had been struck by Ricol's reaction, moments before, to the massacre of Tiantan. The black emotions in the man's face and voice had been genuine, of that Grayson was certain. Ricol was a warrior, not an actor. He was bluff and blunt when he spoke, and seemed to prefer silence on other points rather than to lie.

But was that enough? Could shared horror at a callous and bloodthirsty act provide the basis for mutual trust? Ricol would, after all, also have to trust that Grayson would keep his part of the bargain if he was to commit ships, men, and 'Mechs to combat.

"How many 'Mechs do you have with you, Your Grace?"

"One company. I know it's not much . . ."

"One company! Twelve 'Mechs? With how many DropShips?"

"Six." Ricol smiled. "Understand, Colonel, that all but five of those DropShips are *empty*. I had . . . ah . . . other ideas for them, than dragging my BattleMechs into Marik space!"

Grayson laughed. Other ideas, indeed!

Suddenly, Ricol's admission provided Grayson with the final piece of the puzzle he needed for his decision. To impress Grayson, the Duke could have promised a regiment of 'Mechs to rescue the Gray Death Legion. He could have found a way to promise a rescue, all the while planning to land and grab the cache himself. Yet, he had admitted to having only a single company, and why.

"Your Grace, if I do nothing else, I intend to make certain that the destroyers of Tiantan don't benefit from this."

It was long after sunset when King and Grayson raced southeast across the North Highland Plains, leaving the lights of Helmdown behind them. Their session with Ricol had taken longer than expected. Not that there had been problems with the negotiations. The Red Duke understood that there was no clear guarantee that Grayson would even be able to get into the Star League cache—at least, not without bringing down half a mountain on top of it. He was willing to gamble on Grayson's being able to get in and find something worth taking, though. He did not even quibble, as Grayson had expected, over the number of BattleMechs and other equipment he would get. "That," Ricol had said, "is premature, at best. We don't know what you will find when you enter. We don't know what we will have time to remove when you get in. We don't know where the enemy will be, or in what force. We may be fortunate merely to escape with the lives of you and your regiment." He had shaken his head and smiled. "But, gods of space, what a victory if we win our gamble! There'll be plenty for both of us and we can divide it up later.''

''Oh, so you're cutting us in for a share?'' Grayson had asked.

''My young friend, if this cache is what I believe it to be, there will be far more there than you or I together could ever use.''

Grayson had grown serious. ''I want my regiment . . . intact.''

''And that I will endeavor to provide.''

It was the strategic details of the latter point that had proven time-consuming. Grayson had pointed out that some fifty of his people were prisoner, at last report still held aboard the DropShips in Cleft Valley. Grayson was not sure why they had not been moved, though he suspected that Langsdorf hoped to use them to draw the Legion out of Durandel to battle. The prisoners would not be moved so long as Langsdorf believed that Grayson was still there. When he discovered that the Gray Death had gone, the captives would probably be moved to Helmdown. Or worse, killed.

What Grayson wanted was for Ricol to plan a raid to recover the DropShips. That would not be easy, and could be quite costly in both men and machines. Grayson had pointed out the logic, however. If the *Deimos* and the *Phobos,* could be freed along with their crews, they could go to the place temporarily being called the Rendezvous, a yet-to-be selected landing site somewhere in the vicinity of the weapons cache. That would allow Grayson's people to load aboard their own ships, while Ricol filled his empty DropShips with whatever they could recover from the cache.

Ricol's two JumpShips would carry a total of eight DropShips; his own six, plus Grayson's two. The *Huntress* would carry the *Deimos* and the *Phobos* to the neighboring star system of Stewart, where the Legion's ships could be dropped off to rejoin Captain Tor and the *Invidious.* The Gray Death Legion would then go its way, while Ricol's squadron returned to Kurita space.

In its broad outlines, the plan was simple, but it became a monstrously complex nightmare to consider the individual details. How was a landing zone for the Rendezvous to be chosen? How would it be marked? How could Ricol's twelve BattleMechs hope to capture the *Deimos* and the *Phobos* from a watchful foe? What if they arrived at Stewart, only to find that the Gray Death Legion's evil reputation had preceded them, resulting in capture of the *Invidious* and its crew being taken prisoner? What would happen if Grayson brought down the ceiling while trying to penetrate the Star League cache? And what would be their signal? Though Ricol was willing to offer the Legion a ride off Helm, one way or the other, they needed a signal so that Ricol would not risk more than two DropShips for the Legion's rescue, should the cache be destroyed. The most complex planning revolved around freeing the Legion's two DropShips.

Ricol had no 'Mechs on Helm as yet, but he did have an infantry company numbering ninety men, plus a lance of Galleon tanks. Ricol was certain that this relatively small force could debark by dark from the *Alpha,* and make its way past the spaceport perimeter without exciting undue comment. The spaceport was alive with Marik troops and vehicles; a few more, passing unobtrusively in the dark and would have a good chance of leaving Helmdown and moving quickly toward the east. By itself, this force would be no match for the DropShip's weapons, but after Grayson studied the orbital recon maps that Ricol had brought along, he was able to propose a plan. It was a difficult and dangerous one, but offered the Legion its best hope of recovering the DropShips, the 'Mechs and equipment aboard them, and their fifty comrades still held prisoner there.

It was already three hours past sundown by the time Grayson and King left Helmdown. Their parting with Ricol had been abrupt to the point of rudeness, if only because the plan to recover the DropShips required perfect timing, and that timing was already endangered by the lateness of the hour. The Legion column would be an hour on the road already, and it would take at least three hours more to catch up with them.

THE PRICE OF GLORY

Grayson and King were almost two kilometers south of town when the night lit up above them. They pulled their skimmer off the road to watch as sun-brilliant flares of light descended, one at a time, clearing to sky in columns of flame and thunder.

The DropShips of Lord Garth's fleet were landing.

24

For Lori, the day had been charged with a choking grief mingled with barely restrained fear. She knew with a certainty that transcended the laws of physics that Grayson would not return at the appointed hour.

She had tried to brace herself for his failure to show long before it was time for the regiment to leave. Even as she'd watched Grayson and King speeding toward the northwest hours before, she had told herself they might be late returning. Then again, many times during the preparations to break camp, she reminded herself of how many things could go wrong. Finally, when it came time for her to give the orders to board 'Mechs and load the column's civilians aboard the odd assembly of armored vehicles and cargo transports, she told herself not to panic. King had produced those travel papers he claimed to have picked up from his "contact" on his previous visit to Helmdown. The fact of those papers and his refusal to reveal who those contacts were had made Lori deeply suspicious of the man. She had noted, too, an undefined but quite noticeable difference in the relationship between Grayson and his senior Tech. *Something* had changed between those two. What?

As Helm's orange sun set behind the low ridges to the west, Lori watched the bustle of activity on Durandel's plain spread out below her from Helmfast's bluff. Lights mounted in the Legion's BattleMechs had helped the loading operations continue as the twilight deepened into night. An eerier, piping wail rose suddenly, sending chills racing up her spine. It was the signal for recall. Their last chance to round up any of Durandel's survivors who might be hiding out in the woods. Patrols had been out all day, searching for survivors, but it appeared that every one of the Legion's surviving warriors and dependents had been recovered.

Grayson! Why did you do this to me!

She checked her chronometer. It had been almost two standard hours since Helm's sun had set. Rising from her overlook, she made her way back to where her *Shadow Hawk* stood, huge and silent against the night. The *Hawk* had been Grayson's ever since he'd taken it on Trellwan. He'd passed it on to Lori after her 20-ton *Locust* had been destroyed at Verthandi. She paused, hand on the 'Mech's cold armor, trying to stir some feeling of Grayson's presence, his warmth, but there was nothing beyond the chill of the metal and the noises of Helm's night animals.

Ashamed of being so weak, Lori hurried to the chain link ladder dangling along the *Shadow Hawk*'s flanks and began swarming up the rungs toward the cockpit, ten meters overhead.

It was time to give the order to march.

All together, the muster rolls showed 612 survivors among the Techs, trainees, infantry, service personnel, and dependents of the Legion who had been at Durandel. These were piled into and onto a long, clattering line of vehicles, most of them salvaged from wrecked and damaged hover cargo transports recovered from the ruins of the settlement. These vehicles formed the main body of the convoy as it began to move south. At the rear of the column were the surviving armored and military transport vehicles, including those that had escaped at Durandel and those that had been salvaged from the wreckage. The survivors of the regiment's two infantry companies had been reassembled into a single combat company numbering 130 men and women who rode guard for the convoy's rear.

The unit's eight BattleMechs had been deployed, with Lori herself in the rear, McCall's *Rifleman* ranging far out to the front, and the remaining six 'Mechs deployed three to each side of the convoy, as flankers. The convoy's speed was limited to fifty kilometers per hour. Though some vehicles could make better speeds, most could not. Grayson had insisted that the convoy stay together throughout the march.

They had been travelling for only five minutes when McCall gave warning over the taccom frequency.

"What do you have, McCall?"

"Motion, Lieutenant," McCall replied. "Bearin' a' one-niner-five, at a range a' aboot two hundred meters. Lieutenant . . . ah read it as a man, movin' on foot."

A scout, was Lori's first thought. *A Marik scout. Langsdorf must have thrown scouts out to warn of our movement! Damn . . .*

"Command to all units," she transmitted on the general command frequency. "We have a possible infantry sighting on our front. Be alert for ambush." In the dark, small units of troops masked against infrared observation could be deployed across a 'Mech force's path, waiting in ambush with shoulder-fired infernos and short-range missiles. It would take very little indeed to cripple the convoy's march.

"Lieutenant . . ." McCall's voice came again across the private tactical frequency.

She heard relief in his voice . . . and something else. "What is it, Davis?"

"Two more survivors, Lieutenant. Heard tha' recall but couldnae reach the encampment in time. They just stepped from the weeds an' flagged me doon . . ."

Lori sank back in her seat, weak with relief. They were not ready to fight a battle . . . not now . . .

"And Lori . . ."

"Yes?"

"Let's bring Delmar in on tha' channel. We should ae' tell him his lassie an' bairn are ae' safe an' sound!"

The news of the rescue of two more survivors of Durandel brought cheers and laughter across the general com circuit, and Lori heard Delmar's whoop of joy when McCall told him that Terri and his son were safe. Her own face was wet under the mask of her neurohelmet when, moments later, the convoy began moving again, southward and into the night.

THE PRICE OF GLORY

* * *

"Colonel! Wake up!"

King nudged Grayson in the ribs, dragging him back to a sleep-sodden wakefulness. Grayson's neck and back were stiff from the hours of stolen sleep in the passenger seat of the skimmer.

As Grayson and Lori had worked out the Legion convoy's route south, Grayson knew when the convoy was leaving Durandel, and how fast it would be traveling. It should have been a simple matter of the math to know where to steer across the empty grasslands of the North Highland Plains in a direction to intercept the convoy on its way south toward the mountains.

There was a considerable gap between theory and reality, however. The plains were large, and even so huge an organism as a convoy of 'Mechs and skimmer transports snaking south across the prairie was vanishingly small among so much open space. As for a lone, two-seat skimmer, it was positively microscopic.

Grayson blinked himself awake. King had stopped the skimmer, and the night closed in around them. The sky was bright with stars. He recognized Aldhafera, one of the brightest stars in Helm's sky, high in the east. The dusting of faint stars of the Milky Way outlined the low, dark mass of the far horizon.

"What is it, Alard?"

"This is the place, Colonel. They should be here . . . now. I don't see 'em."

Grayson stood on the skimmer's seat and took a long, hard look into the darkness, first to the north, then to the south. Which way? If the convoy had already passed, it would be to the south now. If he and King raced at top speed, they might catch up with it. If, however, the convoy had not come this far yet, then it would be still to the north.

Grayson climbed out of the skimmer, took a small electric hand torch from King, and made his way through waist-deep prairie grass. Several meters from the skimmer, he stopped and studied the ground.

Hovercraft made little permanent impression on vegetation such as this tough, sturdy prairie grass. Their passage could have been detected on barren, dusty, or sandy terrain, where their fans tended to sweep broad swatches of loose soil or dust from rocks and to overturn lightly rooted vegetation. On these plains, an army of hovercraft could pass without leaving a trace.

A BattleMech, however, was something different. Weighing from twenty to a hundred tons, depending on the type, with all of that weight concentrated across only two foot pads in most models, 'Mechs tended to leave a lasting impression along any path that was not packed to the consistency of poured ferrocrete. Grayson struck out through the darkness, his torch probing this way and that, for a distance of about a hundred meters. It was possible that they could have missed the track; and that the trampled ruin of the convoy's passing might lie just another hundred meters farther east, but Grayson did not think that was the case.

He knew Lori's skill as a navigator. Further, he knew that Lori would not have left Durandel even one minute earlier than she absolutely had to when he had not returned on time. She was too good a soldier to delay the convoy by waiting for him, but she would not have left earlier, either. There was always the possibility of minor problems slowing down the column, however. When travelling with so many civilians, there were bound to be delays.

Grayson was certain that the convoy must still lie to the north. In fact, he was willing to stake his life on that certainty.

He started back toward the skimmer, but King's voice reached him midway. "There, Colonel! I see them!" McCall's *Rifleman* had loomed out of the darkness from the north like a walking mountain. In another ten minutes, Lori was sobbing in his arms, with neither of them caring that they were hemmed in by tens, by hundreds of others of the Legion.

The Gray Death sentry could not see what all the commotion was about. He only knew that the convoy had stopped and that there was considerable excitement up ahead somewhere. Several soldiers ran past him, but he remained where he was, at his post.

Graff the traitor sat in the back of the hovercraft, and the sentry eyed the man warily. If it were up to *him,* Graff would be history. There didn't seem to be a whole lot of sense in dragging the prisoner along with the Legion to wherever it was going. What did the Colonel and the other high-ups plan? A big trial followed by a showy execution? That wouldn't help the poor bastards back in the DropShips, and it wouldn't help the Legion get off this dirtball of a planet.

The sentry shifted in his seat. The hovercraft's pilot had gone off to check on what had stopped the column. That wasn't according to route discipline, and so the sentry hoped that he wouldn't catch hell because the pilot had chosen to disregard orders. He looked at Graff, and Graff looked back.

Graff's eyes shifted past the sentry's shoulder, widening slightly. "Looks like he has big news," the prisoner said.

The sentry turned, expecting to see the hovercraft pilot returning. Instead, the prisoner's hands flashed down across his face, bringing the chain of his handcuffs biting into the young man's neck. He struggled, tried to cry out, but the pressure grew to an unendurable agony of pain and a shrieking need to breathe. The prisoner was strong. He wrenched the sentry to the side, dragging him from his seat. The sentry hung suspended over the side of the hovercraft, his booted feet kicking helplessly against the plenum chamber skirts, centimeters above the ground. The sentry's last clear thought was that he was really going to be in trouble now. Then the night closed in with a whistling clap of thunder, and he died.

Graff released the body and climbed across into the driver's seat. The ignition was still on, the turbine fans purring with disengaged power. He had to get away, had to! He would be running a risk trying to bolt through the perimeter, but he knew how weak the Legion forces were. There were only three BattleMechs along the entire west perimeter of the convoy, and they were widely spaced. If he sent the hovercraft racing into the night at top speed, he would catch them all by surprise, especially as they seemed to be occupied with some problem up ahead. He might escape into the night before they even realized what was happening!

Graff was actually more worried about what Rachan would do to him if the ComStar agent ever learned how much Graff had told Carlyle. Somehow, Rachan did not strike him as being the most forgiving of men. Efficient, yes. Ruthless . . . yes. Forgiving . . .

He engaged the plenum fans and guided the hovercraft in a tight, in-place spin, facing west. The night beckoned. He opened the thrust vents and felt the skimmer race forward. Behind, over the whine of his vehicle, he heard a shout, then a gunshot. By then, he was enfolded in darkness as the wind whipped his hair, and wild laughter burst from his throat. He was free!

Graff knew couldn't go back to Helmport, for Garth and Rachan would be there soon. They might even be on the ground already! No, there was another place Graff could go, and the warning he would bring might put Rachan in a more forgiving mood.

As soon as he was well clear of the convoy, he swung the hovercraft's nose toward the north.

BOOK III

===== 26 =====

The day was still new when the Gray Death Legion found the dry bed of the former eastern half of the Vermillion River, and followed it toward the Nagayan Mountains. There had been an hour's pause on the prairie when Grayson and King had rejoined the column. That had also given their hard-pressed 'Mechs and vehicles a chance to cool, while Grayson explained to the group commanders the results of his negotiations with Ricol.

They had help! Strange and unexpected help, it was true, but help! Among most of the people of the Legion, there was some measure of distrust for warriors of the Draconis Combine, but few hated Kurita's soldiers with the same passion that had driven Grayson Carlyle for so long. A warrior fought side by side with his comrades. The foe might be Kurita regulars one time, a pirate raiding force the next, but most one-on-one combat with the enemy was faceless, impersonal. That made it possible to accept that the faceless foe might become a trusted comrade, at least for a time. Most of the Legion members also trusted Grayson enough to believe that there was good reason for such an unexpected about-face.

Grayson explained that Duke Ricol had dispatched a force of ninety of his troops east toward Cleft Valley. It was possible that the landing of Garth's DropShips had delayed or interfered with that movement, but it was also likely that Ricol would take advantage of any confusion caused by Garth's arrival to move his troops out of Helmdown. He asked for volunteers to form a strike force that would turn around and head north once more. A rendezvous point had been selected in the hills south of Cleft Valley; Ricol's and the Legion's assault teams would join together, attempt to surprise the Marik guards in the valley, and then free the Legion's DropShips. The strike would have to be carefully timed and executed, Grayson told them, because Garth would not likely keep the Dropships prisoners alive beyond tomorrow. By daylight, the Marik command would know that the Legion had not risen to the bait left at Cleft Valley. Lord Garth could easily issue new orders concerning the DropShips and their occupants once he was on the ground at Helmdown.

The rescue would have to take place tonight, or the *Deimos*, the *Phobos*, and the Legion prisoners aboard were lost forever.

Again, there was no shortage of volunteers. The MechWarriors of A Company had to stay with the convoy, and Grayson refused Gomez DeVillar's request to accompany the rescue strike team because he would probably be needed to open the door to the Star League cache. The trainees of B Company volunteered to go, of course, and Grayson accepted them. Tracy Kent insisted on going, and Grayson agreed to that, too, knowing how worried she had been about the loss of her *Phoenix Hawk*. Fifty of the Regiment's infantry were also accepted, with the entire force under the command of Lieutenant Dulaney, the highest-ranking infantry officer that Grayson had. Sergeant Burns would accompany him as senior NCO.

Grayson gave Dulaney and Burns their specific orders, and watched as the strike force disentangled itself from the convoy and whined off on laboring plenum fans northward into the night.

Briefly, Grayson considered replacing the 'Mech technician who was piloting his *Marauder* on the trek, but he quickly thought better of it. Despite his nap while King had piloted the skimmer south from Helmdown, he was still exhausted. As the convoy formed up anew, now minus the vehicles and men and women who had departed, he was curled up again in the skimmer's passenger seat, and fell fast asleep.

When Grayson awoke at sun-up, he was considerably refreshed, despite the cramps in neck and back. The convoy had made good time. Within two hours, they could see the stark, skeletal remains of Freeport to the east, beneath the orange ball of Helm's sun. Soon after that, they found the dry river bed, and turned west to follow it. The BattleMechs moved with easy, long-paced strides, for the ground was firm and level. Occasionally, the sharpest eyes among them would spot traces of ancient, half-buried ferrocrete roads, and once a soldier kicked over a waist-high mound of dirt to reveal the corrosion-ravaged corpse of a Star League-era floater.

It was then that Grayson learned that Graff had escaped during the night. It was regrettable, of course, and Grayson wondered momentarily whether or not to dispatch a unit to try to track him down. He quickly realized the futility of that, just as Lori had the night before when deciding to wait till morning to tell Grayson. The plains were broad, the night dark. Even moments after Graff had stolen the hovercraft, he would have easily eluded pursuit.

Besides, what harm could the man do? Clearly, he wasn't going to return to Helmdown to face Rachan, not after revealing Rachan's plan to Grayson and his officers! If he returned to face Rachan, it would be with a fabricated story that could not hurt the Legion now. No, the convoy would proceed in force. There was nothing to be done about Graff now.

Fifteen hours after the column first set out from Durandel, the Gray Death Legion stood below the cliff that Grayson had first seen on the satellite map stolen from the Marik mobile headquarters. How much more imposing it was in reality than it had been on a satellite projection!

The river valley itself was perhaps ten meters wide at that point, a gentle depression lined with sand, gravel, and ancient, water-worn stones. On either side, the walls of the river valley proper rose more sharply, fifty meters high and capped by a blanket of heavy blue-green vegetation.

As the dry valley curved deeper in among the trees and rocks, there was a point where the valley walls stopped looking like accidents of nature, where even the most skeptical of the Legion's company could look to left and right and see the crisp lines where rock and dirt had been carved from the valley walls, widening the gap for the Wall.

There was no other name for it. Polished by eons of flowing water, it stood just as carefully shaped and set on end by unknown agencies as it had for the past three centuries. The rain and wind of those intervening centuries had softened the crisp contours of the valley cliffs on either side of the Wall somewhat, but they had not touched the granite structure itself. As Grayson stood before it, letting his hand run across its smooth surface, he could imagine that it had been set in place as a dam across that river valley only yesterday, that the builders themselves might step through some hidden door in that featureless expanse and demand to know what the Legion wanted.

Two hundred meters from the Wall was the lone building that Grayson had noticed on the modern map projection. Viewed from above, it had presented a curious sight. It looked even stranger up close, a squat, truncated, four-sided pyramid of cast ferrocrete and gray metal. Though it had no windows, an inset door opened inward on silent, floating bearings when Grayson set his hand against it. He stepped through quickly, with Lori and King close behind him.

"An engineering station," DeVillar said from the doorway, as others of the 'Mech company gathered outside. "Set up as an office or a construction headquarters by whoever built . . . that." Since they had arrived, most of the members of the Legion had avoided calling the structure across the river valley by name. Some called it "the Wall," but most referred to it obliquely as "that" or "it." The sheer scope of such an engineering feat had a numbing effect on those who saw it, for it would be impossible to duplicate it with present-day technology.

Grayson slowly turned, taking in the room. "Could be," he said. "They didn't leave much . . . except for the computer."

Though roomy enough to have stored a number of vehicles or large crates of machinery, which DeVillar suggested might have been the case, the one-room building was empty except for a table with built-in computer terminal and screen. The table was coated with a thick layer of dust, as was the floor and even the walls.

"You mean the engineers who built it worked here during the construction? Used the computer for their calculations, that sort of thing?"

"Seems likely," King said. He was examining the back of the computer. "Gods, how well they built things back then! This is the same sort of computer as up at Helmfast, but it has its own internal power cells, near as I can tell. You could turn it on right now . . . and it would probably work."

Grayson reached his hand out toward the keyboard, hesitated, then turned away. "Lieutenant DeVillar, let's take a look at that Wall. If we have to open it, I want to do it soon. Garth will be here soon, and I don't like camping in a blind alley like this. It would be too easy to catch us with no way out!"

A close examination of the wall confirmed Devillar's earlier appraisal. The granite block appeared to have been balanced on end, then anchored to the opposite sides of the valley escarpments with struts or bolts on the inside. Plastic explosive charges set at the upper corners of the Wall would shatter those struts, sending the wall falling outward, opening the way over the rubble to the storehouse in the tunnel that would be revealed on the far side.

While DeVillar and a pair of Techs clambered along the escarpments looking for places to implant their explosives, Grayson studied the face of the Wall itself. The smoothness appeared to be completely natural, the result of millennia of action by running water. There was one element of the Wall that was not natural. In two places, some twenty meters apart, Grayson found vertical grooves in the rock. They appeared to go straight up the face of the Wall for perhaps twenty meters, then turned toward each other, outlining a huge rectangle in the center of the stone.

A door? The groove was so narrow that Grayson could not force his knife point between the two sections of rock, but it was deep enough that even with a hand torch, he could not see how deeply it cut into the stone. If it were a door, there would have to be a key of some kind. What that key was, Grayson hadn't a clue.

His hand communicator bleeped. He took it from its belt hanger and opened the channel.

"Carlyle."

"Aye, Colonel, it's McCall. Ah go' a wee bit a' fell news."

"Bad news? What is it?"

"Ah'm trackit a large force . . . a *vurra* large force, to the north and travelin' south, fast!"

"You're tracking by their radio transmissions?"

"Aye . . . ah can ae' hear 'em chatterin' away at one another. Multiple signals . . . all in code . . . ah dinnae ken how many targets! Sair . . . usually ah' cannae track it tha' beasties across sae far a stretch. If ah'm tracking them noo . . . it's because there's ae' a great, great many a' them."

"Anything about our DropShips?" The strike force should have attacked the DropShips before dawn, though with the communications blackout Grayson had imposed on the entire force, there was no way to know whether the attempt had succeeded or failed.

"No, sair. No' a worrd."

"Right. As of now, you're our tracker. Keep on them. And let me know if you hear anything about the strike force." McCall's *Rifleman* had the best long-range sensors and tracking gear of any 'Mech in his command. It made sense for him to be responsible for watching the enemy force's approach.

Now that the Marik DropShips he had seen the night before had landed, the Marik 'Mech forces aboard would have been very busy indeed unloading their equipment and joining up with Langsdorf's forces already on the planet. The Marik DropShips still in orbit would have spotted the Legion force not long after sun-up, however, and possibly long before that if they had the correct and functioning technology for identifying 'Mechs from orbit in the dark.

Whatever their technology, it was certain that Garth's people knew precisely where the Legion was now, and they had to be on their way. He wondered if they had some inkling that Grayson already knew where the Star League cache was, that he was already preparing to blast his way in.

DeVillar began to gather his explosives.

Duke Garth entered the room, smiling. "All is in readiness, Precentor. The 15th Marik Militia is already moving. What is left of the 12th White Sabers and the 5th Marik Guards have joined with the House Marik Guard elements we have here. They are ready to move on my command!"

Precentor Rachan turned slowly, his face a mask of black fury. Garth stopped when he saw it, knowing that something was terribly wrong. The Precentor sat at a small tactical battlefield computer, an orbital photographic map projection displayed in color on the screen.

"Your command? *Your* command?"

"Precentor . . . what . . . ?"

"I *suggested* that we would need AeroSpace Fighters in case we had to search for Carlyle, but you said they could not be spared from Irian! I *told* you that we should have landed our ships to the south, near the ruins of Freeport, in hopes of catching Carlyle if his force moved toward the Nagayan Mountains! You refused, telling me that landing at a spaceport at night was *safer* than on open ground! I told you . . . I *insisted* that you set your 'Mechs moving without delay the moment we had grounded, and you found one trivial delay after another, until now the day is almost half gone, and *now,* only *now,* are you are ready to set out!"

"Precentor . . . I was not aware of any rush . . ."

"You fool! You bloody, malfing fool! Look at this!"

Garth looked past Rachan to the computer display. In the center of the map was a miniature galaxy of light pinpoints gathered along what looked like a satellite photograph of a dried river bank. A huge, vertical cliff caught the direct light of the morning sun.

"You see them, Garth? That is the Gray Death Legion enhanced by infrared light . . . Several hundred troops, several hundred civilians, a number of vehicles . . . and at least eight BattleMechs. There is a *Marauder* there. That will be Carlyle.''

"You've found them? Where . . . ?''

"Camped by a dry river valley, close against the Nagayan Mountains, 500 kilometers south of here.''

"Well, he's stolen a march, but he'll be slowed, crossing those mountains. There are mountain passes, of course, but travel through them will be difficult. We can still catch him . . .''

Rachan pointed to the cliff and explained slowly, as though speaking with a not-too-bright child. "You see that, Garth? See it? It is a cliff. A sheer, straight, vertical cliff. It looks perfectly natural, does it not? And yet, can you imagine a soldier of Grayson Carlyle's proven battle skill camping in such a place, with no line of retreat . . . no way out should we come down on him from the north or east? No . . . you wouldn't see that, because you are too dim-witted to perceive a trap when you face one! There can be only one reason why Carlyle and his people are camped there . . . only one!'' Rachan paused and pounded the table viciously as he spat out, "He has found the Star League cache!''

"Found the . . . but how? How? You told me your ComStar researchers had studied the records for years, looking for some clue.''

"I don't know, Garth.'' The Precentor chewed at his lip as he studied the computer projection. "Maybe something he found at Helmfast. Maybe blind, stupid luck. But now . . . *now*, looking at where he is, the artificiality of his surroundings is obvious!''

Garth looked closely. "What do you mean? I see a cliff . . . big rocks . . .''

"You see what you expect to see. What you don't see is why the river that carved out that valley flowed directly into a sheer, blank rock wall . . . and then vanished!''

"You mean that cliff . . .''

"Is a doorway of some sort. It almost certainly leads to what we've been searching for for so long, and Carlyle is about to get it!''

"What's he waiting for?''

"A key, I should imagine. He needs to figure out how to get in."

"And if he finds it?" Garth's face worked uncertainly. "Suppose he turns the weapons inside against us!"

Rachan snorted. "Nonsense. Not in the time he has! Any 'Mechs stored there will not have their weapons mounted, will not be stocked with ammunition. It would take time to power up their reactors."

"Then what's the problem?"

"If he gets in, he will seek to bargain with us." Rachan shook his head, his face set in grim lines. "It is the only thing he can do . . . give us what we want, in exchange for his life and the life of his troops. What he can't know is that we can outlast him. However deep that storehouse is buried, however large it may be, the Gray Death Legion cannot hope to survive in there for long without food and fresh water. Water they may find, if there are underground springs or streams there, but their food problem is going to become critical very soon. There will be no hunting inside the caverns, and his provisions must be running low by now, with that many people to feed."

"So . . . we will starve them out?"

"We will do whatever is necessary. And the first thing that is necessary, Garth, is that you not command the forces against him."

"What? Wait! You can't do that . . ."

"You forget yourself, Garth. *I* am in command of this expedition, and I alone, remember? Colonel Langsdorf showed excellent judgment, speed, and planning at Clef Valley. Three enemy BattleMechs were destroyed, to a loss of only one of our own . . . and the DropShips were captured!"

"With a spy's help . . ."

"That's right, with a spy's help, but it was Colonel Langsdorf who gave the spy his opportunity, who had his troops in the right place at the right time to assist the spy, who managed the battle in a brilliant fashion. I am sorry, Garth, but this campaign is far too important to be left in your blundering, thumb-fingered hands!"

Garth didn't think Rachan sounded sorry at all. "You

cannot treat me this way!'' He drew himself up taller, trying to look down on the ComStar man. "Precentor or not, you have no *right!* *I am* Duke of Irian . . .''

"Consider it a . . . *promotion*. Your Grace. You and I will be on the field as observers only, watching as Colonel Langsdorf closes the trap on our prey.

"But it *will* be Colonel Langsdorf who leads, Garth. I have watched you, and you could not lead your nose to your face!''

Garth bristled, but Rachan soothed him with a motion of his hand, and a tired smile. "Peace, Your Grace, peace. I meant no disrespect. Langsdorf is a trained and talented military leader, and you are not . . . but that is not your disgrace.'' He shrugged. "I have already discussed matters with the Colonel, and he has worked up a plan to overwhelm the Gray Death. Perhaps we can trap him against the mountains, if he does not find the key he seeks. Perhaps we can pin him inside the cache, if he finds a way in. In any case, we must overcome the results of your incompetence.'' Rachan turned back to study the map, dismissing the Duke of Irian.

"You press too far, Rachan,'' Garth said.

"Because I have great ambitions, Garth. Ambitions that someone like you cannot even begin to imagine. Ambitions that will not be stopped by someone like you . . . or a man like Grayson Death Carlyle!'' He stopped then, his eyes aflame. Then, slowly, he seemed to draw back inside himself, to subdue the passion that had gripped him. He passed a hand over his face, looked back up at Garth, and smiled. "I'm sorry, Your Grace,'' he said. "I am . . . tired. There is much to attend to here. Come . . . consider instead what you will do with your share of the weapons from the Star League cache, when you sit on the throne of the Captain-General, ruler supreme of House Marik and the Free Worlds League!

"*That* should satisfy even *you*!''

26

There were rain clouds in the west, piling into the sky above the Dead Sea Flats on the horizon. Bubble tents had sprouted like bizarre, camouflaged mushrooms on either side of the dry river valley. The Legion's noncombatants clustered in the center of the encampment, with the soldiers and armored vehicles around the perimeter. On the outskirts, waiting and watchful, were A Company's surviving BattleMechs.

Grayson stood on a small rise by the river bank, watching the gathering clouds. He had just had the usual experience of speaking by radio with Colonel Addison, regimental commander of a House Kurita special strike force aboard the DropShip fleet. Already inbound, Ricol's DropShips were accelerating toward Helm at a spine-pounding 2.5 Gs. They would swing end for end sometime that night and begin deceleration leg, entering atmosphere above the Nagayan Mountains by late afternoon tomorrow.

Grayson had until then to get inside the cache, find what there was to find, and prepare to leave the planet. There was still no word from the *Deimos* and the *Phobos*, which was not good. Addison had not been in contact with Ricol, and that in itself was strange. Dulaney *should* have joined Ricol's forces long before daylight, and they should have heard *some* word by now, either reporting success or announcing disaster. Grayson wondered if Graff's escape had spoiled the plan somehow, but decided that, at this point, there was nothing more he could do about it. He would have to take care of his own people who were here with him.

They had worry enough in the "vurra large force" spotted by McCall. Those 'Mechs would be here by nightfall, long before Grayson could hope for help from Ricol's incoming DropShips. Their one hope now was to get inside the cache.

He stared across the river bed toward the Wall. He could barely make out the forms of DeVillar and the two Techs working with him atop the wall as they searched for the best places to lay their satchel-charge explosives.

Their basic strategic problem at this point was the approach of the heavy Marik forces. If DeVillar could blow down the wall, Grayson would be able to move the Legion inside the shelter of the cache itself. A small force of 'Mechs would be sufficient to hold the opening against whatever forces Marik was able to bring to bear.

Unfortunately, if Marik forces were encamped outside the entrance to the cache when the DropShips arrived, how would the Legion be able to even approach and board Ricol's fleet, much less load it with treasure from the cache? Various possible alternatives flashed through his mind. He could lead his eight 'Mechs north and meet the Marik 'Mechs halfway. A Company would be destroyed, but it might buy time for the rest to make their escape.

Or would it? Eight 'Mechs could be destroyed easily by a fraction of the army being brought to bear on them. Garth could afford to deploy enough 'Mechs against Grayson's command to keep them busy, while marching the rest on the cache gate. Another possibility was to pull out now, while there was time. They could slip north and west across one of the passes that breached the wall of the Nagayan Mountains, and emerge on the Vermillion Plains to the west. Perhaps a small 'Mech force could stop the Marik army long enough by holding them at the passes. The problem, of course, was that there were three passes to defend. While Grayson was holding one, Garth could slip a large force past his position and into the rear. Besides, to run now would mean giving up all hope of raiding the cache, and Grayson was not sure what Ricol's reaction would be when he found himself with a plain full of refugees, and no treasure. He had agreed to pick up the Gray Death Legion, even if the treasure were lost somehow, but Grayson would still feel he had cheated on his end of the bargain. There had to be a way to salvage at least something of the cache for Ricol, as well as to keep it from the ComStar and Marik forces marching south on their position now.

The key, Grayson realized, as he stared at that blank, impenetrable wall, lay in the doorway to the cache itself . . . and to the cache's nature. There had been a door there, and so there had to be a way of making it open.

One possibility was that it might require a radio command, modulated a certain way, or on a certain frequency. A spoken code word, an ''open sesame'' from the pages of ancient Terran mythology was another. So, too, was a literal key, a device hidden somewhere that, when manipulated, would trigger the mechanism of the gate and cause it to open.

The Gray Death Legion could camp on this plain for a year trying various combinations of code words and electronic modulations in an attempt to reach the door's mechanical guardians. They could search the entire Helmfast district for a century and never find a hidden key, which could be anything—disguised as a piece of machinery, or a decoration on a mantle piece, or . . .

Grayson froze where he was, eyes riveted to the Wall, paralyzed momentarily by a bolt of inspiration. The engineers who worked here would have needed to open the door, both when they were setting it in place, and later, when they were transferring the stock of weapons from Freeport to the cache site. They would have needed a convenient way of opening the door, and an equally convenient way of keeping the door's secret safe. They would have created the key in such a way that it could be passed on, from one of the district's military guardians to another, for generation after generation, if need be. Presumably, whoever was in command of the military district would have the key. It might be that the key's purpose, even the knowledge of its existence, had been lost during Helm's struggles to survive, centuries ago. It would take the death of only one man before he could pass the secret on to his successor for the secret to be forgotten, lost forever.

Or the secret could be rediscovered, now!

Grayson turned and began to sprint for the vehicles that carried what had been salvaged from Helmhold. He, Grayson Carlyle, was the modern-day military governor of the district. As Lord of Helmfast, he was the heir to the lost Star League cache and all it contained. No wonder Rachan and Garth had wanted to get him out of the way. He, Grayson, had had the key to the Star League cache the whole time!

He found what he wanted among the headquarters supplies in one of the trucks, then sprinted back toward the truncated pyramid resting on the gravel banks of the dry river. Lori saw his pounding run and followed. She burst into the engine shack moments after Grayson had plunged inside.

"Grayson! What is it?"

"Maybe . . ." Grayson was gasping for air, making speech nearly impossible, but he was working now, bent above the ancient Star League computer on its table in the half-lit shack. He keyed the initiate sequence and watched colored bars of light chase one another across the display. "Maybe the key . . . we've been . . . been looking for!"

He held up what he had recovered from the headquarters transport vehicle—the map program from Helmfast. That memory clip had been given to him as part of the investment ceremony in Helmdown months ago, a Star League-era map of his domains on the world of Helm. Presumably, that clip had been handed down, Helmfast lord to Helmfast lord, for three centuries. How many of those lords had known the secret it might hold? None, possibly, save for those who had written the program in the days of Minoru Kurita.

Grayson inserted the map program clip into the slot on the side of the engineering computer terminal.

He didn't realize he was holding his breath.

A computer program, whatever its purpose, however it is designed, written, and stored, is a collection of information arranged in electronic form, a systematic and complete list of instructions that a computer can interpret and act upon, step by step. The map program contained instructions and stored data based on old orbital photographs, which could be displayed as a photographic map that allowed the viewer to examine the mapped area at varying levels of clarity and detail, according to his manipulations on the keyboard.

The list of instructions in a program could be designed to be very flexible and subtle. A very long program, or a piece of a program, could be written and stored on the memory clip in such a way that no one would ever suspect it was there. So far as any casual user of the program was concerned, this new section of the program did not even exist. There was no way to get at it, unless the program were instructed to reveal the hidden information. That code could be a series of letters or numbers entered through the keyboard . . . or by uttered voice into computers that responded to voice command.

One particularly elegant solution, though, in cases when the code word might be lost or forgotten, was to build the code into the computer itself. The program might be designed to work perfectly in *any* computer that would accept it. No one would ever suspect the existence of the hidden program section unless the program were run in *one particular* computer, the one that held the secret code. In that computer, the code, set into the computer's own working memory, would be applied against any program run in it. When the program with the hidden program section was run, the code would unlock the electronic door, and . . .

"Colonel! Colonel!" He looked up as a Legion trooper burst into the doorway. "Colonel! Come quick!"

Grayson turned from the terminal. The display had remained irritatingly blank when he plugged the memory clip into the slot. He had not even gotten the ordinary map display, and he was beginning to think that something was wrong with the computer.

"Sir! It's . . . the Wall!"

Grayson and Lori both hurried to the door and looked out. Two hundred meters away, men and women were stepping back, looking toward the towering gray monolith of granite that blocked the valley. Grayson could feel a peculiar vibration in the ground through the soles of his boots, and he was aware of small pebbles along the bottom of the dried river jittering and dancing in time to some massive movement of engines or equipment beneath the surface.

The Wall had opened. The section within the grooves that Grayson had noted earlier was sliding back into the rock, exposing a smoothly cut opening in the rock face. When the section had withdrawn into darkness for a depth of two meters, it stopped with an audible *thunk*. Then there came a grinding of machinery as the rock section slid aside. Ten meters wide, twenty tall, the doorway stood open.

Hundreds of kilometers to the north, Colonel Julian Langsdorf leaned forward in the cockpit seat of his *Warhammer,* willing the bulky Marik column to move faster . . . faster! Several 'Mechs had turned back already due to breakdown or overheating problems, but he was determined to press forward at maximum speed, to catch Grayson Carlyle before another 24 hours had passed. The Gray Death Legion had slipped away during the night, had covered far more ground than he had thought would be possible for a convoy that must include hundreds of civilians, technicians, and wounded personnel. He had not expected such a move at all. After all, where could such a column go? They could continue to hide in the valleys and forests of the Aragayan Mountains for months, if need be, where there was shelter and plenty of water and game. To strike out south, however . . . There was nothing in that direction but the inhospitable wastes of the Nagayan Mountains, the mineral salt wastes of the dead sea, the cratered ruins of Freeport, and endless prairie.

The man who had identified himself as ComStar Precentor Rachan had explained matters to Langsdorf. Carlyle was searching for the lost League cache, possibly with a good idea of its whereabouts, and he was hoping to seize it before Langsdorf could bring his forces to bear.

Rachan had put Langsdorf in direct command of the entire Marik Expeditionary Force. General Kleider was still en route and would not arrive for several hours yet. Rachan had assured Langsdorf that even when Kleider grounded, the final closing of the trap on the renegade Carlyle and his band was completely under *his* command.

Carlyle had escaped Langsdorf before, and the man was determined that he could not escape again.

Langsdorf had twenty-seven BattleMechs in his force. His own 12th White Sabers consisted of six 'Mechs, plus a handful of armored hovercraft and some mechanized infantry he had drawn from perimeter duty at the spaceport, all under Major Sigwell Allendry. There were only two 'Mechs left of the small 5th Marik Guards. Both had been incorporated into the 4th Light Assault Group under Captain Maranov, bringing that company to a full twelve 'Mechs. The 7th Light Assault Group under Captain Chu Shi-Lin was understrength with nine 'Mechs, and five of those were 20-ton *Stingers* or *Wasps*.

Finally, he had a collection of hover tanks and mechanized infantry of the Marik House Guard under a foppish Lieutenant Colonel named Haverlee. Langsdorf wasn't certain how he would be able to use *that* bunch, but he would find something for them to do, one way or the other.

Though his command was a kind of a ragtag throw-together, twenty-seven 'Mechs was a powerful force—almost a full battalion's worth. Meanwhile, reconnaisance reports showed that Carlyle had only eight 'Mechs under his command, plus a scattering of light armor. Rachan had assured him that even if Carlyle managed to penetrate the Star League cache, there was no way he would could ready and power up any weapons in the depot in time to do his renegade band any good. Besides, he would have only a limited number of people who could even operate the stuff. How many MechWarrior trainees might be with him . . . eight? Five? Probably not even that many.

Langsdorf was determined to plant explosives and bring down the entire face of the cliff if Carlyle did man-

age somehow to find a way into the storehouse. Star
League weapons would do Carlyle little good in a final,
desperate battle in the depths of that mountain.

One way or another, Colonel Grayson Carlyle's hours
were numbered!

Grayson stood inside the old Star League cache. It was
difficult to contain his surprise . . . or his disappointment.

The towering blackness of the Wall blocked off the
light behind him, except for the shaft falling through the
open door. The troops and dependents were already fil-
tering in, awed into silence by the size of the hidden
chamber. A grating, mechanical sound echoing through
the rock-walled chamber announced the arrival of Bear's
Crusader, moving carefully across the threshold so as
not to kill or injure any of the people at his feet.

The chamber was a full fifty meters wide and over
twenty meters tall, the rocky ceiling barely visible in the
weak beams of hand torches cast this way and that.
Ahead, the tunnel descended sharply into darkness that
swallowed their lights, giving no clue at all to where the
far wall might be.

Yet this whole, vast chamber, obviously once a storehouse that could have held rank upon rank of Battle-
Mechs with ease, was completely empty. All that
remained was a building similar to the one outside, a
chopped-off, flat-topped, four-sided pyramid with a single door. Holding his torch and trying to keep his hand
from trembling, Grayson approached the small building.
It was probably another engineering shack of some sort.

Was it possible that the cache had not been found in
time before Kurita's invitation? That the chamber was
still being prepared when word came that Kurita's fleet
was materializing at the system's jump points? Perhaps
the Star League equipment had been hidden in the city
of Freeport, after all. A city is an enormous, complex
place. Was it possible that Kurita had *missed* the actual
hiding place during his search, and that the treasure trove
of League artifacts had been destroyed when Freeport
was vaporized?

THE PRICE OF GLORY

As Grayson entered the small building within the chamber, he knew that it was indeed possible, because this building had *nothing* whatsoever to do with a League military storehouse.

27

Rachan looked at each of the faces in turn. These six men with him were Adepts from the hyperpulse generator complex north of the Helmdown spaceport, the highest-ranking ComStar operatives on the planet. They had gathered in this gloomy little basement room of the Helmdown ComStar facility because Rachan was absolutely certain of the security here.

Had Helm been an A-class HPG facility, there would have been another Precentor like himself to manage it. The presence of another Precentor—however awed he might have been by Rachan's credentials—would have complicated matters considerably, for Rachan had taken great liberties with his authority with the hierarchy of the Order. It was entirely possible, even *probable,* that these six Adepts would all meet with unfortunate accidents within the next few weeks, if all went well in the military operation against Carlyle. ComStar Adepts, by regulations dating back almost to the time of Blake himself, never spent more than a year at any one ComStar station or facility in order to prevent undue familiarity among the various staff members. If six tragic accidents did not somehow occur, then within a year, all six Adepts would have been transferred to six other worlds across the Inner Sphere.

Rachan could not permit the secret these six would learn within the next few days to spread to other worlds, even among other Adepts sworn to secrecy. It had to be buried here on Helm.

The Precentor smiled, nodding to each of the men.

"I've brought you together because I know that you all are trustworthy," he said. "What we are dealing with here is a secret that must never fall into the hands of those outside the very highest ranks of ComStar! It is a secret that holds the future of ComStar itself!"

One of the men was Senior Adept Larabee, a man in his late twenties and the ComStarTech in charge of Helmdown's HPG station. "Excuse me, Precentor," Larabee said. "Does this have to do with this weapon cache in the south? Rumors have been flying through this city for days . . ."

"ComStar is not interested in the weapons," Rachan interrupted.

Another Adept looked startled. "I thought that was the whole purpose of the Marik operation! This renegade Carlyle had the key to a lost Star League treasure, and ComStar was helping this Duke Garth recover it!"

"Silence, and attend!" Rachan spoke the time-honored formula used by ComStar instructors with Acolyte apprentices. Having been an instructor for many years, he knew well how to assert his authority over the wills of others. "The weapons cache is a blind, merely a pretext to win Garth's obedience. That Star League facility contains something more precious than BattleMechs or laser weaponry.

"It contains a treasure, and I'll need your help to win it!"

The rising of the sun had not brought the attack on the captured DropShips. Tracy Maxwell Kent lay flat on her stomach on the wooded slope 100 meters from the *Deimos*, practically in the DropShip's shadow, and wondered what they were going to do now.

The plan had depended on their rendezvousing with Kurita troops under Duke Ricol's command south of Cleft Valley. The idea had been to surprise the DropShips with their equipment bays open. When word came that the Legion had marched south, the Marik troops would surely relax security around the captured DropShips.

First of all, Ricol's forces had never shown up. There was no telling what had happened there, though the rumor spreading through the assault force was that the Kurita warlord had betrayed them.

That figures, Tracy thought. *So now we face two DropShips with fifty troops. Great!*

The enemy had not relaxed his security, either. So far as Tracy could see, no one had bothered to tell the Marik forces there that the Legion had gone. The woods were silent, and the BattleMech bay doors were shut, the rampways tucked safely away. Outside each ship, six Marik soldiers in full, bulky combat armor walked nervous patrols. Their attitude suggested that they expected Carlyle's 'Mechs to appear out of the woods at any moment. Tracy turned her head, looking south. Lieutenant Dulaney lay stretched out behind a clump of weeds, and what she could see of his face through all the camouflage paint showed that he was as perplexed as she was. On Tracy's other side, Janice Taylor shifted the position of her TK assault rifle, almost in slow motion, so as not to alert enemy sensors.

So what now? They could lie here in the weeds all day, but it didn't look like the DropShips' captors were going to give them the opportunity they were waiting for, and every passing minute increased their risk of being discovered. Someone among them would sneeze or perhaps be annoyed by some stinging Helman creature, and then the assault force would lose the hope of winning by surprise.

The sun continued to rise. Tracy was sweating heavily now, her face paint smearing into a grotesque caricature. She stared at the *Deimos* with hungry fascination. Somewhere aboard, strapped and racked along with the rest of the Legion equipment stored in the ship's cargo bays, was the *Dutiful Daughter,* her *Phoenix Hawk.* If she could get in, if Tracy could reach her 'Mech, the whole situation would be transformed.

If! If! The word mocked her.

There was a noise, a thrashing in the underbrush 500 meters to the south. She turned her head, searching the light-dappled woods. There was a stir around the *Deimos* as well. Turret-mounted lasers high in the ship's hull swiveled toward the sound, while the guards in the shadows by the landing legs turned, their weapons at the point.

What emerged from the brush startled Tracy so much that she nearly cried aloud. It was a man dressed in the tattered and dirt-smeared coveralls of someone who had traveled a long, long way through woods and rough terrain on foot. He was too far off for her to recognize his features, but there was something about his form, his posture and the way he moved, that was familiar. The next moment, it came to her in a flash who the man was. *Graff!*

Somehow, he had escaped from the Legion, had made his way back here. How? Perhaps he had stolen a hovercraft and abandoned the machine nearby, so that he would not be mistaken for the enemy. He entered the clearing between the DropShips now, his hands upraised, still chained together, a white cloth in his fingers. She could hear his voice as he called out to the DropShips. "Hey! Hey! You in there! This is Captain Grass, Marik House Guard! I have news! Don't shoot! I'm friendly! Don't shoot!"

Two of the *Deimos*'s guards consulted with the others, then left their posts, approaching Graff cautiously with their rifles leveled. Two more sentries approached from the *Phobos,* to the south, joining Graff midway between the two vessels. As Tracy watched, the five men talked excitedly. She could not hear them, but there was much gesticulating and waving of arms.

A moment later, there was a sound from inside the *Deimos,* and the BattleMech bay door ground open, the ramp extending out and down to the ground. Two more sentries took their places on either side of the open door, weapons at port arms. A moment later, a pair of Marik officers strode down the ramp and turned toward the conference in the clearing. Half a kilometer away, Tracy could see a similar delegation approaching from the south. Graff's message could only be that the Legion was far away, and that he had escaped to warn his Marik comrades. She could see the subtle shift among the sentries taking part in the conference, the lowering of weapons, the slouching of their postures.

She let her eyes shift over to Dulaney, and he looked back, and winked. Slowly, very slowly, he raised his thumb in a universally understood thumbs-up gesture. *This* was the opportunity they'd been waiting for!

Dulaney moved his hand, bringing the small hand-held transmitter to his lips. "All units . . . this is it! Go! Go!"

Listeners aboard the DropShips would hear, of course, but they would lose long seconds to surprise and confusion. As a single body, the fifty hidden men and women along the ridges on both sides of the landing zone rose from the weeds and brush and scattered boulders. Laser and submachine gun fire lanced and stabbed into the valley. Tracy saw the sentries under the *Deimos* whirl, eyes wide, their weapons searching the ridge slopes, looking for a target. By the time they found their targets, though, by the time those targets had registered on their brains, they were already dying, cut through by a hail of automatic fire.

Tracy held down the trigger of her TK as she ran down the hill, hosing the entrance to the *Deimos*'s 'Mech bay with a small and deadly cloud of 3 mm slivers. One of the sentries on the ramp threw down his rifle and clasped his face with his hands as blood erupted from the ruin of his face. The other sentry pitched off the ramp, blood pumping from multiple, shattered craters in his body armor.

By the time Tracy reached the bottom of the slope, someone aboard the *Deimos* had awakened to the fact that the DropShips were under attack. A laser battery turret swung from high up along the ship's hull, its double barrels swinging around to cover the woods. Then laser light flared like a star gone nova, outlining in stark and hideous clarity the forms of running men and women, burning them into Tracy's mind like the flash from some gigantic strobe lamp. From behind her, she heard the unmistakable, blood-curdling sound of an agonized death scream.

Then another laser fired . . . and another. Someone at the gunnery controls was firing wildly. Some shots angled off into the trees to the east, where a fire had already begun. Others flashed off toward the south, toward the *Phobos*, and Tracy could hear shrieks of horror and agony from that direction as well.

They would *all* die if they remained where the lasers could mark them down. Their only hope was to gain the DropShip ramp. Men were gathered at the top of the ramp as she approached from the bottom, and she felt a kind of plucking at the left sleeve of her uniform as her boot came down on the ramp's base.

Tracy fired her TK again, seeing gruesome wounds open like red blossoms among the men above her. Then Lieutenant Dulaney was rushing past her, running up the ramp toward the open door. That door was grinding closed now, even as the ramp started to move under her feet. The movement knocked Tracy down, and she scrabbled to find some purchase on the grated surface.

''Tracy!''

She looked down and back and wished she hadn't. The ramp was withdrawing into the ship, its end now meters above the ground. She looked down into the eyes of Janice Taylor, wide and white in her paint-smeared face.

''Tracy! Let go!''

But Tracy clung to the ramp as it swung into the air.

Dulaney was above and beyond her, firing his submachine gun in short, savage bursts. Somehow, the man kept his balance as the ramp moved, somehow he began moving again, step after uncertain step, still firing, moving toward the narrowing opening of the hatch. Why didn't he fall? He reached the hatch when it was three-quarters closed, stepping through into the red light that flooded from the opening. She heard gunfire, submachine gun rattles mingled with the throatier blasts of rifles. She heard Dulaney scream.

Tracy followed, clutching the TK's pistol grip with one hand, the ramp grating with the other, making her way up toward the hatch. She realized the Bay hatch had stopped closing by the time she had reached the top, and squeezed through the meter-tall opening.

Inside, the bay was red-lit and filled with struggling figures. She saw Dulaney's body sprawled nearby, the submachine gun lying beyond one outflung hand. She had only a moment to wonder at how so many of the attacking Legion troops had managed to get past her and up the ramp. Only she and Dulaney had been on the ramp when it began to move. The answer struck her with almost brutal force. The prisoners! They must have been kept on one of the DropShip's lower decks, must have attacked their guards when the Legion strike force's attack had begun!

Seeing two Marik soldiers run toward a hatchway, she cut them down with a swift, accurate burst from her TK. Then she found the bay hatch controls close by Dulaney's body. The Lieutenant had managed to punch the button that stopped the hatch from closing entirely, but had died before he could open the door and extend the ramp all the way once more. She touched the proper controls, then stood guard, crouched above the Lieutenant's body.

Once the rest of the assault force assigned to the *Deimos* arrived, the battle did not last. There had been only twenty Marik troopers aboard, less than the total number of prisoners. No wonder they had looked nervous!

Word came swiftly that the strike force's rush had taken the *Phobos* as well. That ship's defenders had not even had time to fire a laser or to try to cycle their hatch shut. Ilse Martinez had gutted a Marik guard with a combat knife she had hidden before her capture, and led the rest of the *Phobo*'s crew against the bridge, even as Legion troops had poured onto the 'Mech bay deck. Even at that, it had been a close call. Seven of the assault force troops had been killed, including Dulaney. Six prisoners had died in the battles aboard the DropShips. Fifteen were wounded among both the rescuers and the rescued. The ships' doctors and medical personnel began working at once to set up an emergency surgery in an empty cargo bay on the *Phobos*.

They found Graff's body, or what was left of it, some time later. A wild, slicing laser shot from the *Deimos* had exploded most of his body from the waist down. Though Tracy felt Graff had gotten what he deserved, she had other things on her mind.

When she found the *Dutiful Daughter* intact, hung safely in its storage rack, she had been overjoyed.

Now she would show what she could do!

THE PRICE OF GLORY

* * *

Grayson ran his fingers across the deeply engraved lettering in the ferrocrete facing of the building inside the underground chamber, and felt a profound shock to see those words in this place. He and his people had been looking for a weapons cache, and instead had found: STAR LEAGUE FIELD LIBRARY FACILITY, HELM, DE890-2699.

He had heard of such facilities, but had never seen one. Most, he knew, had been set up in the important cities of worlds across the Inner Sphere, urban centers of modern culture and learning. Unfortunately, the vast majority of those cities had fallen during the holocausts of the First and Second Succession Wars.

"What is it, Gray?" Lori said. "What does it mean?"

"It means we might have some trouble explaining it to Duke Ricol," Grayson said. "I don't think *this* is what he had in mind when he spoke of a Star League treasure." The door opened silently at his touch, and light flooded the single room when his boot touched the carpeted deck. This room was not dusty, as had been the engineering shack outside, but it held the same built-in desk and computer.

Grayson quickly sent a soldier for the memory clip still set into the slot of the computer outside. When the clip was plugged into the library computer, the entire wall opposite the computer terminal came to life in color and light. Some words flashed on: *"The Advancement and diffusion of knowledge is the only true guardian of liberty."—James Madison.*

When Grayson touched the engage key, the words vanished and were replaced by what, at first glance, appeared to be a listing of subjects. The room was indeed a library of sorts, and slowly, haltingly, Grayson began to learn how to use it.

Within the next two hours, he discovered a great deal. How a culture handles the dissemination of information to its population can be one of the most critical aspects of its vitality. A culture that restricts information to a select and militant few, or one that reserves learning only for those few able to afford expensive technical devices or expensive schooling—those cultures are flawed to their very cores, no matter how outwardly vigorous and expansive. The Helm library had been one technological answer to the problem that faces every advanced civilization: how do you put an explosion of new information into the hands of people who need it?

Grayson learned that, centuries ago, libraries such as this had been located on every world, in nearly every major city of the old Star League. Their design was simple: it consisted of a memory core that could easily be duplicated onto other cores, and read off the appropriate electronic hardware, either a computer terminal or a simple memory retrieval screen. The technology of the 31st Century, Grayson realized, was no longer up to building a device such as the library itself, but the memory cores and the means for duplicating that knowledge were commonly available. A sampling of the information stored within the computer's memory convinced Grayson that he had found a treasure far greater than any number of BattleMechs.

There was the formula for a simple chemical catalyst, one that would allow silicon, gallium, arsenic, and carbon to be combined in such a way that the material became superconducting at room temperature, allowing the transmission of fantastic voltages of electricity, with no waste heat and no loss of power. That was a secret, Grayson knew, that had long been lost—a secret that could improve the handling of the immense electrical charges required to move a starship into jumpspace. Manufacturers already had devised a method for this crucial process, but even to Grayson's untutored eye, it looked like the new information was much more efficient.

Here, too, was a technique for manipulating the genes of earth-stock dairy animals in such a way that milk production was increased fourfold, as well, as providing certain trace elements, vitamins, and anticarcinines as well.

Grayson was looking for something special among this dazzling array of knowledge that he had managed to access from the library's memories. He touched the display key, and a map covered the far wall in a glowing confusion of color. As he studied the tangled traceries of light and words for a moment, Grayson smiled.

He had found a map of the Star League's Nagayan Mountain Facility.

28

The Star League facility was far larger than anyone had expected. As Grayson had guessed, the main, central corridor was a cavern originally hollowed out by the waters of the Vermillion moving rapidly through a natural cavern system under the Nagayan Mountains. Major Keeler and his battalion of Star League engineers had begun the project by creating a system of subsurface tunnels beneath Freeport, adding to tunnels originally designed to channel flood waters away from the city and into a deep fault chasm known as ''Helm's Pit.''

The Nagayan Mountains, Grayson learned, marked the point where two of Helm's continental plates ground against one another. Millions of years before, an upwelling at that site had created the mountains themselves, and the gradual rise of the land to the east had produced the North Highland Plains. The fault line that marked the juncture of crustal plates existed still, and in one place, the two sides had drawn far enough apart to create a hole into Helm's depths that was, for all practical purposes, bottomless.

Helm's Pit, then, became the drain into which the engineers funnelled the waters of the Vermillion River. The eastern half of the river had dried, leaving a water-polished tunnel plunging into the depths of the mountain. But the mountain, they had discovered, was honeycombed with subsurface tunnels and conduits.

Grayson learned that Keeler had not been the first engineer to work on the Nagayan project, but only the last, and the most successful. The first excavations had been carried out with an eye to creating an underground laboratory. Later, the project was redirected toward an attempt to build a gigantic and impregnable fortress. It had been Keeler who had used the facility as a hiding place for the weapons stored at the League Fleet Base in Freeport.

Keeler had been a subject of the Marik Commonwealth, but he was also a deeply committed advocate of the principle that had created the Star League—that of a limited interstellar community. Grayson read Keeler's own monologues on the subject: the League was disintegrating, the foundations of civilization itself were crumbling. General Kerensky, a powerful warlord whose armies and fleets had, for a time, guaranteed the peace, vanished beyond the Periphery in 2784, taking much of the League's military might with him. That exodus had triggered the final collapse of the Star League, as the lords of the various former League Member-States had risen, each one against the other, in a series of futile and bloody attempts to win control of the Star League's dismembered corpse.

Keeler had foreseen that final collapse. Convinced that the Star League could be rebuilt, that General Kerensky would soon return, Keeler completed the repository for weapons from the naval base at Freeport only weeks before it was learned that Minoru Kurita and his warfleet were bound for Helm for the sole purpose of seizing those weapons. Meanwhile, Keeler had apparently been engaged in a delicate series of negotiations with various factions within the Free Worlds League, who were also intent on grabbing the weapons. By playing them off one against another, he had bought time for himself, and for his project.

There had been no way to buy off Minoru Kurita, however.

"Then Keeler wasn't able to hide the weapons here after all," Lori said, reading over Grayson's shoulder. The screen displayed a report from one of Keeler's subordinates to the Major himself, alerting him of Kurita's approach and mentioning that transport for the main body of the arms depot was not yet available. "That paper seems to indicate that the League storehouse is still located in Freeport."

"I think they must have really pulled together after that, Lori. Look what I found here." He punched several keys, wiping away the report. It was replaced by the intricately interweaving pathways of the map of the Nagayan underground complex. Skillfully, Grayson called up one section of the map, enlarging it until it filled the screen. He pointed to the words spelled out in white letters. "Main Depot Stores", Grayson read aloud. "It's in a room all the way over on the west side of the mountain. The map shows several exits . . . here . . . here . . . and up here. There appears to be a functional transport system, and if I read this right, there are even entrances up on the surface, interconnecting the various mountain passes. This . . . this complex could have held a city without crowding."

"It's magic," Lori said quietly.

"Let's just say our ancestors knew a trick or two that we seem to have forgotten," Grayson replied. "What amazes me is that an awful lot of what we've forgotten is stored right here." He patted the terminal in front of him.

"There are definitely BattleMechs here, all right, Lori. I've seen the manifests. I haven't gone through them all, yet, but I'd say there's at least a regiment stored down there, maybe more. A lot more than we'll ever be able to move aboard Ricol's ships. Right now, though, I'm convinced that the greatest treasure of all is actually this Star League library!"

A transport hovercraft raced south from Helmdown. Six of the seven aboard wore the cowls and cloaks of ComStar Adepts, technicians trained in the inner mysteries of the pseudo-religious order. The seventh was Rachan, still dressed in civilian clothes, but the obvious deference given him by his accomplices revealed his power.

"I see dust ahead, Precentor," said the vehicle's driver. He had pulled his cowl back off his head and donned dark glasses so that he could see better to maneuver the vehicle. The sky was hot and bright, with clouds boiling high in the sky to the east.

"That will be Langsdorf's column," Rachan said. He studied the clouds, and the sky overhead. It would rain by evening.

"Can Langsdorf open the door?" another Adept wanted to know.

"I have carefully studied the satellite projections, my son." It was strange how easily one slipped back into the cant and formula of the Order's speech when one was among others of the Order again. Rachan hadn't used the address form of "my son" in years. "It appears that the barrier erected across the bed of the Vermillion River is supported by some sort of internal bracing, probably of poured ferrocrete and steel. A relatively small charge of plastic explosive at each of several calculated stress points along the barrier should sever those struts and bring down the entire wall. Langsdorf's engineers will know best how to accomplish this."

Senior Adept Larabee studied one of the memory cores. "And these will hold the data from the Star League library. Precentor? It seems more like magic than science."

"Remember, my son, that it is the Order's duty to preserve the Old Knowledge. A Dark Night is coming, and the end of civilization as we know it. Knowledge such as that stored in the League library will be the door to the New Day."

"I understand that, Precentor but I don't understand why we have to destroy it."

Rachan looked past the Adept at the gently rolling prairie unfolding around them as they hurtled south. "Duty is difficult in the best of times, Adept Larabee. Remember, the secret that I have shared with you is one that you six must take to your graves. Those not of the Order . . . even most of those *within* the Order, would not understand what I told you this morning.

"The Divine Blake saw that knowledge—and the communications network that made dissemination of that knowledge possible—would one day be the key to the

Order's ultimate triumph. It is our duty to preserve knowledge, the Old Knowledge, from sources such as this League library, against the day when the Order will usher in a new dawn of civilization and prosperity. But it is also our duty to prevent such knowledge from falling into . . . unsanctified hands.'' He touched the memory core lightly with his fingertips. ''With this, we can transfer the Star League data from the library hidden beneath the mountain. When the transfer is complete, we will destroy the library completely.''

The Adept still looked uncertain, and Rachan smiled at him. ''Believe me, my son. We would not be doing the rest of Mankind any favors by allowing the information contained in that library to fall into their undiscerning hands! It would only prolong the agony. In our hands, however, the Old Knowledge will be safe.''

''I don't doubt you, Precentor. I was just wondering whether . . . we are even worthy of such a trust. Such knowledge could so easily be twisted to evil!''

''In that, my son, you must have faith in your superiors.'' *And I,* he thought to himself, *have faith that all of your wonderings will soon be at an end. Just as soon as you have helped me accomplish what must be done!*

It was sunset by the time the Gray Death Legion emerged into daylight again. One of the passageways marked on the computer map, now transferred to a hardcopy printout in Grayson's hand, had led them to a sealed tunnel door that looked out on the orange sun of Helm descending above the West Equatorial Sea. The hidden computer files had shown them how to shut the East Gate door behind them. Below them lay a broad and open plain descending sharply toward the coast. To their right, northwest, was the glitter of the western half of the Vermillion river, reborn again in cavern lakes fed by melting glaciers. The river surfaced in the Vermillion Valley, one of the three passes through the mountains to the north, and wound twisting out of the mountains and across the plains to the sea.

They had found the Star League cache under the west face of the mountain. It had been filled with silent rows of Star League BattleMechs standing rank upon rank upon metal rank within the support structures of their gantries. There were arms and ammunition, supplies of missiles, and League-issue scanner and communications gear. There were vehicles, most of them powered by the same sort of fusion plants that powered BattleMechs but that were rarely found in non-'Mech vehicles anymore. Grayson had seen dozens of tanks, from Vedettes to Demolishers, apparently armed and ready to roll. After glimpsing a number of transporter vans large enough to transport BattleMechs on broad, flat trailers, Grayson was already picturing how the Legion Techs could move those waiting battle machines out onto the Vermillion Plain, where Ricol's ships could land to pick them up. A broad, ferrocrete road led directly past this western portal and wound down the face of the mountain to a flat plain perhaps 500 meters farther downhill. That would be a good landing place for the DropShips, easily accessible from the western door. The road wound on in the other direction toward the north, through the mountain passes.

"Grayson!" Lori's Mech-amplified voice boomed down at him from her *Shadow Hawk,* from where she stood at the portal fifty meters away. "The *Phobos* has made contact! They're free, and on their way in!"

Grayson whooped and sprinted for his *Marauder,* which stood where a Tech had parked it. As fast as his legs and arms could take him, he swarmed up the ladder and settled himself in the cockpit seat, then began to twist at the dials that would tune into the *Phobos*'s frequency.

"They're encamped on the east side of the mountains, Lori," Martinez's voice was saying as Grayson opened the channel. "We can see them clearly from here."

"Ilse!" Grayson said. "This is Carlyle! It's good to hear you!"

"And it's very good to be heard, Captain! I just told your Exec, we'll be grounding in another five minutes."

"Good! You have coordinates?"

"That's affirmative. We'll set down on the plain below your west door."

"Ilse was telling me that Ricol didn't show, Grayson," Lori added. "It was Dulaney's troops alone that freed both DropShips. It looks like Ricol wasn't on our side after all!"

"I . . . see."

This added new complications. Ricol's DropShips would be dropping in at midday tomorrow. Had Ricol deliberately attempted to sabotage Grayson's attempt to free the *Deimos* and the *Phobos*?

Grayson realized in that moment that the old hatred for Ricol was truly gone. "I'll want to talk to Ricol before I believe that, Lori. There could be another explanation. For now, we assume that we bring Ricol's DropShips in tomorrow, as planned."

"You might not get a chance, Colonel," Martinez said. There was a thin, high thunder audible through the hull of Grayson's *Marauder*. He leaned forward, peering through the 'Mech's forward port, and was rewarded by the glitter of golden sunlight on the hulls of the two DropShips gleaming at high altitude. "I was just telling Lori, it looks like you have company. There's one hell of a big army sitting on the east side of the mountains."

"Are they moving?"

"Looks to me like they may be setting up camp. You'll have to analyze the photos we took, but I count between twenty-five and twenty-eight BattleMechs over there, plus many vehicles and men."

"If they're camping, they must be planning on moving in the morning," Grayson said. "They won't try the passes at night."

Martinez's voice was clearer now as the two DropShips grew larger in the sky. Grayson could make out the pulsing flicker of their main drives now.

"That's my thought, Colonel, but it still doesn't help much. A BattleMech could cross any of those passes inside of an hour or two. If they set out at first light, they'll be on us long before your Kurita friends get here."

The tongues of flame lapping beneath the two Drop-Ships were longer now, and much brighter, as their pilots increased power to slow the nuclear-fusion craft to gentle landings side by side on the Vermillion Plain.

"Maybe not," Grayson said. "I think I have an idea or two to slow them down just a bit."

29

Grayson refolded the map printout, spreading the central portion flat on a convenient rock so that all of them could see. The Nagayan Mountains rose around them, their glacial peaks tinged with the first rays of the new day's light. The sky overhead was the deep, royal blue of evening, with the brightest stars still visible in the morning sky. In the shadowed valley where they had gathered, there was barely enough light yet to see.

"We've got too main problems," Grayson said. "The first is that we're going to have to cover three separate routes—three ways that Langsdorf can try to get at us. We're here." His finger passed across the words "Vermillion Plains" on the map. "Langsdorf's people are camped up here, northeast of the mountains, pretty close to where we were camped yesterday. Between us—" his finger moved north to a mass of tightly spaced contour lines—"are the Nagayan Mountains . . . and these three passes."

It was Captain Martinez who had brought the news that it was not Lord Garth who was commanding the Marik army, but Colonel Langsdorf. While monitoring Marik radio transmissions, she had picked up references to the Marik commander broadcast in the clear. Somehow, that news did not surprise Grayson. He had guessed as much from the speed with which the Marik force had maneuvered south, a feat that Garth probably could not have accomplished in less than three days.

Lori looked up from the map. "You said two problems, Gray. What's the other?"

Grayson smiled. "Our other problem is that Langsdorf probably has enough men and 'Mechs to come through all three passes at once."

"Gods," Clay said. "You're sounding too confident, Colonel. I don't think I'm going to like this."

"Langsdorf has two choices," Grayson continued. "He can mass his army and push it all through any one of these passes. Or he can split his army and move it through two . . . or all three."

Lori looked uncertain. "What do you think he'll do?"

Grayson shook his head. "I don't *know* Langsdorf. I've heard he's a good regimental commander, and he certainly fought well at Cleft Valley. Let's assume he's good . . . and then try to look at it from his side of the map."

"If he divides his army, he'll be committing the classical tactical error," Clay said, rubbing the stubble on his chin. "He'd be setting up his forces to be defeated piecemeal . . . and on ground of our choosing. If he keeps his force together . . . well, there's no way we could more than dent it. That army would just come blasting through and knock us aside like target dummies."

"True," Grayson answered. "But if he comes through as a single force, he's going to have to choose which pass. Look—" Grayson pointed out the passes on the map in turn—"The main road south from the Northern Highlands runs through Drango, in the Drango Gap. There's not a whole lot of problem there. The pass is narrow, but there's room enough to deploy a fair percentage of his total force if we attack him. The ground is high, but pretty smooth. He could move his whole army through, and move fast.

"Now . . . off to the northwest here is Lee's Pass. It's higher and a lot rougher, partly blocked in places by boulders, with twists and turns and kinks and places where sheer cliffs create blind pockets. Langsdorf would have to be a total idiot to put his whole army through there. things are so tangled through here that it would take a week for him to sort things out . . . and we'll be long gone by then.

"Now back here, east of the Drango Gap, is the Nagayan Canyon, and the Vermillion River running through
it to the south. See, it comes in here at the northeastern
end of the Drango Gap, but splits off to bypass Drango,
here. The ground is rougher than around Drango, but not
nearly as bad as Lee's Pass. The main problem is the
Vermillion River. It arises from an underground lake . . .
here. There are fords in the river, but Langsdorf's lance
leaders won't know where they are. It will take time to
find them, and time to get their main force across."

"So what's the answer?" Lori asked. "Are you saying
he'll do the obvious . . . or pull a switch and do the
unexpected?"

Grayson smiled. "A good commander would do the
unexpected, but Colonel Langsdorf doesn't have that option here. If he's going to mass his army and send it
through in one chunk, he *has* to do it here," Grayson's
finger stabbed the map. "At Drango. He'd be risking
losing us and his whole army if he tried it at either Lee's
Pass or the Vermillion River."

"Aye, laddie! You're sayin' he's ae' goin' tae split his
army, then," McCall said, his face brightening.

"He almost has to. As Delmar said, he'd be committing something of a classical tactical mistake, but that's
what makes *that* choice unexpected. If he keeps his force
together, he has to choose the Drango Gap. He knows it,
and he knows we know it. He has to assume that if we
know it, we'll try to do something about it. He doesn't
know for sure what forces we have. We might have
enough explosives to mine the whole pass . . . or we may
have scraped together a large enough army from the local
militia that we could delay his army long enough for our
DropShips to get clear. Remember, it isn't just that he
wants to get through. He *has* to stop us from leaving . . .
capture our transport if he can. He can't risk getting
bogged down in these mountains.

"Now, let's say he splits his force. He could send the
main part of his army through here—" Grayson pointed
at Drango—"Or here." His finger slid east to the Vermillion River. He looked thoughtful. "If it was me, I'd
choose the river. It's more difficult, but less likely. I'd

send enough of a force through Drango to attract the other guy's attention. Maybe send it through fast, try to catch him by surprise and get a strong force in our . . . in the *enemy's* rear, threatening his DropShips. *That* would make them pull south out of the mountains altogether, and solve the whole problem. Then the main force would come through along the Vermillion River. It would take longer that way than through Drango, but it would arrive in time to help the Drango force catch the enemy . . . maybe catch the enemy between our two forces."

"And he'll ignore Lee's Pass?" Lori asked.

Grayson shook his head. "I don't know. Again, if it was me, I'd send a small force—maybe a company or so—through there, too. It might serve as a diversion. Certainly, it would give the other guy something to worry about and might tie down part of his forces." Grayson looked up from the map, and into the eyes of each of the others in turn. His voice took on a new, firmer, and more decisive tone. "We assume that Langsdorf is coming through all three passes. He'll rush a fairly strong force through Drango, trying to catch us off guard and to hold us long enough for the main force to come up. He'll send a small, light force through Lee's Pass, partly as a diversion, partly in hopes of slipping ten or twelve 'Mechs into our rear to threaten our DropShips. And his main force will come down the Vermillion River, through the canyon. He'll figure that we'll try to hold one or another of the passes, and be swept aside or pinned. The rest of his army will reunite on the Vermillion Plains, move against our DropShips . . . and then he'll have us."

Clay looked unimpressed. "So? Where does that leave us? It doesn't look to me as though knowing what Langsdorf is up to is going to help us much. I mean, it's nice to know how the guy's going to kill us, but it doesn't make me feel any better."

"Well, my friend, when we know the other guy is going to commit a classical tactical error, we take advantage of it." Grayson looked at Lori and winked.

Clay's eyes widened. "You bastard! You're going to take them on one at a time!"

Grayson's smile broadened. "Hey, it's unexpected,

right? That gives us quite a nice tactical advantage.'' He pointed at the mountains again. ''Besides, we know some things about these mountains that Langsdorf doesn't. That's worth at least a regiment in itself.''

Clay shook his head, but his smile matched Grayson's. ''Only *one* regiment? Well, then it damned well better be an elite regiment of heavy assault 'Mechs, or Langsdorf's going to cut them to pieces!''

''I've got a question, Gray,'' Lori said. ''This Langsdorf . . . he's probably got orders to find the Star League cache, right? What makes you think he's going to be coming through the passes at all? He might be trying to figure out how to open the east gate right now, and if he can't figure out how to open it, he'll figure out how to blow it down. Like *we* were going to do.''

''Good point, Lori. But put yourself in his boots. You know the Legion vanished into those mountains. You don't know what's inside or where things lead. You don't have a map. You go in after the prey, and you might lose your whole army.

''But suppose you see the Legion . . . or most of it, right out in the open? Like about . . . here.'' His forefinger touched the northeastern end of the Drango Gap. ''You've got scouts and recon patrols out. You see the Legion 'Mechs that you were chasing out in the open now and moving through this pass. What do you do? Keep trying to open the door? Or try to catch the bastard while you can?''

''Gotcha,'' Lori said. ''He won't take the unknown road if he sees us clear in the open.''

''And when he sees us in the Drango Gap, the idea of splitting his force in an attempt to trap us or get at the DropShips will occur to him . . . if it hasn't already.'' Grayson spread his hands. ''After all, he may have decided to send a force through the mountains as soon as he saw the DropShips coming in last night.''

''We'll have a hard march if we're going to get across the Drango Gap before he decides to move, one way or the other.''

''Agreed. But we're not going to march, at least, not all the way,'' Grayson said.

''No, I think what we'll do is give the Nagayan Mountain League Facility's transport system a workout.''

Colonel Langsdorf crossed his arms and closed his eyes. The ComStar Precentor had the most annoying habit of stating and restating the obvious.

''Sir, I understand what you are saying. Lord Garth will be eager to get into that mountain and find the weapons. And I can understand that you are as anxious about that as he.

''But please, sir, understand my position.'' He looked at the Precentor, then let his eyes rest in turn on each of the cowled and hooded ComStar Adepts. Langsdorf's personal belief was that the pseudo-religious hokery of the Order was a mix of superstition and baseless mysticism. If this was the hope of modern civilization . . .

''Perhaps the Gray Death Legion went through that wall. The tracks and signs we have discovered, plus those bubble tents they left behind, suggest that. But on the other hand, we have seen their forces in a pass ten kilometers northwest of here. Seen them, do you understand? It may well be that my engineers *could* open this wall with explosives, as you suggest. But it would take time . . . and a great deal of attention that I simply do not have to spare. I will need my engineers for crossing the mountain passes. It is they who will detect and clear mines ahead of our main forces.

''I *cannot* take my force into an unknown and unmapped network of caves, not unless I know where we are going. I *cannot* expose the rear of my force to attack, should the enemy slip around through the passes and into our rear. And finally, I see no reason to blunder around in caverns when the position of the enemy is known. He is in the Drango Pass, travelling northeast. I have launched *Boomerang* observation aircraft to follow his movements. I intend to meet him in the Drango Pass, and that is where I intend to crush him.

''Now, I'm willing to grant that you, Precentor, and your Adepts have important work inside that cave. I will be delighted to detach an engineer group to assist you, once we've completed this operation.

"But whatever you have to do can damn well wait until I've done my job!"

Langsdorf surprised himself as much as the ComTech people with this outburst. He was normally quiet-spoken, and not given to emotional outbursts.

The campaign was taking its toll on him. There were too many people eager to give him advice, but refusing to give him help. With twenty-seven BattleMechs and a fair-sized armor force, he had an overwhelming superiority against the enemy. Yet, Langsdorf knew 'Mechs well enough to understand a twist of luck, or some stupid mistake on his part, could just as easily wipe out his advantage.

"I understand your position," the Precentor said. "You will do me the courtesy of understanding mine. Whatever you may believe, personally, this expedition is here for *my* benefit. I suggest you remember who gave you command of this force, despite the objections of Lord Garth. It is imperative that I and my assistants enter that cave as quickly as possible. I am willing to grant you . . ." He looked at his wrist computer. "Let's make it six hours. That should give you time enough to crush Carlyle's force and recapture his DropShips. But if you have not won through the pass in that time, I will insist that you dispatch engineers on my command to undertake the opening of this gate."

Colonel Langsdorf burned with a slow, inner fire at the ComStar Precentor's arrogance, but he channeled his anger, brought his anger under control. All that showed was a tensing of the muscles in his hands, closed now in fists at his side. "Very well, Precentor. Six hours should be time enough. I warn you, however, that this man Grayson Carlyle is a resourceful and able foe. He may be a renegade. He may have massacred those people on Sirius V. As an enemy to be met, however, he is worthy of respect—and the most extreme caution.

"The one thing we must not do is underestimate the man. If we fail to understand the way he is thinking, then six years would not be enough for us to beat him."

* * *

Drango was a small village of perhaps three hundred people on the road leading south from Helmdown to the Vermillion Plains. The people were lammen herders, for the most part, though there were many farms scattered along the broad, mountain valley. Ferrisgrass was a nutritious grain that had found a place as one of Helm's few offworld exports, and the tough, fast-growing plant flourished at Drango's high altitude.

It was midmorning when Drango's citizens heard the growing thunder of an approaching army. Some of the town's children had reported seeing army vehicles and BattleMechs earlier in the morning, and there had been rumors of mysterious fires in the night; of strangers, strangely dressed, working in the fields east of the town at night; of spaceships flying overhead on the previous day and landing on the plains to the south; and of strange sounds echoing down from the surrounding glaciers and mountains.

It had been easy enough to dismiss the earlier reports as children's pranks or the overly active imaginations of adults. Not even the most skeptical observer could dismiss the sight that greeted the townspeople who ventured out to investigate that growing thunder.

Altogether, there were twelve BattleMechs travelling slowly at the head of a column of dozens of tracked and hover vehicles. The eagle crest of House Marik was plain to see on 'Mechs and vehicles alike. While the inhabitants of Drango had heard little of the news of rebellion and bloodshed to the north, they knew trouble when they saw it. Most found refuge in the sturdy basements of their homes. A few fled further afield, and by hiding among the rocks and crags that surrounded Drango Gap, they inadvertently won a splendid view of the developing battle.

In command of the column was Captain Maranov, and he was pushing his people hard. Colonel Langsdorf had assigned his 4th Light Assault Group the job of clearing Drango Pass and of securing the village itself, with the mechanized infantry and armor of the Marik House Guard as support. The enemy had been seen in this pass earlier that morning, though there had been no sign of them so far. "Close up, men! Press up!" Maranov barked over his taccom frequency so often that, his men grew sick of hearing it. It kept the column moving quickly, though. If Carlyle's Legion was still in the pass, Maranov wold catch them. If Carlyle had already fallen back through the pass and onto the Vermillion Plains, then the Captain would follow, find him, and hold him until Langsdorf could arrive with the main army. Maranov's *Warhammer* strode ahead with a rapid and determined stride. He was flanked by Colby and Vitner in their two *Phoenix Hawks,* a powerful and impressive phalanx advancing out of the morning sun.

The first explosive charge went off under Vitner's *Phoenix Hawk,* an eruption of dirt and gravel that smashed Vitner's 45-ton 'Mech forward in a cascading hail of smoke and debris. Maranov pivoted his *Warhammer,* searching for an enemy, but his scanners were clear of all but his own 'Mechs and the buildings of the town ahead. Vitner had begun pulling his 'Mech to its feet when a second explosion erupted to the southeast, close beside Benning's *Griffin.*

"Mines!" Bennings called over the comnet. "They've hidden explosives out here, among the rocks!"

Maranov looked around wildly. All along, he had been seeing the Drango Gap as a broad, straight highway through the mountains toward his goal, the plain that reconnaissance said now served as landing field for a pair of enemy DropShips. Get through the Gap quickly enough, and he would have the enemy helpless, right where he wanted him.

With the shattering detonations of the mines, Maranov abruptly saw the pass in a different light. The mountains towered on either side of the gap, needle sharp and capped with glinting ice, barriers impassible by something as clumsy as a BattleMech. Indeed, the Marik Captain now realized that the valley was a splendid place for an ambush.

"Captain!" That call was from Jennings in his *Crusader.* "Bogies at two-niner-five! I have targets!"

"Acquire them and bring them down! Range?"

"Five hundred, and clos . . ."

Another explosion chopped off the radio voice, this time coming from high on a hillside close alongside Jennings's 'Mech. Maranov saw the avalanche started by the mine explosion hurling a mass of broken rubble and rock down on Jennings's *Crusader.*

"I'm O.K.!" Jennings said after a moment. "Just shaken. But gods . . . where are they coming from?"

Maranov had been wondering the same thing. The enemy 'Mechs, each painted with a distinctive grey-on-red skull emblem, seemed to be rising out of the rocks around them. There were four on the northwest side of the pass, and four more to the southeast.

"All units! Fire! Bring them down!"

Maranov lowered his *Warhammer*'s PPCs and opened fire, heavy bolts of charged particles searing through the morning air, striking into the approaching 'Mechs and across the rocks around and behind them. His fire was joined by the other 'Mechs in his group, as lasers stabbed at the approaching 'Mechs, and rockets wove their delicate, white contrails through the sky toward their targets.

Multiple rocket warheads slammed into Maranov's *Warhammer,* exploding, sending chunks of armor spinning wildly in every direction. He returned fire, but he realized with growing alarm that his right arm PPC was overheating with each discharge. That weapon had taken battle damage against Liao six months before, and it still malfunctioned, despite everything he or his Tech could do. That malfunction was a critical factor in his combat now, for if ever he needed heavy and rapid fire, this was it!

Vitner's *Phoenix Hawk* triggered its jump jets and rose clumsily into the air, but Maranov could see that the *Hawk* had taken severe damage to its legs, probably as a result of the mine blast. The 'Mech came down heavily, awkwardly, and nearly fell. One of its backpack jets had been burning roughly, too.

An explosion staggered Maranov, knocking him aside. He fought the controls of his *Warhammer* as his gyros shrieked protest. Then the heavy machine responded and slowly righted itself. He swung around to face the new threat and saw an enemy *Archer* bearing down on him from the east. A second salvo of missiles erupted from the heavy machine's torso launchers as he watched. Then the air was thick with missiles, the ground around him erupting in a nearly continuous cacophony of sound and light and jagged, hurtling chunks of rock.

The *Warhammer*'s instruments shrieked warning at him, red lights reported a fire in his left leg actuator shielding, of a breakthrough in the armor on his left torso, of a critical failure of his left arm actuator. Stubbornly, Maranov pressed through the smoke and noise. His left PPC was not responding to his controls, its barrel dragging on the ground with each step. His right PPC fired . . . then fired again. Lightning arced from the enemy *Archer,* leaving a blackened patch high on the machine's right torso.

Then something slammed into him from the rear of the *Warhammer* once again. With his 'Mech's right leg dragging because of the knee joint jammed by an imploded section of armor, he managed a slow and clumsy turn. Through the smoke, he could make out another 'Mech lumbering toward him—a *Rifleman*—and its horrifying firepower was concentrated on him. Twin lasers fired one after another, opening Maranov's armored torso and peeling back the edges. Twin autocannon sent 80 mm rapid fire shells smashing into the ruin. Maranov could see the twinkle of spent A/C shell casings as they flipped from the rapid-cycling ejection ports of the *Rifleman*'s primary weapons. Shells slammed home into the critically damaged torso of his machine, tearing through red-hot metal. He heard the grinding clatter, felt the vibration under his feet as something massive gave way. He shoved the *Warhammer*'s controls forward and twisted hard to the left, hoping to avoid the charging *Rifleman*'s rush.

The move failed. His gyros were gone, and his BattleMech froze in place. Maranov cursed and smashed at the controls with bleeding fists, but the machine remained as immovable as the mountains around him.

A strange, keening sound was coming across the tac-com net now. It was hard to tell, of course, but the words seemed timed with that *Rifleman*'s movements, and Maranov could have sworn that it was the *Rifleman*'s pilot who was screaming. At him. In a totally incomprehensible language.

Then it was Maranov's turn to scream, as the deck split wide with the stress, and flame licked across his bare legs.

His fist came down on the large red button that would blast him clear of his crippled *Warhammer,* blast him clear of the intolerable agony licking at his blistered legs. Nothing happened, for the same explosion that had torn his 'Mech's cockpit deck had torn the ejection release cables as well. Maranov triggered the firing circuits, again, and again nothing. He stopped his screaming long enough to stare in frank disbelief at the ejection hatch half a meter above his neurohelmet, still stubbornly closed. He mashed the button again . . . and again . . .

Another explosion rocked him. Without gyros to compensate, the *Warhammer* toppled like a falling statue, smashing into the stony, ground with an impact that hurled Maranov forward against his restraining straps and tore the neurohelmet from his shoulders.

The explosion and fall had split open the *Warhammer*'s coolant tanks. With the 'Mech in a head-down position, most of the superheated chemical fluid that had not already flashed into steam flooded into the ruptured cockpit.

Maranov was mercifully unconscious by the time the boiling liquid reached him.

=== 30 ===

Grayson's command and fire lances had caught the Marik BattleMechs between them, with the 'Mechs near the head of the trap caught in a flame-shot crossfire, while those toward the rear could not return fire without risk of hitting their own forces. Grayson's *Marauder* strode forward through the battlefog. As manmade lightning flared and flashed, he found himself confronting a Marik *Crusader* rising from the rubble of a landslide caused by an exploding mine.

Grayson's *Marauder* fired with both PPCs and lasers together, scoring great, jagged hits on the Marik 'Mech's hull. The *Crusader* returned his fire. The *Marauder* took a hit on its right arm, and another squarely in the hull just below the cockpit. Over the general taccom frequency, Grayson could hear McCall's Scots curses, in themselves spine-curdling sounds that might easily confuse the enemy. He brought his massive, 120 mm autocannon down into line and touched off a long, rolling stream of fire that arced into the *Crusader*. Explosions flashed close by the Marik machine, and a hit on its left leg knocked it down into a kneeling position.

Before he could trigger another salvo, however, Grayson was attacked from another direction. As laser bolts struck his right arm again, red lights on his console warned of damage and overheating. He spun his *Marauder* and faced two Marik heavies standing side by side—a *Thunderbolt* and a *Rifleman*.

That *Thunderbolt*'s heavy laser could do horrendous damage to any 'Mech it targeted, and so Grayson wasn't eager to tangle with the big machine. He backed up the *Marauder* quickly, leveling bolt after bolt at both enemy machines. They followed, laser bolts flashing wildly past Grayson's machine.

The *Thunderbolt* looked familiar as Grayson brought the machine up on his main viewer, then magnified the image. The *Thunderbolt*'s right arm laser showed a sharp crease across its surface, and it looked as though the main power connector cable had been cut. It was the same *Thunderbolt* with which he had tangled during that wild struggle for the DropShips in Cleft Valley! Its heavy laser had been disabled then, and there had been no time for the pilot to complete repairs! Grayson sharply swung his *Marauder* onto the attack, striking out toward the *Thunderbolt*'s right flank to keep himself on the Mech's damaged side.

Even with the right arm laser out of action, the *Thunderbolt* was still a formidable enemy. It mounted three medium lasers in its torso, as well as an SRM launcher, and the massive, sewer pipe-sized Delta Dart LRM-15 launcher angled across its left shoulder. Even damaged, the *Thunderbolt* would be a serious challenge for Grayson in his *Marauder,* and this *Thunderbolt* had a well-armed *Rifleman* backing it up.

The three 'Mechs exchanged fire at 200 meters' range, laser and PPC bolts crossing and crisscrossing in the hazy air between them. Grayson tried to fire calmly and deliberately, but within seconds, he found himself snapping off shots as fast as his 'Mech could recycle the power sequence and wink the weapon ready lights green on his console. He saw the *Thunderbolt* stop moving, then shift the heavy long-range missile launcher to a new cant. Grayson paused, measuring the *T-Bolt* pilot's aim, then lunged hard to the right just as the enemy pilot fired. Fifteen warheads smashed into the rock and gravel where Grayson had been standing a moment before. He returned fire with a rapid left-right-left-right pattern of laser and particle fire. The *Thunderbolt* was struck full in its center torso three times, staggered by the explosions. The *Rifleman* laid down a heavy fire that forced Grayson to keep moving. Then autocannon fire was searing in from the left, catching the *Rifleman* in the side and causing damage to one of its arms.

"Hello, Gray," he heard on his taccom. "Need help?"

"I wouldn't mind it a bit, Lori. It's hot out here today!"

Lori's autocannon fire drove the enemy *Rifleman* back thirty meters and left its right arm dangling, useless. The *Thunderbolt* remained where it had been. From the way it was standing, perhaps the 'Mech had shut itself down.

Thunderbolts were notorious for so much heat buildup that their operational governors would shut down automatically to keep the excess heat from killing the 'Mech or its pilot.

But Grayson was suspicious. The *Thunderbolt*'s heavy laser was the main culprit in heat overloads, and this machine hadn't fired its heavy laser once during the fight so far. Of course, it could have overloaded from other sources . . .

Reaching a quick decision, Grayson leveled another volley of laser and particle fire into the big Marik machine. The response was immediate; the *Thunderbolt* stumbled to the side, turning, trying to twist out of Grayson's murderous fire and to bring its torso lasers to bear. Lori opened fire from a different angle, her autocannon and laser tearing gaping craters in the *Thunderbolt*'s side and leg, and opening the LRM launcher with a long, coolant-leaking gash.

The *Rifleman* was firing, this time at Lori. Grayson spun his *Marauder* and opened fire on the *Rifleman*, scoring hits on its torso and on its undamaged arm. When Delmar Clay's *Wolverine* walked up, its autocannon spitting 60 mm shells in short, choppy bursts, the *Rifleman* pilot decided that three-to-one odds were too much, and began backing up. Grayson followed, pouring autocannon fire into the already cratered, smoking machine.

The *Rifleman* pilot appeared to be in trouble. There was a jerkiness about his machine's movements that suggested he was having gyro trouble. Faced with three powerful BattleMechs, he could not turn and run, not with so little armor on a *Rifleman*'s back. There was a fire burning now amid the wreckage of its right arm, and smoke was boiling from a hole low in its center torso. Green coolant fluid leaked from its left arm, and the tracking antenna over its cockpit was twisted and askew.

The *Rifleman* took another step backward, stumbled, and fell. With one arm damaged and the other gone, its pilot was having obvious difficulty getting the machine on its feet again. Abruptly, the damaged *Rifleman* worked its way into a seated position. Then the cockpit armor folded back. In a flash of light and a trail of smoke, the *Rifleman* pilot was gone, ejected, his 'Mech abandoned on the field.

With the fall of the Marik *Rifleman*, the fight seemed to go out of the Marik force. The Marik 'Mechs began to withdraw back down the valley in a ragged line. They had lost the *Warhammer* that had entered the valley in the lead, as well as one *Phoenix Hawk* and the *Rifleman*. Khaled had accounted for an enemy *Stinger*, in a darting rapid-fire and highly unbalanced duel, and Sharyl and Bear together had destroyed another *Stinger* and a *Shadow Hawk*.

None of the Gray Death 'Mechs had been destroyed, but all had been hit several times, suffering considerable battle damage. Sharyl's *Shadow Hawk* had been especially mauled, as had Koga's *Archer*. Grayson ordered both 'Mech pilots to take their machines back to the central underground facility's main depot, where Gray Death Techs were already going through the Star League supplies in search of equipment to maintain the regiment's combat machines in the coming battle. The hope was that they could patch damaged 'Mechs as Grayson sent them in, and then get them back out in the field in time for the next encounter.

Both pilots had protested the order, claiming that their 'Mechs could still move and fight. They had accepted Grayson's command, though, when he pointed toward the south and told them he didn't want to hear any more about it. "You get your 'Mechs spread all over the landscape in pieces, and you won't be one damn bit of good to me," he said. "Rejoin the unit when you've completed repairs!"

The two damaged 'Mechs had made their way through

Drango toward the southeast, as villagers began to emerge from their homes, wide-eyed and wondering. The other six 'Mechs had made their way quickly northwest. Grayson's armor and infantry forces had split up, some moving with his 'Mech lance, some following the *Archer* and the *Shadow Hawk.*

Hours later, a lone Marik *Wasp* made its way back up the pass toward Drango. Its pilot was one of the survivors of the 4th Light Assault Group, and her orders were to observe the Gray Death's salvage operations among the five shattered BattleMech hulks the 4th had left behind. She found three of the lost Marik pilots walking back toward camp, but there was no sign of the Gray Death forces. A *Boomerang* pilot circling high overhead was able to report that the enemy had not withdrawn back down the pass toward the Vermillion plain, but that he could not tell where they *had* gone.

It was as though the mountains had swallowed them.

Captain Chu Shi-Lin was commander of the Marik 7th Light Assault Group, and he was not pleased with his orders. Elements now making up the 7th had been roughly handled several months before at Yalin Station, and now mustered only nine BattleMechs. Of those nine, his heaviest was a *Thunderbolt,* and he had two *Shadow Hawks* and a *Wolverine.* All the rest were light 'Mechs— twenty tonners. Isomoru's *Wolverine* and Kelly's *Shadow Hawk* both still carried damage from Yalin Station besides. Spare parts had been hard to come by, as had the experienced Techs necessary to mend the damaged machines. Chu's unit had been on garrison duty for most of the time since, and he considered it folly to deploy the 7th, completely unsupported, far from the main body of the Marik Army.

During his briefing early that morning, Langsdorf had explained to Chu that his mission was more than a mere diversion. The mountain trail known as Lee's Pass offered both opportunity and danger to the Marik forces. It was narrow, rugged, and twisting. In places, Chu's 'Mech force would have to use its arms and legs to climb or descend like multi-ton mountaineers. In most places, they would have to travel line-ahead, single-file, and there were endless blind turns and pockets where parts of the column would be out of sight of their comrades.

If the Marik forces ignored the pass, the renegade mercenaries might be able to slip through Lee's Pass and escape to the north, or turn south and strike the Marik encampment. On the other hand, if *Carlyle* ignored the pass, a small, light, and fast-moving Marik 'Mech force might slip through and emerge on the Vermillion Plains while Carlyle was bogged down in combat elsewhere. And even Chu's damaged force could pose a threat to the grounded DropShips on the plains beyond.

Chu was not so optimistic about his orders. "That pass looks like the perfect place for an ambush," he had said, apparently not caring whether Langsdorf heard him or not. "A perfect opportunity to throw away nine good BattleMechs!" It was an unusual outburst for Chu, a phlegmatic man not usually given to questioning orders.

Outburst aside, he was a soldier, whether or not he wanted any part of Lee's Pass—soldier enough to salute Langsdorf, return to his *Shadow Hawk,* and form up his troops.

By the time Chu and his men had reached the mouth of Lee's Pass, they could hear the sound of gunfire to the southeast. Captain Maranov and the 4th L.A.G., it seemed, had jumped ahead of schedule and run into trouble at Drango. It might mean that Lee's Pass was unopposed, but Chu was taking nothing for granted.

"O.K., troops," he had said. "Single file. We don't have much choice."

And so they had started to climb.

The Gray Death BattleMechs made use of the old Star League tunnels, first to reach Drango Gap, and then to sprint rapidly northwest to emerge at Lee's Pass. Following the paths plotted by the computer map, Grayson had led his 'Mechs along dark and echoing passageways beneath the mountains, emerging on the surface among the rocks and crevasses along the surface passes.

It appeared that the Star League facility had once been

accessible by numerous routes from the surface. Drango had apparently been some sort of transport center whose surface connected with the underground warrens, though the purpose of it all had long since been forgotten. The villagers were now ignorant of the complex around and beneath them, except for vague legends of strange goings-ons and of supernatural creatures that inhabited secret haunts within the Nagayan Mountains.

The underground passageways had allowed the Gray Death to deploy into Drango Gap early that morning so that they could be seen there in force well before Maranov's force could race across the pass. As Maranov's force had withdrawn, they had used the passageways again to withdraw from the field, leaving the Marik observers completely mystified about where the mercenary 'Mechs and armor could have gone. Sharyl and Koga had been able to follow one branch of the tunnels south from Drango to the central depot, and Techs were already hard at work among the Star League gantries and hoists trying to get the two 'Mechs ready for battle again.

Meanwhile, a single long, winding passageway reaching to the northeast had allowed the Gray Death to reach Lee's Pass ahead of Captain Chu. Grayson had already deployed a force of tanks and armored hover vehicles there, a precaution against a middle-of-the-night movement through the pass in a Marik attempt to flank Grayson's force. Lee's Pass was divided by a razor-backed ridge that marked the highest point in the pass in its course across the mountains. The Gray Death's armor was deployed hull-down behind this ridge, with only their gun turrets exposed. Grayson's 'Mech force arrived behind the ridge only moments before Chu's BattleMechs came into view down the valley.

"Well, Sergeant Burns, how's it going?" Grayson said through his *Marauder*'s external speakers when he caught sight of the dirty, ragged figure directing operations among the infantry from the open, top-deck hatch of his Pegasus armored hovercraft.

"No sweat, Colonel!" Burns had to cup his hands to his mouth and shout up at Grayson to be heard over the keening of the vehicles around him. "We've spotted a column coming this way, mostly light 'Mechs. There's no room to deploy around 'em, so we sit here and let 'em come to us.''

''I leave it to you, then, Sergeant. I will hold my 'Mechs in reserve until you need me.''

A defensive battle was always preferable to an offensive one, at least in terms of minimizing battle damage and casualties. Burns's troops were deployed across the entire width of the narrow pass, dug into shallow foxholes or trenches, or sheltered behind hastily erected barriers of rock and scrap metal. Vehicles, mostly lightly armed transports had been dug in as well, though in such a way that they could easily back out of their entrenchments and maneuver, should the enemy manage a breakthrough. Volunteers made their way precariously along both valley walls, with man-portable missile launchers strapped to their backs. Though the regiment had exhausted its supply of inferno warheads during the raid on the mobile headquarters, they had a number of short-range missiles for their launchers, and the rocky walls of the pass provided ideal sites for firing from ambush into the enemy's flanks. Grayson kept his six 'Mechs out of sight and out of the line of fire behind the ridge that Burns defended.

Chu's force came around a bend in the valley trail and started the climb toward the ridge. Burns waited until the leading *Shadow Hawk* was ninety meters down the slope, then gave the command to fire.

All alone, a transport hovercraft stands no chance at all against even a light BattleMech. Though the vehicle is more maneuverable than a 'Mech, a 'Mech's heavier armor can defend it almost indefinitely against the few light weapons a hovercraft can carry. Indefinitely, that is, in battlefield terms, where an eternity is measured in seconds. In Lee's Pass, the hovercraft's single advantage did not exist. There was absolutely no room to maneuver at all, the principal reason why Grayson did not deploy any of his heavier armor there in the first place.

What Burns's force did have was the ability to mass the firepower of ten lightly armed transports against the enemy 'Mechs approaching one at a time. Even light lasers can cause considerable damage when ten of them fire side by side at a single target.

Beams of coherent light interlaced with one another as they swept across the enemy commander's *Shadow Hawk*. Intolerably brilliant points of light appeared across the *Hawk*'s front armor. No single shot penetrated the big 'Mech's armor, but the *Shadow Hawk* was staggered by the onslaught.

The *Wolverine* traveling behind the *Shadow Hawk* pressed forward, sweeping around the *Hawk* to the left. The defenders' laser fire shifted, catching this attacker in its deadly web. Short-range missiles were now arcing down from the sides of the pass, or stabbing up from hidden shelters at the foot of the ridge. The Marik attackers found themselves in a tangled trap of interlocking fire and hurtling missiles. Explosions smashed and thundered among the 'Mechs in the center of the column, as the lead 'Mechs froze in place, unable to back up or to proceed.

The *Shadow Hawk* dropped its autocannon down across its left shoulder and pivoted, white fire flickering at the cannon's muzzle. Spent casing flew among the rocks at its feet as it panned slowly across the landscape, sweeping the ridgetop with fire and death.

Another salvo of laser fire swept across the *Shadow Hawk*. Its left arm hung limply now, the myomer connectors at the shoulder visibly torn and burned where they were exposed through a blackened gash in the 'Mech's armor. A missile struck the 'Mech's leg with a flash of light, and a meter-wide plate of metal, the *Shadow Hawk*'s left knee shield, went spinning off among the rocks, leaving a visible gap at the machine's sensitive knee joint. Yet it stood its ground, blasting at its half-seen attackers with autofire mayhem.

Grayson listened to Burns' voice over the taccom frequency. "We're not going to hold them much longer, Colonel," he said. His voice sounded raw, as though burned by the hot smoke that hung heavy in the air above the ridge. He was shouting, his words punctuated by the staccato thumps and crashes of exploding shells. "I think they're deploying for a rush, and there's no way we can hold them if they come through!''

"You don't have to hold them, Burns," Grayson replied. "Be ready to step aside as we come up the reverse slope." He was watching out of his combat screens, which displayed the chaos in the other side of the valley. One of Burns's troopers had set aside his rifle for the far more important weapon of a remote camera. That camera was patched into Grayson's *Marauder,* allowing him a view of the battle.

"You got it, Colonel. Watch it . . . they're starting to move!''

Grayson had already positioned the 'Mechs with him in a line that stretched across the valley. His heaviest 'Mechs—his own *Marauder,* Khaled's *Warhammer,* and Bear's *Crusader*—were in the center. Lori's *Shadow Hawk* and McCall's *Rifleman* were on the left. Clay's *Wolverine* on the right.

"They're on their way, Colonel!" Burns said moments later. "I'm pulling out. The lead Marik *Shadow Hawk* is thirty meters from the crest of the ridge.''

"I see it," Grayson said. He was counting 'Mechs as the camera view panned across the smoke-filled canyon. *Shadow Hawk . . . Thunderbolt . . . Wolverine . . .* lots of *Wasp*s and *Stinger*s . . . "Tell your man with the camera he can pull out, too.''

But the Marik BattleMech line moved faster than Grayson or Burns expected. There was a sudden rush, and then the *Shadow Hawk* was striding across the top of the ridge, its laser chopping into fleeing Gray Death soldiers as it came. The sky behind the *Hawk* was filled with flying forms. Several of the *Wasp*s and *Stinger*s had fired their jump jets, and were sailing over the heads of their comrades and landing along the ridgetop in billowing clouds of steam and smoke.

Grayson's monitor lit up with a blinding flash and went dead, and he knew that the soldier carrying the camera had not been able to get away in time. The Gray Death still held one advantage, but that advantage would last, Grayson knew, for an instant only.

THE PRICE OF GLORY

"Gray Death! Charge!" he yelled, as his *Marauder* crashed forward up the slope.

The Marik 'Mechs must have thought they were facing only infantry and light vehicles by the time they rushed the slope. After all, no mercenary BattleMechs had been sighted. As they reached the top of the crest, they were concentrating on the destruction of the mercenary soldiers scattering at their feet, not yet having seen the gray shapes surging up the smoke-masked reverse slope of the ridge.

Grayson's *Marauder* was facing a *Stinger* as he raced toward the ridgetop. He fired both PPCs and watched the light 'Mech's torso armor literally explode in hurtling fragments. He fired again, particle beams probing the already furiously burning inner structure. Then his 'Mech collided with the blazing ruin, sending it toppling back over the top of the ridge.

The shock of Grayson's charge up the slope staggered the 4th L.A.G. 'Mechs. A second *Stinger* exploded as McCall's autocannon and laser fire smashed into and through it, tearing out great chunks of armor in multiple explosions that literally ate their way through the light 'Mech. The lead *Shadow Hawk* stood its ground for second upon interminable second, firing away at Khaled's *Warhammer* as it advanced up the slope, but the *Warhammer*'s vastly superior weight of fire was taking a deadly toll. The *Shadow Hawk*'s damaged left arm was torn away completely under the impact of Khaled's PPC fire, and another hit splintered the *Hawk*'s heavy autocannon.

Grayson turned his *Marauder* to fire along the crest of the ridge, but the Marik 'Mechs were already withdrawing. The leader's *Shadow Hawk* fired its jump jets and vaulted ninety meters back down the hill, landing heavily and with obvious damage, but moving still. Three *Wasps* and the *Wolverine* triggered their jets as well, bounding back out of the battle.

For a moment, the battle swirled around the one enemy 'Mech that remained, another huge and powerful *Thunderbolt*, heaviest of the 4th L.A.'s 'Mechs. Lacking jump jets, it was restricted to a slow, step-by step retreat down the slope. This *T-Bolt*'s heavy laser was still working, however, and it laid down a devastating, highly accurate fire. Grayson's *Marauder* took a hit on its dorsal surface that smashed through already-damaged armor plating and set red damage lights flashing across his control board. Then the heavy Marik machine swung to its right and fired toward the flank, where Lori's *Shadow Hawk* was working down the slope toward a position to cut off the *T-Bolt*. The bolt struck Lori's BattleMech high in its right arm, smashing through armor plate. Grayson fired, and sent PPC and laser bolts chopping into the *Thunderbolt*'s heavily armored body.

"Form up! Form up!" Grayson yelled into his helmet mike. The *Thunderbolt* was firing at Lori again, ignoring the other mercenary BattleMechs in an effort to bring down at least one of its tormentors.

Lori's 'Mech took another heavy laser strike in her *Shadow Hawk*'s leg, almost in the same instant that the concentrated fire from all six Gray Death 'Mechs blasted through the *Thunderbolt*'s armor.

The Marik pilot had had enough. With great sections of armor gaping open and trailing smoke, with his Mech's left arm hanging useless and almost dragging on the ground, he turned and struck out down the ridge to rejoin his fellows.

Grayson gave the command: "Let him go."

31

In the central depot, regimental Techs and astechs swarmed through the gantry structures housing three of the unit's 'Mechs, the two *Shadow Hawks* and Koga's *Archer*. Wavering flares of light appeared here and there at brief intervals, showering sparks as workers welded armor plate in place and attempted to restore damaged circuitry.

Grayson stood with his senior Tech at the foot of his own *Marauder*. The damage to the *Marauder*'s hull had been partly repaired, though the loss of a pair of heat sinks was going to be a worry until they could be replaced.

"Koga's 'Mech will be ready to go in fifteen minutes," King was saying. "They're tacking on a new cover to his port missile battery now. He'll be a bit shy of armor to his left side, but he'll be combat-ready in all respects.

"Sharyl's *Hawk* is in worse shape. We found a *Shadow Hawk* main cam driver for her suspension, but it'll be a few hours before she's moving at speed again. Lieutenant Kalmar's *Hawk* isn't in serious shape, but she lost a lot of armor. I'd say . . . two hours for her."

Grayson ran his eyes across the array of Star League BattleMechs in the depot around them. It was ironic that the Legion was fighting to keep its eight BattleMechs in fighting condition with bits and pieces and patched-together spares, when they were smack dab in the middle of a vast army of clean, new, and untouched 'Mechs.

Unfortunately, it would take days of work to get them

functional, to mount their weapons, load their ammo, test their power systems, and tune their neurocircuitry. The Gray Death Legion simply did not have days.

The same problem faced their reserves down in the Vermillion Valley. DeVillar, Tracy Kent, and a couple of MechWarrior trainees were aboard the *Deimos* at that very moment, unpacking their 'Mechs, but it would be at least another four hours before those machines were ready for combat.

Grayson's scouts had reported a third Marik Battle-Mech force advancing down into Nagayan Canyon, toward the source of the Vermillion River. The Legion was going to have to fight another battle to stop this new thrust, and Grayson had only six 'Mechs with which to face them.

"So, I can take Koga with me, but both *Hawks* are out of action for a few more hours?"

"I'm afraid so. What's happening up there, anyway?" King asked, with a grin. "We're all starting to feel like small, burrowing animals down here."

"We've held them so far . . . but only just. Our biggest problem is that we haven't hurt them *enough*."

"Seven of them for none of us, so far," King said cheerfully. "Sounds like a good scorecard report to me."

"Maybe. But I've got to face six Marik 'Mechs now with six of our own, and this time, the enemy's got some heavies . . . and troops and armor, too. The ground is a lot more open than Lee's Pass. We're going to take a battering, Alard. There's no way to avoid it."

"Then we'll path it."

Grayson shook his head. "The same 'Mechs that get battered now are going to have to face the whole damn Marik army a few hours from now. Don't you understand? We're going to take losses today, Alard. Casualties."

It was hard for Grayson to say the words. He could look at the map and calculate tonnages and firepower, but no matter how he worked his calculations, he always came out with the same answer. If they were to hold the enemy, the Gray Death would have to get hurt.

Who would it be? Clay? McCall? Bear? Khaled? These were the times when he did not feel up to the job of commanding a BattleMech company. He knew and liked every one of the men in his command, yet he was going to have to give them orders certain to result in casualties. He allowed himself a brief thought that at least Lori would be out of the coming battle, then immediately felt guilty about it. He loved Lori, but could he actually choose to save her, while possibly condemning Bear or Clay or the bluff, grinning McCall to death? And what if Lori's machine were repaired in time for the final battle?

King nodded. "Yes, Colonel, it'll be rough going."

"This will be our last chance to stop the enemy before he can join forces down below. Whatever we have left after this battle—that's what we'll have to face him on the Vermillion Plains."

"That's what you mean when you say you haven't hurt him enough."

Grayson nodded "He still has twenty . . . twenty-one 'Mechs . . . minus whatever we knock off in this next battle. We have six . . . minus whatever we lose, plus four from the DropShip, if they're ready in time, plus Lori and Sharyl, if *they're* ready in time." Grayson shook his head. "We have to keep going . . . have to meet them on that plain with whatever we have left. There's no alternative."

He turned away from King for a moment, looking at the surrounding 'Mechs. When he turned back again, his eyes were bleak and cold. "Alard . . . I think we're going to lose this one."

King shook his head. "Don't talk that way, Colonel. A lot could happen yet."

Grayson shrugged. "Maybe there comes a time when your luck runs out, when the breaks stop going your way . . ." He stopped, then took King's shoulder under his hand. "I need you for a special assignment."

"Eh? Colonel . . . I'm *needed* here."

"No. Not as much as *I* need you. The other Techs and astechs can handle the repairs, and they've plenty of spare parts and equipment to do it. I want you to take a squad of soldiers and a couple of Techs you can trust, and head back to the East Gate.''

''The library? Why?''

''Because these—'' he waved his arm at the silent, cold 'Mechs around them—''these are not what this battle is about.''

''But I thought . . .''

''Look at them! How many regiments might be equipped with all of these? Three? Five? Weapons for maybe five infantry regiments? A treasure . . . right?''

''By today's standards, yes. Certainly.''

''Alard, the real treasure is that library. We have got to save it. *You* have got to save it.''

''Me? Why?''

''There are memory cores here, in storage. They're up the tunnel, there, to the left.''

''I've seen them.''

''The data stored within the library can be duplicated on one of those cores. The library itself will show you how.

''Detail one of your Techs to take over here, and get back to that library. Make the copy . . . no! Make two! Then get one aboard the *Deimos,* and one aboard the *Phobos.*''

''You . . . you think Langsdorf is going to destroy the library . . . deliberately?''

''No. Not Langsdorf. Someone else. That Precentor who Graff told us about . . . Rachan.''

''The ComStar Precentor? Gods, why?''

''I don't know. I've been over it and over it, and I don't know.'' His fingers came together in a fist, and fist smacked into open palm. ''But it was Rachan who orchestrated this whole thing, ever since Sirius V. He arranged the Legion's disgrace, so that he could get this cache. Sure, the BattleMechs are valuable, but how much of them could Rachan hope to keep? I don't see a ComStar fleet anywhere about to carry them off! My guess is that the weapons are payment to the Marik forces who are helping him!''

''But why does . . .''

Grayson plunged ahead, letting his words order his

thoughts as he spoke them. The puzzle was clearer now, the pieces fitting together. "Think, Alard! A ComStar Precentor arranges the deaths of millions of people—in order to seize weapons that he cannot use or keep himself! Which he will give away in payment to the people helping him!"

"ComStar could take some of the weapons . . . payment for the mercenaries they use."

"Maybe . . . Possibly . . . *but is that worth the lives of twelve million civilians*?"

King started to say something, then closed his mouth. He shook his head mutely.

"ComStar knew about that library. They must have found references to it somewhere, maybe in archives that they uncovered somewhere. Maybe there were old Star League records that mentioned a library on Helm. I think that ComStar . . . or Rachan, if he was operating alone . . . looked at those records and realized that the real treasure was that computerized data center, the library!"

"But it still doesn't make sense," King said. "If they want to preserve that knowledge, they could have come to you openly, could have said, 'Hey, Colonel, it turns out there's an old Star League library hidden in your landhold. Would you mind if we went in and made a copy of the data?' Would you have turned them down?"

"No. Of course not. That's why you have to go make those copies. ComStar doesn't want to preserve that data so much as they want to destroy it!"

"But why? I've always heard that ComStar was interested in preserving old knowledge. They make mystic religion out of it . . ."

"That's why. They have twisted learning and technology and Star League science into . . . into something different. Their Order is based now on ritual and incantation and hidden mysteries. Maybe it wasn't always that way, but that's what it has become. Look, you know as well as I that most Techs laugh at Adepts who mumble incantations over a hyperpulse generator to make it work, right?" King nodded. "What happens when enough people realize they don't need ComStar incantations to operate the machinery? What if ordinary people start building . . . hyperpulse generators, say? My guess is that Rachan is here to copy the library for himself if he can, and then to destroy the library, whatever the cost." Grayson passed his hand over his eyes. He was very tired. "That library has cost twelve million lives already. That alone makes it precious. You have got to see that the information it contains is preserved . . . and spread."

"Spread?"

Grayson pointed up the passageway. "Make sure those extra memory cores are loaded aboard the DropShips, too. There are ways of making duplicates of a core's data using a large computer like the navigational computer aboard the *Invidious*. We can see to it that copies of the data are made and that copies of the copies are made, and maybe we can see to it that some of the data the library contains can be spread around a bit. ComStar wouldn't be able to stop it, not if it was spread to enough worlds. Any computer can be hardwired to read data off one of the cores. Even a simple viewer can be hooked up to read it. Make enough copies, and you can beat them!"

"You say I can beat them. What about you?"

Grayson smiled, but it was a pained and broken one. "Because I'm going out with six 'Mechs to face . . . whatever Langsdorf is gathering to throw at us. I've got to stop as many of his 'Mechs on the Vermillion River as possible.

"After that, I'll meet him again on the plains in front of the DropShips. I'm going to try to buy you time enough to make those copies and load them aboard the DropShips. But I don't see how I can hold him . . . and let you get away clean."

"Now wait just a minute . . ."

Grayson held up his hand. "I don't want to hear it. You scramble—*now!*—and obey my orders!"

Then he turned and started toward his *Marauder*.

The Nagayan Canyon was broad and flat, rimmed by steep and rocky bluffs. The Vermillion River flowed out from under a massive block of granite as a deep, clear pool that extended far back into the hillside as an underground lake. The river flowed from the lower end of the pool across the canyon floor in broad and looping sweeps that crossed from one side of the valley to the other and back. Along most of its length, it was broad, up to fifty meters wide in some places, and as deep as six meters at others.

There were fords, however, shallow places already spotted by Grayson's infantry scouts and specialists, who had worked through the previous night with long steel probes and instruments to test the firmness of river bottom mud and sand. Grayson's 'Mech force emerged from an entrance hidden close beside the underground pool and moved downstream, using the fords to position themselves in such a way that the enemy 'Mechs would have to cross the water to get at them. Scouts had already reported the approach of Langsdorf's third force. It was a column of six 'Mechs, all but one of them massing more than 55 tons.

"Spotters up, Colonel." The antenna on McCall's *Rifleman* was twisting this way and that, as though testing the air. "Five thousand meters, straight up. They're ae' watchin'."

Grayson acknowledged, then shifted frequencies. "Sergeant Burns? *Boomerang*s are aloft. Move out."

Grayson had brought Burns and about half of his command southeast from Lee's Pass. A small guard of infantry still held that pass, but more to sound the alarm if the Marik forces should try that route again than to present the enemy with a serious challenge. But Grayson had wanted Ramage's experienced infantry sergeant in the Vermillion Pass with him.

Boomerang spotter planes meant that the Marik 'Mechs were on their way. The sergeant and a handful of experienced troops from Ramage's Special Ops moved in the shadows under the rock at the source of the Vermillion, preparing.

The surviving BattleMechs of the 12th White Sabers appeared at the far end of the valley less than ten minutes later. They strode forward with a resolution that at first made Grayson wonder if they had already spotted the fords.

That resolution faltered at the water's edge. The *Warhammer* in the lead began wading into water that rose to the big machine's hips. An *Archer* took up a covering position on a hill in the rear, as the other 'Mechs—a *Wolverine*, a *Shadow Hawk*, a *Wasp*, and yet another of the monster *Thunderbolt*s—began spreading out along the river, looking for a shallow place to cross.

BattleMechs are able to fully submerge and can operate for considerable periods of time under water. A 'Mech's weapons cannot be fired through water, though, and so most 'Mech pilots prefer to keep their weapons clear when facing a watchful enemy.

Grayson wondered if Langsdorf himself was piloting the *Warhammer*, then decided he was not. BattleMechs, even those of the same design, become as individual as people after a firefight or two. He had seen Langsdorf's 'Mech before, but this one sported a completely different set of armor patches, numerals and unit patches, oil streaks, rust spots, and ancient wound scars.

It was just as well. He had begun to feel a sneaking admiration for Langsdorf. *This feeling of being inside the enemy's head is getting to me,* Grayson thought. It was hard not to sometimes when the enemy seemed to be struggling against the same things as Grayson and his men.

The Gray Death BattleMechs held their fire. The enemy 'Mechs were 600 meters away, still too far for accurate fire with most of the weapons at their disposal. The *Wasp*, ranging upstream, had found a ford and was moving across. The others began to make for the spot along the far shore. The *Warhammer*, almost halfway across, hesitated, then began moving back toward the far shore.

Grayson clicked open a channel. "O.K., Burns. They're in position! Go."

Still the mercenary BattleMechs held their fire. The *Wasp* was across now, the *Shadow Hawk* and *Archer* close behind. The *Thunderbolt* and *Wolverine* were in midstream, the *Warhammer* still on the far bank. Armored hovercraft were moving farther up the valley. Those could be trouble, Grayson thought, for they could speed straight across the river at any point without slowing. The timing was critical now. If there were enough of them . . .

Grayson watched the surface of the water. The *Thunderbolt* stopped, then canted forward, as though examining the water as well. There was a rainbow slickness to its surface, as though something oily were coating the water.

The 'Mechs in midstream suddenly thrashed about, churning at the water with their arms. "Fire!" Grayson shouted, as laser and particle beams instantaneously lanced across from the waiting mercenary machines. Meanwhile, the troops concealed under the overhanging rock had emptied twelve 50-liter drums of CSF onto the surface of the river.

CSF, which stood for "Concentrated Synthetic Fuel," was the generic nomenclature for any of a variety of fuels. With far greater explosive potential than gasoline, and with a much higher burning temperature, several CSFs formed the basic combustible component of inferno warheads and the high-temperature jet in flamers.

Laser fire flicked across the water, and the fuel flashed into flame. The resulting fireball that rose from the river's surface was sun-bright, rimmed with orange and shot through with swirling, stabbing vortices of black. The surface of the river vanished in a literal sea of flame.

The Gray Death 'Mechs approached at a slow walk in line abreast, firing as they came. The enemy *Wasp*, *Shadow Hawk,* and *Archer* stood their ground, inferno at their backs, pouring fire into the oncoming mercenary line. Moments later, the *Wolverine* rose from the flames, fire still clinging to its legs, but its autocannon continued to hammer away at Bear's *Crusader*.

Of the *Thunderbolt,* there was no sign.

The trap had worked well, but now came the hard part. Grayson had hoped to trap a substantial portion of the enemy force on his side of the river, cutting it off from armored forces and at least one or two of their heavier 'Mechs. He had accomplished precisely that, but the four 'Mechs they now faced were capable of putting up a very tough fight, indeed. It was vital they they destroy as many as possible here, before the final confrontation. Grayson picked up the pace and closed in, lasers and PPCs blazing.

===== 32 =====

Duke Ricol's fleet of six DropShips landed late in the afternoon, descending out of a gray and drizzly sky. The *Alpha,* the DropShip Ricol had grounded at Helmdown, had lifted off from the port still disguised as a merchanter, then shifted course in time to join Colonel Addison's fleet on the final leg of its passage to the Vermillion Plains. Grayson was there to meet him, as was Captain Ilse Martinez.

"You can't trust the man," Ilse was shouting as Ricol stepped down the ramp onto the muddy, rain-sodden ground. "I heard the entire story from MechWarrior Kent! The Kurita bastard wasn't at their rendezvous. He wanted the raid to free us to fail . . ."

"And would you care to hear my side of it, Miss?" Ricol said archly. He was dressed in habitual reds trimmed with black and gold at cuffs and collar. A laser pistol and power pack hung from his belt.

Grayson gave a shallow, stiff bow, that was little more than a nod. "So just what *is* your side of things, Your Grace?" Could the man be trusted, or was this yet another plot within a plot within plot?

"Duke Garth landed before I could even return to the *Alpha,*" Ricol said, spreading his hand open for emphasis. "Actually, I thought at the time that the confusion would help us, but I was wrong. When we arrived at the port, there was a full platoon guarding each gate, and BattleMechs everywhere. An order had been posted, practically closing down the city. No movement in or out." He looked at Grayson. "You were lucky, my friend, to get away when you did.

"At any rate, I had no radio and could not communicate with my ship. I returned to Deirdre's to decide on what to do. I considered using the starport transmitter facility to contact the *Alpha* . . . or you . . . or your troops, but thought better of it when I realized that the starport communications facility on Helm is staffed by ComStar Adepts—the same ones who run the planet's HPG.

"Martial law was in effect in Helmdown and around the starport until late yesterday evening, until after yet another Marik DropShip grounded. I watched through binoculars from Gresshaven. That one had a general aboard . . . Kleider, I believe. At dawn this morning, the curfew was lifted and I was able to return to the *Alpha*. By that time, the only thing left was for me to come here."

Ilse turned to face Grayson, her dark eyes blazing. "You're going to believe that?"

"Evidently *you're* not, Captain." Ricol smiled. "I suppose you could check with someone in the city to corroborate my story . . . but then, that is rather out of the way now, isn't it?"

"Conveniently for you."

"Enough," Grayson broke in. "Captain Martinez, please be so good as to prepare the *Phobos* for lift-off. Coordinate the launch checklist with Lieutenant Thurston."

Ilse looked at him for a long, deadly moment. "Yessir," she said at last, then whirled, and stalked off toward her ship.

Grayson considered the Red Duke. If he had indeed attempted to betray them, if he was lying about his failure to muster his force for the rendezvous, Grayson was under absolutely no obligation to follow through with his own end of their bargain. True, Ricol's DropShips outnumbered Grayson's on the Vermillion Plain, but Ricol had no BattleMechs at all, and Grayson did. Assuming that something could be done to further delay the approaching Marik forces, Grayson would be within his rights to load what he could of the Star League treasure aboard his own ships and depart, leaving Ricol to negotiate with Langsdorf and Rachan. Alternatively, Grayson could keep the League cache out of Rachan's and Garth's hands by arranging to take the library records on board, leaving the Star League tomb forever sealed behind him.

There was little Ricol could do about it, either, short of attacking Grayson. The Gray Death commander was reasonably certain that the Red Duke would not risk damage to any of his DropShips so far from the borders of Kurita space.

"Well, Your Grace, do I trust you?"

Ricol watched Grayson for a long moment. "Anything I say could be . . . prejudicial, Colonel. Let's say . . . I am here to offer my services. If you want to avail yourself of them, the decision is yours. If you see fit to carry out your part of our agreement, that decision, too, is yours. And as for *trusting* me . . . well, Grayson Death Carlyle . . . even *I* wouldn't go that far!''

Grayson watched Ricol for a moment more, then turned, pointing up the side of the mountain above them. "We found the cache, Your Grace, up there, where you see the *Archer* standing guard. There are fusion-driven prime movers in there, more than enough to load whatever you can carry aboard your ships. Munitions, spare parts, electronics, infantry weapons, CSF canisters, infernos, even Star League-issue uniforms. If you set your people to work immediately, I may be able to buy you enough time to get loaded.''

Ricol's brows lowered. "The situation is that critical?''

Grayson shrugged. Exhaustion was creeping up on him again, and it was an effort to stand, to talk. "We have engaged the Marik forces three times. So far, we have taken no casualties among the MechWarriors, though we've lost nearly fifty infantrymen and armor personnel. By rotating our most badly damaged 'Mechs through a field repair facility that we set up inside the Star League depot, we've been able to keep all eight of our 'Mechs running.''

"Eight 'Mechs! That's all you have?''

"For the moment. Four more should be on line within the hour. They were in storage aboard my DropShips, and had to be broken out, powered up, and retuned.

"At the moment, my greatest concern is for my people. They've been in combat almost continuously for the past ten hours, and are exhausted. Their 'Mechs are in bad shape, despite the repairs—most of which were purely temporary in any case.

"Meanwhile, my opposite number on the other side of the hill must be reorganizing his forces for a final push through one of the passes. By this time, he knows just how strong a force I have, and knows how battered it must be. I believe he will move his entire force through one pass—probably the Drango Gap—hoping to meet me either in the pass or on this plain. I intend to oblige him."

Ricol looked aghast. "Eight . . . twelve 'Mechs . . . against how many?"

Grayson closed his eyes to concentrate for a moment. The enemy *Thunderbolt* and *Shadow Hawk* had been destroyed at the Vermillion River, and his men had damaged the *Wasp, Wolverine,* and *Archer*. Probably not damaged badly enough, however. Those 'Mechs would be undergoing repairs at this very moment and would be back in the field in another hour or two. "Nineteen. Possibly twenty. We don't know yet if Colonel Langsdorf's *Warhammer* is in the field."

"The odds are not good, my young friend."

Grayson smiled weakly. "Well, there are ways and ways of calculating odds, Your Grace. The odds of my 'Mech force surviving are small. But the odds of us achieving what we want look good."

"And what is it you want?"

"My senior Tech is gathering data," Grayson said. "There is a Star League library under that mountain, and I have reason to believe that is what brought ComStar here. The Marik forces . . . they're just puppets. It's ComStar . . . or a renegade ComStar Precentor . . . who is our enemy here."

"I've heard of such libraries," the Duke said thoughtfully, "though very, very few have survived . . . and none of them are intact. It would almost seem that there is a deliberate campaign to vandalize them. Of course, most were destroyed in the earlier wars.''

"I'm beginning to think you're right about the deliberate destruction,'' Grayson said, grinning wearily that Ricol seemed to be on the same track of thought. "Anyway, I intend to buy my Tech the time to copy that library and get that copy safely aboard one of my DropShips. I do not expect to have the chance to board myself. Langsdorf's forces must be kept a safe distance from the DropShips. If I can get some of my MechWarriors out, too . . . all well and good. But right now, those library copies have absolute priority.''

Ricol nodded agreement. "But will you do something for me?''

"What?'' he asked.

"Arrange for additional copies of the library to be made . . . as many as your Tech has time and material to make. When we leave here, I will carry the library with me as well.''

They waited on a flat and muddy river plain. From the mouth of the valley a kilometer ahead, a small host was emerging in line-abreast formation. 'Mech after steel-armored BattleMech. Twelve 'Mechs waited south of the river to meet them. Some of them—DeVillar's *Griffin,* Tracy Kent's *Phoenix Hawk,* the *Stinger*s piloted by the raw trainees Gary Brodenson and Jason Morley—were in perfect condition. But McCall's *Rifleman* still trailed debris where it right arm had been blasted away, and Delmar Clay's *Wolverine* could barely stand, its internal structure starkly visible through the craters in its chest and sides. The other 'Mechs showed varying degrees of wear and tear, from Grayson's *Marauder* with heavy damage to its torso, to Lori's *Shadow Hawk* with most of the damage patched and repaired.

"Private channel, Gray.''

"You've got it, Lori.''

"Gray . . . it's no good. We can't make another attack.''

"What do you suggest?''

There was a long silence, as though she were studying the advancing Marik force.

"I don't know, but look, if we board the DropShips now, we could launch before they got here."

"Duke Ricol is still loading, Lori. And Alard King isn't back yet from the library. We've got to hold a little longer."

"*Damn* Duke Ricol. And *damn* the library!"

"Do you suggest we abandon our 'Mechs? Run?"

He was answered by another silence. Was she arguing the question inwardly, one way or the other? "No," Lori said at last. "Of course not. But Gray . . . there's no way out."

"No, there isn't." He paused, considering. "Some of you may be able to get out. If . . . two . . . maybe three 'Mechs follow me, we could hold them long enough, *just* long enough, for the rest of you to board ship and go."

"*Grayson Death Carlyle* . . . if you are suggesting that *I* leave you to face all of *them*!"

Grayson chuckled. "The thought *had* crossed my mind, Lori, along with the thought of knocking you unconscious, tying you up, and tossing you aboard the *Phobos* like a side of frozen meat. But you'll notice I didn't suggest it."

"It's a damn good thing you *didn't,* or you'd have to take *me* on, along with our friends over there. I'm in this with *you,* you idiot!"

"You always did show terrible judgement, my love."

There was another long silence. "Grayson," Lori said softly. "I love you."

"And I love you," he said, but the endearment was almost matter-of-fact as Grayson studied his instrumentation. "Range, nine hundred meters, and closing" were his next words.

"Company, sir!"

King looked up from the computer console. The Special Ops corporal, Janice Taylor, had leaned into the library door with the warning. The TK assault rifle clutched in her hand was pointed at the ceiling, a fresh magazine of caseless 3 mm rounds rammed home, a second 80-round magazine taped upside down to the first to allow her to change quickly when the first ran dry.

"What is it?" He had found the Star League computer easy to activate, easy to understand. Its long-dead programmers must have assumed that its operators might not have the same grasp of programing mechanics as they did. Step-by-step instructions had led him to connect the half-meter-long memory core to a slot that opened in the desk beside the terminal on his command. The pressing of a key had started the copying process. On the screen, characters spelled out:

Program: Copyall
Complete: 23%

As he watched, the figures changed to read "24%." He had tried to imagine just how much information, in bits and bytes, was being manipulated silently within the library computer's framework.

"I don't know, sir, but we can hear people working on the other side of the Wall. Corby thinks they may be setting explosives."

King sagged back in the seat. *No! It was too soon!*

"I'm afraid I have no advice to offer," he said. "If it comes to combat, that's your department."

"I've deployed my people around the cavern, and we're watching. But if there's a large force out there, I can't promise to protect you here. This building is more exposed to fire from that doorway than I'd like."

He gestured at the screen, which now read "28%." "There's no way to hurry this," King told her. "Do what you can, and keep me informed."

"Yessir." Janice vanished back through the door, and he heard her calling orders to her troops a moment later. He wondered how long eight men and women could hold out against whatever was beyond the Wall. He touched the uncomfortable pressure of the flare pistol in his belt, thinking, *That's no defense. You'll just have to get the job done . . . and get out!*

His eyes met those of one of the two Techs in the library room. They were scarcely more than teenagers, and both looked scared.

''Go on, you two,'' he said. ''There's nothing more to be done here. No, wait—'' His words stopped them as they started toward the door. ''If something happens to me, get this core back to the DropShips. Promise me! It is vitally, vitally important!'' *So many have died for it already!*

The youngsters assured him that they would, and vanished.

King wondered if he would ever see them again.

''Range eight hundred meters. Closing.''

Lori tried to analyze Grayson's voice through the faint hiss of static on the taccom's general frequency. The other MechWarriors had been completely silent ever since they had assumed their places in the line. She had had better luck determining the other warriors' moods than Grayson's. They, like her, had reached the absolute limits of their endurance and their abilities. Before they had mounted their 'Mechs, Lori had heard Sharyl saying over and over, ''He can't make us do this . . . he can't make us do this . . .'' Even the normally jovial Davis McCall had been stonily silent, the pain stark in his eyes. Something seemed to have broken inside him with the near-dismemberment of his beloved *Bannockburn*. Delmar Clay had tried to argue Grayson out of the attack.

''We've lost, Grayson!'' he had said. ''We simply don't have what you're asking of us! Look at them!'' Clay had pointed at Burns's infantrymen standing sullenly beside their vehicles, which were spread out in a long, ragged line ahead of the 'Mechs. ''They're burned out! At the point of collapse! We still have time to pull back aboard the DropShips . . .''

Khaled had said nothing, but Lori had seen him looking off toward the mountain valley and shaking his head. Koga had been as imperturbable as ever, until Lori caught him striking his right fist hard against his left palm in an unguarded moment. Seeing the fury in his expression, she had approached him. The impenetrable mask had dropped silently into place once more. ''Vengeance cannot always be answered,'' he had said, and without further explanation, walked away toward his *Archer*.

Vengeance against whom? Lori said to herself.

Of all the old hands of the unit, Bear alone seemed unaffected. She had spoken to him before they'd boarded, but his response had seemed to come from a great distance, as though he were removed, on some higher, colder, and far-distant plane.

It was a different story among the newly fielded recon lance. The two recruits showed widely differing attitudes, with Gary Brodenson frankly terrified and Jason Morely passionately announcing that he could not wait to come to meet the enemy. DeVillar was grim, at one point, having joined Delmar's questioning of Grayson's orders. Tracy Kent was ecstatic over having regained her BattleMech once more, though the approaching Marik army had sobered her.

"He's not going to . . . going to make us stand to the last, is he?" Tracy had asked Lori. "I mean, what if he's down, but the rest of us are still fighting?"

"Then we carry on without him," Lori had said. The words had come with savage, inner pain. She could have chided Tracy, reminded her of duty, of honor, but she added, simply, "We'll have to see when the time comes, I suppose. But you'll do fine."

With the possible exception of Bear, who came from a culture markedly different from her own, Lori could identify with all the different responses she found among her comrades. Yet, it was Grayson, of all people, who puzzled her the most.

He was grimmer, lonelier, and more isolated in a way that she could not touch or reach. Just before they'd boarded their 'Mechs, she had asked him to wish her luck. He had turned on her then, and she had seen agony behind his eyes. But she still did not understand.

"Seven hundred meters. Closing," she heard now over the taccom.

Lori began to switch the power systems of her *Shadow Hawk* to combat mode, checked her fire extinguisher automatics, and made certain the first of the autocannon reload cassettes was properly seated in her cannon's receiver. In seconds, she was too busy to worry about anything else.

33

The explosion smashed down on Alard King's body like a living thing, knocking the air from his lungs and leaving him gasping on the library floor. The shock wave had been transmitted through the floor of the cave and the deck of the library structure almost as though the deck had leaped up and hit him hard enough to knock him down.

For a moment, all he could hear was the ringing in his ears. Only gradually did he realize that there was noise trying to push through the ringing, that the noise was growing in volume, an almighty roar magnified tenfold by the echoing enclosure of the cavern. He pulled himself shakily to his feet. Miraculously, the computer still ran, the screen now reading completion at 89 percent. Or was it a miracle? The League engineers must have known that they were building over an earthquake fault; they would have designed the electronics of their facility accordingly.

The noise increased. Still dazed, King stumbled toward the door, which hung open now, the bearings smashed from their tracks.

He blinked in unaccustomed light. The Wall was open.

Langsdorf's engineers had placed their charges in hopes of bringing down the whole wall, but ten million metric tons of rock had been beyond their capabilities, at least with so little time in which to work. Light spilled now through a gaping hole on the north side of the Wall. Rather than falling, the ancient granite of the wall had split along an old and invisible seam. Perhaps a quarter of the wall had crumbled, and was lying as a vast pile of black and grey rubble. The shaft of light flooding the room was harshly visible in the dancing motes of rock dust thrown up by the blast.

Against the light, shadows moved.

The shock of the blast had struck Janice and her troops as hard as it had King, but they had been braced and expecting attack. They lay in their positions just outside the pool of dusty light, arrayed in a semicircle, with their weapons turned toward the invaders. The roar of noise was the firefight erupting within the cavern. Heavily armored Marik infantrymen were spilling through the gap in the wall and clattering through the fallen rubble. TK rounds stitched through armor, flesh, and granite wall alike, erupting in miniature suns of destruction. Submachine gunfire lanced out of the darkness, grabbing at armored men and spinning them around, or slamming them down beside the dark, bloody forms of their comrades.

And the invaders replied. Gunfire flashed through the darkness. A young mercenary soldier shrieked as an invisible hand lifted him from the cavern floor and hurled him backward, leaving him crushed, bloody, and still.

King darted back into the library. The screen read 96 percent. *Come on! Come on!* He didn't know what would happen if he tried to stop the machine and remove the core. Perhaps nothing, or perhaps the attempt would cause him to lose everything. He gripped the edge of the table, watching the screen.

There was an odd, double bang that filled the room and made him look up. Two small holes had been drilled through the library's walls, high up, near the ceiling. Two companion holes marred the wall on the opposite sides. Someone was adding long, keening screams to the roar of gunfire outside. King remained transfixed, watching the percentage of copied data creep with infinite slowness toward the magical, three-digits of completeness. *Come on!*

There was a new sound, one that drowned out the screaming, drowned out even the hammer of gunfire. It was a deep, full-voiced thunder, and it came with the steady beat of someone knocking slowly to be let in. He looked out the library door again, and his eyes widened. The hole in the granite Wall was wider now, and something very large moved against the light outside.

There was a chiming note from the computer. He hurried back to the table as the memory core rose silently from the desk top recession. He grasped the core and lifted it free. The screen now read: DATA COPY COMPLETE. DO YOU REQUIRE ANOTHER?

''No thank you!'' King shouted at the machine, though he knew the computer did not hear him. The shipboard computer could be set to make further copies, if required. This one copy would have to serve. Clutching his treasure before him, he stepped out of the library.

There was a further, shattering roar from the Wall, and King held up one hand to protect his face from splintered, hurtling shards of rock. The gap in the Wall was opening further.

The light spilling through the opening was blotted out by something large stepping through the enlarged opening. For just a moment, it looked like a, a gigantic, primordial, insectoid monster come to claim its cave and prey. Then it shifted in the backlight, and King recognized it even as the powerful spotlight mounted on its shoulder came on, bathing the interior of the cavern with light.

The *Archer* took a step forward into the cavern . . .

Grayson studied the 'Marik Mechs spreading out on the plain on the far side of the river. The odds were not so great as he'd first feared, though they were certainly bad enough. In all, he counted sixteen 'Mechs in the enemy line. That meant that at least four of those hit in earlier battles had been too badly damaged to join the Marik line now. That *Archer* at the Vermillion River, for example, had been savaged before it had finally managed to make its way back across the steaming river. Not bad . . . but not good enough.

One of the 'Mechs, a *Warhammer,* remained well behind the others. *That will be Langsdorf,* Grayson thought.

Grayson could make out a cluster of vehicles close beside the distant 'Mech. Who? Langsdorf's staff? Rachan? Garth?

They're getting closer. We're almost at the end.

How long would their twelve 'Mechs last against sixteen? There was no way to answer that question. In fact, the question was largely meaningless, for numbers alone could not give a true picture of the relative power of two opposing forces.

A more accurate image could be drawn by comparing the total weights of two opposing forces. Grayson had long since used his *Marauder's* computer to tally the figures for the 'Mechs he saw arrayed against them. The figure he'd come up with was 795 tons. The total weight of his own force was a respectable 649 tons, which gave Langsdorf only a narrow 16-to-13 lead.

Even comparing BattleMech weights did not always indicate which side had the best chance to win. There was a concept, known as "CLG" among MechWarriors. The letters stood for "Combat Loss Groupings," and it referred to the fact that in 'Mech combat, 'Mechs of a single unit often received critical levels of damage at about the same time. For example, a twelve-Mech company might get into a firefight and battle for an eternity, in combat terms—as much as three or four minutes—and while they would take hits, none would appear seriously damaged.

Then, several more minutes into the battle, a 'Mech would be knocked out of action. Almost immediately, another would be lost, then one or two more. Within the space of thirty seconds, half the combat strength of the company would be gone. This was because it took a set space of time for even light 'Mechs to accumulate enough damage to threaten them, and it was likely that several 'Mechs in the unit would be brought to the same point in about the same time. Further, once some 'Mechs had been lost to one side, the enemy could concentrate more weapons on fewer targets, accelerating the rate of damage among the survivors. Grayson had heard one story of a company entering combat, fighting valiantly for five minutes without losses, then falling apart within thirty seconds. There had been, he'd heard, only three surviving 'Mechs in that company.

MechWarrior commanders knew about CLG and tried to keep close tabs on the damage sustained by their people's machines. A good commander was one who realized when a particular battle became hopeless and withdrew *before* CLG began taking its toll.

In this battle, CLG was already working against Grayson's force, and there was not a thing he could do about it. Two of the team's 'Mechs—McCall's and Clay's—were so badly damaged that only a few more hits apiece would knock them out completely. Once they were gone, the odds of 16 to 13 would drop to something closer to 8 to 5. Grayson's own *Marauder* would not take many more hits, and the enemy was certain to concentrate their fire on the mercenary leader. How long would it be before 8 to 5 became 2 to 1? Or 3 to 1?

Yet, these crucial numbers said nothing of what was burning within Grayson's mind.

He was going to die. He knew it with a calm certainty that would have belied the numbers and odds even if it were the Gray Death outnumbering the Marik forces by almost 2 to 1.

The enemy 'Mechs were splashing across the broad, shallow Vermillion River now, as hovercraft whined across farther upriver. There were Marik troops upriver, too, watching, Grayson knew, for a repetition of the CSF in the water. That was all right, because he had not expected that trick to work twice.

In fact, Grayson was all out of tricks. There was nothing left but a last, forlorn charge.

"Range, 500 meters," he said. "Up weapons! Prepare to attack!"

He wondered if anyone would follow the order to charge. There had been so much grumbling when he'd held his final briefing an hour before, and there were dark looks on some faces, questioning or confused or simply scared expression among others. Was this the final measure of a combat commander's skill, whether or not his troops would follow when he gave an order that amounted to suicide?

He checked his rear screens. The line of vehicles winding down from the cache continued to move, fat and vulnerable. The DropShips remained on the plain five kilometers away, hatches open, taking the treasure aboard. As yet, there had been no word from King, no white flare over the mountain to indicate that he had come through safely with the library memory core. Where was he? The Star League 'Mechs be damned . . . *where* was King?

The Marik BattleMechs opened fire. Explosions geysered up in the wet ground, and a long, ragged line of missile trails arced swiftly overhead. Grayson wondered what would happen if he gave the order, and no one followed? For one thing, Lori might live, which he so desperately wanted.

There was no chance that the Marik forces might take prisoners, not while they believed the Gray Death was responsible for the massacre at Tiantan.

There was no way out. The Gray Death Legion would end . . . *here*.

Grayson opened the general command frequency again. ''Forward!''

He engaged his *Marauder*'s drives, and the damaged machine lurched forward, its primary pusher links rattling in their casings, charred circuit wiring dangling from a gaping hole high on its starboard flank.

Fire from the enemy forces swept across the flood plain, converging on him and him alone.

King yelled and threw one hand over his eyes, while the other still clutched the memory core. The *Archer* fired its right arm laser, the beam lancing past King and into the library building.

The library did not so much explode as burn. The walls softened, folding in one another. Intense heat consumed it, melted it, and weird shadows chased one another across the floors and walls of the caves. King stumbled forward, away from the heat. Around him, the battle had stopped. The appearance of the lone *Archer* had been more than sufficient to stun the battling soldiers into motionlessness. One by one, the soldiers on both sides rose to their feet. Weapons clattered to the floor as the Marik soldiers began to assume control of the situation, and the Gray Death mercenaries surrendered.

More figures made their way into the cavern, following the *Archer*'s trail of flattened debris. There were more soldiers, wearing the gray and purple body armor of Marik Guards. There were also ComStar Adepts, six of them in their robes and hoods, walking carefully with their skirts raised above the rubble.

And that could be none other than Rachan. He bore his authority like a cloak, and even in the semidarkness of the cavern, his physical presence was as commanding in its own way as that of the 70-ton *Archer* towering above him. Though Rachan's eyes were invisible against the brightness behind him and the glare of the searchlight overhead, King felt his gaze upon him. The Precentor raised his arm, and pointed a bony finger at King. "You. You have what I want. Bring it to me."

Somehow, King found his voice. "Why? So you can destroy it?"

Rachan's laughter surprised him. "You cannot possibly understand the import of what you hold, mercenary. Bring it."

King took a step forward, the memory core seeming very heavy in his arms. He stopped again. "You're wrong, Rachan, I do understand Star League knowledge, preserved for three centuries . . . it's priceless, invaluable . . ."

"I represent the ComStar Order, my son. The data you hold will be safe with me. Trust me."

"This knowledge could be the deliverance of mankind!"

"Bah! You don't know what you're saying, youngster! Deliverance or damnation, pure knowledge is not as important as the uses to which it is put. Bring that memory core to me!"

"No."

"Soldiers!"

"If your soldiers fire," King warned, "they might hit this!"

"Fool! You don't understand, do you? It doesn't matter to me in the least whether that cylinder you hold is preserved or not. If I can save a copy for ComStar's files, well and good. But my mission here is to destroy that library!''

''Like you destroyed twelve million people at Tiantan?''

''Be quiet!'' In the dying light of the fire behind him, King caught a glimpse of Rachan's wild and contorted face. He was breathing heavily, his hands twisted into trembling claws.

King had sensed the sudden and uncomfortable stirring among the Adepts standing behind Rachan. He knew that, like him, they were Technicians. They were trained . . . disciplined. Though he could not see their faces under their cowls, King suspected they must be young . . . and, therefore, idealistic. Was that idealism directed toward an ideal of service to Order or to the race? Or was it a fanaticism twisted around the solitary figure standing in front of them?

King decided to take a chance. He raised his voice so that the Adepts would hear him. ''Did you know? Did he tell you? It was Precentor Rachan who planned the murder of twelve million civilians on Sirius V!''

''*Quiet!*''

''We heard it from a Marik Captain!'' King went on, barely missing a beat. ''He did it so a Marik Duke could legally take this planet away from Grayson Carlyle! Is this the man you follow?''

''Precentor,'' one of the hooded men said. ''What this man says *cannot* be true . . .''

''Fools! All of you!'' Rachan's voice was wild now, closer to a scream than to words. He vaulted on top of a pile of rubble close beside him. In the light of the *Archer*, something flashed in his hand, a small and wicked-looking laser pistol. ''What does it matter . . . a few worthless lives? *They were expendable!* You are *all* expendable!''

The laser fired wildly, stabbing. Janice Taylor shrieked in pain, falling backward several meters from King. A young, red-haired soldier standing at her side screamed with her, but in rage, not pain. He dropped to the ground, rolled to the left, and came to his feet with a TK assault rifle in his hand. Gunfire erupted from the weapon, spraying wildly toward the Marik soldiers.

Blood gushed from the Precentor's leg as he pitched back off the mound, the laser pistol flying from his hand. Marik soldiers scrambled for cover as the boy with the TK stood in the open, his face twisted with rage as he swept the rubble at the *Archer*'s feet with a hail of explosive rounds.

King was already moving, but so was the 'Mech. As the shots rang out, it stepped forward, one hand coming up in ponderous slow motion, its target the red-haired boy with the wildly stuttering rifle. King could hear Janice Taylor's voice, raw with pain. "Nik . . . *Nik!* It's O.K.! I'm O.K."

King fumbled with one hand under the memory core. As a senior Tech, he had a MechWarrior's understanding of BattleMechs, of how they were designed and how they were assembled. He could look up against the spotlight on the *Archer*'s shoulder and make out the curve of the cockpit's armored screen, could see the cluster of stubby snouts just to the right of the insectlike face where an *Archer*'s IR and scanning gear are mounted.

His right hand came up from under the memory core, clutching the flare pistol that had been tucked into his belt, and concealed by the core. He took three running steps toward the looming *Archer*, took aim, and fired. White light burst against the 'Mech's cockpit.

"Run!" King shouted. "Everybody run!"

The mercenary soldiers were already falling back into the darkness of the cavern. A Marik soldier rose from where he had dropped to the floor, and brought up his rifle. Gunfire crashed in the cavern again. A mercenary returned the fire. Bullets sang off the 'Mech's armor and the partly shattered granite wall.

The red-headed boy named Nik threw his rifle aside, stooping to help the wounded Janice Taylor. Another soldier joined him, and together they helped her to her feet. King dropped the empty flare gun, put his head down, and ran as hard as he could. The *Archer*'s IR gear—and its pilot's dazzled eyes—would clear in seconds.

It was less than seconds before the three mercenaries had plunged into the sheltering darkness of the tunnel. King did not think the lone *Archer* would pursue them into an unknown labyrinth.

Behind him came the roar of gunfire.

Grayson's *Marauder* set off alone against the Marik army. Behind him, the BattleMechs under his command stirred or stood still as their pilots watched, dazed by mind-numbing battle exhaustion. It was not mutiny so much as it was the complete breakdown of men and women pushed too hard, and too far.

Then a second 'Mech began to move. McCall's shattered *Rifleman* started forward, wires and twisted strands of myomer sheathing still dangling from the gaping hole where one of its twin-cannoned arms had been mounted. In the next instant, Delmar Clay's battered *Wolverine* was moving out, with Lori close behind him. Then the entire band of twelve 'Mechs was moving forward, a ragged, battered line, to meet the enemy at the Vermillion River.

Colonel Langsdorf stood on the ground next to his *Warhammer*'s foot, on the crest of a hill a kilometer from the river. Lord Garth was with him, as well as General Kleider and officers of his staff, all recently arrived from Helmdown.

"I don't believe what I'm seeing," Kleider said. "The idiot is *charging* our line! And after the battering they've already taken!"

The *Marauder* at the head of the mercenary forces was among the Marik BattleMechs now. The sounds of battle were muted and distant, but the men on the hilltop could clearly hear Carlyle's heavy autocannon as it engaged Captain Tarlborough's *Warhammer*.

White fire lanced out from a Marik *Shadow Hawk* and a *Wolverine,* catching the mercenary's *Rifleman* in a blistering crossfire. The watchers could see that the Gray Death 'Mech was already severely damaged. As they raised electronic binoculars to their eyes and zoomed in on the scene unfolding below, several of Kleider's aides began to bet with one another on how many shots the damaged *Rifleman* could take before it went down.

"Twenty C-Bs . . . he won't last thirty seconds," one said as he checked his wristcomp.

"You're on. The *Wolverine*'s going to have to shift to that *Marauder* any second . . . Ah! There! That'll give the *Rifleman* a breather!"

"Nah! Our boys are charging now. He's surrounded! Look! Our *Crusader* is up close now. This won't take long!"

"The merc *Crusader*'s coming up to the rescue!"

"Not in time! Ha! There goes the *Rifleman* . . . fourteen seconds! You owe me! Gods, look at him burn!"

Langsdorf felt a twisting in his stomach as he watched and listened. "Carlyle is a brave man . . . and a fine commander," he said at last, in a voice deliberately loud enough to interrupt the comments from the General's junior staff.

"You forget yourself, Colonel," Kleider said. "The man is responsible for the deaths of millions."

"Is he, General? I wonder . . . I have been engaging him in combat almost continually now for several days. I find him resourceful, daring, brave, intelligent . . . Frankly, it's hard to reconcile this warrior with the mad dog butcher you say massacred a city on Sirius V."

To that, Garth and Kleider made no reply.

McCall was down. Grayson had seen him go, his *Rifleman* spouting flame. "McCall! Are you there?" Grayson yelled into his mike. There was no answer, but a moment later, Grayson saw the *Rifleman*'s rear escape hatch open, and a ragged and bearded figure climb out and drop to the muddy ground. A Gray Death hovercraft hissed close by, risking laser fire and the swinging of the Mech's foot as one of the crewmen pulled the dazed McCall aboard.

Clay's *Wolverine* stood near, pumping cannon fire into a gut-damaged Marik *Shadow Hawk*. Bear's *Crusader* closed with an enemy *Crusader,* both fists upraised, then swung them down in a splintering crash that tore one arm from the enemy 'Mech and left it lying steaming in the mud. Lori's *Shadow Hawk* was behind Grayson's embattled *Marauder,* chopping into an enemy *Wasp* that tried to circle the Gray Death's commander for a shot from behind. Infantry from both sides tangled wildly between the legs of the thrashing, struggling 'Mechs, weaving in close for a quick shot, then darting away again on shrieking cushions of air.

Suddenly, Lori's *Shadow Hawk* staggered under the impact of a rapid-fire volley of missiles, striking her down from behind. Grayson swung his *Marauder* and opened fire on her attacker, a heavily damaged *Griffin.* The two stood there, dueling over Lori's fallen 'Mech, until Grayson's more powerful PPCs melted through the *Griffin's* armor, setting the lighter 'Mech ablaze.

"Lori!"

"I'm . . . all right, Gray! Armor's burned through in my back! Fires . . . but my extinguishers have them under control!"

"Get up if you can! They're closing in!"

Lori struggled to bring her terribly damaged *Shadow Hawk* to its feet. Grayson, meanwhile, continued to trigger his 'Mech's heavy weapons at the advancing Marik 'Mechs. He was drenched in sweat and the *Marauder's* computer was warning of imminent shutdown.

This can't go on much longer, he thought.

34

"This can't go on much longer," Garth said, looking at his wrist computer. "Are they going to smash each other to pieces? What about the DropShips?"

"What about them, Your Grace?" Langsdorf asked, with barely concealed contempt. "We can't approach them until the enemy has been beaten, which, at the moment, he most obviously is not!"

The general's aides cheered. Another enemy 'Mech was down, the big, combative *Wolverine*. "Yah!" One junior lieutenant yelled as a comrade tugged the binoculars away from him. "Step on the pilot! Step on the pilot!"

"Damn! The bastard got away! Maybe our boys should start potting at those hovercraft!"

"Hey, another one's burning!"

"Idiot. It's one of ours!"

"No, no! That one! One of the merc's *Stinger*s! Ho! Man! Did you see that? What PPC fire does to a *Stinger* is *not* to be believed!"

Langsdorf turned at the sound of a hovercraft approaching at high speed from behind. The maneuverable little transport slowed as it approached the *Warhammer* and the coterie of officers. There was a single man at the control stick, his Adept's robes soaked with blood.

"Here . . . what's this?" Kleider said. "What are you . . ."

Before he could finish the phrase, the Adept vaulted over to the side of his vehicle as it came to ground on its plenum skirts, and stalked toward Langsdorf. The blood that stained his robes, it seemed, was not his own, yet his face showed the mark of some terrible, inner wound. The personal escorts of Kleider and Garth stepped forward, their weapons up, blocking his way.

"Let him come," Langsdorf said. "It is one of the ComStar Adepts."

At the sound of a dull, hollow boom signaling some enormous explosion. Langsdorf turned and raised his binoculars. A Marik *Wasp* had exploded, sending a huge ball of fire rocketing into the sky, and scattering burning chunks of metal across the battlefield.

The explosion seemed to mark a breaking of the Marik force's will. Langsdorf noted Captain Tarlborough's *Warhammer* leading the rest of the Marik 'Mechs as they splashed through the broad, shallow water of the Vermillion toward the rear. The mercenary 'Mechs advanced to the water's edge and waded in, taking advantage of the water to cool their hot drive and combat systems. The Marik 'Mechs formed up on the north side of the river, milling about uncertainly. Some of them appeared to be in bad shape.

Langsdorf turned back to the Adept. "Can I help you, Adept? We're a little busy right now . . . ."

The Adept scarcely looked the part. His cowl was back off his head, and his wispy, straw-blond hair was matted across his forehead in sweat and grime.

"Colonel Langsdorf . . . ?"

Langsdorf nodded.

"I am Adept Larabee, of Comstar's Helmdown Station. I . . ." He hesitated, suddenly unsure of himself. "You . . . you must stop the battle, Colonel!"

"Nonsense!" Kleider pointed. "Arrest this man!"

"Touch me and you risk a ComStar Edict!"

Kleider's troops froze where they stood, bewildered. A ComStar Edict could deprive a world . . . or a number of worlds . . . of the services of the ComStar HPG transmitters. Loss of access to an interstellar communications network was of little personal import to the soldiers who stood there, but they knew *Edict* as a near-magical word of curse and dread. They looked back toward their leaders, uncertain.

"This . . . this . . ." Garth sputtered, then brought his tongue under control. "This Adept has no authority here, Colonel!"

"Perhaps," Langsdorf said, in a low, almost deadly calm tone. "But I think I'd like to hear what he has to say."

Larabee pointed toward the battle plain. "Colonel, this whole operation was mounted to destroy the Gray Death, an outlaw mercenary regiment"

"Yes."

"But they're not outlaws! The city of Tiantan on Sirius V was destroyed on the orders of Precentor Rachan! This whole thing was *his* doing! *He* is the outlaw!"

"Lies . . ." Garth began, but the Adept cut him off.

"We met a senior Tech in the caverns, trying to save a Star League library."

"Library?" Kleider looked startled. "What library? What does a library have to do with this?"

"Everything! Rachan brought me and my brothers here to copy the data stored in a Star League computer, and he planned to destroy the computer when he was done! But we met a senior Technician who had been on Sirius V. He knew that Carlyle's regiment had not committed the atrocity. *And Rachan admitted it*!"

"Seize him!" Garth screamed. A Marik soldier reached for the Adept, who twisted away. A second soldier swung his rifle, knocking Larabee to the ground, senseless.

"Stop!" Langsdorf barked, bringing his sidearm, a large-caliber automatic pistol, out of its holster. "Everyone, stop!"

Kleider pointed toward the battle. "Listen, man! Never mind this lunatic! The mercenary force is falling apart. Only six of them still on their feet! One more charge and you've won! *Won!*"

Langsdorf eyed Kleider bleakly. "Won? Won what, General?"

"Why, victory, man! A glorious victory!"

Langsdorf's gorge rose in his throat, almost making him sick. He pushed past the general and started toward his *Warhammer*.

"Langsdorf! Where are you going!"

"To give my orders, General." He grasped the rungs of the 'Mech's ladder.

"Excellent! Excellent! I suggest you use your BattleMechs to crush their line, then press on to the DropShips. Your infantry can deal with the survivors! My congratulations, Colonel . . . on your *glorious* victory!"

The word made Langsdorf pause, two meters above the ground. He hung there a moment, swaying on the ladder, looking down at Garth and Kleider. "No, General. There is no *glory* here. And no victory!"

"What do you mean?" Kleider shouted.

"I mean, General, that I will not order what is left of my forces to charge. The battle is over. I will not throw away more of my men . . . not for you." He glanced over at Garth, who stood in the *Warhammer*'s shadow, a dumbfounded look on his fat face. "And certainly not for *him!*"

Rachan lay on his back in the dark. The fire that had consumed the library was almost gone now, and the only real light filtered in through the smoke and dust from the smashed-open entrance to the tomb. He had regained his senses and found himself alone. The Marik soldiers who had survived the insane attack by the young merc soldier and the *Archer* he had commandeered from Langsdorf's encampment were gone. The troopers must have assumed he was dead and left him here, helpless in the dark.

When he tried to get up, his leg was a leaden, useless thing that pinned him there to the rubble-strewn floor of the cave. Pain throbbed and pulsed in his thigh. Looking down at it, Rachan could see where his upper leg bent off to the left at a sharp and unnatural angle well above his knee. *There was so much blood . . .*

He heard a noise, a deep and echoing sound from the darkness. He reached out, scrabbling through broken rock, looking for his laser. Suppose the mercenaries were coming back? Suppose they found him? They knew that it was he who had placed the blame for Tiantan on them. If they found him . . . alive . . .

The sound came again, and Rachan stopped searching for the laser. That noise was nothing made by men. It sounded like the roar of some monstrous subterranean animal, echoing up out of the dark. The floor of the cavern moved, and Rachan shrieked in agony. The movement had been sharp enough to twist his leg, reawakening the torture that seemed ready to tear the limb from his body.

The roar sounded again, lower, deeper, a rumbling that went on and on and set the broken stones to quivering and jittering all around the wounded man.

The fleet of Prime Movers made their way across the river flats toward the battered group of 'Mechs. Grayson watched them from his *Marauder,* but could muster no emotion. It was as though he watched from an enormous distance, remote and detached.

"I said, this is Ricol!" The voice on Grayson's general frequency repeated itself. "Have your people ready for pick-up!"

Grayson turned his *Marauder* back toward the north. The enemy 'Mechs were . . . withdrawing. *Withdrawing!* But another charge would have been certain to overwhelm the remaining Gray Death 'Mechs. Only five 'Mechs still stood with him. His command lance had been wiped out, with the 'Mechs of Lori, Delmar Clay, and Davis McCall all out of action. Fortunately, the pilots had all been picked up, exhausted but unhurt.

Though Khaled's *Warhammer* was down, he was alive, but wounded. The two recruits were dead, their *Stinger*s smashed or exploded. What were their names? Morley and Brodenson. Grayson remembered their faces at the briefing . . . one excited, the other terrified. Neither emotion touched them now.

Koga, Bear, and Sharyl stood to his right. DeVillar and Kent stood on his left. All of the surviving 'Mechs were battered and smashed to the point where they could barely stand. Koga's *Archer* was out of missiles and had lost two medium lasers. Grayson's own *Marauder* was out of autocannon rounds, and his left arm PPC had gone dead. The cannon on Sharyl's *Shadow Hawk* had been torn away, and the laser on her 'Mech's arm had been shattered.

One more charge by the enemy 'Mechs and what was left of the Gray Death Legion would have been smashed flat.

He tried to concentrate on Ricol's words, still coming over the radio. ''We're picking up the damaged 'Mechs, Grayson. Our commtechs on the DropShips have confirmed it. Langsdorf is pulling back. We picked up his order. They're retreating. You've won, Grayson! You've won!''

He looked through his *Marauder*'s forward screen. The tough plastic had been cracked by a near-miss from an enemy missile. Three bodies lay sprawled in the mud a few meters in front of him, infantrymen cut down by machine gun fire as they'd tried to get close enough to an enemy *Wasp* to attack it with satchel charges.

Strange, thought Grayson. It doesn't feel like victory.

The feedback through his neurohelmet brought a strange, queasy sensation through his middle ear. He worked with his controls a moment, trying to isolate the problem.

Three must be battle damage to the Marauder*'s sensors,* he decided. *It feels like the ground is moving.*

Colonel Langsdorf sat in his *Warhammer*'s cockpit, struggling with the heavy machine's controls. His neurohelmet was transmitting sensations of vertigo and unsteadiness through his middle ear, sensations that made him feel as though the ground were shifting beneath his BattleMech's feet.

Soldiers were running past him, and hovercraft skittered off toward the north. Garth, Kleider, and their escorts were long gone back toward Helmdown. Once Langsdorf had reached his 'Mech's cockpit and given the order to withdraw, there had been nothing more they could do.

Nothing they could do here, at least, the Colonel corrected himself. *But my career is finished.* Court-martial and death by firing squad awaited him. It all seemed distant and unreal.

"Colonel Langsdorf!" A voice came through the radio. "This is Boomerang Two!"

"Recall, Boomerang Two," Langsdorf said. "Land at the encampment, and prepare your aircraft for evacuation."

"Sir! Sir . . . you've got to see this! Open one of your monitors for a video feed!"

Langsdorf turned his main monitor on. After flickering with static for a moment, it then cleared to show the image transmitted by a camera in the belly of the little spotter plane circling high above. It took Langsdorf a moment to figure out what he was seeing. It looked like a geyser, a column of steam and boiling water mounting in a white pillar toward the sky. How very curious, he thought. Then he caught sight of buildings at the pillar's base, and the scale of the thing made itself clear. Langsdorf sucked in a sharp intake of breath. "Boomerang! What is that thing!"

"Those buildings you see . . . that's part of the ruins of Freeport! I'm east of the mountains, circling above our encampment. That geyser started up a few seconds ago!"

"It's . . . huge . . ."

"The water jet reaches two thousand meters, Colonel! There's steam shooting up farther than that! The geyser is four hundred meters across the base!"

The ground was definitely shaking under the *Warhammer*'s feet, and there was a growing, subsurface, almost subsonic rumble that transmitted itself through the ground and into the body of his 'Mech. "But where is it coming from?"

"From the ruins of Freeport. It's as though a huge body of water underground started turning to steam! It started coming up through a spot on my map that looks like some sort of dam or flood-control equipment, down where the river bed meets the dry sea floor!"

Langsdorf watched the explosion of steam and water mount higher into the sky.

The Yehudan Sea was returning to the light.

35

Rachan screamed. The pain in his leg was unendurable as the ground shook and rumbled with accelerating fury.

He had not seen the records of the Star League's underground facility's building, had not seen the survey plots of the huge system of pipes that the League engineers had built beneath Freeport in order to drain the eastern half of the Vermillion River and open the cavern into the mountain.

The water had been rerouted, channeled into Helm Pit, an ancient faultline fissure that plunged for kilometers into the planet's crust. Later, when Freeport was destroyed, the channels had been opened, and a large portion of a small sea had funneled into the pit.

For three centuries, a small sea had existed at the core of the Nagayan Mountains. In a geologically active area, this could have created considerable problems, but fortunately, no large magma pockets or other thermal sources existed in the area. The area had once been much hotter, too, the site of considerable tectonic activity as the continental plates that had bumped and forced the Nagayan Mountains up from an ancient ocean continued to grind together. But the area had been quiescent for millions of years.

For three centuries, the Star League base's fusion pile had remained quiescent as well, providing the trickle of power necessary to keep the library's memory alive, and to be ready to open the Eastern Gate when the proper code was received. There was always the possibility, however, that someone would come who did not know the code, and would simply blast down the Eastern Gate rather than use the computer to unlock the door. Even a wall of granite weighing ten million metric tons could not keep out a determined invader. Major Keeler, the engineer who had created the whole system, knew very well that a few properly set charges of plastic explosives or a determined application of heavy lasers would smash the wall down, or burn through it.

He had, therefore, set other monitoring devices to watch over the integrity of the Eastern Gate, and other places throughout the complex. If the gate were ever smashed or the library destroyed, it would mean that it was not Star League personnel who had returned, but barbarians. Barbarians who must not be allowed to rifle the storehouse's treasures.

Deep below the mountain, the fusion reactor was generating heat normally found only at the core of stars. As it grew hotter, an underground sea turned to steam, and an eons-old balance of geological forces was overturned.

The crust of the planet moved.

Rachan could know none of this, of course. All he could tell was that the rumbling from beneath the mountain was louder now, with quake-loosened stones splattering down from the ceiling of the cavern in the darkness. The stones grew larger, as head-sized rocks broken fresh and jagged-edged from swaying cavern walls smashed to the ground around him.

Desperately, one hand clenched in agony around his shattered leg. Rachan began to drag himself toward the opening in the wall. A searing, claustrophobic fear possessed him in the roaring darkness, throttling him with the same intensity as the fire searing his leg.

A new sound ground through the dust and dark, the sound of stone splitting. As light burst suddenly down upon the ComStar Precentor, he looked up and shrieked.

The Wall across the mouth of the river-carved cavern had been severely weakened when Rachan ordered that its support struts be cut. It had been weakened further by the movements of the *Archer*. The earthquake shattered the last of the aligned-crystal steel braces, and sent ten million tons of granite toppling into the cavern opening.

The roar of tortured rock continued long after it had cut off the man's single, sharp scream.

The DropShip fleet accelerated at 1G, outbound from Helm. Under acceleration, Grayson could walk normally on the 'Mech Bay deck, talking to the tired and dirty men and women gathered there. All were exhausted, yet suffused with the flush of victory.

Lori and Alard King walked with him. As they approached a group of refugees, a ComStar Adept named Larabee stepped forward, his robes still bloodied from the fight in the Star League cave.

"Adept Larabee," Grayson said. "I heard that it was you who found Alard King and brought him to the ship. I was busy seeing to the boarding operations and hadn't heard the full story. I wish to thank you personally."

The Adept took Grayson's hand and shook it. "My pleasure, Colonel. I was on my way toward your ships anyway, in a transport hovercraft. I found your people— King and five of your soldiers—making their way down the slope of the mountain."

"Ha! It was more like we were clinging to the side of the mountain, waiting to die," King said. "The quake was going full-force then, and we couldn't even stand. He saved us, Colonel. I know damn well he saved Janice, that young corporal in charge, because she would have bled to death if we hadn't been able to get her back to the ship in time."

Grayson looked the Adept in the eyes. "I . . . I don't agree with what ComStar was doing on Helm, Larabee, but that doesn't lessen the importance of what *you* did, for me . . . and for my people. I appreciate it."

Larabee studied Grayson's face for a moment. There was still an inner pain there, a bleakness that victory and rescue had not erased. "Listen, Colonel . . . ."

"Yes?"

"I don't want you to judge the Order by the actions of one man."

"Rachan?" Grayson shook his head. "We'll probably

never know the whole story. It's possible he was working alone."

Larabee looked torn, indecisive. "I tell you the truth, Colonel. I don't know if he was working alone or not. It's almost impossible to believe that such a hideous, evil plot could have been concocted by one man, but neither can I believe that the Order to which I have dedicated my life is capable of such monstrous deeds!"

"Whatever happened," Grayson said gently, "it is a failure of your Order's *system*. The power that ComStar wields, concealed by its mysticism . . . it is enough to corrupt an army of men like Rachan."

"I swear to you that I knew nothing of it, Colonel. I swear to you, too, that your name, and the name of your regiment, will be cleared! If the plot was something concocted by men high up in the ComStar hierarchy, they will not dare to admit it, for there are too many people alive who know what really happened. They will find other scapegoats for Tiantan . . . Kleider and Garth, to begin with."

A fierce light burned in Larabee's eyes. "I will speak with my superiors on Terra. I think they will publicly support the . . . the *theory* that Rachan was an isolated madman, that Tiantan was his idea alone, but carried out by the Duke of Irian in exchange for the promise of loot from the Star League cache. You, Colonel, will no longer be considered a renegade."

Grayson nodded. "That's . . . good. It doesn't much help the people who died on Sirius V, though. And it doesn't help Morley, Brodensen, Dulaney, or the others who died."

"Never forget the living, Colonel. There are *always* the living."

The living. Ramage was alive, barely, recovering now under the ship doctor's care. Clay had his arm in a sling, but was happily reunited with his wife and son. Janice Taylor was alive, and Lori. Grayson reached out, putting his arm around her waist, drawing her close. *Lori is alive!* he thought joyfully.

"Yes, there are the living," Grayson repeated. "And

for that, we have to thank you, Adept Larabee. We cannot repay you.''

''But you can. Alard King explained to me your suspicions concerning ComStar during the ride to your ship.'' Larabee looked down at his hands. ''Perhaps I can settle some of my own doubts on that score if I know you are carrying out your original plan . . . allowing that library data to be spread across the stars.'' Larabee turned his hands, examining them. ''I just wish I knew.''

''Knew what?''

''I wish I knew whether, by helping you, by helping to spread that data . . . I will be helping to make up for the evil done by one, mad renegade of my Order . . . or whether it will make of *me* the renegade . . .''

Epilogue

Grayson never did learn whether Adept Larabee became a renegade fighter or a renegade. As the man had promised, the First Circuit, ComStar's inner council, did declare Precentor Rachan an outlaw and disavowed his actions. They claimed that the tragedy on Sirius V was the result of a madman's megalomania and the corruption of a small clique of Marik nobles and officers.

During the year following the nightmare of Helm, Grayson heard isolated bits of information about the incident from various sources. It was discovered that Garth and Kleider, for example, were behind a plot to overthrow Janos Marik. Their connivance at Sirius V, it seemed, had been part of a plan to discredit Janos Marik by discrediting the mercenaries he had hired against their wishes. The rift within Marik's staff would have resulted in civil war and a chance for Garth, Kleider, and several of Kleider's brother officers to seize the Captain-General's power. The plot failed when unknown sources—widely suspected, but never proven to have been ComStar agents—alerted Marik to the plot, which allowed him to react with loyal elements of his army. In the clash that followed, Garth was captured, tried, and executed. Kleider escaped with a handful of 'Mechs and men and was not seen again.

Grayson and Duke Ricol had parted company at Stewart, where the *Deimos* and the *Phobos* were reunited with Captain Tor and the JumpShip *Individious*. As promised, Ricol had shared the booty from Helm with Grayson. There were 'Mechs enough to fill out three full combat companies, plus spares and repair materials enough to fully refit the A Company 'Mechs damaged on Helm. Afterward, the Red Duke vanished toward the Kurita frontier.

"I imagine we will meet again as enemies, I'm afraid," he said in parting to Grayson. "It is inevitable, I suppose. And . . . who knows? Perhaps things will change. I can always use a good mercenary regiment in my employ, with a commander I can trust."

"Perhaps, Your Grace. I'll have to think about that one."

The library data was copied . . . and copied again. Captain Tor used his old merchanter's contacts to find people who would transport those copies along the trade routes, scattering the old Star League library files among the stars.

There was no way to tell whether the effort would be worth it. Though Grayson had recognized the importance of the library, as had Duke Ricol, how many of Tor's merchant friends and contacts took the memory cores in order to sell them? How many found that no one was interested enough to buy them . . . or even to take them when offered free?

That was beyond Grayson's power to control. He had done his best in trying to disseminate the data as widely as possible. If mankind was to benefit from the lost Star League treasure, it would have to *prove* its worthiness by recognizing the value of the data. Perhaps, the rediscovered farming methods, old genetic manipulation techniques, and long-lost manufacturing processes would one day make a reappearance. Perhaps man's lot would improve, and the long, dark slide into feudalism and technological ignorance would be arrested . . . even reversed.

But it might be centuries before any such change. Man—and his ignorance—covered one hell of a lot of ground.

Grayson floated in weightlessness in a lounge aboard the *Invidious*. The stars shone with crystal and unwinking clarity through the chamber's transparent panels. The ship's jump sail had already been retracted, and preparations made for the first jump toward Lyran space. There was talk about a new contract in service to Katrina Steiner. The Gray Death's reputation had grown on Helm, along with its strength in 'Mechs. On Galatea and elsewhere, there would be more recruits waiting to join the Legion.

Lori stirred in Grayson's arms, and he drew her closer. There were advantages to being regimental commander, he thought. The ship's lounge, with its magnificent view of space, could be locked at his command. An hour's privacy was a treasure without price aboard ship. His lips found Lori's, and they kissed in a long and deep embrace while drifting in the afterglow of their lovemaking.

"What are you thinking?" she murmured in his ear.

He smiled, and squeezed her closer. The movement set them turning, very slowly.

He had been so certain that he was doomed to die . . . that there was no way out, for him or for his regiment. Though the conviction had not left him, it no longer held him prisoner. His . . . what was it? Call it luck . . . or destiny . . . it had brought him so very far from Trellwan . . . Yet were not luck and destiny his to make and shape for himself? They were not outside forces to be waited on . . . or relied upon. Not as he relied on the people around him.

He smiled, remembering the words of the old, old warrior's song:

Home is the regiment, the price of glory high.
We stand with brothers at our sides
to pay that price, and die!
The blood of comrades cries to us
long after glory's passed:
Home is the Regiment, our family and our own!"

He clung to Lori. "I was just thinking," he told her, "how good it is to be home."

The End

CRUSADER

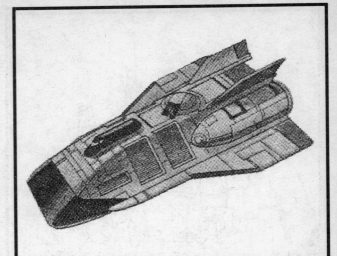

LEOPARD CLASS DROPSHIP

UNION CLASS DROPSHIP

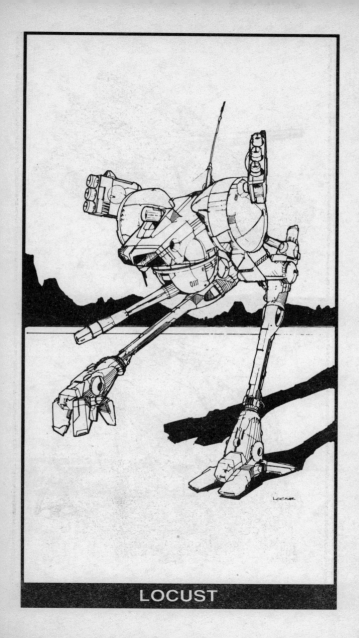

LOCUST

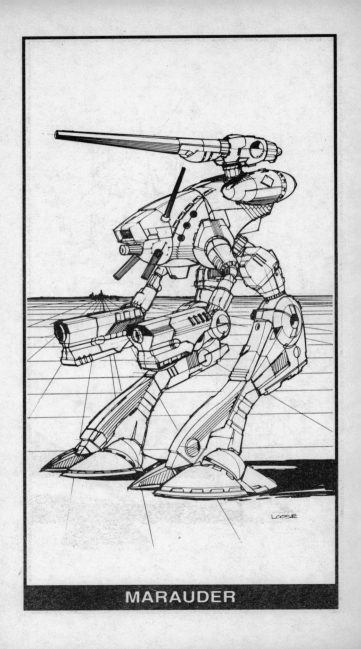

MARAUDER

PHOENIX HAWK

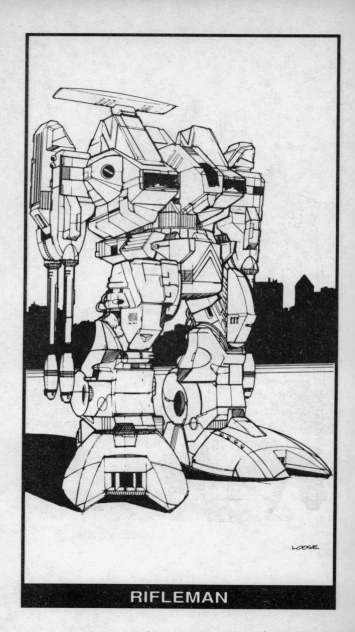

RIFLEMAN

SHADOW HAWK

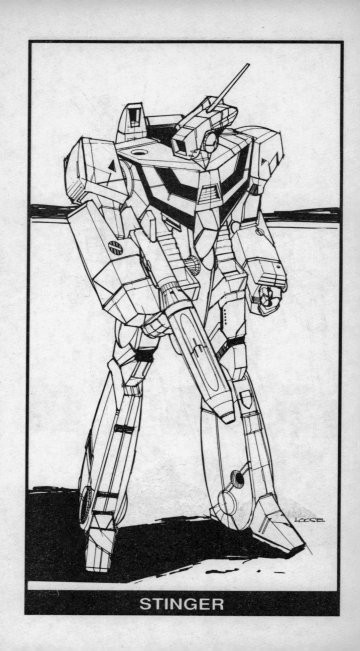

STINGER

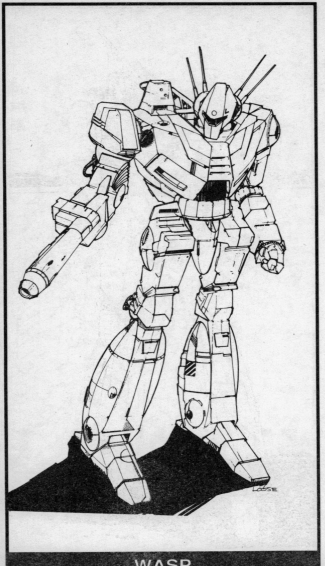

WASP

WOLVERINE

ABOUT THE AUTHOR

William H Keith, Jr. likes to travel. This is fortunate because he has been doing a great deal of commuting recently between the 31st and 69th centuries. During his very few side trips to the 20th Century, he has considerable difficulty remembering what year it is. Those who know him think this makes him lovably eccentric, but he insists this is only the temporal equivalent of jet lag. His analysts are studying this trait in hopes of shedding light on his monomaniacal compulsions to cover blank computer screens with small dark words.

When not time tripping and/or time stumbling, Bill lives in the hills of western Pennsylvania with Nina, his mercenary warrior wife; Heather, his alien-genius daughter; an ancient Egyptian cat goddess named Merneptah; and four hyperactive computers. Determining which of the members of this menagerie is in command at any given instant may possibly unlock the key to quantum mechanics and reveal the Ultimate Secret of the Universe.

RoC